To Grace

FOREWORD

Several years after the Ohio State University Press first published Helen Hooven Santmyer's " . . . *And Ladies of the Club,*" Press Director Peter Givler got a letter from a Mrs. Bertie Dell, of Galena, Ohio. She wrote that she had a novel manuscript in hand, titled *The Earth Abideth.* It was written in 1938 by her father-in-law, George Dell, and she thought that it might be as good as the monumentally successful Santmyer novel. Dell's novel, like Santmyer's, was set in Ohio during the era following the Civil War and leading into the 1900s.

Givler asked to read it, and what he got in the mail was a manuscript so reflective of a particular time and place—and also so impressive—that one is tempted to reach for such comparisons as *Main Street, Sister Carrie,* or *Winesburg, Ohio.* It was like finding hidden treasure, and that the book had gone unpublished all these years creates the notion that maybe out there stored in attics around the country are yet other undiscovered literary works, the authors of which are now likely in their graves, their genius unshared and unknown.

In today's world of commercial publishing, full of agents, schools of writing, "How to Sell" workshops, and even whole magazines devoted to helping authors get published, the idea of a writer being discovered by accident or fate seems quaint. But George Dell's family speaks of him as a man who for much of his life (he's now eighty-five) wrote primarily as an expression of personal growth and the pleasure of the creative process. They say that, in any case, *The Earth Abideth,* with its German immigrant characters, would have been a political risk for any American publishers in 1938 because of the general anti-German sentiment immediately prior to World War II.

The recent discovery of this novel is important to American literature in two central ways. First, its author of a half-century ago wrote about his ancestors and their fellow Ohioans yet another half-century before that, having the advantage of firsthand living resources no writer today can have. Yet because of its publication today, it can reach a popular contemporary audience—an improbability for other books written at the time, most of which are now long out of print and forgotten.

George Dell, an intellectual, teacher, and writer of considerable gifts, wrote about a time in America and a way of life which are largely gone but which helped shape who we are today. He focused on the American heartland of rural Ohio—then considered the West and part of the westward movement—and unearthed our roots at a time when they still could be found. He dramatized the essential American experience of man's struggle to conquer new land, characterized the Protestant work ethic, understood modern psychology as well as religious mythology, and through all this portrayed the indomitable frontier spirit.

Mark Twain tried to define the American novel by saying that we have to write fiction from long-term and heartfelt experience, not intellectual analysis or outside observation and judgment. He also said since fiction was best rendered in small settings with few characters, it probably would take a thousand or so able novels to capture all of America. The novelist, wrote Twain, "lays plainly before you the ways and speech and life of a few people grouped in a certain place—his own place—and that is one book. In time, he and his brethren will report to you the life and people of the whole nation."

Twain was assuming that regionalism would dominate the future of the American novel, whether critics called it realism or local colorism or naturalism, and he was right. From Hamlin Garland and Dreiser to Sherwood Anderson, Faulkner, and Tony Hillerman, much of this country's most distinctive fiction has been grounded in "the speech and life of a few people grouped in a certain place." For a century or more, these novels have taught us about ourselves: where we came from, where we have been, where we find ourselves. And those who have written about the past of specific American places have made a vital contribution to our understanding. For people who live in Ohio, George's Dell's book is especially important. With a skill equal to his contemporaries, Dell writes about a particular time and place in rural Ohio, yet transcends regionalism and makes lasting universal statements about humankind.

Dell wrote at a time when this country had just passed through a traumatic and prolonged economic depression accompanied by social upheaval, and when it stood on the brink of a major war. He tried to capture, at a time of crisis, some of the sense of what had gone into the making of a specific part of our experience, and by doing so to help his readers recognize and comprehend their past. We can use such help today as much as our parents could have almost five decades ago. That Dell's book remains alive to us today is a tribute to its enduring virtues: he was able, through knowledge and imagination, to make a part of the American experience vivid and real.

Ultimately, *The Earth Abideth* will take its place not with the works published today but with the works of the time in which it was written. And, as " . . . *And Ladies of the Club*" demonstrated, many of us still want the kind and quality of reading experience afforded by that bygone era.

WILLIAM W. ALLEN
Ohio State University

AUTHOR'S NOTE

In general the material of this novel is true, although plot inci-
dents and characters have been fabricated. Belonging to local legend, tradition, and geography, however, are the following:

Geography and topography. The Standing Stone is famous. Rock
Ladder is known locally as Jacob's Ladder. Hockhocking Creek and
such may be located on the Lancaster sector of the U.S. Geological
Survey for Ohio.

The story of *Mary Elizabeth Sherman,* sister to General W. T.
and Senator John, is local legend, narrated in Wiseman, *Centennial
Lancaster.*

Material about the *Ohio Centennial* and the G.A.R. encampment at Columbus is taken from the files of Columbus newspapers.

Folklore and all that curious body of manners and customs de-
tailed in the story are in general from relatives of people who lived
in this time and place.

Religious services are from a Lutheran liturgy, and have been
translated from the German with the exception of the marriage
service.

One generation passeth away,
and another generation cometh:
but the earth abideth forever.

BOOK ONE

I

1   On a late Sunday afternoon in April 1866, Thomas Linthorne waited behind the thick Osage orange hedgerow on the lip of Chilton's upper pasture field as was his wont for the two Sundays past.

He was almost apathetic, for the smoky sun was already low in the sky. He had been anxious the first Sunday, afraid that someone from the cold brick house might spy out the bay horse dragging the buggy after her as she grazed. The second time there had been more green in the hedge, less likelihood of detection. Today there was a solid mask of woven leaves.

But today, for the third time, there had been no signal. Kate had said, "If they go off to church, or visiting like they sometimes do, I'll hang out the tablecloth. Don't you come down unless you see it. Rancy's got half a mind that something's wrong already."

Thomas needed no prompting about Rancy's suspicious nature. When first he had called on Rancy as an agent for Wells and Benton's line of trees and shrubs, Rance had closed the old oak house door tight behind him to keep Thomas shivering on the porch. Later they had gone out to the barn to talk for a quarter-hour between the stalls. Rance finally thawed enough to ask what a half-dozen Russets and another dozen Vandermains would cost, and Thomas let him have them for a dollar under the quoted price because he was sadly in need of business.

But when eventually they parted under the frost-blanched sky, he was still wondering what made the man so queer. It seemed as if there was some mystery about the house.

It was the second time he called that he saw the girl. He had driven up from Lebanon in a blinding storm that hardened his harness to ice. Rance took him in for coffee, changed his mind to offer whiskey instead. Kate came in while Thomas was swigging from the cold stone jug, his head back-tilted to show the ice on his thick black brows and mustache.

"Get out!" Rance immediately lashed out at her. At that she slid through the paneled door like a brown mouse, but she was not quick enough to avoid Thomas's eye.

He pretended to have taken no notice, but when an hour later he drove on toward Blue Ball, he purposely left behind the bone-handled knife with which he had scaled the sleet from the backs of his hands.

Thomas found shelter in the covered bridge until he saw Rancy's lantern swinging in long arcs toward the barn, then came back afoot. He had to wait interminably before someone came to the door at the end of the passageway. The door grated a bare two inches to show the tallowy face of an old woman huddled in a mulberry shawl.

"Sorry," said Thomas politely. "Must of left my knife."

"Heh? What say?" the creature creaked at him.

"My knife!" Thomas repeated. "You remember me, don't you, Aunt Bess? Just called on Mr. Chilton an hour or so ago. Mr. Linthorne, Wells and Benton, Cincinnati."

"Ain't seen nothin' looked like a knife," Aunt Bess grumbled. "Got a mind, you can go look."

Thomas had a mind. As he had supposed, the girl was in the sitting room. She was paring potatoes beside the yellow stove.

"Left my pocket knife," Thomas said when he saw her start. "Somewheres in the passageway, I reckon."

She jumped up immediately, brought a lamp from the table.

"You won't find it without a light, mister," she said. "That place is so dark the rats bump their heads."

Thomas carefully closed the door behind them. He knew where the knife was, for he had deliberately wedged it into a moldy cranny, but that matter was inconsequential.

"You related?" he asked at once, unwilling to believe that Rance could have married so gorgeous a creature.

4

"No kin," said the girl. "You look in that crack down there by the baseboard?"

"Been here long?"

"Since Pa died. He owed—"

At that moment Aunt Bess stuck out her ugly head. She had a milk bucket and a heavy coat in her hands.

"You'd best git along down to the barn if'n you know what's good for you, missy!" she grinned mirthlessly. "Or maybe you don't mind the taste of that cane of Rancy's."

The girl threw on the coat and took the bucket at once.

"I hope you find it, mister," she said as she moved off.

Thomas watched her until the heavy door at the end of the passage jarred shut, then quickly retrieved his knife and followed.

The blast of wind around the elbow of the house almost beat his breath away as he hurried into the dark after his quarry. She was not surprised when he caught up with her on the farther side of the smokehouse.

"Listen!" he had to shout to make himself heard. "You don't owe these people anything, do you?"

"I ain't no way beholden," she answered. "What little Pa owed I guess I served out long ago."

Thomas drew himself to his full height, a good six feet four.

"Minded to marry?"

"Maybe. Some day."

"How'd you like me?"

"Ain't seen better as I can remember of."

"Well, I don't never expect to see no better myself," Thomas said prettily. "Maybe—"

She made an uncertain step toward the barn, and then thought better of flight.

"I ain't but seventeen," she confided. "And Rancy's got notions that—"

"You listen to me!" Thomas stopped her. "I'm going up as far as Springfield this trip. Coming back I'll stop in again. You be thinking whether you want me."

He heard her laughter.

"What if I know already, mister?"

Thomas kissed her then, roughly, passionately. The next

5

moment she had broken away and was running for the black bulk of the barn.

When he came back weeks later, they had a few stolen moments in the orchard.

"I ain't got nothin' but my clothes," she confessed. "Strikes me it might be a hard scratch if we're both Job poor."

"I been thinking so too," said Thomas. "Maybe we'd best wait a while so's I can save up a little."

They waited a whole year, largely because Aunt Bess came down with a hacking cough that kept her bedfast until her death. Afterward Kate's lot was almost unbearable. Rancy was moody at first, then violent. Kate endured his long silences, his drunken brutality, but when he brought home a profane red-headed woman, she wrote Thomas the letter: "If they go off to church, or visiting like they sometimes do, I'll hang out the tablecloth."

Thomas stopped his whittling long enough to glance toward the house as he repeated the quotation for the hundredth time.

At what he saw his heart lurched. Down in the dish of the farmland on the far side of the stony fallows a willowy figure in blue percale had just finished putting the second pin into a large white square that flapped languidly in the breeze.

Thomas ran to rein up, jumped into the buggy, and cut out along the hedge for the wagon road. A minute later he was letting Winnie take the long downgrade at her swift stride, holding her in only enough to keep her from stumbling.

2   Kate was waiting behind the honeysuckle vine.
"Best tie behind the house," she suggested. "Maybe that locust would be a good place."

"No sense tying," said Thomas. "Be gone long, will they?"

"I don't know whether they will or won't," she said anxiously. "Didn't do nothing but sit around all afternoon. Mayme kept whining about first one thing and then another—how she'd like a glass of dandelion wine and there wasn't any more down cellar, how she wanted to sleep and have him let her alone, and how she wanted to visit down the road a piece. Finally he just got up and went out and hitched. That's all I know."

"No danger they got a notion about us, is there?"

"Not this kind of notion . . . but we'd best hurry." She ran to throw open the cellar door. "I got some stuff packed in them boxes right down there at the bottom," she said. "'Tain't much, and it's all last year's, but it'll keep our stomachs from sticking to our backbones. You carry it up and tuck it away in the buggy."

Thomas hesitated. "Not if it belongs to Rance I won't!" he said firmly.

"It belongs to me. Guess I did all the work. All that Rance did was own the land it grew on . . . Now go do what I tell you!"

Thomas obeyed. There were several wooden boxes full of tin cans rimmed with red sealing wax, and one that held three stone jars. When he came up with his third load, Kate was staggering out from the house, her arms sagging under a weight of bedclothes.

"I don't know," Thomas protested again, his brow wrinkled. "Guess most people'd call this downright stealing."

"I ain't like most people and there's no call for you to be!" she returned coolly. "Get a move on and fold up them comforters so's we can sit on them."

Thomas was all thumbs at the task. As soon as she had inspected his disposal of goods in the back of the buggy, she hurried to help him. "Go shut them cellar doors, Thomas," she directed as she took his task away.

Thomas did, and was horrified to see her going back to the house.

"Don't you get no more!" he said sternly.

"I ain't taking anything I didn't mean to."

"Well, I'm a-telling you not to take any more at all! I won't put hands on more of Rancy's stuff!"

He followed her into the musty sitting room to see that she did as he bade, shuffling uneasily around the room while she reached down a bottle of brown ink from the clock shelf.

"Where you aimin' to tell him you lit out for?" he interrupted the scratch of her quill.

"Cincinnati, that's where. Hunt a long time down there afore he finds out he's barking up the wrong tree."

Thomas went out then to water Winnie. When he came back

from the trough with the bucket, Kate was already in the buggy, her legs tucked under the blanket.

"Lock the door?" he asked.

She didn't answer him. Instead she said, "I wouldn't wait too long if I was you."

Thomas needed little urging, especially since at that moment the planks of the covered bridge began to rattle staccato under the swift passage of a trotter.

"Turn around and go back past the barn!" Kate ordered quickly. "Don't whip up. That's Rance—I can tell by the way he drives."

Thomas coaxed Winnie into a gentle trot. Behind the barn a field road led through a snarl of sassafras and hazel, first down to a rocky run, beyond the run through a serpentine of woods to the green depth of oak and maple timber a half-mile from the house.

Thomas stopped to look back when he was certain they could no longer be seen, but the dusk was already so gray and the trees so dense he could not have seen if anyone was coming after them.

"Best listen," Kate suggested.

They listened, holding their breath to make their ears more acute. Through the dark wood they could hear the wind like many mice among the old leaves, the far-off purl of water as it went over the limestone rocks. Beyond that there was nothing.

3 They passed Blue Ball, its few houses sulphurous with candles and kerosene; went on to Franklin, already blue with sleep; from Franklin turned east toward the hills. Their farm was bedded in the heart of Fairfield County, a good two days away.

"Sleepy?" Thomas asked when he felt Kate snuggle against his side.

"Ain't sleepy," she answered. "But I'm awful cold and hungry, Thomas. And these pots and pans down under keep scratching my legs something awful."

"What pots and pans?"

"The preacher's," she said jauntily. "Will we get us a preacher, Thomas?"

"Not tonight!" he snapped, angry that she should have stolen some of the kitchenware while his back was turned.

She didn't seem to mind.

"Course, preachers cost a dollar or two," she said. "I thought maybe we'd have to get along without."

Thomas took the remark as intentional criticism. "I ain't that poor," he said tartly.

Kate sighed. "I'd like to have my lines written down, of course, Thomas. But I reckon I could do without if I had to. Only I don't feel like doing without something to eat much longer. You like ham and pickles?"

"See here, girl," Thomas said more gently as he put his arm around her, "you ain't got something to eat too, have you?"

"Maybe . . . only you'll have to find a field first."

Thomas found a field, the long swell of the uplands deep violet against the gray sky. On the right was land plowed for corn, and beyond that a black wood; on the left an ominous ravine. The grass was wet and the stars cold. They shivered as they limped down from the buggy to stretch their cramped legs. A mile or so away a hound heard them and set up an eerie baying, to be seconded by the crisp bark of a house dog.

"Want I should make a fire?" Thomas asked as he hooked out his big gold watch to trace the time in the starlight. It was just twenty-three minutes past ten.

"No need," Kate told him. "I'm going to spread the blankets. The bottom one'll get plenty wet, but we can dry it out in the sun tomorrow morning."

Thomas led Winnie out of the shafts and lifted off her harness while their bed was being made. For the first time he began to feel nervous. It was not so much the danger that Rance would follow as that the woman was stranger than he had expected, more assertive, less inclined to be docile. Moreover, they were not married—it would be awkward to sleep beside her. He had heard his father tell of bundling, how in the old days it was customary for young folks to save the fire by crawling into bed fully clothed. But this was different.

When he had tied Winnie at the end of a long rope, he went

back to the buggy to find that Kate had spread the blankets over the roots of an oak tree.

"None too particular, are you?" he asked uncivilly as he shifted the covers to the open grass.

"I could sleep on thorns," she said.

Thomas crawled between the comforters after her, a wad of bread and meat in his hands. Lying there in the dew together, they looked up at the foamy sky and ate slowly, a bit afraid, a great deal more expectant. Most of all they were overwhelmed by the repressive strangeness of each other.

4 In the night, the rain of stars like fire on their faces, Kate crept close while Thomas told her of his boyhood, his years in the war, and of how he had been shot through the thigh at Manassas. It was the opportunity she wished—her story was more bitter:

She had been a girl in Franklin, her father a cobbler whose trade provided little more than bread and molasses for his three children. The mother was dead, had been carried off by scarlet fever. Peter Harewell supplied her place as best he could while the children were very young. Afterward the care of the tiny house devolved upon Kate. Courtright and Hans helped as soon as they were able, scratching rows of potatoes like little old goblin men.

They had moved to the country then, first to a stony farm near Germantown, afterward to a few boggy acres on the farther side of Lebanon. Peter Harewell was earnest, hardworking, God-fearing, but it was plain from the first that he would never squeeze a living out of the marshy ground. The farmers around shook their heads, on rare occasions sent over a pork loin or a bushel of garden stuff.

Harewell always accepted their offerings with great dignity, in fact, sometimes tried to repay them. But his doom was written in the too-wet furrows. When first one and then the other of his boys came down with diphtheria and lay under the soughing cedars behind the board church, Peter gave up. For a time he tried to go back to bootmaking, and for another period of a few months he made and vended brooms—learning the new art from the Shakers of Union Village. Then came obliquity of mind, and at last doddering imbecility. By the time he died, he was no better than a baby.

Kate had gone to the Chiltons then, when she was only thirteen. Rancy and his mother, whom the entire countryside called Aunt Bess, at first treated her with some kindness. Rance may have flattered himself into thinking Kate would grow up to love him. That first winter he used to sit for hours at a time twisting his hands through her hair and making little effort to conceal his caresses while Aunt Bess made a blear-eyed attempt to spell out the chronicles of the paper.

Kate thought no evil of the fondling, did not really know what the man was about. She had been reared in the strictest seclusion, had had no girl friends with whom to exchange confidences. While her father lived, her life had been steeped in the dogmas of the German Lutheran church. Once each Sunday, and sometimes twice in the summer, Peter Harewell took his children to hear the homilies of white-haired Schlegel, a man whose angelic mien was belied by the vehemence of his pulpit utterance.

Then, when she was fifteen, there came a day when she no longer dared to doubt Rancy's meaning. They had been out haying, together with a simple-faced fellow known in Blue Ball as "Whistle John," had stolen down to the brook to get away from the heat of the afternoon. The ragweed and wild sunflowers were heavy with dust, the leaves hung flaccid and lifeless, the very air was sick with heat. It was Rancy who suggested wading after they had splashed their wrists and sloshed their flushed faces. Kate, vaguely uneasy, dissented at first, but at length gave way to his importunity.

In they crept together, holding hands because of the sharp rocks hidden beneath the green water. That had been all at first. And then Rance had wanted to go upstream toward what was known as the Sink-hole. Reluctantly Kate let herself be led. There was a high ledge of shaly bank topped with haw trees just before they came to the bend—at the ledge Rance unexpectedly kissed her. She was soon to learn what the hungry look in his eyes meant.

When she told him he was silly he said nothing, simply waded on into the oily black water, dragging her after him. She pulled up her skirts at once to keep from getting slopped. "I don't want to go no farther, Rance!" she kept protesting. He was so strong that she must follow him against her will. They were mid-thigh, and she was noticing with distaste the hairiness of his muscle-knotted legs when suddenly Rance gave a spring and dragged her down. She could not swim, remembered only that she had screamed. Then she was choking, drowning. Before her eyes in that awful moment her whole life's story was vivid.

That was all, except for the horrible awakening on the sandbank. He was sitting naked beside her, apparently unconcerned over the fact that he had forced her, his eyes fixed on the swoop of a kingfisher over a rotten log upstream. Kate said nothing to him, simply struggled to her feet and dragged her aching body through the weeds, her feet and legs bleeding from the blackberry thorns.

That night when he came in for supper, Rance looked at her again in that queer way of his, but he was as though dead to her eyes. From that day his brutality began. A week later he had beaten her—for the first time. Aunt Bess might protest, but against the flood of Rancy's passion she was a single straw. Rance forbade Kate to go to church or to visit the neighbors, saw her walk through winter without soles to her shoes, broke all the mirrors in the house, even threw away her comb and brush. Worst of all, he allowed himself to become bestial in appearance.

That was all before Thomas had appeared. Kate knew the first time she saw him that there was destined to be something between them. She had felt all hot and sick, had been glad to go when Rancy ordered her from the room. And when Thomas had come back later, she was not responsible for anything she had said. She wanted him, counted the days until he could take her away, had seen her best plans spoiled by the sudden shifts of fate—and had found the courage to hope again.

She had no fear for the future. Come life, come death, there could be nothing worse than she had already gone through. That was why she had told him he need not marry her unless he willed. Once he knew about her, she was not certain he would want to go on with his bargain. But if he did, she would give him everything, would make his home for him, bear his children, work for him her life through, love him as long as she lived.

Patiently Thomas lay on his back and heard her to the end. Overhead the wheel of the sky had turned an hour toward dawn; in the farmyard the melancholy hound had long since stopped his baying.

"Well, Thomas?" he heard her ask, and suddenly knew that she had withdrawn from him, as if she feared he did not mean to accept her.

For answer Thomas pulled her back into his arms.

"We'll hitch, I reckon!" he said. "Ain't you sleepy?"

"Kind of."

"Then you just go ahead and drop off. And in the morning you forget that bad dream you just told me about. I never did do my fishing in water that's already gone on down stream, and I don't aim to begin now."

He heard her sigh contentedly and knew that she had relaxed in his arms.

5　On Tuesday morning they bought the license at the courthouse in Circleville and drove around town looking for a minister.

"Guess you want it Lutheran anyway, don't you, Kate?" Thomas pondered when they learned that the Methodist minister was out making a sick call.

"I ain't particular," she said. "But they do say the Lutherans tie awful tight, Thomas."

"Then it'll be Lutheran," he said at once. "Don't want any slip-knots in this family."

He inquired at the livery stable, was routed to a rambling white house on the north side. Once there, they tied Winnie to the parsonage hitching block and went timidly to the porch together.

The white-haired woman who came to the door immediately revived their courage by the German homeliness of her face.

"Ja, ja," she kept saying in answer to Thomas's inquiries. When she learned they meant to be married, she ushered them into a bare, cold parlor. They stood in awkward silence while she disappeared behind a yellow pine door, at last heard voices, the one urgent, the other raised in mild protest.

"Strict, maybe," Thomas murmured. "Don't like to marry unless he knows the people."

Kate said nothing, but Thomas could tell by the perkiness of her chin that she didn't mean to wait in the cold room forever.

Then, just as they were both edging toward the door, Schatten-dorn came in, a little black book in his hand. He was an elfin man with a bush beard of sandy gray, his eyes quizzical behind his gold-rimmed glasses; and he was evidently suffering from a cold, for he sniffled and made apologetic efforts to relieve himself by applying a large red bandana.

"Sprechen Sie Deutsch?" he inquired when he had finished a leisurely surveillance.

"Guess not," said Thomas, uncertain of the question. "We just want to get married. How much does it cost?"

For answer Schattendorn went back to the door and called, "Mutter! Mutter! Komm' herein!"

His wife had her apron off and was evidently sure of her mission, for she immediately said, "Der Herr Pfarrer, he don't versteh mooch English. Aber auf Deutsch, ja, es ist joost as goot."

"How much does it cost?" Thomas repeated.

She shrugged her shoulders, as if to bargain for whatever he wanted to give.

"Tell him to go ahead," said Thomas, and took his place with Kate in front of the bare mantel.

Schattendorn took one last solemn honk at his nose, planted himself with open liturgy on the bare pine boards in front of them, and began portentously to read:

"Da ihr euch Beide, meine Geliebten . . ."

Outside the shuttered windows of the parsonage, the fern-like tracery of rose leaves on the square panes of glass wove a rhythm of shadows richer than the mottled light through the most glorious rose window. Overhead the smudged pattern of the high ceiling re-treated farther than the long arches of the dimmest Gothic cathe-dral. From the street came the screech of cartwheels and the distant shouts of children playing hopscotch, more harmonious than the choric responses of any massed choir.

" . . . Es ist nicht gut, sagt der Schoepfer, dasz der Mensch allein ist, ich will ihm eine Huelfin schaffen."

Their marriage day! From dim-visioned Eden, ambrosial with flowers; from the archeologic plains where the sons of God first saw that the daughters of men were fair; from slave marts, palaces, huts,

14

castles, hovels, halls; by seductions, rapes, and honorable betroth-als, the lordly community of those joined male and female together stood massed around the two of them, Kate Harewell and Thomas Linthorne swearing together before God and man that till death did them part they should be as one flesh.

"Weil nun die Ehe eine so wichtige Sache ist."

One man and one woman. Never to lust after another or give oneself completely into confidence of another mate, to share all, dare all, endure all, taste the bitter and because of fellowship call it sweet, by the sweat of the brow earn one's daily bread, by the pangs of parturition bring children into the world—for love's sake only.

Schattendorn's hand was shaking a little as he paused to ask their names. Lindorn, he repeated; Harevell. Thomas thought he was finished and reached for his wallet, but Kate restrained his arm.

"Thomas Lindorn, wollt ihr diese gegenwaertige Kathrine Harevell zu eurer ehrlichen Gemahlin haben; versprecht ihr dersel-ben alle eheliche Treue, Liebe, und Fuersorge, auch sie nicht zu verlassen, bis Gott dies Band trennt? so bekennet es vor Gott und dieser Zuege und sagt, Ja."

Thomas saw as if from trance the nodding head of mother Schattendorn and heard her prompting his response. "Ja, ja," urged the good old soul; and when he looked sheepish, "You say it, ja—yes."

"Yes!" said Thomas deliberately.

"Kathrine Harevell, wollt ihr diesen gegenwaertigen Thomas Lindorn."

"Yes!" said Kate, almost before he had finished speaking.

The pastor stopped again and made frantic signs to his wife, who at once stripped from her pudgy finger a broad gold wedding band.

"Der Ring ist ein Sinnbild der Ewigkeit."

Forever and forever. Like the starry procession in the skies, the seas forever flowing, the seasons, the sun, eternity itself, so the path of marriage, once begun, never ended. Twenty miles to the east lay the farm that Thomas had bought, its miserable rusted plow the only equipment with which they would start life. What lay twenty years toward the east? Or, for that matter, twenty months, or days?

Birth and death, joy and sorrow, prosperity and adversity. Thomas looked down at the brown hair of the girl he had chosen and found her good. Her flesh was firm to his touch, her eyes honest in his eyes, her voice sweet to his ears. From her lithe body his children would be born. Her hands would rock the cradle, and her hands might stitch the shroud. At the churn, in the furrows, before the fire, with needle, skillet, hoe, and loom she would serve him; and at night when he came home to her he would find her body soft to his caresses.

"Der Friede Gottes sei mit euch. Amen."

Thomas felt in his pocket for a handkerchief to wipe his moist brow. There was no longer any doubt of it—he was married. His heart raced a little when he thought of the awful finality of the bond. Between the two of them, himself and the girl who until this quarter-hour had been mistress of her own destiny, they could count less than ten dollars. They would have to work like slaves to get the ground broken, the corn in.

"You'd better kiss me, Thomas," Kate recalled him to his senses.

He was followed by the good housemother, and then by the fatherly peck of her clerical consort. Thomas reached into his pocket again, this time for the worn one-dollar bill he had carefully folded.

"Guess it ought to be worth that much, anyway," he attempted to be jocular as he handed the money to Schattendorn.

He froze when he saw the look in the other man's eyes. It was not admonition so much as contempt, not contempt so much as horror. Schattendorn may not have understood the words, but he could not mistake the tone; he was not to be bribed into any flippancy toward the mysteries of his faith. He might never have seen the money, so regal was the way he stalked out of the room and shut the door behind him.

Thomas felt downcast. He helped Kate with her coat, fumbled his hat from the torn plush rocker.

"Guess you'd better take care of this, missus," he said uneasily as he hesitated before the door, the proffered bill in his hand.

Mrs. Schattendorn made no scruple about tucking the money

into the folds of her dress. Outside might be the promise of another year, but in the manse too many of the days were gray, the harvest all too little. A dollar would pay for the doctor when Schattendorn came down with another of the dizzy spells that had begun to plague him.

6 At four that afternoon they reached home.

The farm lay on what was almost the north shore of the Ohio hills, just east of a side road called Gregory Lane after the richest man in the community. It might be good land, it might be bad; for the last ten years its worth had not been tested. Ragweed, thistles, fennel, docks, and daisies covered the rolling loam. The worm fences were down, the fields encroached upon by scraggly hedges. With some help the discolored frame house looked as if it might succeed in supporting the chimney for another year. As for the barn, it was only a great slatternly shed, and the few lean-tos that served for springhouse and smokehouse would have to be replaced.

It was the land that caught Thomas's eye—the long, low swell of the fields, undulant to the brow of woods at the back line. There was walnut and oak in the woods, walnut and oak that would have to be sold to satisfy the demands of the mill that would supply him with new timbers. Better yet, just across the pike, rising up behind the two red-brick boxes of church and school was a green-black crown on a massive head, the richest woodland he had ever seen. Who owned the hill now Thomas did not know, but he was certain who would. Ten years from now that would be his land. By that time folks hereabout would mention the name Linthorne with awe.

And in twenty years—

II

1   Kate became pregnant the first month. That year they worked from first dawn until long after dark. Thomas was strong, no novice with plow and disk, but he was often so tired that he fell asleep at the supper table. Kate went with him to the fields every day through the summer, was sometimes weak and sick, but never unwilling. He scolded her for her persistence in the face of danger.

"No sense in it atall!" he would reprimand sharply when she had to grab at him for support after rising too quickly. "First thing you know you'll lose the baby, and then where'll we be!"

"I won't!" she always replied. "And he'll be big and strong like you, Thomas. You'll have to have a big boy to help you get these fields in shape."

The neighbors were kind. Spence Vitt, who owned a few hilly acres on Goose Ridge a quarter-mile or so down the road, had insisted that Thomas take for his own a harrow, drag, and the miscellaneous odds and ends around his barn. Spence had no use for them, had set his land to fruit. "You just wait and see," he was wont to reply to those who understood nothing but the rhythm of corn and wheat. "Come five years, I'll have enough apples on them trees to feed everybody in the county. Plant corn, I'd have to get me a big ladder before I could cut it."

Thomas fully agreed with him. The Vitts might be poor (Spence lived with a single sister, Cora, who at twenty-five had the flavor of quince), but they wouldn't always be eating hominy grits. Secretly Thomas vowed that once he had the lower acres in rotation he would put apples on his own hills. By the end of the next winter most of the good timber would be gone anyway. A Lancaster firm

18

had given him nine hundred dollars for the privilege of sawing, from which he had managed to save out two hundred for a team.

That was his pride, the span of grays. He couldn't rightly afford them, but neither could he afford to be without them. Bill Sapooney had gone with him to McGruber's place on the Cedar Hill pike when he made the bargain and had stuttered admiration all the way home.

Bill was a twisted, wry little man, no more than twenty-seven, but he spoke always with the authority of the pontiff. His nose was forever running, his hands covered with warts, his clothes ready to fall off despite the contraptions of pins and hitches he used to hold them together, but Bill was not disturbed. Neither did he seem to mind that his farm was overrun by weeds and rats. It was enough to satisfy Bill that folks always said "Whyn't you ask Bill Sapooney?" whenever there was a moot point in argument. No one ever did. No one had to.

There was an ugly story that the Sapooneys, Bill and Celia, his almost toothless wife, ate "taller" soup in the winter; and an uglier one that they ate rats. "I know tam vell it ain't squirrel like he says," Tanterscham would grimace with sour emphasis, and go on to tell how he had left the Sapooney table in disgust.

Thomas could not but be impressed by the tales. He began to regret that the Sapooney farm bordered his own, warned Kate that she should keep her weather eye open. "No sense putting harness on the wrong horse," he told her. "Things people say are true, you could plant potatoes on the kitchen floor over yonder. Ain't no wonder they made Lute Tanterscham sick to his stomach."

It was Celia Sapooney who came down the road one day in late September. Thomas was out with prong and hook trimming the thorny hedges and Kate was kneading bread in the trough when she glanced up to see the ugly woman letting herself in at the gate. Kate had to look a second time to make sure she was not having one of her dizzy spells. Celia, whose face looked like a piece of yellow pine with knotholes for mouth and eyes and whose figure was a file, was wearing some kind of outrageous bonnet frippered up with fruit gew-gaws and lemon-striped ribbons. Her walk as she came through the grass would have been grace to a grasshopper.

Kate made hurried inspection of her kitchen. She wasn't in the mood for company, had too much work ahead, but the fact that Celia had put on her best indicated that she must think her visit of momentous importance.

"Come right on in and sit," Kate invited before Celia had a chance to knock. "Real nice weather we been havin'."

"Well," Celia sighed while she bounced a wad of bacon rind from tooth to tooth, "it's a mighty blessing the good Lord don't make all the days bad. Been so lately that all Bill can say is if 't don't rain, it'll pour. Hay's mouldy, corn's half a crop, fruit's rotten, and wheat didn't amount to hardly nothin' atall."

Kate went on with her work. It was no news that nothing ever prospered on the Sapooney farm. It might rain white flour and tenderloin, but the Sapooneys would scrape up only smutted corn and sowbelly.

Celia took off her bonnet to admire it and revealed a frowsy mass of sun-bleached hair.

"Guess you're sort of wonderin' what on airth I come over here for," she teased Kate.

"Sakes alive, no!" Kate protested. "Seems to me with our houses side to side almost, there ain't no reason to make calls formal."

"Well, don't you take it wrong, Mis' Linthorne, that's all I ask. It's just like I told Bill this morning: I feel the good Lord wants every one of us to do their bounden duty and I guess I know when mine's plain as the nose in front of my face."

Kate left off working at that. She was a little scared when she saw the curious way Celia was working her jaws.

"Guess you're fixin' to have you a young un, ain't you?"

Kate flushed, her mind racing to discover the other woman's intention, but she gave no word of confirmation.

"Course, if I ain't right, all you got to do is up and say so," Celia said. "But I ain't lived twenty-three years growin' on twenty-four for nothin'. Long about three months after the weddin' I always look for signs."

"There's no law against it, is there!" Kate said angrily.

"Why, course they ain't! Don't you go gettin' riled now—I ain't meanin' nothin' but your own good." Celia wiped her eyes with the hem of her dress. "Take me and Bill, now," she sighed. "Might think to look at us we ain't tried to do what the good Lord says we should. 'Tain't that, though, Mis' Linthorne; 'tain't that atall. Seems just like He ain't a-lookin' on our efforts with favor."

Kate wanted mightily to laugh at that, had to twist her fingers in her apron to keep her face straight.

"It's just because you're so awful young I come over," Celia said earnestly. "Maybe you know everything you're supposed to know about havin' young uns, and then again maybe you don't. Certain sure there won't be no harm repeatin'. It's just that I don't want that precious young un of yours to be marked."

"Marked?"

"You've heard tell!"

"Why, yes—I guess I have. Only—"

"Well, maybe you ain't saw what I've saw! Down Sugar Grove way there was a big woman named Schoonover. Had a brat most every year. Worked out in the fields she did, a-plowin' and a-reapin' and all such truck, just as hard as any he. Trouble was that goin' after the plow all day long, she looked too much at the horse's tail. You know what happened? Well, you can just believe it or not, but every one of that woman's kids was born with a hare lip."

Kate laughed outrageously although she realized that Celia expected her to look tragic; when she saw Celia's anguish, she tried to cover the cause of her mirth.

"And then there was Bill's own brother. While she was a-carryin' him, his mother cut her finger on the butcher knife. When he come along he had the biggest strawberry alongside his nose you ever did see."

"I've heard of things like that," Kate said dutifully.

"And cats and snakes and things!" Celia whispered as she glanced fearfully about her. "Why, I tell you, Mis' Linthorne, sometimes what's born ain't a baby atall."

Kate got up at that, suddenly half sick. She didn't believe the woman, didn't believe the crazy stories of monstrosities and enormities she had heard whispered by Aunt Bess, didn't believe that she and Thomas could have such ill fortune if they lived a thousand years. But there was always the chance that what people said might be true. Certainly midwives should be reliable. A midwife in Franklin had circulated the tale that she had once delivered a child with two faces.

"Guess there ain't much I can do about it," she said, thoroughly miserable.

"That's just what I come for!" Celia leaped at her. "That's just exactly it. There is somethin' you can do about it. You got to be awful careful. Don't never look at nothin' bad, not even the least little bit. That's pretty—that picture of roses over there by the stove. You stand and look at that a couple hours a day. Pity is you don't have an organ. There ain't nothin' nicer'n sweet music."

"I'll try real hard to take good care of myself," Kate promised. She was glad to hear Thomas stomping the dirt from his boots.

Celia also heard and hastily put on her bonnet.

"You remember now—you be mindful!" she called over her shoulder as she went out the door. "And remember, if they's anything I got you want, all you got to do is stick your head out the window and yell."

Thomas watched her go with evident distaste, his lips compressed.

"What'd she want to borrow?" he asked as soon as Celia was beyond earshot.

Kate felt like crying—it was indecent to have people make such calls.

"She didn't ask for anything," she said.

"Well, don't you let her get her paws on nothing! Not her. Spence Vitt was telling me the ugly old buzzard run around all last winter in a coat made out of ratskins! And from the looks of her house—"

"You hush!" Kate stopped him.

Thomas kept right on grumbling. "Want me to shut up, you better start dishing out," he said finally. "Wouldn't take a whole lot more till my stomach fell right out of the bottom of my shoes."

2   By Christmas Kate began to feel proud of the way she had carried the baby. There had been almost no discomfort after the first month—a little swelling in the ankles, but that was to be expected.

"Best be looking around for a doctor one of these days," Thomas remarked one night toward the end of December.

He was proud of her bigness; he was sure the baby was going to be a boy, hopeful it might turn out twins.

"There's one at Hooker."

"Old fool!" Thomas commented. "Heard tell he'll saw a man's leg off to get out a splinter."

"We won't have to send all the way to Lancaster, will we?"

She was afraid of that. It would take Thomas hours to drive to the county seat, hours during which anything might happen. There was no one around to get in. Celia Sapooney had never had a baby, would be positively dangerous because of her dirtiness. For all Cora Vitt knew, babies grew on gooseberry bushes. Up the road the other way there was only old man Brewster, and across from him Lucy Jordan, a stuffed woman who looked like a moulting owl. Down Gregory Lane there were no houses, not unless the hovel of the horrible Schraders could be called a house. Of the Schraders people told stories that could not be repeated.

"Why, no, I don't think I'll have to go all the way to Lancaster," Thomas finally answered. "Asked Spence the other day about that fellow up in Carroll. Piggin, or Pingin, or something like that his name is. Spence says he don't think he'd charge any more'n ten dollars."

"Don't be always figuring what it costs, Thomas! Thing to ask about is does he know his business."

Thomas was a little hurt. "Guess somebody has to worry about the money," he muttered.

"Is Dr. Pin—whatever his name is—is he a good hand at bringing babies?"

"Heard tell he was. Tell you what I'll do: come Sunday afternoon, I'll hitch up Winnie and we'll drive up to scout around a little bit. You can put on a couple coats and bundle down in some blankets to keep warm."

Kate really wanted to go. But on Sunday it was raining, had rained for a good twelve hours. The roads were drab, the hills dirty white where the snow was streaked.

"Better wait until some other time," Thomas said when they came home from church. "Dangerous taking Winnie out when it's freezing up like this. She'd fall and break a leg, we'd be in a pretty fix."

Kate let him break the appointment. And somehow, chiefly because of the failure of either of them to urge another particular day, the whole of January and the first of February drifted away, and they waited every day for the pains to start.

3 On the fourteenth of February, Thomas took a load of corn to town in the morning. After dinner Spence Vitt came to help haul rails, already split and stacked on the edge of the woodlot. Spence hired out almost every day, and though it was hard for his neighbors to find him available, he gave Thomas at least two days a week.

It was a gray, cold afternoon, the sun long a mere blur of light, then entirely obscured. Along toward half-past three or a quarter till four, Thomas noticed from the hill how the cattle were frisking about Jordan's barnlot.

"Looky there, Spence!" he called as he pointed his numbed finger.

Spence's face, when he turned around again, was hard to read, but Thomas knew that there was something the matter.

"Figure your missus is all right?" he asked strangely.

"Was," said Thomas. "You make out it's going to snow?"

"Sure looks like it," said Spence, and Thomas did not at all like the way he said it.

After that he worked but halfheartedly, his senses acute to the utter stillness, the gelid, gray menace of the day. There was not a single whip of wind, not the slightest movement through all the wood. Dry and bare along the gullies and matted around the worm fences the weeds stood brown above the light crust of snow, a bunch of berries or a snarl of forlorn bittersweet the only color.

Spence too seemed to have taken fright. Now and then he would lift his head as if to sniff the sky, then go hesitantly back to dragging rails. Over in the east and under the curl of the hills it was already dark.

Thomas was loathe to call the work done, especially since he

24

meant to carry in all of the pile, but he was becoming more anxious with every passing moment. Unexpectedly he gave up trying to break loose a locust post frozen into the clay, instead stumbled toward the team to strip off their blankets. The big horses stomped and flinched, the breath from their nostrils like white plumes.

"Come on, Spence!"

Spence picked up the ax and followed along behind, unwilling to be jostled over the rough ground.

Almost as soon as they started, they met the onrushing wind and felt the sting of the hard-driven pellets it carried. By the time they reached the run, a short two hundred yards away, the ground looked as if it were streaking out from beneath the howling gale.

"Blizzard!" Spence yelled as he trotted up alongside, his long lope as ground-hungry as that of an Indian.

Thomas slapped down the reins, succeeded in quickening the team for only a few yards. Monumentally strong, resistless as fate, the heavy horses might with patience bury the plow under a stubborn soil all day long, but it was not in them to run.

"You go on!" he shouted to Spence. "Go on, I said!"

The icy wind drove his breath away. His arms were white, his hands frozen, his face coated with ice. It was all he could do to keep his eyes blinking open, but even then he could not see. In five minutes it had become as dark as midnight, a black through which the sandy snow stung like needles. The team had slowed down again, why Thomas could not tell unless the wheels were piling up against ice.

Then, suddenly, the load lurched sidewise as the near front wheel struck a rock. For a second the wagon teetered precariously, as if it might go over into the gully. "Giddap!" Thomas roared in fright, and used the ends of the lines for a whip. Ahead came the mighty surge of strength, pawing relentlessly toward safety and home. "Godamighty close!" he muttered as they snagged back out to the lane.

Spence had propped open the gates as he ran on ahead—there was that to be thankful for. It could be but a little way now, no more than several hundred feet. Thomas strained his eyes to spy out the barn. He caught himself thinking that this was like death, consciousness without connection, the soul islanded, lost, unknown, unknowing. Only, there could hardly be as much pain in death, once the first sharp pangs were past.

If by instinct the grays could find the barn! There it was, a lantern hard to the left. The glow danced nearer, veered ahead while Thomas shouted. Then in a sworl of white, Spence was at the horses' heads, turning them in through the big doors.

Thomas half fell from the wagon, his legs little better than pieces of jointed wood. Behind him Spence pushed shut the doors, rolled the salt barrel to hold them against the thrust of the wind.

"You'd best go right on up and take a look at your woman!" he said when he saw Thomas eyeing the heaving team. "Don't have to worry about the horses—I can take care of them all right. Only I can't—well, you'd best get along up."

Thomas refused to be frightened, helped unhitch, glad for the chance to do something to make his blood start again. Outside the wind lashed in fury against the walls, moaned and howled like a being in pain. *Who-who-whoooooooo!* it screeched as it bore down savagely, its rush the charge of a mad bull. The heavy-timbered barn shivered before the impact.

"You get along up!" Spence ordered for the second time.

Thomas knew his meaning. If it was fate that Kate should have chosen this night of all nights—but the idea was unthinkable. A man was queer that way: he was always trying to smell out disaster. Some fellows crossed so many bridges before they came to them that when they did actually reach a stream they fell in. Thomas knew how he would find Kate, huddled before the fire, with the teakettle singing and the water in the reservoir hissing a little. Her eyes would be worried, but the moment she knew he was safe she would be happy.

He burrowed toward the house with his head between his knees, kept himself from falling over the wellhead by grabbing onto an arm-thick link of the old grape vine. Funny that there was no light in the kitchen! His heart raced for a moment, and then quieted thankfully. There was a light after all, but from the middle room. Kate must have carried the lamp in there to hunt something in the closet under the steps.

"Kate! Kate!" he kept calling as he forced his weight against the door. "Kate!"

And then he heard her groan, heartsick, quavering, as if her very soul was in torment.

Thomas barely took time to bar out the wind. He found her lying on the floor, the lamp beside her. Thank God that she had been able to set it down, had not fallen with it! She might have been burned to a crisp. She was breathing rapidly, her eyes bloodshot, almost unrecognizing. Thomas went down on his knees beside her, panic-stricken.

"How long's it been going on, Kate?" he forced his voice into her consciousness. "Kate! Kate! How long?"

She looked at him blearily.

"Two hours," she whispered at last, and then stiffened out and held onto a chair leg as her pains came on again.

Thomas waited for nothing more. It might still be possible to go to Carroll after the doctor. Winnie was good. The snow could be no more than two inches deep; in places the road would be swept bare. Winnie would race through that, as long as she could go away from the storm.

"Spence!" Thomas was screaming before he was half near enough to be heard. "Get the mare out, Spence! Spence!"

Spence met him at the barn door, knowledge written large on his face.

"She bad?" he asked fearfully.

"Two hours gone. You'll stay with her, won't you? I got to go after a doctor."

He was already urging Winnie out of her stall.

"Go where?"

"Carroll. That doctor you told me about."

"You can't get through to Carroll tonight, you big fool!" Spence half snatched the harness away. "Ain't no man living could drive that road tonight!"

"By the Lord, that's what I'm a-going to do!"

"You're crazy, Thomas! Horse like Winnie can't run in a blizzard. You can't even see the road. And that old doc's seventy— think he'll come out?"

"I'm going, I tell you!" Thomas protested stubbornly. "Take your hand off my arm and help me hitch."

Instead Spence looked up earnestly, his eyes pleading like the eyes of a hound.

"Don't do that, Thomas!" he entreated. "You can't get through. I know this country. You don't. I been man and boy here. You ain't but just come. And I ain't got nobody, you might say, while you got your woman to look after. What'd she do if you never come back?"

Thomas saw that his eyes were wet, knew that Spence Vitt would be his friend as long as he lived.

"I got to have a doctor!" he kept insisting. "I got to, Spence. I don't know what to do."

Spence nodded his head, hesitated a moment as if uncertain whether he should tell Thomas of his intention, and then bolted for the door.

"You go on back up!" he yelled just before the night swallowed him.

By the time Thomas picked up the lantern to follow, he was nowhere to be seen.

4 Thomas sank wearily to the chair. His body ached, but his nerves were still taut. Now and then there was some mysterious sound from the icy room upstairs, but it was no longer Kate's voice.

Spence had gotten through to Rock Mill for a midwife, had run back leading the horse, the rawboned woman and her husband in the buggy behind. Now the old man sat dreaming by the kitchen stove. He was a cracked-clay fellow, long, lean, brown as leather. There was nothing about birth that could excite him in the least.

"What you goin' to call the kid?" he broke in upon Thomas. "Valentine?"

Valentine's Day! Thomas had forgotten. Once, a long number of years ago, he had carried a homemade lacy heart to a flaxen-haired girl on Valentine's Day, only to have her tear it up before his eyes.

"That'd be nice," he said in an effort to be agreeable. He was a little afraid of the old man's opinion. "Course, maybe it ain't a boy."

"Course 'tis, course 'tis!" the miller disagreed. "Girls ain't no earthly use! Always a boy till they tell you 'tain't, and even then you keep right on hopin' they looked wrong."

Thomas nodded eagerly. "That's what we'll call him, then," he said.

The old fellow worried off a hunk of black twist before he demurred.

"Hopin' you wouldn't," he said. "Me, I always wanted somethin' I could call Hocking. Can't name a she Hocking. Not in this part of the country, anyway."

"Hocking?"

"Hail, yes! Hain't no name better'n Hocking. Crick out here's called Hocking, ain't it? Goes on down and makes a pretty good river, an' they call that Hocking. Injuns said Hock-hocking. Means bottleneck."

"Seems a little funny, don't it? For a boy, I mean."

"Funny!" The old man shifted his chair for emphasis. "Son, you listen to what I tell you: you call that young un like I say. Man named Hocking Hunter was the grandpappy of this whole part of the country. First kid born in Lancaster, 'long about 1800. Pappy come clear from Virginy. Got to be one of the best danged lawyers in all Ohio."

Thomas heard a step on the stair, knew the big woman was coming down. He looked up hopefully when she entered, although he knew he was less than dust in her eyes. What she had called him for not making Kate a bed in the kitchen he would never forget.

"More'n you deserve, you big brute!" she greeted. "Fine a boy as ever was born."

Thomas tried to force his way past her, but she barred the door.

"You go up there now and I'll knock your ears off!" she said quietly. "Guess if she got along without you this long, she can get along a while longer."

"She's all right, ain't she?" he implored, his hands twisting at his black hair.

"Course she's all right!" said the midwife. "Any woman's all

29

right. Only men that're born addled and get worse every year they live."

Thomas had to go back to the fire, where he stood forlornly watching the graybeard suck his quid.

"Sorry I got to cause you all this trouble," he said in a weak attempt to conciliate the woman who was puttering about the stove. "You can go on home tomorrow."

The midwife snorted. "Go home when she's able to be up and doin', that's when I'll go home," she said. "Two whole weeks, maybe. And you'll just pay me a dollar a day until I do! You can put that in your pipe and smoke it!"

Thomas relapsed into total defeat. Through the vague aura of his muddled thoughts, he heard the miller say, "Know what he's a-goin' to name that young un, ma? Hocking! Always said they'd be a Hocking born some'eres hereabouts."

His wife's silence chastened him. Thomas gathered that she too was disappointed, that she would have given her eyes not to have it said that she had not been able to redeem her man's desire for a son.

5   That winter all the talk was of the way Luther Tanterscham avenged himself on Bill Sapooney.

For years Bill's hands had been pebbled with warts. He seemed to be proud of his affliction, was in the habit of exhibiting his treasures whenever he could find someone not too queasy to look at them.

"T-ta-take that there one now!" he would blubber fondly. "That there one's a new one. D-didn't have it atall two weeks ago, and now it's b-bi-big as the best one I got!"

Then, unexpectedly, some of his beauties began to bleed.

Celia ran down Gregory Lane to Tess Sellers, who had the reputation of being able to stop blood, cure swinney, take fire out of burns, and do a hundred other things. When she came back, she was mysterious with a secret—all Bill had to do was rub each wart with a single white bean, put the beans in a bag, and then drop the bag on the road. Whoever found it would also pick up the warts.

Bill dropped the muslin bag in a rut in front of Tanterscham's house that same night, and as luck would have it Ralph Tanterscham, a year old toddler, lifted it the next afternoon. In two weeks' time his hands were a sight for sore eyes.

That should have been the end of the matter, but Celia wasn't able to keep Bill's mouth shut. As well latch the lane gate to keep crows out of the corn as counsel Bill to prudence.

"G-go on down and see what I done done to that Tanterscham brat!" he kept boasting. "H-hands look like as if he h-held 'em in a hive of b-b-b-bees."

It happened that one day Spence Vitt wanted a crosscut and went over to Tanterschams to borrow Luther's. Lottie said Lute was down in the barn feeding, and sure enough Spence found him forking down hay. The minute he walked through the wagon door, he was attracted by the yellowed piece of paper tacked on the outside of one of the stalls. It hadn't been there before—he could swear to that. What puzzled Spence was that it was no more than six inches from the floor, and right over a big rat hole.

"What's that thing say, Lute?" he asked when he saw the writing was all in German.

Tanterscham grinned craftily, but he obliged Spence by rattling it off:

NEHMT OBACHT
Mit dem seyd ihr benachrichtet dasz ihr bey Empfang dies, die von euch bisher bewohnte Gebaeud verlassen mueszi. Im fall ihr dies nit thut, werd ihr die Straf empfangen von die vorgeschrieben Gesetz.

Ich wuensch dasz ihr zum Bill Sapooney gehn solt.

Spence had a good notion there was something in the air when he heard Bill's name.

"Turn it over, turn it over, Lute!" he said. "Know I can't understand anything out of that side of your mouth."

Tanterscham was pretty shy for a while, but finally told what the paper meant. It was nothing less than a notice to all his rats to leave their domiciles under pain of punishment, and to go over to Bill Sapooney's. It had been his father's, he said; all he did was rub out the original name and write in Bill's.

Spence managed to keep a straight face.

"They go yet?" he asked.

"Dey have to talk it over a vile first."

"Figure Bill's got about all the rats he can handle already."

"He get some more . . . You shust vait und see!"

Spence had a lot of devilment in him that day. He went out and moseyed around the yard until he found a piece of charcoal. "Trouble is we got all English rats in this part of the country," he told Lute when he came back in. And on the stall right beside the German he wrote the English:

WARNING
All rats get out of this barn soon as you read this. If you dont youll catch it.

Go down to Bill Sapooney.

Spence spread what he had done up and down the road so that everybody could come in and have a good laugh. Thomas went down and so did Joe Jordan and Lonzo Brewster. Lute Tanterscham himself wasn't laughing.

"You shust vait!" he said whenever anybody teased him. "Dey go. You shust vait!"

Sure enough, three nights later the rats must have made up their minds. Thomas was in the kitchen when he heard Celia screaming. He ran, and so did Spence from the other side of Sapooney's house. It was a fine white night, the moon all lonesome in the sky, so that the whole Sapooney yard was lighted up. And there out behind the house with his corn knife was Bill, whacking away harder than he'd ever whacked in harvest time. Every now and then the house door would open and Celia would go *whoosh* with a big bucket of water from the reservoir. It was so hot it fairly smoked on the cold ground.

Rats! They were all over the yard, tens and dozens of them. Bill would chase one a while and then take out after another, his chance of catching any about the same as that of finding a flea in a strawtick.

Thomas and Spence just stood in the yard and screamed with laughter. Spence couldn't even look, he was crying so hard. Time she got rid of all the hot water, Celia came out into the yard with the hickory splint broom. Only she wasn't much help to Bill. Just let her see a gray streak sliding toward her skirts and she'd yell bloody murder.

And then Bill missed and smacked right down through his shoe. Celia went crazy when she saw the blood. "You got to take me down to Sellers, Mr. Linthorne, you just got to!" she kept bawling. Thomas wouldn't. Instead he carried Bill into the house while Spence ran home after some clean cloth for bandages.

Celia must have gotten down to Tess Sellers somehow, because about an hour later the bleeding stopped. Just seemed to dry up, the blood did. Thomas and Spence were the most thankful men alive—for a time it had looked as if Bill might bleed to death. He hadn't done anything but cut off the whole end of his big toe. Just as fast as they'd get one bandage on it, the cloth would be all soaked and they'd need another. They used up one of Cora Vitt's best petticoats—it was the only thing Spence had been able to get his hands on.

The two of them stayed over most of that night. They couldn't depend on Celia. "Bat had brains like that woman, it wouldn't live long!" Thomas commented angrily to Spence when Celia finally came home and started running around the house like a chicken with its head off. First thing she did, for example, was take a lantern out in the yard and hunt the corn knife Bill had butchered himself with.

Thomas was thoroughly put out when he saw what she meant to do. She didn't pay any attention to Bill; old Tess had told her that it was the knife that was hurt. She laid it on the kitchen table as tenderly as if it were a newborn baby, got out her bucket of hog-fat, and greased it up and down both sides. Three times a day she had to do it, she said, and when the knife was over being hurt, Bill's toe would be all right.

Bill recovered, but he never liked Tanterscham very much after that. "D-d-d-dam Dutchman!" he always sputtered whenever any-one reminded him of his warts. "G-get even with him one of these days, you just see if I don't."

Spence voiced the thought of the neighborhood. "Bet you Cely'll get her a new fur coat sure'n for certain," he said.

III

1 The year was good to them.

By March, Kate was as hale and hearty as ever—Thomas knew her again as the sprightly child of their early marriage. Motherhood had made her a little more dignified, but sometimes she was still a wilding as she romped on the floor with the baby, rolling him over and over on the blanket she had spread or teasing him with a tarnished ring that dangled just out of reach of his chubby fingers.

The wheat was good; the corn stood thick and strong. When the neighbors came to help with the hay, their flashing scythes were almost choked by the heavy grass. Thomas set out a few apple trees back of the house, brought home more than a barrel of syrup from the sorghum mill. By Thanksgiving, if it was cold enough, he would butcher one of his pigs, and after Christmas the three others. With the meat, molasses, wine, berries, and wild honey, they would manage well indeed.

There was even money in the bank. The Lancaster Lumber Company offered an extra hundred for the few oaks on the shelf over the lower pasture, and Thomas found no reason to regret the bargain. He loved trees, almost as much as Spence Vitt loved them. Lordly and sentient things they were, flowing with life, sharing their abundance. His heart still beat quick whenever he looked across the road to the dark height of Church Hill. But the big oaks in the pasture had to go because they were dangerous to cattle in a storm.

Their greatest advance was that everyone in the community accepted them now. At church, the little nondenominational box called Union Meeting House, they met the Shreets and the Peterses, the Wagrams, Chenoweths, McGrubers, Prides. When there was a threshing or a barn raising, Cory, Barker, Canaway, and Wendell talked in neighborly fashion. The Tanterschams and Jordans exchanged weather signs whenever they came down the road; old daddy Brewster, the hermit soul who grubbed out his last years on the next farm east, tottered over daily for his milk; and, greatest wonder of all, the rich Gregorys drove into the yard one day as nonchalantly as if they had always visited.

Only the Schraders were unknown, aloof, hostile.

Thomas had first heard of them from Spence, and Spence was not one to let his tongue gibble-gabble. "Just you go your own way and let them go theirs, Thomas," he advised. "There's some kinds of poison a man can't do without, and there's some kind he can't do with. Schraders is the last." Thomas had not commented then, knowing hearsay half-lies. But it was peculiar that Spence should have bothered to give him warning—and that right in the thunder of threshing.

The more he thought about what Spence said, and in later weeks the more of the ugly stories he heard of the tribe who lived down Gregory Lane behind the big woods, the less he liked having Matt, Gorm, Harrison, and their women and kids near. Never farmed and always ate, people said. Butchered with a bullet after dark—a mile or so away from home. Lived dirty, thought dirty, acted dirty.

Through the big woods the Schraders roamed, guns in hand, exactly like the squatters of a hundred years before. They would have been champions in a tomahawk fight. But now, in the year 1868, with the current of civilization strong all around them, tomahawks were out of date.

2 Two things happened that winter that were destined to be of great importance.

Coon came.

And they, or rather Thomas—for Kate was distinctly cold toward the transaction—bought Black Belle.

It was a snowy night in the middle of winter that they heard the low whine at the door, hopeful-hopeless, part of the wind and yet somehow detached from it. They were still at the supper table, their plates greasy cold from the fried hominy.

Kate had the baby in one arm, the hungry pig nursing as usual, with the other was lifting the coffeepot from the hot stove when she suddenly stopped as if arrested.

"You hear that, Thomas?" she asked anxiously, and held her breath to make sure she was not deceived.

"Hear what?"

He was indolent and luxuriously warm after a long day in the cold barn, could not be bothered by trifles. Kate waited until the ominous call came again. "That!" she said as she crept close to him.

Thomas was on his feet as quick as a cat, his muscles hard.

"Sounds a whole lot like a dog," he said as he went toward the door, but he was careful.

It was a dog, a big black mongrel with burning eyes, part collie and part hound. He stood in the fresh snow on the stoop, begging, his right foreleg held close to his breast as if it might be broken.

"Been through hard times, that boy!" Thomas said as he coaxed the dog into the warm room.

Kate put the baby in his cradle at once, oblivious to his cries. "Best be careful!" Thomas warned, but he was proud of the way she started right in to pick the burs out of the black pelt and break the ice from the sore paws.

"Looks like he come an awful long way, Thomas," Kate was compassionate. "Think he's hurt much?"

"Been kicked, I suppose."

"His leg ain't broke, is it?"

"You let his leg alone! Fool with it, he might bite right through your hand."

"He won't bite," Kate said positively. "Just you wait till I give him something to eat, and you'll see how well he likes me. We can keep him, can't we?"

Thomas made quite a ceremony of unlacing his left boot before he answered: "Why, that I can't say. Keep him if he don't belong to nobody. That is, in case we want him."

"I want him!" Kate said instantly. "And what's more, I'm a-going to keep him."

When Thomas went up the road next day and told Spence Vitt, Spence came back with him.

"Just wanted to make sure afore I said anything," he remarked when he had taken one good look at Coon. The dog lay in a corner of the kitchen, his leg bound in one of Hocking's diapers. "No doubt about it, though, Thomas—that's Gorm Schrader's dog. Been treated plenty bad."

Thomas looked worried. He didn't want to get into trouble with the Schraders, certainly not over a cur.

"Don't think we ought to keep him, then?" he asked, hoping that Spence would agree with him.

"You do what you like," Spence said. "Wouldn't if it was me. Course, maybe you're different. Gorm mightn't care a little potato. And then again he might throw a conniption and come over here with the idea of burning you down."

Thomas stood abject after Spence had gone. "Guess maybe we better just turn him out," he told Kate, knowing how much his words would hurt her.

"We will not!" she said. "Just because you hear bogey stories about this Gorm Schrader, you're afraid of him. I'd just like to see him come and get Coon if I was a man. You can just bet your boots I'd do something about it all right!"

Thomas let her challenge his courage—he was really afraid. If the barn or house did suddenly catch fire some night, who was he to say that the blaze had been set?

He thought a lot about unpleasant possibilities during the next few days and on Saturday, when he drove to Lancaster, went to a hardware store and bought himself a rifle.

3   There was no unpleasantness. Gorm didn't care a wormy buckeye for the dog—he wouldn't tree. Coon went with Thomas to the woods a week later, on a day when Thomas was lucky enough to see a rabbit on its form and bowl it over. That night when they had fried rabbit for supper, Coon got his share.

All through the late winter they hunted, if hunting it could be called, for luck or Thomas's aim was generally bad. Some of the days he certainly could not spare. It was unlike him to indulge

37

himself when there was harness to stitch, fences to mend, dung and fodder to haul. But there was a strange perversity in him. Instinctively he sensed the need of knowing how to shoot well, to scout the woods, to break the back of danger against the root of new-developed craft.

He and the dog never wandered south over Church Hill where the deep ravines led to a half-mile of dense woods that bristled over the blunt shoulder of Rock Ladder. But north and northwest they loved to roam, in and out of the crannies of Goose Ridge or into the deeper silence of Black Man. Most of Black Man was on the Barker farm, acreage totally disproportionate to the owner, who was little, timid, inept, a ghost-haunted individual who swore the long Kentuckian still walked with his blacksnake.

It was more than a year after Thomas moved in that he first heard the story.

It was in '53 or '54, old-timers said. Chenoweth's father was living then, a patriarch with long red beard and apple-green eyes. He had stemmed from New England, for years had ridden circuit through the Virginias. His health was finally broken by long exposure to frost and sun, but his spirit took fire within him. If there was anything he hated, it was slavery; anyone he despised, a slave-owner. After he gave up preaching, his tirades against the traffic in blacks were so bitter that people avoided him. They agreed with him in principle, but his words were the words of a madman.

A year or so after old Chenoweth moved onto the skirts of the ridge, everyone knew he was running a station. The lantern in the front window of his house on the hill burned at all hours of the night; often through the dead stillness of the dark the neighbors heard the rumble of his wheels. Chenoweth brought up runaway blacks from farther down in the hills, hid them through the day in a cave on the ridge, the next night spirited them away toward Columbus.

One night a big black harbored in the cave. And the very next morning the Kentuckian rode up on a horse that had been hard pushed. He was big, the slave-hunter, and soft with that sly softness of a tiger's pads. Chenoweth met him before he got down, but the old man was no match for the hunter. He knew all about the preacher, all about the cave on the ridge, and he was going to carry back his darky or have a big piece of his hide to show for his trouble.

Chenoweth's cave was a long L under a sandstone ledge, the entrance so well concealed in laurel that an eagle couldn't have spotted it, but the Kentuckian poked around until he found it. Never once left the spur it was on, Chenoweth said afterward. Whoever had told him about the place had given a pretty good description.

"Won't take long now, mistah," he remarked with all the dignity of a man handing a dancing partner to her chair, and crawled in head first.

Only thing he didn't know about was the L. The black must have slugged him there with a piece of loose rock. All that Chenoweth knew for sure was that he heard a funny hollow sound, and then he waited and waited. After what seemed too long a time, there was a scrunching noise, and then the feet of the Kentuckian began to wriggle out. It took several minutes to clear his body—all that was left of it. There wasn't much head.

Chenoweth buried him that night up on the ridge. Some people said that he gave the Negro ten dollars in hard money as a kind of reward, but Charley, his son, always denied that his father thought a slave-owner was worth that much.

Years passed, the war began, and the name Black Man stuck onto the north hills.

Then one night in '64 (Barker himself told Thomas this last over a pint of elderberry), Barker was coming home with a load of coal. Just at the bottom of Sunset Hill he bogged down in a chuckhole. There wasn't much to do except go home after another team because Tanterschams were away, Bill Sapooney without any horses at all, and the farm that the Linthornes later bought was untenanted.

Barker cut off across country so that he wouldn't have to walk two sides of a triangle. He was going along the run just off to the right of the ridge when a big fellow came out of the dark and started to walk along beside him. Barker wasn't very much scared, although the man's appearance was strange. Tramp or hunter, he thought. There was something a little peculiar about the way he walked and talked, but not much, and Barker was thinking about telling him to come along up to the house when the stranger asked a light for his pipe.

Barker gave it to him. He waited while his companion broke a match off the block, but when it bloomed into a head of light Barker's eyes almost popped out. The man's face was all smashed away so that there wasn't anything left but a bloody mouth, and there was a big blacksnake under his arm that trailed on the ground behind him.

"You run?" asked Thomas, shivering a little in sympathy.

"Any man says I run's a liar!" Barker answered proudly, his sparrow chest inflated with importance. "Didn't run, Thomas; I just up and flew! Offer me a thousand dollars cash money to go back tonight and walk along Black Man, I'd spit right in your eye! Yessir, I'd spit right in your eye! Why, man, I wouldn't go that way after dark with Sherman's whole damn army!"

Thomas was more or less inclined to agree. He walked home by the road, his rifle cocked, the hair on his neck on end whenever Coon suddenly veered toward the bushes.

He was glad he had heard the story, but he wouldn't tell Kate. It might be hard on her, might make her see things, now that she was carrying the second baby.

4   It wasn't two weeks later that Thomas had to pay Barker back for the elderberry. The little fellow came down one morning all in a dither. One of his horses was down, he said: he had tried everything and couldn't get her up. He suspected wolf teeth.

Thomas tried to argue with him, but Barker got mad and said he knew what he was talking about. And at any rate there couldn't any harm come to the horse—not if she was going to die anyway.

It was a disgusting operation to Thomas. They tied the mare's head down, propped open her jaws, used a hammer and cold chisel to knock out the two big teeth Barker indicated. The second one broke off; try as they would, they could not lift the roots.

"Won't do any good, I'll tell you that," Thomas said when he was leaving. If there was anything he hated, it was cruelty to a horse or dog.

"Yes, it will, too!" Barker spat out. "Much obliged to you for coming over. You let me know when you want someone to tend to your hogs next spring and I'll be down."

Thomas said he would, but he vowed secretly he wouldn't keep his word. Wanted anybody to work for him, he'd get Spence. That was the proper kind of man to have around—not a coward who got drunk and reported he had seen a dead slave-hunter.

5 Just before Christmas that year Spence came over to show Thomas a bushy cedar that would be nice to hold candles for the baby. Hocking was toddling everywhere now, would be two in February. He was a handsome fellow, brown-haired like his mother. Celia Sapooney had paid one frightful call on Kate, during which she suggested in her inimitable way that the baby's head was too large and that he would likely turn out to be an idiot, but Thomas was not worried. "Takes lots of skull to go around brains," he quieted Kate. "Any woodpecker can have a head like Cely Sapooney's."

It was while they were on Goose Ridge cutting the tree that Spence told Thomas about the shooting every Christmas afternoon. It was to be down at Sellers's this year, the big place at the bottom of Gregory Lane. Quarter a shot, Spence said, the money to go toward buying the steer that would be the prize. Sometimes barbecued it when the winner was agreeable. But he could drive it home if he liked.

"Sure I'll go along down with you," Thomas said eagerly. "Only thing is, I don't know about this gun of mine. Seems sometimes like it shoots high and right."

"That case, I'd aim low and left," said Spence. "'Tain't the gun atall nine cases out of ten."

Thomas and Kate fixed the baby a nice Christmas. There were popcorn strands on the cedar, and some red paper knickknacks Kate had cut out of the privy catalogue. Thomas bought a little cart with a wooden horse when he went to Lancaster, pampered himself by taking home a half dozen oranges and a pound of chocolate drops. His prize was a spray of holly he had had the good fortune to pick out of a gutter on Columbus Street; it lacked berries but was cheerful when Kate tied it over the frame of the sitting-room door.

41

For Kate herself Thomas bought nothing. She would have thought it wasteful for him to use money that way, saving as they were for stock, to say nothing of the land he hoped to buy. "Never got a thing for Christmas in my whole life I can remember of," she observed when he tactlessly suggested he shouldn't forget her. Nor had Thomas, at least not after the first few years.

But there was a good dinner, a goose that was only a little too tough, and for dessert a pumpkin pie and some wild grapes that Thomas had stored in a stone jar frozen into the garden soil. They were wrinkled and somewhat bitter, but their spiciness was very suggestive of Christmas.

"You sure you don' want to come along down?" Thomas asked as he rose from the table and got his rifle.

"My goodness no!" said Kate positively. "What'd people think if I went traipsin' after you everywhere? Say I had you hooked fast to my apron strings, that's what they'd say."

It was good logic. Women were born to be inconspicuous. They were always in the kitchen—at least seldom out of the dooryard. Once a week when they went to church, they took off their dark percales and put on black skirts and white blouses; but as soon as service was over they hurried back to drab. Spence Vitt had their description perfectly. "Put me in mind of walkin' pictures!" he said.

"Look like they'd bust right open if they cracked a smile." He made exception only for Celia Sapooney.

Thomas drove up the road for Spence before he headed south for Zeke Sellers's place. Winnie skimmed the hard-rutted roads without seeming to touch the bad places, so that they were down in no time at all. There were about twenty rigs and saddle horses at the hitching rail ahead of them, their owners congregated in the field behind the barn where the shooting was to take place. When Thomas and Spence arrived, they could see the dot of blue denim and gray flannel jackets around the stake where the steer was tied.

Sellers, a big, black-browed, frost-bitten man, met them as they hitched. Thomas thought he looked to be two-thirds bone, but his "Howdy!" was affable enough.

"Hoddoo!" said Thomas stiffly. He stood slightly in awe of the man whose mother was said to be a witch. The time Lonzo Brewster stepped into a scythe blade he would have died, folks reported, if someone hadn't hurried for old Tess. She stopped the flow of blood without using even a cobweb.

"Got a crowd, ain't you, Zeke!" Spence said when Sellers stood back in moody silence.

Sellers turned slowly around as if to make sure, unwilling to trust his memory and the obvious display of rigs. "Tol'able," he finally assented. "Seen a whole lot more, an' I've seen a whole lot less. You boys aimin' to throw a little lead?"

Spence jerked his head at Thomas.

"Guess Mr. Linthorne means to try once or twice," he said.

Thomas was embarrassed by the hard scrutiny of the older man. It was all very well to carry out the rifle for a try at a skunk or groundhog, but to shoot mark before the eyes of the whole neighborhood was a different matter.

"Well, only costs a quarter," Sellers said. "Can't lose much. You make up your mind, you tell me."

With that he started through the frosty grass toward his big gray brick. Thomas thought his attitude something of a rebuff; if anything, it hardened his resolution to try.

They joined the group in the field: men and boys of all ages, no more than half of them known. Thomas was glad whenever he saw a friendly face or could exchange greetings. Some of the eyes were hostile, particularly those of old Brame Slosson from down Sugar Grove way. Brame nursed an ancient flintlock that had an immensely long, heavy barrel—it was the only gun he'd trust, and he never missed shooting for a turkey or a steer. Some of the younger fellows might jostle him a little and make fun behind his back, but they had a wholesome respect for Brame and his "Angel 'f Death." The gun had been Brame's daddy's. "Kill one Injun, killed a hundred an' one!" Brame always bragged. The men he harangued didn't know about the Indians, but they did know that in Brame's hands the flintlock had killed their hope of wresting any prize away.

Spence took care of Thomas in an offhand manner, managed to introduce him to a few men without being obtrusive. "Friend of mine name of Thomas Linthorne, Mr. Benter," he would say. "Shake hands!" And after they had held out their paws suspiciously: "He's got that piece up my way Fargot used to own."

So besides Benter, Thomas met Smith, Brierley, the two Carter boys from near Basil, and several others whose names he couldn't remember. Brierley interested him more than any of the others. He was a horse trader who ran a Lancaster livery barn and had a couple of blooded stallions at stud. Brierley and he talked horses as naturally as if they had known each other life long, but when Thomas became boastful of Winnie's speed, Brierley grew respectfully contemptuous.

"Course, Linthorne, 'tain't that they ain't lots of good nags in this world," he said as he rolled his quid. "And you got to remember they's lots of reasons a man buys him a horse. One fellow wants somethin' that'll go hell-fersartain, an' another's got his mind on a gentle mare for the missus."

"Guess that's so," said Thomas. "That wasn't what I meant about Winnie, though. She's like a kitten, but she's got git-up-an-go too."

Brierley got stiff for an instant, made as if to turn away, and then changed his mind.

"Where is this horse you got spread out all over your mind?" he asked sharply. "Ain't drivin' her, are you?"

Thomas took him down to the rail, instantly regretting he had done so when he saw the harsh way Brierley forced Winnie's mouth open.

"About five, ain't she?"

"Five or six," said Thomas.

"What you want for her?"

"She ain't for sale."

Brierley laughed and spit.

"Listen," he said, "they ain't nothin' ain't for sale. Got the right kind of money, you can walk off with this whole universe."

"I ain't thinking about selling, anyway," said Thomas. "You see, Winnie's the only horse I ever had that was all mine. Sort of seems to belong to me. And I sort of seem to belong to her."

Brierley looked as if he wanted to laugh, but instead became confidential.

"I ain't sayin' she ain't good," he said. "And I ain't sayin' she is. Only it don't take long to see she ain't the best. Guess maybe you never noticed that right front hock."

"Nothing the matter with it, is there?"

"Maybe not. But it looks a whole heap like a spavin to me."

Thomas thought hard while they were going back to the field. He loved Winnie, but it might be he would think more of another colt. And if Winnie was spavined, then it would be sense to get rid of her.

"How much would you be willing to give for that horse of mine?" he surprised himself by asking.

Brierley was indifferent. "Depends," he said. "Hard cash, I wouldn't risk no more'n a hundred. Trade, maybe a little bit more."

"Not much, is it?"

"Now looky here!" said Brierley, and stopped so that Thomas had to look down his mouldy mouth. "Seems like you're the right kind of fellow—kind that likes to have good legs and wind in front of him. Want to go somewheres, you want to go in a hurry. And don't much stomach the idea of havin' to carry the nag back. That right?"

"Guess it is, just about," Thomas was flattered. He was smiling like a simpleton.

"Well, then, tell you what I'll do. You drive on in town some day next week and look me up. I got a filly by Thunderhead out of Jenny B. Name's Black Belle. You've heard tell of Thunderhead, hain't you?"

Thomas hadn't, but he lied. "Guess most everybody has," he said.

"Thought so. Swept all the tracks before I put him to stud. Wasn't nothin' could pass him this side of Zanesville. And this little girl of his is the spittin' image of her daddy."

Thomas began to tingle with the excitement of possible ownership.

"Guess she might be more'n I could pay for," he tested.

Brierley took off his hat and scratched his bald head.

"Maybe so," he said. "Three and a quarter is all I want now. Say I'd take that horse of yourn in for one and a quarter and leave you an even two. Pay it all on the nose, you can knock off ten percent of that. I like a man, I believe in treatin' him right."

"I'll think it over," Thomas told him, and was glad to see

45

that Brierley didn't seem to care one way or the other. Back of the barn they walked away from each other and never met again all afternoon.

6 The target, at fifty paces, was little bigger than a dime-sized bull's-eye, and was set just above an inverted black V. It looked like an easy shot, but the first hour wore away and no one was successful in carrying away the black without tearing into the surrounding white. Sellers held a piece of paper and called out the names of those who were to shoot, kept them moving along, settled whatever disputes arose.

Thomas stood a little back and to the left so that he could get a good view, Spence and a couple of strangers close beside him, all of them stomping and slapping their mittened fingers against their legs. Since morning the day had grown steadily colder.

"Trying it, Thomas?" Spence asked at last.

"Think I ought?"

"You don't, I will. Only seeing as how you been getting your hand in, you ought to have more chance than me."

Thomas went over to Sellers while the targets were being changed and after paying his quarter had the satisfaction of seeing his name added to the bottom of the list. When he rejoined Spence he asked about Brame, having noticed the old man posted on a pile of logs a hundred feet away, his long "Angel 'f Death" aslant his legs.

"Brame always shoots last," said Spence. "Sort of a privilege he has. Leastaways nobody ever tried to take it away from him."

Thomas watched closely while Benter, Danielson, McGruber, Shreet, the two Carters, and Marty took their turns. McGruber surprised everybody by putting a ball three-quarters in the black. It was the best shot of the afternoon, and Mac's previous reputation was that he was only a dumb critter whose value to the community was in helping butcher. Thomas felt shaky when he heard the flurry of laughter that followed the next attempt. He wouldn't like that if he missed.

"Thomas Linthorne! Thomas Linthorne!"

He was conscious of craning necks as he walked over to the line. Never before had he been so much aware of his body. "Big brute!" he heard someone behind him whisper. He was inclined to agree. He had daydreamed on the way over how he would have to ease Winnie home so that the steer could plod along behind the buggy. Now he would give anything if only he could throw a ball near the black.

At that his arm was steady enough as he brought the sights down. He held them on the mark, curled his index finger ever so slightly. It seemed the gun would never go off. The pointer wavered out of line to the right, then swung a little too far left. Thomas brought it back carefully and—

"My God, Zeke, there's Gorm Schrader comin' up the hill!"

—his gun cracked. Instant before his eyes was the triangular tear four inches above the bull's-eye, one of the worst attempts of the afternoon.

"Gorm Schrader! Gorm Schrader!" ran the whisper. There was a strange hush on everyone's lips. Nobody moved. Even Sellers, who should have been bawling out the name of Abraham Slosson, looked as if he were frozen, his white paper held almost at arm's length in front of his steel-rimmed spectacles.

Schrader's muscular bulk was ill-protected against the weather, his neck wide open to show his hairy red chest, but he was indifferent to the cold. He walked with indolent grace, a great red human cat. His eyes were small, green, set deep in their sockets, but it was the hands that claimed Thomas's attention, big, black-nailed hams, the one holding a rifle, the other swinging pendulum-like.

"Twenty-five cents a try!" Sellers greeted acidly as soon as Gorm got near enough to make the mistake of his meaning impossible. "Steer's over yonder; pay your money to me."

Gorm walked right on into the middle of the group, his head turning neither to right or left.

"Let's see the targets!" he said bluntly.

Sellers pointed to them, the lot displayed on an upturned packing box. Gorm was slightly interested in McGruber's—that was the only one.

"Twenty-five?" he seemed to bargain.

"Spot cash!" snapped Sellers.

"Cheap for a steer."

Sellers bit his lips. "Hain't won it yet that I've heard tell on!" he said.

For answer Gorm reached into his pocket and threw a quarter into the grass at Sellers's feet. Then, almost before Thomas knew what he was about, he had leveled and shot. There was no mark perceptible unless one looked close, and then one saw there was something wrong with the middle of the black. It seemed now to be grayish.

"Guess that wins it, don't it?"

"Not by a jugful it don't!" Sellers said tartly. "Brame Slosson's got to shoot yet." And turning, he yelled, "Brame! Hi there, Brame!"

Brame was already on his way down from the woodpile, his gun held cautiously at arm's length.

They made a respectful semicircle around him, Sellers and Gorm within the ring. It seemed impossible that the old man could match Gorm's skill, but they were all hopeful. Sellers ordered a fresh mark in place—he wanted Brame to have every opportunity.

The long gun came up slowly. Brame seemed to quaver a little while he drew bead. Then, suddenly, he stiffened. There was a deafening report, and the whole bull's-eye disappeared.

Gorm immediately started toward the steer, but Sellers grabbed his arm.

"Ends it, don't it?" Gorm pretended surprise. "Ball touched the white. Mine didn't."

"Tie," said Sellers. "Brame's gun blows a bigger ball, and you know it! You'll have to shoot it off."

Gorm's face was ugly when he heard that.

"Godamighty, mister, I ain't got any more quarters to throw away on your old cow!"

"You'll have to shoot it off!" Sellers repeated. "Know you don't have to pay to shoot off a tie."

Gorm cocked his rifle without further words and waited, his back to the target but his eyes avoiding any encounter.

"Ready whenever you are," said Sellers.

48

Again the gun swung to the shoulder with precise smoothness, again there was the almost instant discharge, and again the black rim showed around the hole.

"Brame!"

Brame shook in a little powder, patched a bullet and rammed home, then sighted more carefully than before. The explosion seemed to rock him back on his heels, but he again carried away the black.

"Use a shot-gun you ought to be able to hit something!" Gorm bullied him.

"'Pears like I do," said Brame as he shook his head up and down. "Want to swap guns for the next one?"

Gorm knew when his bluff was called. This time he took a little longer to aim. If anything, the shot was worse. Sellers had to pull down his spectacles before he was convinced that the ball had not struck part of the white.

They all stood rooted while Brame leveled and held for the third time. He was swaying from the weight of the heavy barrel, seemed not to be able to freeze. Then, when at last he came to rest and they all tensed themselves against the expected report, he had to drop the muzzle until he had hold of himself.

"Shoot, you damn old guinea!" Gorm ordered harshly.

"Take all the time you want, Brame!" Sellers instantly corrected.

Brame did, but it was asking too much for him to hit again. The heavy ball smashed out only half of the bull's-eye, and the steer was Gorm's.

They went home silent, their Christmas spoiled. Thomas saw the tears on the old man's face as he hurried away, no one daring to console him. Then, from the hitching rail, he looked up across the frosted pasture to watch Gorm flog the steer up the run. Gorm had a club in his hand, stopped every now and then to whack the hide of the reluctant beast.

Thomas shivered. He had thought that he wouldn't be afraid of Schrader, that the stories told of Gorm could not possibly be true. Now he knew that he was afraid. And he was beginning to believe what people said.

7 On Tuesday, Thomas drove Winnie into Lancaster for some sugar and five yards of gingham. He had not intended to see Brierley at all. But once in the county seat, he thought he might as well run around, now that he was so near.

He could have choked himself afterward when he remembered how he had been putty in the trader's hands. He had hated to part with Winnie. But the black horse he drove home moved over the roads like silk over flesh. She would carry him fast and far, there was no doubt of that.

There was doubt about something else, though—what Kate would say when he told her he had thought it worth two hundred dollars of their money to be so carried.

IV

1   The purchase of Black Belle was an extravagance, but it had good effect on Thomas. The next spring he ripped up both the good fields and the land that had never been laid to the plow, grubbed, blasted, burned, ran the marking sled clear against the fences in his endeavor to use the waste margins. He began, too, to pasture on Church Hill, a privilege that none saw fit to deny him. After all, the land belonged to Fargot, and Fargot couldn't sell grass in his Lancaster grocery.

The second child, a girl, was born two years after Hocking. Three months afterward Kate was pregnant again, and almost a year to the day bore a third, this time another girl. Thomas was proud enough, but wished they had been boys instead. The naming of the girls he left to their mother, who called the first one Charlotte, after her own mother, the second Faith. The latter name was indicative of her changing character.

Not a year after marriage, she had insisted that Thomas buy a big Bible. After that when he came in at night, he often found her reading while she waited supper for him. Or else she would take down the heavy volume and spread it in the pool of light on the red-checked cloth after the dishes were washed. Sometimes she read aloud while Thomas relaxed in the rocker she used to sing the babies to sleep, his long legs stretched out to toast his stockinged feet at the fire.

Thomas approved her selection of passages. Not since he was a boy had he heard the stories of Esther, Ruth, Samuel, Saul, David, the terrible suffering of Job, the trials of Paul, the fervor of Isaiah, the wrath of Ezekiel. The Psalms were beautiful—if sometimes egotistical; the Proverbs plain common sense that he mightily approved. But the strange book called the Song of Solomon and the fantastic horror of the Apocalypse he could not stomach. The first he thought indecent, the second lunatic.

2 It was the summer Hocking began finally to say a few words that Kate startled Thomas one evening by suggesting that they ought to say a table prayer.

"What for?" he demanded, his brow furrowed.

"Folks do," she said quietly. "Call it returning thanks."

"Who?"

"Well, almost everybody that's had the right bringing up. Even Sapooneys, I've heard tell."

"You don't know anything about Sapooneys!" said Thomas. "You ain't never ett there, and if I can help it you ain't a-goin' to."

She was not to be drawn into digressive argument.

"I think it'd be real nice," she said in the level voice Thomas by now knew meant that she had her mind set.

He let it go for a day, thought it over while he was following Bill and Charley through the corn the next afternoon, and at last decided to agree. That night when they sat down he reached for the bread as usual, but while she washed up and he got out the last to put new soles on his Sunday shoes, he reopened the subject.

"About this—this praying—before we eat," he drawled with his mouth full of tacks. "Tell the truth, I wouldn't mind it—not a whole lot. Trouble is I don't know what to say."

He wouldn't look up, even when he realized that Kate had her hands out of the dishwater and was staring at him. When, finally, he did glance at her, he was puzzled to see the luster of her eyes. It was almost as if he had come home from town with word that eggs were up a cent.

"You really mean, Thomas?"

"Mean what?"

"You will—offer the blessing?"

"Ain't never denied you nothing in reason, have I?" he grumbled.

She went back to her dishes then, but as soon as she was finished scouring up the skillet she sat down at the table with a pencil and a sheet of wrapping paper. It was a full half-hour before she was finished, and by that time Thomas was trimming the edge of the second sole.

"I been writing down the ones I've heard," she said as she handed him the paper. "Course, you won't want that first one in German, but I put it down 'cause it was Pa's and it just sort of popped into my mind."

Thomas read the English.

All eyes wait upon Thee, O Lord, and Thou givest them their meat in due season. Thou openest Thy liberal hand, and satisfiest the desire of every living thing. Amen.

We praise and thank Thee, O God our Father, for all Thy gifts, of which we are not worthy. We pray Thee to feed our souls with bread from heaven, through the mercy of Jesus Christ our Lord. Amen.

"What's that first one?" he asked when he had spelled out the words by holding the paper close to the lamp chimney. "Sounds like somebody with a sore throat."

Kate read the words with great dignity:

Herr, wir gehen zu dem Essen,
Lasz uns deiner nicht vergessen.
Hilf uns, dasz wir nach der Erden
Deine Gaest im Himmel werden. Amen.

"I can't help it," she apologized when he caught the tears streaking down her cheeks. "That was Papa's. You can't use it, of course."

"Why put it down, then?"

"Well, the others mean the same thing. I just thought that maybe you'd be choosy."

"Wouldn't take Dutch if I was," said Thomas. "My name ain't Tanterscham."

He felt somewhat displeased, wanted her to know it. While he got the lantern ready for his final inspection of the stables, he thought up what to say.

"Course, there's just this much about it," he remarked just before he went out. "I work awful hard for what I get. Praying ain't a-goin' to plow any corn. Guess a man could pray himself blue in the face and still starve if he didn't—"

"You hush up now!" she commanded as she came toward him defiantly. "Ain't a true word in your mouth, and you know it!"

"Humph!" Thomas grunted. He hadn't thought she'd be so touchy. "No use getting your dander up. I was just pointing out that—"

"I don't want to hear it!"

"All right, don't then!" he shouted at her. He slammed the door behind him, stayed in the barn a full hour before he came back.

That week, however, he searched for the paper one day, found it in the Bible where she had hidden it away. Out in the fields in the afternoon, he practiced the prayers on the corn and circling buzzards, clearing his throat solemnly to preface every attempt. Charley and Bill didn't seem to mind, as long as he held on to the corn plow.

And that was why when the threshers came Thomas did not call on Cory or Pride, as was usual. With deep-voiced majesty he said grace himself—and glanced up quickly when he was done to see Kate gaping, the big blue platter of fried chicken tilted precariously in her hands.

3   That was all right when a person got used to it—starting off the meals with a prayer. It made everybody equal, sort of told when it was the right time to reach.

And going to church was all right, too. At church one could relax comfortably and think of all manner of queer things while the preacher was droning. It was a good place to lay plans for the week, to hear what was doing on farms miles around. When there was a

54

woman lying-in who might need help, or a sudden plague among the cattle, that was the place to offer aid and suggest cures.

But about baptism Thomas was not at all easy in mind.

Kate had been screwing him down a little too tightly—he had deferred in so many things that she had come to believe he would never raise his back. Not that it would hurt the kids any. Only trouble was that it meant saying things he didn't rightly believe.

Thomas took his problem up the road to Spence Vitt, the only man he felt he knew well enough to trust. Cory or Pride would have been better able to talk—they knew ten times as much as Spence. Cory was always reading books, had once been a preacher; and Pride was always buying ink tablets and writing down things that never happened. But a person might as well approach a graveyard monument as go see either one of them. Time they finished their gabble, they had a man more muddled than he was before.

Spence was picking kernels from a big blue bowl of cracked hickory nuts when Thomas eased down beside him on the kitchen stoop. For some ten minutes he forgot what he had come for, simply helped himself whenever he saw a nut-meat that was almost whole.

"Get me some of these this year," he vowed.

"Right good in cakes," said Spence. "Blame things are hard to pick, though—only things worse is beechnuts."

"Cora making for the social?"

"Reckon she is. Sort of goes in strong for hick'ry nut icings."

Thomas smoked a pipe, unwilling to tell what had brought him up the road. "You'll be gettin' some apples this year," he said at last. "What's on them trees back there, Seek-No-Furthers?"

"Some. Mostly Ramboes, though. Won't be more'n a hundred bushels this year. Reckon I'll have to give 'em away couple years from now."

"Want you to save me some. Havin' a parin'?"

"Think so, maybe. Cora ain't strong on dried apples, but I like 'em. Ain't nothin' nicer for a man's pockets when he's out all day."

"Guess that's about right, Spence." He knocked out his pipe, packed it again, and again sucked it to its last bitterness. "Cora in?" he asked then, as if she might be eavesdropping.

"Somewheres around—why?"

"Oh, nothing much. Just wanted to ask you something to see what you'd say." Thomas arose and walked down to the well as if inviting Spence to follow. Once there, they had to wind up a fresh bucket of water.

"What I'm after is just to get your idea," he said when he could delay no longer. "I just wanted to—well, it's like this: How much you think there is in this blame business of takin' a kid to church to have him baptized?"

Spence was none too willing to answer.

"Guess it's all accordin' to what you believe, Thomas," he said. "In the Bible, if you know the right place to dig it out."

"Think it's true?"

Spence shied a clod at a stray hen.

"Well, Thomas, here's how I figure," he said when he came back to the well. "Lot of things a man knows what to think about, and lot of things he don't. Cutworms in the cabbage, rats in the corncrib, horse foundered, or something like that he can figure out. Then there's some things he thinks he knows, like snakes sucking cows, or carrying a buckeye to keep rheumatics away. But when it comes to things about God—well, he ain't no better'n a rabbit with its head in a hole."

"Ain't the point of baptizing that it's just what everybody does?"

"Maybe," Spence admitted.

"You baptized?"

"Got me a certificate, anyhow. Bet you are too."

Thomas had to confess that he had been.

"All I'm a-tryin' to get at's the reason," he explained. "Don't seem right to me that God's up there a-watchin' to see whether a young un gets a little water on his head."

"'Tain't that exactly," Spence said. "Mostly obeyin', as I get it. You tell your boy to do a thing, you get mighty put out if he don't. Mightn't be much you ask, and he mightn't know the reason. But you want him to mind all the same."

Thomas nodded his head as if persuaded.

"Think I ought to give in and tell my woman we'll take the kids, then?"

"Would if I was you," Spence said. "Can't no harm come of it. And you ought to get a lot of peace of mind."

Thomas mulled over the idea as he kicked home through the sticky night, his boots furrowing the dust. Just so Kate didn't get the idea she was running the family and could have anything she hollered for! Only, she never did ask for much. She had gotten a little funny about church, but that might be because she didn't want people to think she meant to go kicking over the traces.

Thomas knew that some of the members of Union Meeting had been asking about the babies, had seen their chins droop and their brows go up when Kate admitted no one of the three had been baptized. Only, he wouldn't have them pushed under Hocking Creek— that was asking too much. Kate would have to wait until a sprinkler came along.

He told her his decision as soon as he reached home, went on down to the barn without waiting for her thanks. But when the time came—about the middle of August—he knew that she was happy. She sang "Nelly Gray" about the house from morning until night, and that was something she hadn't done since their first year.

4 What troubled Thomas more than anything else was that the baby was too puny. Little, pindling thing she was, always whimpering, but not for food. Kate's breasts were full, but the milk wouldn't agree with the child. Before the summer was out they were trying everything to keep the spark of life in her. Kate made sugar teats and soaked them in diluted cow's milk, fed spoonfuls of tea and potato gruel, barley water, chicken broth, anything that people recommended. But the bones still stuck out of Faith's skin, and her flesh was blue. "I'm so afraid, Thomas!" Kate would cry when she came out from the cradle at twilight. They tiptoed around the house to keep the child from waking, and even then were constantly called up in the dead of night. It seemed that nothing would quiet the baby but paregoric.

As usual Celia Sapooney heard of their plight and came over to offer her advice. Thomas got out of the house as soon as he saw her, but he could not forbear asking what she wanted.

"She thinks we ought to have Faith measured," said Kate, her cheeks smudged with tears. "Old Mrs. Sellers does it, she says."

Thomas fairly growled. "You put that right out of your head!" he commanded. "That baby's either going to live or die, same as everything else. Won't do any good to have an old witch hex her, and you know it!"

Kate was far from convinced. But neither did she say anything more about going down to Sellers's. Celia Sapooney, when she met them at church, turned up her nose with fine disdain.

September and October wore away, and Kate as usual made her tomato figs and apple butter. A bright November followed, the most glorious they could remember. Almost every day was warm enough to let the door stand wide, and for once Thomas had his corn all in before the first sift of snow. "Fixin' up to do something afore long," he would say every day when he glanced at the sky. He had good authority for dire predictions. The corn-husks were thick, the hornets high, the caterpillars almost solid black.

But the good weather held through the early part of December. Then, just ten days before Christmas, Hocking came down with whooping cough. They pounded him, tossed him, stood him on his head to help him clear his throat of phlegm whenever the fits were upon him. Little bright-eyed Charlotte, like quicksilver upon the kitchen floor, caught it next. Between the two of them there was little peace in the house.

"Baby comes down, she's goin' to be a goner sure!" Thomas said one night when they finally succeeded in pummeling Hocking back to life. He was almost as limp as Hocking, his face flushed and his forehead beaded with sweat.

Kate had no spirit to answer him. From hour to hour and day to day, she fairly held her breath, her eyes swollen and staring, as if she could face down fate. Thomas himself went about the farm like a wooden man, seldom speaking, often not remembering what chores he had finished and which were still to do.

In the house all was silence, save for the spasmodic coughing of the children. It was useless to speak—there was no topic worth discussion. It occurred to neither of them that it might not be a curse if the baby did die, since it seemed she could never live to become robust. She was a part of their life, perhaps even more so than Hocking or Charlotte. With neither of the others had they suffered the trouble and heartache they knew because of her.

But by some miraculous providence, Faith was spared. The dreary months of winter, blurred with icy rain or at times glorious with sparkling snow that drifted in long hummocks over the fences, gave way at last to the winds of March. When the valley lilies began to shoot up under the lilac bushes, Kate took heart. "It ought to let up with warm weather," she said now whenever Hocking was racked by a spasm.

"Say it does," Thomas would answer. "Never shake it off while it's cold and damp."

Gradually things came back to normal. April sent Thomas again to the earth, his muscles a fair match for the obdurate clay. In the house Kate went about her work with some composure.

"Lord sends everybody trouble, I guess, Thomas," she sighed when he dared to remark that they had been sore tried.

Thomas winced a little, but he did not immediately answer. There it was again, her insistence that there was a supernatural disposition to interpose in the affairs of earth. He had tried hard to believe as much as she believed, but his mind would not readily admit faith. It didn't seem reasonable that there existed somewhere a gigantic being called God, a being interested in what men did, able to reward or punish, inclined to chasten, to repay patience with largesse, send suffering for sin, in the end save or damn.

Of course, preachers always insisted that God wasn't like a man. But this essence they talked about was a mere nonentity, a gaseous emanation of the imagination. From what Thomas could see in the world about him, it was manifestly untrue that God hated the sinner and loved the righteous.

"Figure it ain't so much the Lord as a man's luck," he said, unwilling any longer to pretend by silence that he agreed with her.

"Some fellows I know never seem to have anything happen to them. Others could hang up all the horseshoes in the smithy, and it wouldn't do no good. Just look over yonder at Sapooneys."

"You know what's the matter with Sapooneys! They're shiftless!"

"Go to church every Sunday, don't they?" he argued. "Accordin' to you, they ought to be God's children as much as anybody else."

She couldn't answer him. That was what made him mad—that nobody could answer him. Preachers who came down to Union Meeting all had the same sort of talk: wanted a man to believe that everything good that happened was to be laid to God, and everything bad to a man's own orneriness. That wouldn't hold water any more than a leaky bucket.

Ordinarily Thomas wouldn't go out of his way to get into a fight about it, but he wasn't going to shut up if he was pressed, either. There were too many hypocrites who kept their mouths shut just so they could be buried under granite markers decorated with angel wings.

5   That spring he drove to Lancaster to see Fargot, conscious that he was at last able to make an offer for the hill and woods he had so long coveted.

Now that he was near possession, it seemed as if he no longer cared. He catechized himself as he looked out passively on the exuberance of the fields. Something was the matter with him, had been the matter for months. He was bigger, stronger, harder, more the master of his destiny. He had more friends, enjoyed a more respected place in the community. He had done wonders with the farm. The neighbors spoke of him and his achievements with a little awe, mixed with more envy. "Good corn, but it ain't a pinch of snuff to that stand of Tom Linthorne's!" they would say. Or, "Beats me how some fellers can make grow and others can't! Only crop Fargot ever had to beat mine was pea-vine."

He wondered idly as he guided Black Belle through a dry run if his fear of the Schraders could have poisoned his mind. Silly to think that! They had never stolen a thing, as far as he knew, not even a ham from the smokehouse. In fact, after that Christmas when he had gone home sour because of the ease with which Gorm outshot Brame Slosson, Thomas had rarely seen any of the swine. "Feared of them, I wouldn't be buying Fargot, would I?" he mumbled to himself as the buggy banged out of the wash.

That left only Kate to cause his mood. He let his mind walk around the idea, afraid to send it any nearer to what he had long guessed the heart of the truth. Kate! Quieter, a bit stouter, more given to hard silences, less inclined to defer than she had been when he brought her to the farm. She had a mind of her own—that was the whole trouble. Most women were content to let their husbands do the thinking. Enough for them to take care of the house, cook, bake, churn, scrub, milk, hoe, and bear children. On their lips always "Clem thinks—," "My man says—," "Well, when Bill gets it into his mind—," "I'll ask Charley," and suchlike statements.

It had been that way at home for a while, too. Not that he was inclined to browbeat or bully. He liked to see a woman have a little spunk. Time Ruth Tanterscham wouldn't kiss Barker when he found the red ear, Thomas had admired her for it. To say nothing of the Danielsons. When the wind was from the northeast, he and Kate could hear Jessie laying it on Henry more than a mile away. But even that was better than the kind of cold silence Kate served him. A whip-tongued woman like Jessie Danielson a man could knock down once in a while, kiss her back to forgiveness when she cried.

By the time Thomas drove into Lancaster and hitched in front of Fargot's store, he was too sorry for himself to be fit company for any man. That was unfortunate because Fargot was a knot himself. He was never one to bargain.

"Hello!" he bawled out unceremoniously when he saw Thomas standing by the notions case.

Thomas snapped back the same kind of greeting—one would have thought they were mortal enemies. Fargot didn't mind. He was too busy cutting up a cheese to be very much interested in anything or anybody.

"Corn good?" he finally yawned without looking up.

"Middlin'. Plant a few hills over, I reckon."

Thomas blew his nose and folded his handkerchief carefully to prove he was a person of consequence.

"Any excitement out your way lately?"

"What sort of excitement?"

Fargot's face leered across the coffee-grinder. "Just trying to make talk," he said, his big mouth shutting over his teeth like an oyster shell. "Got the habit from my wife running around to all these Ladies' Aid meetings."

Thomas made an effort to be agreeable when he saw that Fargot meant not to be.

"Guess you mean Schraders," he said. "They ain't been up to nothing. Keep pretty quiet down in the woods all to themselves.

Fargot must have forgotten his peeve, for when he went up to count out some peppermint lozenges he leaned across the counter to whisper, "Not near as quiet as I'd like to see 'em, Linthorne, not near as quiet. Guess you know what I mean."

Thomas nodded and made a ceremony about his pipe—the swagger intended to show Fargot he was the right kind of man. The storekeeper was deeply appreciative.

"Near a size with Gorm yourownself," he said approvingly when he came back along the counter. "Shows you can't always call a skunk by the stripe down his back."

Thomas took the speech for a compliment.

"Gorm and me never had much truck with each other," he said. "Hopin' we won't when I—that is, if I—fact is, I come up on purpose to see you about that."

"What?"

"I been mindin' to buy the hill."

Fargot deliberately took the weight off the flat of his hands and went back to the rear of the store. Thomas watched out of the corner of his eye, saw him step out into the back-lot with several coal-oil cans, come in again and stopper the spouts with potatoes, then cut himself a sliver of cheese. Thomas was not too much embarrassed—he knew Fargot would have to beat his brains awhile.

"How much you offering, Linthorne?"

"How much you asking?"

"Plenty lumber up there on the hill."

"Big ash and a couple oaks all I ever saw. What I want it for's pasture."

"How about them beeches?"

"Past prime, I'd say. Rest of the stuff's just paw-paws and persimmons mixed in with the maples."

"Well, what about them? They're sugar maples."

"A lot of them sugars was so rotten they blew down in that big storm last winter," Thomas complained. "Fellow wanted a woods, he'd have to plant up there again."

Fargot kept moving his hands over each other as if he were washing the grease from the mottled skin.

"That so!" he pretended surprise. "Guess I ought to get out there once in a while. What you say's true, I'll have to change my price a little. Was figuring on asking two thousand, but if the hill's all cleared off it ought to be worth a little more . . . Say three."

Thomas was stunned. "Three thousand dollars!" repeated unbelievingly.

"I don't need the money," Fargot said with deliberate rudeness. "What I want to sell for?"

"Wouldn't come down any?"

"What for? Money in my pocket every year I hang on. You want it, you'll have to give what it's worth."

Thomas wiped the cold sweat from his forehead. It was useless to haggle with such a man—he might as well save his breath. He could back out, of course. But what Fargot said was too near the truth—the land was increasing in value. It might not be worth three thousand for twenty years to come, but in the meantime it would be constantly productive.

"Not asking it all down, are you?" he inquired feebly.

"How much you got?"

"Guess maybe I could manage twelve hundred."

"How soon you be ready with the rest?"

"Five years—maybe."

"No *maybe's* about it! I want to know sure."

"Better make it ten, then," Thomas floundered.

"Make it ten it'll run you eight percent." Fargot lit a stogie and blew the acrid smoke right into Thomas's eyes. "You think it over day or two," he said coolly. "Ten years, eight percent, twelve hundred down. Want to go through with it, drive in some day next week and we'll hunt up a shyster to make it stick."

6 Thomas was sick when he left the store. All the way home he told himself that he would not mortgage his family's future for any lump of earth covered with timber. But driving up Gregory Lane (he had purposely come home the south way in order to go along the length of the ridge), he felt his resolution weaken. If a man couldn't cut fifteen hundred dollars worth of lumber off the tops of those deep ravines, it would be only because he couldn't get a saw-mill in. And deeper in the woods were other trees: red and bur oak, walnut, ash, hackberry, chestnut. Most of the beeches he would like to keep. They did something to him every time he saw their smooth gray trunks and regal crowns, green or golden or brown as the seasons shifted. Even in the winter they were beautiful against the hill, white-streaked by the snow on their gray branches, the roots black-burrowing into the shadows.

By the time he came up from stabling Belle, he was in better humor than he had been all day. Kate met him at the door, something in the taut lines of her face he did not like.

"You ain't a-goin' to tell me one of the kids is down again, are you?" Thomas asked apprehensively, knowing that she had looked that way through all the winter and spring.

"Gorm Schrader was here, Thomas," she whispered. "He says Coon's been over killing his sheep. Says if we don't keep him tied, he's a-goin' to shoot him."

"Gorm Schrader don't have no sheep!"

"Says he does, anyway. I got Coon shut in the smokehouse. I tell you I was that scared I could have run. That man's a fright!"

Thomas snapped his teeth shut, too angry to talk. That clinched the business with Fargot. Schrader would have to be put in his place, and one way to do it was to put up signs around the woods telling him to keep out.

V

1 Kate was angry the way Thomas threw away the money to
buy Church Hill and the big woods, what with the new baby
to be born about the end of summer and the furniture so bleak she
hated to ask anyone in. To quiet her he told her to go ahead and
pretty up the house. He himself cared nothing for fripperies. A few
good oak chairs and a table, with a cord bed to sleep on, that was
all he asked. The way some houses looked, a person didn't know
whether he was supposed to ease himself or not.

Kate made most trouble over the front room, a place where she
might have a potted fern and a mess of fancy stuff to show when the
neighbor women came to help with dinner for the threshers. The
room had been bare until now, although half an eye could see it
could be a pleasant enough place.

She bought two big rockers—one on its own cradle—a square
oak table with twisted legs that ended up in eagle claws, had a fern
stand and an old oval mirror from Mrs. Wendell, took her rags to
the carpet-maker to be woven into a scatter pattern, and hung a few
vivid lithographs on the walls.

What she really wanted was a wedding picture with deep gold
frame like the Jordans, Tanterschams, and Wendells had. Lacking
that, there should have been either Thomas's parents or her own.
Lace doilies and cross-stitch tidies gave tone to a room—there was
no denying that—but nothing could beat the big pictures and a
red-leather Bible with gilt clasps. A body had fairly to whisper when
she walked into Flory Wendell's parlor. Flory wouldn't be taken
aback if the minister or the Gregorys called right in the middle of
the week, or if for that matter—God save the day—Baltimore sud-

denly succumbed to one of his fainting spells and had to be laid away.

Kate kept her improvement tight shut away from Thomas's eyes until she was really finished, and that wasn't until she had an opportunity one Saturday to go along to Lancaster to buy the motto. Around the border it had red roses against a black background, the whole center being taken up by the white scroll with "God Bless Our Home" in raised gold letters. She hung it right over the mantle, the most conspicuous place in the room.

That same night she took Thomas by the arm and led him in, unlocking the door with as much ceremony as if she were entering the holy of holies. When she held down the lamp to inspect his boots, he pretended not to know what she was hinting.

"Uh-huh!" he said vacantly when she pointed out where she would have hung their wedding picture if she had had one. He kept turning around absent-mindedly, as if he saw nothing he looked at.

"Like it?"

"Uh-huh! Guess you done yourself proud, all right!"

She was disappointed, but comforted herself with the certainty that a man would never be able to pass judgment. First time she saw Lucy Jordan passing down the road, she'd call her in and watch her face. If that old war horse puckered with envy, she could be certain the parlor was good enough to marry in or bury from.

2   Thomas kept Coon close to the house after Gorm Schrader's warning, although he would not consent to shut him in the barn or smokehouse. He told Spence Vitt about the visit, and Spence, after looking on all sides of the matter, gave his opinion that Gorm might have been drunk. Thomas took that possibility back to Kate, but she was positive Gorm had been sober as a stone jug.

"I watched him, Thomas," she said, her face still betraying her scare after all the days that had gone by. "Stood right there on the step with his gun in his hands, he did. Wasn't teetering like a drunk at all. 'Thomas hain't to home,' I said, soon as I seen who 'twas. 'Don't mind about that,' he said in that big voice of his, his eyes all glassy hard. 'You just pass word on to him that if he don't keep that dog he stold from comin' after my sheep at night, I'll cripple him up so's he won't go nowheres.' Coon was right behind me all the time, a-barkin' and a-growlin' fit to kill, like as if he knowed who 'twas."

"He'll get shot himself if he tries anything funny!" Thomas muttered as he always did whenever he got to thinking about Schrader.

In reprisal he put signs along the edges of the woods as he had threatened. He had the feeling Gorm wouldn't stop at a piece of board, even if he was able to read it, but the warnings would make it possible to law him if necessary. Thomas didn't want to be mean —he could understand a man's need to get off alone once in a while, especially if home meant the company of Matt, Hetty, Harrison, Bette, and Bette's parcel of filthy brats. All the same, he couldn't help feel vindictive.

After the sawmill was gone, he was not often down below the crest of Church Hill because of the constant drive necessary to keep things moving on the home place. He was up to his ears in debt, could be ruined by the slightest slackness. He was raising chickens now, an added chore; then, since Kate was almost always busy with the babies and was sluggish because of the fourth she was carrying, he had to milk, slop, and scatter grain in addition to all his other work.

That sometimes meant going back to the fields by moonlight. It was pleasant then, the curl of cool loam about his feet, a solitary owl sometimes breasting the moon, but it made craggy muscles the next day. Often late at night he could hardly stagger to the house after pitching down hay for Bill and Charley. Kate would be waiting for him, the door locked, but once Thomas was in she would go straight to bed. He never disturbed her. If ardor was any measure, love was not as real as it once had been.

So the bad feeling against Schrader smoldered for a good many weeks without any further provocation on either side. Thomas began to feel that he had called Gorm's bluff, that there would be no further trouble.

And then, out of a clear sky, there came the hardest deluge of hate he had ever known.

3   No one could have guessed that Black Belle would have had anything to do with it.

Thomas drove her down to Marty's to be shod one Sunday afternoon, unwilling to spare the time on a weekday. It was stifling hot in the smithy; to add discomfort the flies kept stinging maddeningly. Belle was so irritable that Thomas had to gentle her to keep her from kicking Marty clear through the doors. When the last iron was finally hammered home, he was as wet and worn-out as if he had just come in from a day in the corn.

Marty came out to help him hitch, teetering from side to side on his bandy legs, his eyes caressing the black horse as if he had part claim to her himself.

"Say she was a stepper, that lady!" he admired as he patted Belle's withers. "Yessir, I'd say she was a stepper!"

"Best there is in the county," Thomas agreed. "Do a mile in just about two. Timed her myself. Just sit back and hold onto the lines, that's all I got to do."

Marty started to say something in return but stopped when he heard the trotter on the highroad slow down just outside his lane.

"Sounds like somebody else has to have a little shoeing!" he said with eyes strained on the opening between the trees. "Don't really like to do it on Sunday, but—"

"Sorry I had to ask you," said Thomas, and gave him an extra quarter.

He was startled then by Marty's look, more so by his muttered "It's Gorm Schrader, Tom! Thought 'twas when I heard the horse."

Thomas climbed up at once, anxious to get away before any trouble could start, but when he turned Belle out into the lane Schrader was right in his way. He thought for a moment to pull right, had to give up that idea because Marty had a row of beehives so close to the edge of the grass that turning out was impossible. What made matters worse was that Gorm was already stepping down, indifferent to the fact that he had Thomas penned.

Thomas got hot around the collar, uncertain what he might be expected to do, and knowing full well that Marty would report every word.

"Pull over a little, Schrader, will you!" he bawled as he reined Belle in.

Gorm hardly glanced at him. "Won't be but a minute or two," he flung out of the corner of his mouth, and shoved by to talk to Marty.

Thomas waited, fuming. The minute dragged to ten, and then to ten more, and still he heard the low blur of conversation behind him where Gorm and Marty stood beside the syringa bush.

He got down then, mad enough to eat clay. It was but a few steps to Gorm's horse, a good-enough bay blind in the right eye. Thomas had hold of the bridle and was pulling her over before Gorm knew what he was about. When he did, he came running.

"What's the hell the matter with you?" he demanded. "Told you I'd only be a minute or two."

"Can't wait all day!" said Thomas. "I asked you to get over."

"Well, I heard you. I don't have to get over if I don't want to."

"I can't wait all day!" Thomas repeated as he made for the buggy. "I got work to do."

Gorm laughed sarcastically. "Seen a little of your work over in the woods," he flouted Thomas. "Right pretty signs you got nailed onto them trees."

Thomas was in no mood to debate the matter.

"Thought maybe you'd read them," he said. "Mean just what they say."

Gorm laughed again. "Figured maybe they did. Was on my way over to knock down a couple squirrels when I stepped right into one of them. Know what I did?"

Thomas hesitated, uncertain whether he should reply or let anger rest content with what he had already said.

"I just turned right square around and walked back home," Gorm answered his own question, and slapped his thigh for emphasis.

The effect was so comical that Marty joined in his laughter— the two of them made Thomas feel like a fool.

"You read the same one next time you go over," he said, and bit his lips to keep them from quivering.

Gorm's face went suddenly sober.

"Like hell I will!" he said, and suddenly came closer, swinging his long arms like an ape. Thomas grasped the whip when he thought Gorm meant to climb into the buggy after him. "Trouble with fellows like you is they think they can buy everybody else clear off the whole goddam earth! Never ready to let good enough alone. Soon's you get a little money ahead, you got to try to take the bread out of somebody's mouth so's you can go around bragging—like you do about this black horse you paid Brierley two prices for!"

"My business what I paid, none of yours!"

"I'm a-makin' it my business! Had Brierley talked into letting me have her for a couple hundred afore you butted in."

Thomas felt himself growing cooler, more confident.

"No law against outbidding you, is there?" he asked.

Gorm sniffed. "Just keep on busting your head around!" he warned. "Come a day, you'll knock your goddam brains out—unless somebody knocks them out for you! Telling you one thing though, Linthorne, first time you or anything you claim belongs to you comes across my line, I'll write a little note of my own! Only it won't be daubed on with paint. Lead pencil's good enough for me!"

Thomas slapped down the reins, angled Belle around Gorm's buggy. Lead pencil! He knew from firsthand evidence what Gorm's lead pencil would be!

And the worst of it was that Gorm made no curlycues when he used it.

4   By the middle of August, Kate was so heavy she could hardly move. Cora Vitt came in to help now and then, and even Celia Sapooney was welcome when she dropped in one afternoon and stayed to fry up a mess of potatoes. Celia had two of her own now, squally, dirty brats she had named Lotus and Adolph.

At that, though, they could hardly be more dirty than Hocking and Charlotte. Kate let them run wild, able to do little more than boil oatmeal for their breakfast. They would totter down to the fields after Thomas, their faces tear-stained from some real or fancied hurt. Or he would find them playing on the cellar door or around the wellhead when he came in to the house. He was sick with the thought that they might be injured, but he could not see how to do more than he was doing. Half the time now he got his own meals.

One thing he was thankful for was that Coon followed everywhere Hocking and Charlotte led, his big eyes hungry for their love. He seemed never to mind when they pulled his ears or tried to straddle him; on such occasions he would simply sit down while they tumbled in the dirt. Coon let them go to the run or ferret around the barn, but the minute either of them tried to cross the road, his wild bark drove them back through the gate. Once he even caught Hocking's cotton pants, his white teeth slitting through the sleazy cloth and scratching the soft flesh of the thigh. Thomas brought the crying baby home and put liniment on the wound. Hocking fairly tore down the house with the pain of the burn.

The danger Thomas feared most of all was that of copperheads. Never a month passed during the summer that he did not have to kill at least one of the snakes. They lay tangled in the shrubs along the fence rows, or hid in the long grass of the pastures. Haying, a man often slit one of them in two with his scythe. It was even worse when they crawled under the wheat sheaves or the swaths of timothy left to dry.

One burning hot day Thomas was forking out the stalls when he heard Charlotte scream. He ran as fast as he could, pitchfork in hand, but Coon was ahead of him. What Thomas saw when he got out in the light was the blur of the dog's head as he snapped it from side to side, a copperhead held tight in his jaws. Thomas snatched up Charlotte and tore every stitch from her body, but she was untouched.

He didn't tell Kate, but he told Spence Vitt.

"That dog means more to me than anything else I got!" he said proudly as Coon lay between his feet.

"Should," Spence said, and helped Thomas pat the long head. "Have to get me one of them hound dogs some day."

But three nights later when Thomas went out to the barn, Coon wasn't to be seen. He whistled the high note that always brought the dog running; when he didn't appear, called several times. He thought then of what Gorm Schrader had said about the sheep, but the story was too preposterous to think truth. Coon very likely had a possum treed, too far away to hear his whistle.

Nevertheless Thomas was worried. When he went to the fields the next day, he took the children with him, setting them in the shade of a big honey locust near the fence. That afternoon he quit early and had the chores done by suppertime.

"You're not going down in the woods!" Kate pleaded when she saw him ready to go out with the rifle.

"Got to," said Thomas. "Want to find that dog. Be back before dark, or soon after, anyway. You don't have to worry your head off every time I turn around!"

He pulled up Church Hill through the blackberry tangles, headed down across the middle of the woods so that he would not have to struggle in and out of the ravines. It was dark and still under the trees, a little fearsome. From time to time as he walked he whistled, waiting always to hear the quick rush of pads or at worst an answering whine. It would be like Gorm to set traps! But there was never more than echo, that and the traitorous protest of the nesting crows.

So he came down at last to the rim of trees before the precipitous scale of Rock Ladder, and was none the wiser for his pains. From the ragged cliff, the last inch of his possession, he tried to spy out the Schrader shack, but it was already too dark to see much in the woven thickets. Above the trees a thin curl of lavender smoke twisted up from the hovel hidden deep in the rocks and box elders —that was all.

"Beats me where he's got to!" Thomas muttered aloud in his disappointment. He had wanted so much to bring the dog back to the children that he was bitter. They had cried half the day, had worn him thin by their incessantly repeated questions.

On the way back he made a wide sweep to the east. It was blue-black in the woods now, the little sounds hushing to absolute quiet. Disconsolate, his gun trailing, Thomas was plodding along stolidly when he stumbled over a root where there was no tree. Almost at once he guessed the truth. His match made him sure—it was what he feared. Coon had been on his way home when the bullet caught him, had dragged himself forward a few feet before he crumpled. The long scar through the dried leaves showed that, showed also how he had pawed the ground with his forelegs before he died. Thomas held the second match very carefully to see if there was wool matted between the teeth. There was not a single fiber.

"Killed him to spite me!" he said with hard finality when he had fully satisfied himself. "Only reason he done it at all—just to spite me."

It was hard to scoop out a place to bury, but he covered the body somehow and then rolled a log to cover the shallow grave.

He was cold mad when he went home. Either he or Gorm Schrader would have to leave: there was not room in the same county for both of them.

The next morning when Hocking called the dog as he always did, Thomas shut him up in a hurry. "Won't do you no good bawling like that!" he snapped. "Coon run away!"

Hocking cried at the reprimand. What he could not know was that his father was innocent of any desire to scold him, that his hard tone was really meant for Gorm Schrader.

5 The pains came about ten o'clock one Friday night. Kate had to wake Thomas—he was always so dead tired he could sleep through flood or fire.

He had made plans for the baby, wanted none of the struggle they had gone through when Hocking was born. Flora Wendell, who lived next to Sellers's on the Cedar Hill pike, had said that she would come over, as she had when Charlotte and Faith came. Flora was a little twisty—she liked to have her own way, but she was the only woman Thomas would trust. Her own three children were like little plow horses. Thomas hated to call a neighbor so late at night, but Flora could take the back lane to the Jordan line, and from there cut down across pasture.

The proper arrangements had been made with the doctor, too. It was Sankey from Lancaster, a youngish man with a lot of common sense to make up for whatever he lacked professionally. There was just the chance that Sankey would be already out, in which case he had instructed Thomas to go for Turner or Betts. The three of them traded off with one another.

Thomas hurried out under the wealth of stars, buttoning his

coat as he ran because he knew there must be a little delay at the Wendells. Black Belle wouldn't mind the run in and back—she hadn't been worked since Sunday. She nickered as he jogged into the stable and hooked the lantern onto a harness peg, trotted out the moment he threw the stall open.

It seemed no time until they were flying up past the house. The lamp shone dimly from the bedroom window—he had carried it in for Kate before he left. He hoped the children would be quiet, particularly that Faith would not whimper. She had been a little better lately, but was still so thin that she wouldn't throw a shadow.

Black Belle took the long slope to the head of Gregory Lane without slacking pace. She ran without effort, seemed fairly to flow into the dark. Thomas noticed the speed with which the laurel bushes rushed by. She was alive, that horse! He had never regretted the day Brierley talked him into buying her. Of course, Winnie had been good, too, but there was no telling what might have happened to her. As well let someone else have the trouble.

Down to the bridge over Hocking Creek they swept, Thomas's hands firm on the lines to give just the right touch as they curved into the rattling tunnel. Not that Belle would need to be reminded. He would take his chance on driving her blindfold, if need be. Perhaps horses could see at night, like cats. Certain sure they seemed more than human in some other respects. Just let Death prowl about the house, and they'd go half crazy sometimes.

There was a sharp, curving hill just beyond the bridge, thick with the shadow of interlaced trees. Place where on a June night a person could almost always find buggies off to the side of the road, in them young bucks sparking their girls. He had been doing the same thing himself not so many years ago. Seemed like a lifetime, though, considering all that had happened since. To think how he had used to borrow a folding accordion down in Cincinnati and drive up the river. Big boats churning down on the Ohio, their lights flickering, other lights over on the Kentucky shore, the dismal moan of whistles through the dark. The lonesome sound always made the girls hug a little tighter.

Nonsense! Over on the left his woods, the scar that the lumbermen had made showing against the star-stippled sky. Loved that piece of land more than he had ever thought it possible to love soil. It would be nice to keep. The kids would like to gather shellbarks and hunt in it when they got bigger. Every spring there would be a sugar camp. And with Coon buried way back among the beeches it would be almost like getting rid of the body of a friend to sell it.

Schraders! Fire going out in the open, why God only knew! Unpredictable, that tribe! Thomas didn't like fire. The woods were pretty wet from the recent rains, but in October when the leaves came down and the grass was tinder Schrader might get even in an ugly way. Only, if Gorm or Harrison ever set fire to his woods, he'd shoot on sight! Might mean hanging, but he'd have a sense of being responsible for the biggest improvement the township ever knew.

He slowed Black Belle for the turn into Cedar Hill pike when he saw Sellers's cold gray house. This time of night Zeke and Naomi would be sawing wood. Couldn't tell about the old witch, Zeke's ma. She must be way up in the eighties now. If half of what was reported was true, she should be out in the kitchen stirring a pot with dead kittens, live frogs, toe-nails, and fifty other things mixed in. Wonder was that Naomi didn't kick. Too fat to care much, maybe. Never a threshing that somebody didn't tell the story of what she had said when her first man fell out of a cherry tree and broke his neck. "Might've been worse," she had commented. "He might've broke his leg!"

Wendells showing up now. Speaking of Naomi Sellers, Balt Wendell would make her a good match. Both of them looked three hundred pounds, and maybe a bushel of corn atop that yet. Shame to wake Balt and Flory this time of night. Everything seemed so peaceful: the drowsing trees, starlight reflected from the front room windows, faint silver over the barn roof. Even the windmill was motionless.

Thomas pulled up in the yard, cupped his hand to his mouth: "Hey-ah! Hey-ah there, Balt!"

That got up the dogs. He could hear Sellers's and McGruber's, both of them nasty curs; in turn they roused up Jordan's collie and Pride's old bull. *Yap-yap-yap-yap*, just like a lot of nagging women!

"Balt! Hey, Balt!"

The window on the west side creaked open at last.

"Who's down there?"

"Me, Balt! Tom Linthorne. Tell your woman my wife thinks it's a-comin'!"

The window creaked down again, just as sluggishly as it had gone up. Balt was a crank about night air. Never wanted anything at all open when he went to bed, even in the middle of summer.

Thomas waited impatiently, after a time pulled around so that he could go the minute he knew he could depend on Flory. He noticed with satisfaction that Belle was eager. No noticeable laboring for breath after the run, as one observed in the common lot of horses.

"Tom!"

Thomas jumped—Balt had crept out the back door and slid through the grass in his bare feet.

"Whyn't you just yell?"

"Might as well come out if I was awake. Flory says for you to skit along down after the doc. She's a-goin' to hustle over just as soon's she's dressed and has all her things together. Your woman ain't bad, is she?"

"She'll be all right," said Thomas. "Fourth, you know. First one's the one that counts."

"Well, you get along. She'll go right on over, Flory will!"

When Thomas clicked his tongue, Belle moved off instantly, her head thrust forward as if she sensed the long run ahead.

Liquid silver the night, cool at last after the breathless day. The road pearl-gray in the starlight, tawny when the moon shuttled across open sky, blue under the trees and the hill shoulders. Off to left and right the harvest of the year: orchards with fruit plumping to scarlet, great rectangles of corn hardening to gold, growth of sweet clover and alsike.

Thomas reprimanded himself for dreaming so luxuriously, the wind cool upon his face after the heat of the day. At home in the hot bedroom, Kate was in labor, her face covered with sweat, her hands clutching for help. He hoped that she would not have a hard time, that Flora Wendell would remember to put a twisted bedsheet into her hands. It was a little easier that way, they said. Pity it had to be at all. Not much indication of a benevolent Providence when one thought of birth. If he, Thomas Linthorne, were God, he'd have all babies born some other way. And maybe not until they were two years old. That was as soon as they left off being smelly nuisances.

Lancaster at last. The first huddle of houses and the fields beyond, then railroad tracks, junkyards, factories, a few poor shacks mixed in. The canal, livery barns, hitching lots, warehouses. Main square, stores that catered to the swells. Ahead the hill. Up there the house where Sherman had been born, across from it the Ewing mansion where he was reared. Aristocrats in the town in the old days —Rising, Brough, Stanbery, the Shermans, Medill, MacCracken, Hocking Hunter, a dozen others. Gotten to be senators, governors, judges, generals. They had entertained some of the biggest men of the day: Daniel Webster, De Witt Clinton, Henry Clay, General Jackson, old Tippecanoe Harrison. There was even a story that the Duke of Saxe-Weimar had gone to the Standing Stone to carve his name.

Thomas headed down Broad Street, swerved to Chestnut, let Black Belle climb the steep hill as slowly as she liked. Dr. Sankey lived just at the summit in a rambling white house with green shutters and U-shaped veranda. His heart leaped thankfully when he saw that there was still light behind the heavy curtains. Sankey read a lot. The walls of his office were lined with books, not one in fifty of which had the flavor of medicine.

The heavy brass knocker echoed through the house. Dr. Sankey hurried to answer—he acted like he didn't want his old mother to be disturbed. Deaf as a stone she was, too.

"Hello," he called out as he opened the door; and then when he saw who was on the porch, "Oh, hello, Linthorne! On its way, is it?"

"Was when I left," said Thomas.

Sankey didn't lose any time talking. Thomas liked a man not to gab. "I'll be right back," he flung over his shoulder and started to throw off his dressing gown. "Come on in if you like."

"I'll just wait here."

Sankey brought his bag within three minutes, handed it to Thomas to carry while he buttoned his coat.

"When did she start?" he wondered as they were climbing in.

"About ten o'clock, I guess."

Sankey whistled.

"Where did you lose all your time? Stop to get a beer?"

"She didn't wake me up right away," Thomas answered sheepishly. "And I had to stop to send a woman over."

"Third, isn't it?"

"Fourth."

Sankey stretched back so that he could settle his long legs more comfortably. "How's your horse," he asked. "Stand a little rough going?"

Thomas was scared by his question.

"Think maybe we'd better get along?"

"I expect maybe we'd better. Course, she's built all right, there's that to be thankful for. Baby might come without one bit of trouble. Useless to have a doctor around. Only if it doesn't—"

Thomas touched the lines to Belle's back. The wheels clacked through the deserted streets, the echoes of Belle's hoofs reverberant behind them. Thomas held her in a little at first for fear he might meet someone racing down one of the cross streets, but beyond the canal he let her have her head.

Sankey hung on, his body wedged tight. Once he opened his mouth to call out some admiration of the horse, but the words were lost. It was futile to try to talk against the rhythmic thunder. The steel struck sparks like tiny fireflies from the pebbles in the road.

Thomas had to wonder if Belle could possibly last. The pace was a little too strong—most horses would have been throwing their legs six or seven different ways by now.

"Whoa, girl!" he gentled. "Whoa! Whoa, girl!"

Belle pricked up her ears, but it was hard to draw her in.

"Got a real mare there!" said Sankey when they had to slow against the hard ascent of a hill.

"Best there is!" Thomas answered. "Reckon she'd keep it up all night if I let her."

"Chances are we'll get there in time."

Chances! Chances? That wasn't satisfactory! Thomas didn't want there to be any chance. For Kate not to have a doctor would be almost as bad as that first time.

They passed the railroad, the lower course of Hocking Creek, McGruber's, Wendell's, Sellers's! Then came the sharp turn into Gregory Lane, and the last mile home.

"Get up, Belle!" Thomas urged, and let her have her way.

The wheels whined as she struck into her stride. *Clatta-clap, clatta-clap, clatta-clap,* she galloped down the darkness. It was almost as if the sound were poured through a big funnel and spilled out into the distance behind them. Thomas felt Sankey pressing up for support again. He himself was bigger, held the seat better. He'd rub the mare down while the doctor was doing his business, see to it that she didn't cool off too fast. God! how she raced! He should be able to win with her at the fair—it would have to be a wonder that beat her.

Schrader's, Rock Ladder, the big woods, a long arc along the edge of the hill—then the dark of the leaf tunnel curving down hill to the creek. It would be but a few minutes now.

"Up, Belle!" he nudged again, and again she answered him.

On the brow of the plateau they poised for an instant before they shot over the crest and down toward the covered bridge. Thomas knew every inch of the road, inky black here under the trees, knew just when to angle the reins. Even if he made a mistake Belle would right it. She was fairly flying now, had wings in her feet, was a disembodied spirit of motion. "Hold her in, for God's sake!" Sankey yelled, but he might as well have tried to stop a comet. His bony fingers dug into Thomas's arm, pressed through the weight of muscle clear to the bone.

Thomas had no chance to reassure him. He was calculating with hair-breadth thinness. Out of the gloom of the arch, they would curve in another second to the bridge. He judged the moment, threw his weight to the left, caught the protest of the straining wheels, the blur of thunder ahead of him.

The impact of their crash was terrific. In that last instant before he hurtled out into the dark, Thomas knew that the shafts had snapped. He must have pitched fully fifty feet down the road, tumbling over and over in the heavy dust. Belle slid along on head and shoulders, the buggy little better than matchwood on her back.

Then, after a second of shattering silence, Sankey groaned from the deep ditch at the left, his voice drowned by the screaming of the horse. Thomas tried futilely to get up. His left arm was pinned beneath him, was crazed with stabbing pain. He reached around with his right to feel the broken bone sawing through the flesh. The blood was warm and sticky.

Again that horrifying cry as Belle kicked convulsively! If only his knees had not struck like sledgehammers he might be able to go for help. Surely Bill Sapooney would have heard, to say nothing of Flora Wendell. The two houses, his own and Bill's, were almost equidistant from the head of the lane, neither of them more than shouting distance away.

The night was so peaceful, save for those awful moments when he heard either Sankey or Belle. The persistent pulse of the crickets! The slow fire of the glowworms beyond the trees! The scratch of falling stars! If only his head were not bursting with pain! If only he might waken from the ghastly dream to find Kate sleeping beside him! If only Sankey didn't die! Belle would have to be shot. And he himself might never walk again without a cane. They would have to move to town . . . Wouldn't somebody hurry and come!

Of a sudden he was nauseously sick and rolled over to vomit in the road. The spasm past, he lay quiet, aware that Sankey no longer groaned. That must mean death. Somehow the thought was no longer terrifying. Up there in the house Kate was facing death to bring into the world a life that might not be worth one of her moans. She had made no protest, shown no fear. Perhaps death was simply an island of peace. One might lie in the churchyard unprotesting, knowing that the heat of summer and the frosts of winter were powerless to cause the old agony. If only he might hold on for several minutes longer, to tell whoever came about Sankey lying over there in the ditch!

"Hurry!" he heard himself cry out, and knew immediately it had been someone else who shouted. His voice had never been that weak. If big Tom Linthorne shouted, Bill Sapooney would be sure to waken. That's what he'd have to do, shout with all his might!

He sucked his lungs full of air for the effort, pushed himself up with his good right arm—and saw the whole sky bloom with fire as he fell up through it.

6 They told him afterward that his home was a madhouse that night.

Ten minutes after the thunderous report, the head of Gregory Lane was alive with people, few of them fit to be seen. Lute Tanterscham, who beat everyone else, came clad only in his long underwear. Spence and Bill Sapooney ran with lanterns soon after the old German; next Joe Jordan, Wagram, Lonzo Brewster, Pete Promise.

By the time they got Thomas and the doctor up to the house, Balt Wendell was puffing down through Jordan's pasture despite his leaky heart. Before morning Barker, Shreet, Chenoweth, Marty, Canaway, and their womenfolks had all been in and out.

It was Spence who saddled Tanterscham's big bay and galloped to Lancaster for help. It took him only a minute or two to stop in the lane to finish Black Belle. He couldn't bear to hear her crying, knew that she might last until morning that way, both forelegs broken, the spear of shaft sticking into her belly.

Spence rode back ahead of the two Lancaster doctors at about a quarter past two. Neither paid any attention to the new baby. Flora Wendell and Lottie Tanterscham took care of Kate when her time came, going about their business as if neither of them had ever heard of a doctor.

The crowd in the kitchen made way hopefully for Turner and Betts, pushed back from the kitchen table where the two men lay side by side, Thomas with his eyes wide-staring toward the rings of light on the ceiling, Sankey hardly breathing, so deep was his sleep.

Betts stripped off his coat, vest, and shirt as soon as he had taken one look. He was a short, stocky fellow, his arms immensely powerful, his hands like clubs, but he knew what he was about. Turner was finer, thinner, far more dignified, an academician. They might work until morning, but when gray light came his silver spectacles would be perched on his nose and his black bow would be as debonair as ever.

Dr. Betts bawled for hot water. While it heated, he cut away every stitch of clothing. That done, the two of them washed, made splints, bandaged, held smelling salts, put on hot applications and cold, Betts swearing every inch of the way like the born fighter he was, Turner never once going astray by so much as the loss of a syllable. When they set Thomas's arm and Barker began to blubber like a baby, Betts swung his foot against the man's buttocks. "Cry about that for a while, damn you!" he muttered savagely. His own face looked as if he might break down at any minute.

They brought Thomas around without much trouble, made a bed for him on the floor of the living room, and then put him to sleep. Sankey was hurt far worse, a skull fracture that might mean death. Neither Betts nor Turner would admit it, neither had given any reason to believe it, but they would not have traded Sankey's life for a hundred Tom Linthornes. When Betts heard the suspicion that Thomas had been driving too fast, he went black with rage, for a full ten minutes uttered not one word that could be repeated.

Morning came, and noon, and night again without either of them deserting his post. For that matter, neither did any one of the neighbors for more than an hour at a time. Out under the dooryard trees they clotted, talking in low tones as if they had come to a funeral, or breaking away with a word to perform the necessary work about the stables.

Dr. Sankey died at three o'clock the next morning. Betts went crazy with grief when he finally knew Sankey couldn't live. "Pray, God damn you, you big clodhoppers, pray!" he raged at them, his hands feverishly applying cloths soaked in well water. He had cut away all the bandages in a faint attempt to relieve pressure.

At just three minutes after three he called for the mirror. They waited breathless, their eyes staring, hoping against hope. There was not the tiniest bead of moisture on the glass.

Betts took just one look before he smashed the mirror to bits against the stove and went out into the yard sobbing like a broken-hearted child. He was still crying when Spence drove him home an hour later. All that long way to Lancaster not one word was spoken.

In the kitchen Flora Wendell cleaned up the bits of shattered glass and put on the pot of coffee. From the grim purse of her lips it was easy to tell what she was thinking. Seven years of bad luck to come after the seven years gone by would be enough to put Thomas, Kate, and all their children six feet underground.

VI

1 The long weeks of Thomas's recovery were as unreal as the fabric of dreams, phantasmata of noons and midnights in walls, on roads, around the dooryard and barnyard, or in walks across the fields to Goose Ridge and Black Man. Before his eyes nothing any longer was reality. Sounds of the seasons: of katydids and crickets, the whistle of scythes and the voices across the corn, the monotone of rain and the rasp of falling leaves; colors: of the thistle, goldenrod, lobelias scarlet and blue, cream white of milkweed pods, gold of beeches; the musk pungence of chrysanthemums; the gelid constriction of frost—all sharp etchings of the senses that had once meant so much to him now were void of inference.

Neighbors seeing him drag down the road uncertainly, his eyes fixed on infinity, thought better of their intention to ask about his health and pass the weather signs. "Looks bad!" they whispered one another behind his back, and tried so hard to be natural in front of him that they achieved only awkwardness.

He did not see—he saw nothing. All he could think of was meaningless defeat, frustration. The crops would be saved—Tanterscham, Spence, and Jordan had seen to that. There would be enough money for the note when it came due. But the next year when the dogwoods bloomed and he should be putting in his corn, and the next after that, followed by endless others down the long corridor to the grave, it would be useless to make any effort. There was no longer any heart in him. So brave, so certain, so ruthlessly insistent on his own way he had been. Now he had no way.

It was fate that mattered. In moments of black despair his mind toyed with the thought that some divine malevolence might have marked him. Nobody knew anything about God. Legends were legends, traditions traditions, but there was no more reason to believe the All-powerful good than to believe Him bad. All that a man knew was that there was smut in the corn, frost on the orchard blossoms, hail that tore to ribbons the fields in blade. Or, in other years, the absence of all these, a harvest so plentiful that it proclaimed waste.

Often he sat for long hours behind the closed doors of Kate's parlor, her Bible open on his knees, searching for plan and finding confusion, seeking blessing and discovering blood mixed with the manna. It was partially because of the selections Kate had read aloud that he turned most of all to the prophets and the books of the Hebrew kings. Back in the vast domain of the past, he traced the golden chariots of the Assyrians, heard the whips of the Egyptian masters, saw the maiden led to sacrifice, listened to the wails of those lost in ruined cities. Jeremiah might mourn, Ezekiel flash with fury, Isaiah rebuild the pinnacles of hope. But it was all so far away, so long ago, so dismally uncertain.

Sometimes he raised his head from the book to look out with amazement at his well-known fields, so cool and calm after the burning heat of centuries-old Palestine. Almost always his mind flashed at the recognition of things known. These were the realities, these squares and rectangles of obdurate clayey loam, not those ancient turmoils of an embittered, race-conscious people crying to a tribal god. The Assyrians, Philistines, and Egyptians too had had gods—and they were lost in the mists of obscurity.

There was nothing sure—nothing but death. A man might cry out ceaselessly for counsel and help, but the rains would lash him and the suns burn as if he had never spoken. Accident, sickness, misfortune, hate, lust, fear were bright swords that could slash through any shield. The rich, the wise, the strong had for a little while the good fortune to escape the traps of time; but when the steel jaws snapped, they too would be powerless.

He would get up slowly, then, so broken that it was painful for him to move. It would be getting dark in the room, the shadows stagnant in the corners and under the windows. Outside the panes he would see the trailing tendrils of the white clematis or the shroud of honeysuckle with the wren's nest hidden away in its depths. "Help me!" he would half mumble, knowing full well that there was nothing he believed in to which he could cry for help.

The light in the kitchen would hurt his eyes as he came out to find Kate setting bread or frying meat for supper.

"Feel any better today, Thomas?" she would ask, her voice dry as a withered leaf.

"Just about the same," he always said.

It was the pretense they kept up between them: the pretense of loving communion, of mutual trust, of belief that they might renew their struggle.

2 It always puzzled Thomas that Cory drove over. He did not know that Spence Vitt had prompted the visit, fearful that Thomas's mind might be shattered.

Cory lived opposite Barker far up Locust Lane. The farm was tiny and poor, unable to sustain Como, Maude, and their three children, but Cory never complained. A bulging, unwieldy, pock-faced man, short of breath and of sight, he had reputation locally for knowing more and saying better than anyone for miles around. His voice was as big as his body, molasses-slow save when he was aroused, always as deep as a drum. It was enough in itself to make anything Cory said portentous. One had to listen close for the man's meaning. Seldom if ever did he take pains to remember that he should talk in terms of frostbite, glanders, whey, and brine.

Thomas led at once to the front room—Cory was not one to sit in the kitchen or stand under the strawstack. They sat heavily, Thomas from sheer hopelessness, Cory from failure to calculate correctly the pitch of his chair. They rocked in awkward silence while they measured each other, their eyes avoiding, the sound of Cory's breathing like the drone of a bluebottle.

"Broken bones," said Como without giving proper introduction to his mind, "are somehow reminiscent of civil war in nations.

The cleavage discovers weakness, the weakness must be mended, the mend makes for greater strength. You ought to know that you wore blue in the war."

Thomas nodded, rocking slowly.

"I'd say it was like that, somehow," he agreed listlessly.

"Then there's every reason for you to believe you'll come out of this stronger than you were. Not only in body. I refer to the value of misfortune in healing the spirit."

Kate brought them in a pitcher of cider and her two good tall glasses with ruby scrolls. Como watched her pour greedily, his eyes more appreciative of her person than of the expected drink.

"You've got a fine wife there, Thomas," he said when they were alone once more, the door closed tightly. "A good wife is a man's first blessing. Oftentimes I look at my Maude with tears in my eyes to think how barren the years would be if she was suddenly snatched from me."

"Things like that happen," said Thomas dismally.

"In one way, yes. In another, no. It's part of my creed to believe that nothing in this universe ever just happened. Every drop of rain, every hurt and ache, our sadness and our joy is all part of some divine plan. The poet put it right: 'We are but parts of one mysterious whole whose body nature is and God the soul.'" Como licked his lips at the rich harmonies. "There's nothing surer than that," he said.

Thomas felt uneasy and resentful. It was all right for the man to be a windbag—he certainly had read a lot and knew a lot of hard words. But there wasn't any point in his coming over to deliver one of his bombastic sermons. Wanted to do something to help, he should get on his old clothes and husk corn or haul fodder.

"Sounds like so much nonsense to me!" he said rudely. "Wouldn't call it right for Dr. Sankey to die the way he did, would you? Or for me to be laid up like this, not even able to fork out a stall! Wouldn't call it right for me to have to shoot my best horse and pay a lot of bills for something wasn't my fault!"

Como Cory sat with his mouth open, his body pitched forward, heavy hands resting on his knees.

"I would!" he said emphatically. "I'd call it part of the plan, part of the divine plan. You can't understand it, and I can't understand it. But I can't understand sunrise, either. Or for that matter, why there should be a sun at all."

"There's some good in that."

"You happen to find it so, just because you need light and warmth. If you were caught out in the middle of a desert, you'd find the sun a curse."

"Wouldn't you?"

"No," said Cory, "I wouldn't. I'd say it was part of the whole idea then, just as I say it is now. That is, I hope I'd be big enough to see myself in proper perspective. The only time a man makes himself really unhappy is when he tries to measure the whole universe by the length of his foot."

Thomas fidgeted.

"Don't rightly know what you're getting at," he said bluntly. He felt no obligation to make Cory easy. If he wanted to talk nonsense, let him talk it to himself.

Como opened his heavy lips several times as if he was minded to go on, but always rolled his tongue over his teeth instead. Then, suddenly, he beat down Thomas's guard.

"Do you believe in a God?"

The vibration of his deep voice echoed in the room as if the question were embodied and stood between them.

"Off and on—I do a little," Thomas said, knowing well the possible penalties for such a restricted admission. "Mostly I don't."

"Why don't you?"

Thomas held up the arm that had been broken.

"That's one reason," he said truculently.

"Don't believe in an immortal soul either, then?"

"Don't know anything about it. Maybe when you die, that's all there is."

"You happy? Living like this, I mean; not believing that at the last day God will take you up to high heaven."

"Couldn't expect me to be very happy, could you?"

"Then why don't you go out and shoot yourself! Or just tie up somewhere down in the barn and swing off!"

Thomas felt the shiver run up and down his spine. The man had read his mind, had asked the question he had been posing these many weeks: Why not go out and kill himself? Cory was mercifully too nearsighted to see how his face twitched.

"I'll tell you why!" the big voice boomed at him. "You may try to reason yourself out of believing! You can say the Bible's a lie, God's a myth, Jesus Christ the creation of the distorted imaginations of a group of poor fishermen who were trying to feel important, the prophets no better than the Delphic Oracles, the saints and martyrs fools and maniacs—you can say all these things and deny all the evidence that has come down to us. But there are two things you can't deny: nature, and your own heart. Nature would show plan to a blind man. Who ever taught a spider how to spin a web? Who tells the birds it's time to migrate? Or for that matter why don't everything run down and stop like a clock? You can't answer a hundred questions like those! But you'll be a whole lot better able to tell why an egg turns into a chicken than you'll be able to deny that there's something in you that knows the difference between good and evil, and that tells you to do what's right. It's the same with that feeling inside you that you're going to live forever."

Thomas was little persuaded, but he saw no reason to prolong the argument.

"I'll think about it," he promised, and hoped that that would make Cory go.

He was not to escape so easily.

"Once you have that straight—that you're going to live forever, either in hell or heaven—you're fairly sure God isn't just fooling with you. He means for you to do your duty! And your duty's whatever you see ahead of you that has to be done! I tell you, nothing would make me so mad if I was the Lord as to look down and see a big, overgrown fellow like you moping around. Know what I'd do! I'd give him a good celestial kick in the behind!"

Thomas went hot. "I'm doing everything I can do!" he said sharply. "Guess I'll have sense enough when I get well to pay back anything that's been done for me."

Cory's skin was too thick to smart with burning words.

"You won't do everything you can until you start to smile a little!" he said. "Going around looking like you're dead-beat all the time don't do anybody any good!"

Thomas was at last able to shut the door on the man. He was mad through, fairly quivering. There had either been some loose talk, or else Cory could see a lot better than people said.

"Don't ever let that old buzzard in again!" he told Kate spitefully. "All he needs is a beak."

"Wouldn't call him a buzzard unless I wanted people to think I was fit to be buried," she answered without sympathy.

Thomas went right out to the barn. It would be easy to fix the hay hoist to the center beam, to step off from the mow. All he needed was a half-ounce more inclination.

3 But from that bad hour with Cory he might date his rebirth. His anger at being taken for a moony despondent made it easier to live with him. Instead of staring dreamily when he walked now, he was as like as not to go plowing through the dead leaves, his feet kicking at every impeding weed.

"Looks like we got Tom back," Joe Jordan remarked on Sunday in the churchyard after Thomas had been vehement against paying the preachers more than three dollars a trip.

"Yeah, he'll be all right," Ory Shreet whispered back. "I think he'll be all right. Don't you?"

"He'll be all right."

"Little changed, though."

"Yeah, he's a little changed."

"Sterner."

"Looks sterner."

"Think he is sterner."

"He can stand being a little sterner."

"Thought for a time he was a goner sure!"

"That's just what I said to Phillipy, 'Tom Linthorne's a goner!'"

"Looks all right now, though."

"Yeah, he'll be all right."

"Hope he will . . . Always liked Tom."

"Same here. Always did like Tom."

"Well, looks like we got him back."

4 Before the arm was out of splints, Thomas went down Gregory Lane with Spence Vitt.

Spence had come around purposely, it seemed, since he was busy grading and sorting his fruit. He wouldn't say anything significant—just thought that perhaps Thomas would like to stretch his legs a little. Thomas would, but he knew there was more than that to the invitation. Spence never left work for a lark.

They moved along briskly, for the air was cold, the heavy cloud shadows like puffy pouches under an old man's eyes.

"Be getting that arm of yours in use pretty soon, won't you?" Spence asked while they stopped to gather a few hazel nuts from the bushes along the run.

"Seven weeks tomorrow," said Thomas. "Doc says he's going to keep it tight for eight. I'm using it a little but it's hard to do much on account of my fingers are so blamed stiff."

"You better just do what the doc tells you."

Thomas knew when Spence turned down the lane that he must at last relive the accident. He had avoided the spot. It was not so much the thought of his own hurt, not even Sankey's lying in the ditch and moaning his last life away. But to think of Belle, one moment beautiful as running fire, the next a misshapen black mass of flesh—that was hard to bear! He had never loved a horse as he had loved Belle. As yet he had not thought of buying another.

They passed the bridge over the creek in solemn silence. There was something fixed about Spence's face, a look that Thomas had never seen before. He glanced away in embarrassment, allowed his eyes to steal back to make sure.

"Just about here's where it was, I guess," he said in an attempt to break the tension.

Spence was very quiet. "Not here," he said. "Little farther on."

Thomas wondered how he could know so well. He remem-

bered then that Spence had helped carry him home before he went
back to shoot Belle.

"Right there opposite the big hackberry, I figure, Thomas."

Thomas nodded. He looked on all sides, as if there should still
be marks in the road.

"Reason I asked you to come up was I wanted you to see the
place yourownself. Notice anything funny about it?"

"Don't rightly know what you mean, Spence."

"You just stand here, then, and I'll show you."

Spence slipped down into the west ditch and dug around in the
frosted weeds. His fingers began to twist at something that refused
to obey them. The air was suddenly filled with the fragrance of
crushed mint, bruised in the attempt he made to pull away the
tangle.

"What you got there, wire?"

Spence shook his head up and down. "Part of the line fence
along Gregory's pasture," he confirmed. "One end of it still fast to
the hackberry yonder."

"What of it?"

"Just wait a minute and I'll show you."

Thomas waited, trying without much success to lend his good
hand. Spence at last came crawling back on all fours with the un-
snarled skein, his feet pawing furrows in the wet bank.

"Always thought there was something a little funny about Belle
stumbling that way, Thomas," he said. "Wasn't a stumbling horse.
Ever notice the way she picked her feet way up in the air?"

"What's the wire got to do with it?"

"I ain't saying. Just had sense enough to be real careful the day
after, I might be able to tell you. Wasn't until just this morning I
was going down to Marty's I saw the piece sticking out back of the
hackberry. Struck me as funny, so I got out. All I know is Gregory's
fence was cut through. There's just enough wire on the hackberry
to carry clean across the road to the elm over yonder. Make anything of that?"

Thomas was breathing very hard.

"See if it reaches," he said.

When Spence pulled the strand taut, it lacked just an inch or two of touching the elm tree.

"Guess he must've seen me go out that night, Spence," Thomas said thoughtfully. "Knew about Kate 'cause he'd been up to the house. He could tell she didn't have long to go."

"Didn't see anybody down at Schraders as you drove along, did you?"

"Wasn't nothing but a fire. Didn't see nobody around it."

Spence rolled the coil and threw it back down in the mint.

"Just be able to prove it on him, you'd have him for murder!" he said slowly. "Only I reckon that'd be pretty hard now."

Thomas was the calmer of the two.

"Just keep it quiet," he advised. "Just between ourselves."

It was good for him to know at last that it was not Belle's fault, that she had been the victim of spite. If only she too could have known before she died, could have realized how much he would always praise her and never blame!

"Won't do anything about it, then?"

"Won't do a thing," said Thomas.

He meant what he said. But from that day he never looked again at the beam high in the barn. Without conscious knowledge of any change within him, he felt that there was again something to live for.

5 That winter was the happiest Thomas and Kate had known. He was at work again, his arms and legs strong as steel. There was purpose in everything he did. Fencing, ditching, butchering and boiling down gray soap, putting a longer flue to the chimney and sealing the seams of the house against prying frost: all these he did with mechanical promptitude and efficiency. It was not work that made him happy, although he would have been miserable without it. What really inspired him was his new feeling about Kate, and in turn Kate's reacceptance of him.

Instead of long silence they talked now, laid plans for the children, discussed the wisdom of going into Lancaster to church. Thomas joined the Ben Butterfield Post of the G.A.R., thought of getting into the Odd Fellows or Woodmen. He did not solely because he disliked to leave Kate alone at night.

"I think we're happy just as we are, Thomas," she would respond to his suggestion that they might find better land east of town. "Not very many places we could have school and church right across the road. I wouldn't like for Hocking to have to walk a mile or so through the woods."

He generally agreed with her.

At other times they played checkers, using hickory nuts for the white men and walnuts for the black.

"Wouldn't cost nothing to buy a board," Thomas always reproached himself when they set out the men on the checked cloth. "Only, seems like I can't never think about it."

"I like it better this way, Thomas. Get through playing, we can crack and eat, and get more nuts next time."

They made elaborate plans for Christmas. Thomas was to go back on Goose Ridge for the tree and hide it in the barn. There would be a knitted sweater and some kind of toy for Hocking, a pair of shoes and a toy for Charlotte, a doll for Faith, who was jealous of Charlotte's rag baby, and a dollar for the last-born to spend when he was big enough to appreciate a present. Thomas was to buy two whole pounds of chocolate drops and a dozen oranges.

Then, on the twenty-fourth, they woke to icy rain. All that day it fell, to sheathe whatever it touched. The roads became impassable—long, rounded ribbons of ice, bare of all travelers. The huckster could not get through, the mailman was unable to move, the sleighs with their bright jangle of bells were strangely lacking.

When at three o'clock dark began to fall with the continuing drizzle, they looked at each other in bitter disappointment.

"I don't know what to tell them, Thomas," Kate whispered. The children had been prating of Christmas for weeks.

"Might say old Kriss'll be a couple days late on account of the roads being so bad," he suggested gravely.

When she laughed at him, he was at first surprised, and then caught the point of her mirth.

"Well, we'll fix it up somehow," he promised.

The somehow proved to be an all-night task. For want of an

evergreen Thomas chopped off the satin-bright limb of a cherry tree, a miracle of crystal when he brought it into the kitchen. They placed it by the stove so that it would melt free, later wound it with bits of colored paper and hung sugar cookies on the branches. Kate stuffed doll heads and sewed dresses feverishly while Thomas went to the barn with his lantern and saw. When along toward midnight he came back to the house, he was carrying a bushel basket full of the most elaborate blocks Kate had ever seen, triangles and squares of all sizes.

"Think these'll do?" he asked as he dropped the heavy basket to the floor.

She was so glad she kissed him.

"They're just beautiful, Thomas!" she said with real admiration. "I'm right proud of you!"

"Shucks, Kate, I didn't do nothin' only saw up an old piece of oak," he declared deprecatingly.

But Thomas glowed with her praise. She was the finest woman in the world, he thought, the woman he would choose a thousand times over.

He was drinking a cup of coffee to take the frost out of his bones when the clock struck twelve. "Merry Christmas, Kate!" he called, still florid with her appreciation.

"Guess we got a right to be happy, Thomas," she said. "'Tain't everybody can say things are as all right as they are with us."

VII

1 It was a good Christmas in all but one thing—their concern for old Lonzo Brewster. Thomas had been keeping an eye on the ancient fellow for a good many years, had helped him in innumerable ways when he saw Lon was failing. Lon had at last given up trying to do more than take his frow and maul to the woodlot to split a few white oak shingles. With the help of the neighbors and the few dollars he made from these, he was able to get along. From the Linthornes he had milk and butter in plenty, and Kate invariably took him a round white loaf when she baked. Others did their share, too. Pete Promise was often down at the ramshackle house, and Lucy Jordan was too good a manager not to keep her eyes open. She made Cynthia and Henry hunt the eggs and feed Lon's chickens every day.

So when about ten o'clock on Christmas morning Kate suggested to Thomas that he go up and bring the old man back for dinner, Thomas had no notion he would find trouble. He hitched plodding Charley to the field sled, fearful that Lon might snap one of his brittle legs on the ice if he had to walk, and so drove into the road with mock gaiety, waving his mittened hands to Charlotte and Hocking, whose snub noses were pressed against the steamy kitchen panes.

When he failed to return in a good hour, Kate became worried. She glanced down the road whenever she went to the oven to baste the two chickens she was roasting for their feast, but it was impossible for her to see clear to Brewster's because of the screen of branches along the line fence. To add to her anxiety Hocking kept dinning his eternal question, "Where'd Papa go, Mamma? Where'd Papa *go?*" He was lying flat on the floor, building towers with his blocks, too sensually happy to listen for her answers.

Kate was considering the wisdom of throwing a coat over her head and going out to the road when she finally saw Charley creeping back home along the icy slope. Thomas was standing on the sled, but Lonzo was not beside him. At the moment Kate supposed only that the old man had accepted an invitation to go to the Jordans.

"Here he comes now," she told the children. The three of them scrambled on chairs to force her away from the glass, futilely shouting and waving their tiny hands. "He can't see you!" she told them a dozen times, but they persisted nevertheless.

Kate knew there was something wrong when she saw Lon lying on the sled. Thomas had made a blanket bed. From the way he kept turning around every few seconds, he appeared to be greatly concerned.

At the moment Kate felt only a flash of resentment. If Lon was sick, their Christmas would be spoiled. It was a pity his own children thought so little of their father they could not spend even this one day with him. Jim was said to be a drinker; and *De*troit, Lon's girl, had run off with a man from the east ten or fifteen years ago.

"You stay away from that hot stove, Hocking! You hear!" she ordered, and threw a shawl around her to go meet Thomas.

He had stopped opposite the kitchen door, seemed to be making ready to carry Lonzo in his arms.

"He sick?" Kate asked as she picked her way over the icy flagstones.

Thomas made a face and shook his head the least bit, then came close so that Lon wouldn't hear his reply.

"Got chills and fever!" he whispered. "Might not amount to a whole lot."

"Shouldn't ought to bring him down here with the children if he's got something catching!"

Thomas knew that would be her word.

"I couldn't let him up there alone, could I?" he defended himself. "House was awful cold, Kate; wasn't no fire atall. Nothing to eat neither. Thought yesterday one of us ought to go up."

"Well, you cart him on in," she resigned herself. "Only I don't know where to put him."

They finally bedded him down in a corner of the kitchen. It was the only warm place in the house, nor was there a single extra bed in any of the other rooms.

"Just you fix me up some turpentine and lard and I'll rub his chest real good," Thomas said. "And save out some of that chicken broth before you make gravy. That oughtn't to make him sick to his stomach."

Once Lon was settled, Kate accepted him as if the charge were really her own. It was a bother to keep the children from being too noisy and to make them stay away from the bed, but the old man's eyes were so grateful that she did for him willingly.

"Maybe I'd better put on some irons to get hot," she suggested to Thomas when Lon had one of his chills.

Thomas agreed. "Gets any worse, I'll borrow me a horse and go in for a doctor," he promised.

That night, however, Lonzo was feeling a little better. He still had fever, how much they could not say, but he made an effort to sit up when Thomas carried him a cup of mullein tea. "Gaddin' around too much fer an old man, that's what did it!" he quavered, his skinny hand shaking so much that Thomas would not release the cup. Then, as he saw the decorated limb of cherry, "What's them pretties you got over there for?"

"Christmas tree," said Thomas.

"Christmas tree! 'Tain't Christmas, is it?"

"Today is."

"Criminently!" Lon swore. "Had me a notion Christmas ought to be comin' 'round pretty soon. Tell you what, though, Thomas, you ought to should get you one of these here cedars if you want a Christmas tree."

"You drink your tea and lay down again!" Thomas ordered.

Lon was too weak to disobey. All that evening Kate saw his bright eyes watching her and the playing children. When she undressed the babies for bed, she took them behind the stove so that Lon should not see their nakedness, but he was watching for them to reappear.

"Say," he hailed her as she was opening the middle room door, "maybe you can tell me. I been wonderin' what that thing is stickin' up over there. That thing with all the papers on it."

Thomas was proud of the patience of her reply.

"That's our Christmas tree, Lonzo." she said, as if she heard the query for the first time. "You go to sleep now so's you'll feel better in the morning."

2 "Der Loeffel der Mann," said Kate, and grabbed hastily for the spoon she had dropped.

It was New Year's Day and they were having sauerkraut, of course—it would have been inviting bad luck to eat anything else. Lon was spooning the juice from his second plateful when he glanced up suddenly and said, "Hey, Thomas, there comes Joe Jordan down the road."

"Ain't a-comin' to see me," Thomas grunted disinterestedly. He didn't want to be interrupted—he liked sauerkraut.

They all knew he was mistaken when Joe rattled around the house a few minutes later.

"Hate to bust in on you thisaway, Thomas," he was apologetic as he stood in the doorway. "Thing is, that red mare of mine got her leg kicked wide open last night. You still got that receipt for King Oil?"

Thomas pushed back from the table immediately and went into the middle room to rummage through the table drawer. He had a long search. Just when it appeared he must shout for Kate, he found the yellowed paper and carried it out in triumph.

"Copy it down for you, Joe," he said as he made a place for his paper by shoving back the dishes. "Wouldn't like a whole lot to lose the receipt, there ain't nobody else around here knows it."

And on the bit of newspaper torn from the wall he scrawled with slow hand: 1 oz. green coperas, 2 oz. white vitriol, 2 oz. salt, 2 oz. linseed oil, 8 oz. molasses, 1 pint urine. Mix and boil 15 minutes. Let it cool, then add 1 oz. oil of vitriol and 4 oz. turpentine.

Joe was appreciative, but Lon's presence seemed to have dropped a blacker pall than usual on his spirits. Thomas noticed his nod, and followed him out-of-doors where Joe hung solemnly on the snowy walk.

"Guess you know Lon's snowball bush bloomed two times last year, Thomas," he found heart to say at last. "Know what that means. Might be getting yourself in for a whole peck of trouble."

Thomas simply laughed at him. He was glad to get back to the sauerkraut. He and Lon sat at the table until the light wore away, doing honor to the day by drinking a full quart of Kate's wild cherry.

3 They kept Lon a half week longer. He swore he was as fit as a fiddle, but Thomas wanted to make a good job of the cure. So by the hour they must listen to his stories, his favorite the one of Mary Elizabeth Sherman.

"'Twas 'long about the spring o' the year," he would begin. "Mary 'Lisbeth—she was big sis to Gineral an' John, you recomember—Mary 'Lisbeth was up on Standin' Stone with a parcel o' other young uns. Pickin' poseys they was doin', an' havin' themselves a real fine time hilabalooin' and makin' wishes on the fellers they loved.

"Well, just a little afore that time a young feller had come to town name o' Reese or Rush or some such name. Fine young feller that followed the law. Took a shine to Mary 'Lisbeth first time he laid eyes on her, an' hung around pretty close to see nobody beat his time. Don't know what finally happened to him, but heared tell he went back east an' made a real fine mark to shoot at.

"Mary 'Lisbeth an' all them other young gals was pickin' Johnny-jump-ups on Standin' Stone when she sodden saw young Reese right smack behind her. Had snuck up close, maybe, so's he could steal a kiss without her bein' any wiser.

"Well, she up an' screamed a wee mite, just to show him how glad she was to be that way surprised. Wouldn't have been good bringin' up to do nothin' else. There she was, the feller close as a rabbit to a blackberry patch, an' the open side o' the rock before,

99

caught halfways betwixt heaven 'n earth, with nowheres to run but out on air.

"Don't believe I told you this young feller was a lawyer. Name o' Rush."

"What did she do then?" Thomas would always ask, obedient to Lon's wish to be prompted to his climax.

"Well, now, what could she do? Most young gals would have looked just oncet down the drop off Standin' Stone afore they got real sick to their stummicks en' give in real lady-like. But Mary 'Lisbeth wasn't built like the ord'nary gal. Thinks she to herself, 'Ain't but few chances I'll get to find out if'n or not he really loves me, an' most-like won't never come another such chance as this.' So what does she do when she sees him a-leapin' towards her but step right off on air with no more howdy-do than she'd make comin' downstairs to her front parlor . . . Wanted to see if'n he'd come after her."

"Did he?"

"Well, now, Thomas, here's the truth on it: that feller never even took a little look round. One minute the gal went flyin' off in front o' him, an' the next he was right after her. 'Bout two hundred feet high Standin' Stone is there, with nothin' in the way of earth but couple laurels stickin' out from the rock. Down they dropped together, he a little bit behind her 'cause he got such a late start. Looked fer a minute like they'd make pancakes out of theirselves. Then, just about time they was makin' ready to land, seemed like somethin' slowed 'em up, an' when they lit 'twasn't no harder than hens hoppin' down off'n a roost.

"All he did was tuck her arm in his'n an' walk her right on down to the courthouse. Time the other folks got there, they was comin' out man an' wife, just as big as you please."

Thomas always contrived to show amazement.

"Don't rightly seem as if it could have happened!" he'd say while he scratched his head, or "How do you figure they kept from hurting themselves, Lon?"

At that Lonzo would hitch himself high in his chair, his thin finger crooked for emphasis.

"Angels," he delivered his opinion. "Says in the Good Book angels are always around hankerin' to do tricks like that'n. Way I

100

figure it is God didn't want her to turn that young feller down an' was powerful feared she was notioned thataway. So all he did was put the idee in her head to jump, an' then sent out a call for a couple o' his angels to git down in a sodden hurry an' catch the two o' them on their wings."

Thomas would nod his head gravely and get up to go about some necessary work while Lon tagged after, his eyes still blazing.

"Figur' maybe I got that right, Thomas?" he would ask, perhaps a quarter hour later. "What I said 'bout them angels!"

"Right as the smooth side of a plank, far as I'm concerned, Lon," Thomas would satisfy him, and be happy to see the old man's face light up with satisfaction.

4   They persuaded Lon to come down both noon and night to take his meals with them when at last he insisted on returning home. Mornings, he said, he wanted nothing but hot water.

It was about mid-March that Thomas trudged up after him one noon when he had failed to put in an appearance, his emotions a mixture of concern and anger. For all his dislike of having to tend Lon like a newborn calf, it would be a load off his mind to find him propped up against the kitchen stove, his hat tilted down over his forehead so that the brim rested on the bowl of his clay pipe. Kate could hardly be asked to go through the ordeal of nursing him again. She was still cheerful, but her face looked drawn. It would be good for her to get out into the spring sunshine with the babies and scratch dirt for a while.

There was no one in the dirty house where Lon hoveled, nor was the stove warm. In the bedroom a heap of covers lay tangled together, in itself no evidence that Lon had even slept at home.

On a notion Thomas went across the road to ask the Jordans how recently they had seen their neighbor. Mrs. Jordan came to the door, her sharp eyes hostile. "Why no, I hadn't set my eyes on him!" she said prissily. "Cynthy! You hain't seen Lon Brewster putterin' around, have you?"

Cynthia and Henry hadn't, but the query brought along Joe to the door, his sad gray eyes watering.

"I wouldn't take no oath on it, Thomas," he said forlornly. "But while I was out digging post holes this morning there was somebody went down in the woods. Just caught the back of the feller's coat out of the corner of my eye. Time I turned around to take a full look he was too far gone. Might've been Lon."

Thomas twisted the possibility in his mind while he trudged back home. The woods were no place for Lon in mid-March—they were still too wet. The maples might be showing color, but the ground still held the chill of winter. Now that Thomas thought about it, he remembered that Lon had said something about the medicinal properties of skunk cabbage. Thomas did not believe a ton of the stuff would do a man the least good—it might, in fact, poison him. But if Lon had gone to the woods, it was likely he was hunting the unsavory plant.

Thomas gulped down his sausage and boiled potatoes, his mind made up to take the afternoon off in order to scout Lon out.

"Don't you worry about me none, Kate," he said as he rose from the table and grabbed his hat off the pegboard by the door. "Got an idea Lon's down there all right. Probably got his feet good and wet by now."

He saw her face go a little gray, the way it did whenever she suspected he might be cooking up a mess for himself.

"I mean that!" he repeated to soothe her. "I won't be gone more'n a couple hours."

He would have liked to take his gun, but that would give the lie to his apparent unconcern.

The wind had whipped up new chill while he ate; he shivered when he stepped out of the warm kitchen. It looked like rain in the east, a possibility he did not like. He wanted no rain—there had been too much already. The streams had their throats full of it.

On the top of Church Hill he stopped to cut a heavy hickory stick to help him prod up and down the slippery cuts. As he walked, he kept looking anxiously to the left and right, scanning the springy mat of soaked leaves for footprints. It would have been cheerful even to see fresh knife marks on one of his beeches.

But there was nothing, nothing but the ever-deepening gray of the afternoon. Once when he felt a few stray drops of rain, Thomas glanced anxiously at the sky, balancing the probable wisdom of returning home against the awful doubt he would entertain if Lon did not come back for supper. On the whole it would be better to go on, to follow the crest of the hills along the curve of Gregory Lane, then to swing wide and come back up the east side of the woods as he had that night he stumbled over Coon.

Such a course meant to go clear down to Rock Ladder, on the very verge of Schrader land. He wouldn't like to be seen, to have the tribe think he was spying on them. On the other hand, it was his woods. He could certainly walk in it if he pleased.

It was beautiful even in March, the ground littered with the frolic and spite of winter, the gray-brown slashes thickety with berry canes. In the pockets of leaf mold under rotten logs and between the roots of trees, rosettes of new leaves were already pushing back their covering. Thomas saw in anticipation the glory of spring: green mist as soft as the haze of remembered happiness. Spring and autumn, those were his seasons. Summer and winter he loved tentatively, but in the mournfulness of death and the miracle of resurrection there was something very near his mood.

He had crossed the last ravine and was angling up the long slope that led to the bare table-top of the precipitous mass called the Ladder when he first thought he heard someone. He stopped suddenly, his senses alert. It was foolish for him to come down this far unarmed, knowing what had happened to Coon and what Gorm had done to kill Black Belle. He was fairly certain that the man would not dare open murder, but the risk was not well taken. A shot might be heard by no one, or thought of any importance if it was heard.

Thomas shivered as he conjured up the specter of his own sudden death, almost regretted the necessity of breathing in his endeavor to pick up any strange sound. If there was another man in the woods, he too was immovable. Perhaps even now he might be peering out from covert.

Thomas decided to go on to the top of the hill. He did not want to return the way he had come, and the only decent path led east from the Ladder before it swung north.

Then, just as he started, he heard the noise again, almost as if it were the echo of his own footsteps. He tightened grip on the hickory cane. In another minute he would command the summit where it would be possible to spy out the hiding places in the rock. He made almost no sound now as his feet rested in the ledges covered inch-deep with blood-red sandstone ground to finest dust. It was raining again, almost imperceptibly, the silver beads like powder on the blue wool of his coat.

"Come down to put me off, maybe!"

Thomas turned as if struck. There was no one behind him. The hair on the back of his neck stiffened when he heard the other man laugh. Gorm was enjoying his discomfiture.

"You did, you can go right on back home!"

There was no place a man might hide. On the open sweep of the hill there were only a few butts of rock, none big enough to offer much cover, and but one tree, an old sycamore. The experience of a lifetime had strengthened Thomas's belief that a man could not well hide behind a tree. Either some part of his clothing would project on one side, or the curve of his cheek and forehead on the other.

"Wonderin' what you can do about it, ain't you!"

The sound was certainly from the direction of the sycamore. Could it be hollow? Spence had said something of a bee tree down near Rock Ladder, had promised to come with Thomas to chop it down. They had never gotten around to the task.

Without giving himself away, Thomas took a good picture of the contour of the sycamore. There was a great spread of branches fifteen or twenty feet from the ground, a few arm-sized limbs that a tall man might grasp to pull himself up the trunk. If Gorm was in the tree, he wouldn't have his gun with him. By rights it should be somewhere near the bole, unless he had not brought it. On impulse Thomas walked rapidly down slope in hope of picking it up. He was not rewarded for his trouble.

"You in that tree, Schrader?"

Silence—feathered by the almost imperceptible hush of the freezing rain.

Thomas backed away slowly, circled the big trunk, the mist beading his lashes when he attempted to look up. It would be as well for him to go on home. It looked as if it might rain harder any minute—the whole sky was the color and weight of lead. After all, he would like nothing better than to avoid further trouble with Gorm. The man was arrogant, but arrogance would break no bones.

He had taken a hesitant step or two downhill, not yet sure of his own mind, when he heard Gorm's taunting laugh.

"You'd best run away if you know what's good for you!"

That was the last straw.

"You come on out of there and you'll find out what's good for *you!*" Thomas shouted back.

Gorm came at once, his Judas mane tangled with strips of bark. He was exactly as Thomas remembered him: bloodshot eyes, dirty jeans, bare chest, knotted arms, barrel torso. Seeing him swing easily down from the perch, his hands and feet barely touching the branches, Thomas thought he looked like a great red catamount.

Thomas's impulse was to run, but there was no escaping fight now. If he was afraid, he was also glad. A mad swinging, kicking, wrestling match would be infinitely preferable to what he had so long feared—a shot from ambush. If only he could teach Gorm Schrader that he was not to be trifled with, he might in future be let alone.

"Throw down that club if you ain't a coward!"

Thomas flung it with the same motion he freed himself from his coat. They stood facing each other at a distance of some ten feet, both cautious, both searching possible advantages, watchful for any trick. Thomas noticed that he stood downhill and circled east so that Gorm would get the beat of rain in his face. Unfortunately his maneuver brought him too close to the sycamore. Gorm rushed immediately, hoping to pin him against the tree.

Thomas met him with a sledge-hammer swing that went wild when Gorm ducked under. Then they were down, clawing frantically for each other's throats, their nails leaving streaks of blood. Gorm had what little advantage there was, but when he brought his thumb up to gouge, Thomas caught it between his teeth. Gorm howled with pain. His instinctive leap backward allowed Thomas to regain his feet.

"I'll break every bone in your goddam body!"

Thomas's fist caught him right in the mouth. It was a vicious blow, so vicious that Thomas feared he had broken his hand. Gorm came up lipping blood, the light of the killer in his eyes. He said nothing now, only crouched and crept close, feinting with head and shoulders to throw Thomas off guard. Thomas was panic-stricken. If Gorm rushed again, his only hope was to try to knee him.

Luckily Gorm parried a long time. Thomas saw the trick he intended—to play for position on one of the rock ledges and crush him under the force and weight of his body when he sprang. To meet the danger he himself backed up hill. That brought them out on the smooth top of Rock Ladder, the sandstone slippery with rain. Thomas realized instantly it would not do to try to fight here. In the grass he had been able to keep his footing, but on the stone Gorm would overmatch him. He leaped aside in the attempt to flank a rush but was not quick enough, and again the two of them were down.

Gorm had him this time. Thomas fought desperately, his body thrashing to keep the clawing hands out of his eyes. His left hand, the only one with which he was able to resist, was tangled in Gorm's hair, pushing back so hard it should have torn the scalp loose. Gorm knelt on the right arm, his heavy knee crushing the biceps against the rock. Thomas had to twist his head to keep the fingers away. They caught in his nose, slit one nostril open, reached nearer, nearer their mark. On the instant he saw Gorm's plan—he did not mean to kill. Larger satisfaction would be to make Thomas go through life blind.

Thomas knew he could not hold out much longer. The weight on his chest was crushing the breath out of him, making the contest more uneven every moment. Gorm was sure, so sure that like a cat he could take his time. He might hold for a quarter-hour, half choke Thomas to death before he hooked in his thumb to lift the eyeballs from their sockets.

There was but one thing left to do and Thomas did it, shaking, lashing, writhing in the hope of getting Gorm into position. Once he tried, twice, three times. The sky was gradually going black! For the fourth time he attempted to hook his legs around Gorm's head, and for the fourth time he failed. As last resort he let go the red hair and smashed Gorm full in the nose. That sent the head back for an instant, and in that instant Thomas wrapped his legs around the neck and snapped Schrader's head back so hard the skull struck the bare rock.

Gorm should have been hurt, but he had weathered harder blows. He kicked savagely, caught Thomas in the shoulder and plunged free, shaking his head from side to side to clear it.

It was raining so hard now that they but half saw each other as they fronted on the tabletop, the jagged file of ledges on Thomas's right. The Ladder was more than a hundred feet high, almost sheer. If they went over that, neither of them would live. It was all very well for Lon Brewster to tell his fairy stories about angels, but any angels out in such foul weather would be angels of darkness.

Again Gorm crept in. Thomas kept a wary eye on him, rubbed his right arm to restore circulation. His hand still throbbed, but he meant to try it again when the time came. All his hope now was in trickery.

He got out of the way of the rush when it came, sidestepping so that their positions were reversed. His right arm hung down as if useless, only the left warded impact. Again Gorm tried to crash him down, and again Thomas managed to escape. He knew what he wanted—he wanted Gorm to sneak in. If he did, Thomas meant to let him have it right between the eyes.

The Ladder was again on Thomas's right. He caught himself thinking of home, Kate. She was likely building the fire bright against the afternoon gloom. What if he should not return to her! If she never knew exactly what had happened to him! Gorm was being more careful. It was apparent now that he meant to move in from the side so that Thomas should have to leap for the edge of the cliff. If they met, they would both fall perilously close.

Thomas saw the custard-colored whites of Gorm's eyes, heard the heavy intake of his breath. His arms were open pincers, his shoulders hunched like the shoulders of a bull. He was only six feet away (it was time to jump), five, four, three!

Thomas swung. The right caught under the jaw and Gorm went down like a plummet, to lie absolutely inert.

Thomas circled cautiously, afraid of some trick. But Gorm's eyes were rolled up in his head! It could not be true—that he was unconscious, that Thomas had won! Lying there on his back, the only good Schrader who had ever been seen in the county, he looked little more frightening than scary Tom Barker. He would be coming to any moment now, would find some latent power to send his body surging forward again. And if in the meantime Thomas did escape, then Gorm would lay for him. Somewhere, sometime, there would be a day, a place, an opportunity. The bullet would be sure.

Thomas looked about carefully. The blue smoke of the rain was like a curtain. From Gregory Lane came the sound of no traveler. People were staying indoors, glad for a fire and the luxury of dry flesh. Down in the bottoms, their hovel tangled in brambles, Matt and Het were likely quarreling over a clay pipe while Harrison lay flat on his back and bawled at Bette to keep her brats quiet. They were the only ones who would miss Gorm, and they largely because there would be one less mark for their curses.

The man was heavy, but Thomas cradled him. With meticulous care he thrust his left arm under Gorm's knees, got the right beneath his armpits. Laboriously he pushed to his feet, feeling for the first time the bruised muscles where he had been kicked.

And then, deliberately, he carried Gorm Schrader to the face of Rock Ladder, poised a second so that he should not slip, and with all his strength smashed the man down over the face of the cliff.

5 It was raining rivulets by the time he got home, his feet so heavy with mud and water he could hardly lift them.

"Lon must be up at the house," Kate greeted him. "Leastaways there's a light." And then as she turned and saw him, "Where in heaven's name you been you got all scratched up like that!"

Thomas pushed her into the cold middle room so that they should be away from the children.

"I just killed Gorm Schrader, Kate!" he said calmly. "You're the only person on this whole earth knows it besides me, and I don't ever want to hear you repeat it!"

When he came down after changing into dry clothes, she was singing at the stove.

VIII

1 Lonzo Brewster was dying. Soaked through by the rain that fateful March day Thomas pitched Gorm Schrader from Rock Ladder, he had coughed through the spring and summer apologetically, his body shrinking to a mere bag of bones. When the rains of October and the hard frosts chilled the air again, it was too much to expect that he would last long. Now, in mid-November, he was lying up at the Linthornes, making a pitiful attempt to go so that he would not have to be troublesome.

Thomas had bought a bed for the middle room and had kept the stove going, although they ordinarily depended on the kitchen fire. "No need you puttin' yourself out, Thomas," Lon protested, but Kate agreed with Thomas that they should make their guest as comfortable as possible.

On his last afternoon Lon called Thomas to his bedside and told him about the farm.

"All yourn, Thomas," he rasped as he tried with his skinny claw to hold Thomas's big hand. "Want it to be thataway. Jim, he ain't never took much shine to ownin' a piece o' land. An' Detroit, she up an' flew the coop. Never cared a hoot fer her pappy, that gal didn't. So you just take down the fence an' call it all Linthorne."

Thomas fuddled around until he finally provided himself with ink and paper.

"Best put that down in white and black, Lon," he said when he came back to the bedside. "Don't want Jim lawing me."

Lonzo smiled when Thomas handed him the pen.

"Can't scribble none, Thomas," he shook his head. "Wasn't

never learned to do it. You just put down whatever you want, an' I'll make my mark."

Thomas sent Kate down the road for Spence and Cora Vitt while he tried to improvise a will. They were back long before he was done puzzling. Finally he called them in to hear and to see Lon subscribe the paper.

"Reads this way, Lonzo," he said:

I, Alonzo Brewster, 74 years old, farmer, Bloom township, Fairfield county, do give my farm and farmhouse with the buildings and everything in them, to Thomas Linthorne, 32 years old, farmer, Bloom township, Fairfield county, to do with whatever he wants to, either keep it or sell it.

"Is that all right," he asked when he was finished.

" 'Xactly what's in my head," Lonzo confirmed. "Bring me that pen again."

They watched him make his cross, and afterward Spence and Cora signed as witnesses.

Lon died in his sleep that same night. Thomas had meant to sit up with him; but he was already so worn out by night watches that, when about ten Lon seemed to be sleeping, he went to bed. Kate found the old man cold in the morning. There was a smile on his gray face that might mean anything. Thomas preferred to believe that at the last he had been happy.

2   Thomas invited Joe Jordan and Lute Tanterscham to sit up with the corpse. He would have liked to include Spence, but Spence had to go to Columbus to see a man who had asked a price on Greenings and Rome Beauties. Lute and Joe had known Lonzo better than any of the other neighbors, so it was fitting they should share the last watch.

It happened, however, that Joe brought fidgety Tom Barker with him and that later on Bill Sapooney blundered in without being asked. That made five instead of three. Thomas told Kate to fry up some more meat and open another can of pickles before she went to bed. There was cider and apples in plenty, and Thomas would fill the coffee pot and slice bread as often as was necessary. The wine would have to wait until someone showed inclination for something harder than cider. Some folks always set out a jug of whiskey, but Thomas did not approve the custom. When he was a boy he had heard it told on good authority that at one such wake the watchers became so much befuddled that they allowed rats to chew the whole face off the corpse.

For warmth they clung to the kitchen, one of them going in with a lantern every quarter hour to be sure that nothing had happened to Lon. The night had started in to be clear and cold with a custard moon hanging low over the woods, but along toward midnight when the moon went down the wind crept up the road. They looked at each other apprehensively when they heard it, the thought of an icy graveyard in their minds. Out on the bald dome of the burial ground, there would be only the little cover of the spindly cedars.

They sat around the stove, squatty, apple-checked Tanterscham nearest the wall, then in semicircle Sapooney, Barker, Joe Jordan, his droopy face made sadder by the occasion, last of all Thomas.

Their talk was of omens and awful events, as it always was when they sat up with the dead: of clocks stopping; people buried alive— the fact proven when disinterment found them turned in their coffins, or half-naked, their grave clothes torn away in their last agony; of others disentombed whose beards and hair filled the caskets; of body-snatchers, blood-suckers, walking and talking ghosts, rappings, haunts; of corpses sneezing and changing position; and of all other unholy things. Before two hours had passed, they were all so wrought-up that when of a sudden the wind pried open the door and howled in their ears, they all jumped with fright. Thomas was the nearest and threw the bar to prevent any further intrusion.

"Thought sure the Old Man was a-comin' after us that time!" he admitted as he regained his chair.

They were all glad to be locked in.

"Horses knows it same as owls," Jordan drawled. "Bird flies up against the window or owl sits a-hootin' somewheres near the house, you can be pretty sure. Horses gets kind of skeery. Mind me of an old mare I once had. Time grandma passed beyond she near kicked the stall down."

"Well, I'm a-tellin' you it's b-bad luck countin' k-kerridges!" Bill Sapooney said. "See a funeral goin' down the road, best thing to do is turn your head away. C-c-count 'em an' it'll be just that many weeks till you have to put away one of your own. And t-tell you another thing, Tom, Cely was dumpin' our pot out the back window last night when she s-su-sudden saw a light flash over your house. W-what do you make o' *that!*"

Thomas was unconvinced.

"Ain't much reason to think them stories is any more than just made up," he rationalized.

"Mein Vater alvays sagt you go joost the same you don't see noddin'," Tanterscham chimed in. "Der ain't no goosts!"

Joe Jordan took issue immediately. "Know what Tom Barker here run into up on Black Man that time," he reminded them.

Tom was immediately a-tingle.

"Hopin' you fellers wouldn' think of that!" he piped. "Can't get that feller out of my mind. Walkin' right alongside me he was, just as natural as daylight. Hadn't of struck that match, I wouldn't of knowed him from Adam. That's why he done it all right—wanted me to see his face."

Tanterscham laughed at Tom's pop-eyes and the excited blur of his syllables.

"Goosts sind joost people," he said, his little eyes winking. "Maybe I ain't never told you vat happened to mein Vater:

"Ven he coom over to dis coontry he vent to Salzeck in Pennsylvania. Von night two fellers vent out to steal poompkins. Got two sacks between 'em, und ein ander big poompkin dey couldn't put in. On der vay home dey haben in ein graveyard to split up gestopt. Only der big poompkin dey couldn't take over die wall because it vas too heavy.

"Vater war joost a boy den. He vas down die road not makin' a sound mit his bare feet gecomin' ven he saw die Schatten onder die

112

trees. You joost bet he vas afraid. 'You devil!' he heard von say, und den der andere sagt, 'Mein Gott! Mein Gott!' "

"Vater vas too scairt to move. He vatched a vile, and den dey started countin', pilin' up vat looked like heads. 'Dies ist meins und dies ist deins! Dies ist meins und dies ist deins!' he heard 'em say und thought it was Gott und der devil splittin' up die souls.

"Vater vanted to run, aber er couldn't. 'Dies ist meins und dies ist deins!' dey vent on, und den der von countin' yelled, 'Dies ist deins. I'll take dot big von out in der road!'

"Vater hat heim so fast dey all come out to see vat der matter vas gerunned. Ven er sagte, dey all vent in und locked die doors. Vasn't ontil die fellers got heim mit die poompkins dey knowed vat Vater saw.

"Dot was der letzte Mal he efer beliefed in goosts."

They all laughed a little, but it was noticeable that Tom Barker crept over to his coat and brought back a bottle of brandy. Sapooney joined with him and Jordan in rekindling their courage.

"Think what you want to, but I know what I know," Joe said, his solemn eyes resting hopefully on their faces. "I ain't never told this before because it sort of gets under a man's skin."

"Wait a minute till I pour some coffee," Thomas interrupted.

"B-b-better put in a ch-chunk too," Bill Sapooney chattered. "It's a-gettin' cold."

It was getting much colder. They could all feel the draughts from the door and windows. Outside it seemed to be sleeting a little.

The persistent scratching as of icy fingers on the frost-wrinkled panes did their nerves no good.

"Happened down Clear Creek way," Joe began. "Know it's a true fact 'cause I've seen the cemetry myownself. And not only that neither—I knowed the man that saw the marks. Name of Joe, same as me.

"Here's the way it was: there was a no-account family on a farm down there near the big knob. Name was Matheny. Leastaways the mister wasn't much good. Way he treated his woman wasn't fitten atall. Carried on with other women he did, mostly with an old she slut that had a pile of money, but no good common sense.

"Well, it went on that way awhile, with folks seeing him drive up and get the widow almost every Sunday. Gave out his wife didn't much hanker after going to church, but truth was he didn't ask her. She was a little woman—his wife, I mean. Come to think about it, the widow was little too. Only she had a lot more git-up-an-go.

"Well, to get down to the point, this Mrs. Matheny passed on pretty sudden one night with her neck broke. Fell down stairs and banged against the door at the bottom, he said. Wasn't no one believed him much. There was a lot of blood around, but he gave out it was his'n, and that she got her marks coming down. He had a cut on his hand, all right; he was smart enough for that.

"Buried her way up in the old churchyard down by Sprossen's place. Not a gosh-danged thing behind it but woods a mile deep, and woods on both sides. Nearest house was Sprossen's, and that was over a half mile.

"Funeral was one day in the middle of winter. Don't guess her body was real cold before this Matheny was down on his knees to the widdy. Anyways they got married in two-three weeks and went to living together right in the same house where he'd killed his wife.

"Well, along towards dark one Saturday night this fellow named Joe decided to drive in town for a load of truck his missus had been nagging after. Hadn't meant to go till Monday, but it come on to snow in late afternoon and he figured he'd better get in and back before the roads got real bad.

"He was going by the old church graveyard when he saw something awful funny. Backed up and got out to take a sure look. Wasn't no doubt about it—there was a line of foot tracks in the fresh snow where a woman had walked out of the graveyard and hadn't walked in. Knowed it was a woman by the size, too little for a man and too big for a kid. What struck him as funny was what I told you about there being nothing but woods on the other side. So what'd he do but let his horse stand while he followed on up hill to see where the tracks come from."

"Kn-knowed a case like that once myownself," Bill Sapooney broke in the moment Joe stopped to drink the rest of his coffee. "There was a c-c-coffin restin' on a—"

114

"Joe ain't done," Thomas stopped him when he saw Jordan's pain at being interrupted. "Maybe one of us better look in and see Lon before we hear the rest of it. It's almost three."

They all looked at Barker, since it was his turn, but Tom showed no inclination to take the lantern.

"Think he's all right!" he blubbered hurriedly. "Night like this won't be any body-snatchers out. You got the door locked tight, ain't you, Thomas?"

"Won't take me very long to finish," Joe mercifully suggested.

"Well, as I was a-sayin', this fellow named Joe followed the tracks on up hill, wondering what a woman could have been doing out there that afternoon. Prints didn't curve any, just led straight back towards the woods. But just when it begun to look like that's where they come from, they stopped. Just went right up to a fresh grave, and didn't go no farther. And the funny thing was that the only person that had died and been buried all winter was this Mrs. Matheny.

"Joe thought about it all the way into town. More he tried to add things up right, the skeerier he got. Never opened his mouth to a soul, though, 'cause he was half afraid he was plumb batty. Just got his stuff together and hustled back to the hitching lot soon as he could.

"Mustn't have been no more'n seven when he got back opposite the cemetery. Snowing hard it was, everything all white, even his legs and the bottom of his rig. Knowed the only peace of mind he'd get would be to go on over to the gate and strike a match to see if them footprints was really there or not.

"He come up from the side like, so's not to rub out any marks there might be, and got down on his knees to strike a match. Sure enough, there they was, almost marked out, but he could still see the little hollows the snow had filled in.

"Joe was a-kneelin' there, holding the match in his hands and thinking it was danged funny when all of a sudden a wind blew out of the road at him so cold it felt like a knife blade laid down his back. Match went out like a snuffed candle. He got another one out fast as he could and struck it on his teeth, 'cause everything else was wet. You know what he saw?"

Barker was shivering, his body huddled as close to Sapooney as he could squeeze.

"What?" he voiced for all of them, the sound hardly escaping from his dry throat.

"Tracks going back, that's what," said Jordan. "That's the reason his first match went out—her a-rushin' by him like that. Wasn't no point to Joe's going on up hill this time to see where the steps led. He *knew*."

"Wouldn't be any sense in the body getting up and walking around like that," said Thomas, his voice so sepulchral it frightened him.

"That's what Joe thought," said Jordan slowly. "Wasn't till next morning he heard they'd found Matheny out in the barn with his head bashed in. Looked like he'd been hit with a poleax."

3   It helped none to have the clock strike three just as Jordan was finished.

They sat silent after that, feeding the fire to roaring heat and pretending to drowse, all of them so much on edge that sleep was impossible. Jordan huddled with the fortitude of a Stoic, hopeful for nothing, ready to answer at any moment if the great bird flapped its cold wings against the window. Even Tanterscham tippled at the bottle, and Sapooney was trying to get stupid.

But the most miserable of them all was undoubtedly Tom Barker. Half-past three struck, and then after a century, four, and still Barker sat on the edge of his chair, gripping hard to keep from crying. When finally he could stand seeing his distress no longer, Thomas pushed his chair over close to the shivering man.

"Buck up, Tom!" he whispered so that the others wouldn't hear. "Won't be more'n a couple more hours until daylight."

Barker lifted a stricken face. "'Tain't only that, Thomas," he whimpered. "Maybe—if you'd—"

"Ain't sick, are you?"

"I ain't real sick. Only I ain't feelin' good atall. I got to go see Aunt Mary, and I'm scared!"

Thomas went with him, their feet hollow on the creaking

boards of the privy walk. The ghosts of the desolate dead walked all about them, laid icy fingers on their faces as they passed. Beyond the gray light of the lantern was only horror, black and shapeless as death itself.

They hurried to get back to the living reality of the fire in the kitchen. That might be the most primitive, but it was also the most effective of all exorcisms.

4   The minister who drove out from Lithopolis was a big-boned, raw-faced man sent by Braun, who was himself the victim of laryngitis. It made little difference who read the service; the important matter was that Lon be decently buried.

The sleet had made the rutted lane into the graveyard so bad that six of them had to carry the casket up the hill on their shoulders, the minister leading the way. After the pallbearers came the two dozen mourners, their heads wrapped against the cold.

Around the open grave they circled solemnly, uncertain if they should uncover in the biting wind. The minister slipped the black book from his side pocket, forced his frosted fingers to find the burial service. They were all rigid as he began to read:

"I am the resurrection and the life, saith the Lord. Whosoever believeth in me, though he were dead, yet shall he live; and whosoever liveth and believeth in me shall never die.

"Blessed are the dead which die in the Lord from henceforth. Yea, saith the Spirit, that they may rest from their labors; and their works do follow them."

He paused then for a moment, motioned to Thomas that the pallbearers should begin to drop the body. The ropes were covered with ice as hard and sharp as glass. Thomas saw Tanterscham working hand over hand and took cue from him as the deep voice began again:

"Man that is born of woman is of few days and full of trouble. He cometh forth like a flower, and is cut down; he fleeth also as a shadow, and continueth not. But the mercy of the Lord is from everlasting to everlasting upon them that fear Him, and His righteousness unto children's children.

"Dust must return to the earth whence it was taken, and the soul to God who gave it.

"Since it has pleased God, the almighty Lord of life and death, to take the soul of this our brother out of time into eternity, we return his body to the earth. Earth to earth, ashes to ashes, dust to dust, in the certain hope that at the last day Jesus Christ shall wake his body from the grave, reunite it with the spirit, and preserve it forevermore. Amen."

They stood for a minute in silence when he had finished, their eyes moist as they thought of other graves, other loved ones to return no more from the little plots where they were lying. Then, slowly, they broke circle to permit the minister to go back to the road. After him in ragged line the women and children wavered, their shawls and mufflers caught close around their faces to hide their eyes.

The men stayed behind until they were decently away. Then someone brought spades and a crowbar from their hiding place behind the nearby cedars, and in a little while the ugly yellow mound was the only proof that Lonzo Brewster had ever lived.

5   Thomas was sobered by the funeral. In anticipation he had seen Lon's interment as a bit of necessary routine, the scalding wind of the open burial ground menace to the health of all who walked after the farm wagon that served as hearse. He had not let Kate and the children go, of course; decency required no such extreme measures.

At the grave, however, something had happened to him. That was the sum total of life, then, of the long years of labor sweetened by the harvests drawn from the bitter soil—to be swept down as the meadow grass before the scythe! To be remembered no more, perhaps not even by a crumbling stone! Stranger and pilgrim upon the face of earth, having no continuing city.

When he returned home, he took Kate's Bible into the cold parlor—there was a word in Ecclesiastes he wanted to read again:

All things come alike to all: there is one event to the righteous and to the wicked; to the good, and to the clean, and to the unclean; to him that sacrificeth and to him that sacrificeth not; as is the good, so is the sinner; and he that sweareth as he that feareth an oath.

This is an evil among all things that are done under the sun, that there is one event unto all; yea, also the heart of the sons of men is full of evil, and madness is in their heart while they live, and after that they go to the dead.

For to him that is joined to all the living there is hope; for a living dog is better than a dead lion.

For the living know that they shall die; but the dead know not any thing, neither have they any more a reward, for the memory of them is forgotten.

Also their love, and their hatred, and their envy is now perished; neither have they any more a portion for ever in any thing that is done under the sun.

6 Thomas was silent the rest of the night. His thought was not so much of Lon, silent now after his threescore years and ten, as of Gorm. Ugly as his life had been, it might have been useful. Even now Het, Matt, and all their brood might be suffering because of scanty provision.

The next day Thomas hitched the team without telling Kate, filled the wagon bed with corn, potatoes, baskets of apples. From the smokehouse he brought two of his best hams, dared even go down cellar to run off with some of Kate's canned stuff.

He drove boldly into the Schrader wheel-tracks, angled right up against the shack. Harrison was in the yard chopping wood. Like Gorm big and red-headed, he was wary when he saw Thomas. He wouldn't leave off chopping, seemed to want to keep his hands on the ax.

Thomas had to get down and go over to the woodpile.

"Guess me'n you's pretty near strangers," he said as he held out his hand. "I'm Tom Linthorne."

Harrison nodded imperceptibly. He wouldn't take the proffered hand, although he did not seem entirely unfriendly.

"Heered tell about you," he said. "Guess you'n Gorm had a couple run-ins."

Thomas didn't mean to waste time talking about anything like that.

"Got a whole lot more stuff up to the house than we'll ever need this winter," he said. "Wondered whether I couldn't trade you a little of it for some of your time. Some things've been getting away from me lately."

Harrison didn't know what to make of that. He cautiously circled over to the wagon, looked in over the tailgate.

"Didn't know whether you'd have any use for that kind of truck or not," Thomas apologized. "Won't find nothing wrong with them hams, though. They're A No. 1."

Harrison was hungry, but he wasn't to be sold into slavery. The moment Bette blustered from the door, he whipped her back to the house.

"How much time I got to give you next spring for all that?" he wanted to know.

"Oh, day a week for a month or two, maybe . . . Say from along about middle of March to end of May."

Harrison started to unload when he heard that. He kept his dignity, acted as if the shack were already overflowing with milk and honey, even if Matt had that very morning walked into Lancaster to try to sell his steel traps.

Watching him, Thomas began to wonder if he had not been misjudged. Harrison Schrader didn't look like a thief, didn't act like a thief. Given a chance—a team, fertilizer, the tools he needed, help at harvest, he might prove to be one of the most respected men in the community.

Thomas vowed he'd have that chance.

IX

1   The old stake and rider between his land and that which had been Lon Brewster's Thomas hauled to the house for firewood. As for Lon's cabin, he decided to let it stand for the present. He had already begun to anticipate the day when Hocking and Grover would marry, perhaps make their land and effort one with his. The girls, of course, would have to go elsewhere.

Now that he was the owner, he began to look at the adjoining acres with new eyes. In the fields where once he had noticed only thistles and sourdocks, he visioned corn and oats. He would plant Chinese cane in the ancient garden plot, dig a new well, clean out the spring, put down corduroy through the mudholes in the back lanes. Possibly—he knew this thought almost a daydream—possibly he would try tobacco. Land elsewhere in the county was said to be good to raise a kind of yellow leaf that was used in dyeing. The crop was a nuisance, of course, but if he repaired Lon's barn a little, he couldn't want a better drying shed.

One day in January he went up to the old barn to look around for a snaffle. It was raw weather, the wind both violent and cold, so that his eyes were watering and his nose dripping by the time he found refuge in the bay of Brewster's house. He was twisting his red woolen scarf closer about his throat when he heard a sudden, sharp, slapping sound in the barn. The wind was enough to hurl the structure into the next field if it were so minded, but the noise seemed to be the kind made by a man.

Thomas went down warily, knowing how often tramps loitered in disused buildings to get away from the cold.

The man in the barn was not hiding. He was as much surprised as Thomas, showed his uneasiness by a strange way of laughing too often and turning his eyes away when he spoke. He was a big, sandy-haired fellow, his eyes sometimes blue and again gray, his hands too soft to belong to a man who followed the plow.

"Live hereabouts?" Thomas asked after they had exchanged greetings.

The fellow shook his head. "Not any more I don't," he said, but he volunteered no further information.

It was only by chance that Thomas learned he was speaking to Jim Brewster. He had seen at a glance that there was no old harness about, but a good hickory pole across the mows reminded him of his intention to shape up a new ax handle.

"Ain't what I come over for," he said as he climbed the ladder. "What I really was after was a snaffle."

The sandy-haired man huddled on the damp dirt, his body shaking with cold. Thomas pitied him because he looked so much like a fence post dressed up to scare crows away. That he seemed not to hear, to care if he had heard, was of little importance.

He must, however, have given Thomas's remark passing thought, for as soon as Thomas crawled down he volunteered, "Want you a snaffle, I think I know where one is." Thomas followed in confusion to the end stall where the stranger pawed a jointed piece of rusted metal out of a litter of rubbish in the feed trough. "Knowed it was there," he said. "Laid it there day before I run away."

Thomas held out his hand at that, although Jim seemed hesitant to remove his from the warmth of his jacket pocket.

"Just up takin' a last look-see," he explained. "Heard tell pap willed you the place."

"Didn't know you was in this part of the country," Thomas apologized.

"That's all right—I ain't thinkin' hard of you. Or of pap, either. Just because we couldn't see eye to eye when I was a kid ain't no reason for keepin' a grudge. Only, I really didn't know he was real sick. Not till after it was all over, anyway."

Thomas unlocked the house door so that Jim could look his fill.

They walked slowly from room to room, Jim even climbing into the loft. "Slept up here nigh on seventeen year," he shouted down. "Some mornings was snow all over the bed."

Thomas found himself liking the man better. He seemed little more than an overgrown boy, for all the tales told of his hard drinking. Thomas couldn't get over feeling like a thief. No one he talked to had thought that either Jim or *De*troit would ever turn up again.

"Like to farm?" he asked as they were walking toward the road.

"Done most everything. Sailor, blacksmith, shoemaker in Lynn, Massachusetts. Under the ground in Pennsylvania a while. Even was out west . . . Guess farming's about as good as anything else."

"Like to have the old place back?"

"Ain't particular. Pap wanted me to have it, he'd of willed to me in place of you is the way I look at it."

Thomas led him along home.

"Make mistakes, all of us," he said. "Your father was always pretty lonesome, long as I knowed him."

"Tell me he took it pretty hard when I pulled out," Jim admitted. "Know he did when *De*troit left."

"Well, what I thought of was this. You got nothing to do. Strikes me there wouldn't be nothing nicer than for you to settle back on the land again. Only trouble is you wouldn't have anything to work with. So maybe you would use what I got, and pay me with a cut across whatever you make clear money."

Jim smiled wrily. "Don't figure I'd be gettin' rich very fast, do you?"

"Don't for a fact. Point is, I've always heard you couldn't stick at anything very long."

Jim took the criticism with good grace.

"How many years I have to keep paying you off?"

Thomas considered for a long time. "Tell you what," he finally came to decision, "you get it going in five years, I'll deed it over. Reason I won't right now is you got to prove you're man enough to handle it."

Jim wouldn't commit himself. But when late that afternoon he set out to walk to Hooker he looked at Thomas significantly. "Guess maybe I'll try to do that—what you said."

Thomas laid a hand on his shoulder.

"Be looking for you to move on down," he said. "Don't see why you shouldn't eat here until you get a few things laid by. Don't have a woman, do you?"

"Not certain sure yet," Jim laughed guiltily.

"Well, you'll need one. Best thing you can do is start looking in dead earnest."

2 Jim came back in a week.
He was a good worker, showed no disposition to hide a bottle, was friendly to Thomas, courteous to Kate, kind to the children. It was a rare night he did not take one of the babies on his knee while he told of his travels: of the year spent in a freighter on Lake Michigan, of the black maze under the coal hills, of riding herd at night out in Wyoming. They loved to hear the gentle blur of his voice as he spun the fabulous with known fact.

From the first Charlotte was his favorite. She was six now, a little dark-eyed beauty, already showing she could be a creature of moods. If there was to be a war in the barnyard, with files of imaginary gray-clad men slipping somber-eyed around the corners of smokehouse and chicken shed, she would almost certainly be the leader. But at other times, generally on rainy days and in the company of her mother, who was teaching her to spell out the primer, she was a different being. Not until Jim came in and swung her up for a pick-a-back ride would she show the slightest interest in anyone.

Then, suddenly, all Charlotte's happiness came to an end. At the table one night Jim made the simple announcement that he meant to be married. Every Sunday afternoon he had been borrowing the buggy, but he had never appeared with his girl.

"Why, Jim, there ain't hardly any fixin's left up at that old house!" Kate protested. "No carpet, no bed, nothing but a couple broken chairs."

"Countin' on makin' most everything like that," Jim said.

Kate pondered. "Course, there's a few things Thomas and me

124

can let you have the use of. Chest upstairs I ain't at present in need of. And—well, I guess maybe we can fix you up."

Thomas winced at mention of the chest of drawers. He had bought it cheap when a family sold at auction to go out to Iowa, had carted it home proudly, thinking how much Kate would like to have the extra drawer space. True enough it was only black walnut, nothing pretty like poplar or oak.

"Guess you'll be wanting some money too," he said loudly to cover his confusion. "Got a ten dollar bill upstairs I'll loan you. Pay me back when you feel like you're able."

Jim muttered thanks.

"Course, I told her all about the house," he said, still unwilling to answer their unspoken questions as to the identity of the bride. "Said it didn't make much difference to her—long as summer's comin' on anyway."

"Didn't make no difference to me neither, Jim," Kate said fondly. "And we didn't have no more'n you when we come here."

Thomas, she saw, hung on her every word. She could not know that he was studying her face, that he had begun to be a little jealous.

"When'll you be moving up?" Thomas asked when he saw Jim mopping up his plate with a wad of bread.

"Fixin' on Saturday right now. Course, Lucile may have plans I don't know about. But if it's all right with you, I'll take one of the horses and drive in after her Saturday about noon."

Thomas turned the proposal over in his mind.

"Best take the team instead," he suggested. "Be some truck I want hauled back. No sense going light both ways. Guess maybe the girl'll have a little fancy stuff she don't want to get rid of, too."

3 Jim's wife was very young.
   She was a tall girl, her corn-silk hair in natural ringlets about her cheeks, her ivory skin frosted with shell-pink. In a way she was beautiful. What made one hesitate to pronounce final judgment was the almost complete lack of light in her eyes. Seeing her for the

first time when Jim brought her down for Sunday dinner, Thomas was disappointed in his endeavor to discover if her teeth were good. In all the time they were eating, and afterward when they sat in the middle room, she never smiled once.

Her name was, or had been, Lucile Carbery, and she was from Glendale, a little hamlet over in Perry County. She had first met Jim while she was in Lancaster visiting her sister. Afterward she had contrived to get work in one of the fashionable homes on Main Street Hill, and so had accumulated a small sum to dower herself. In her three years of service she had alternated hope with despair. Jim was always running off somewhere, seemed never able to master himself sufficiently to hold a job.

That was why she was so happy to come to the farm. Out where there was wind and sun she felt that she would have allies in her attempt to shape her man to some semblance of her ideal. She asked little, entertained no illusions. It would satisfy her to see Jim no more successful than any one of a hundred farmers she had known and could name, no wiser, wittier, kinder, more resourceful. Men, she knew, were to be accepted as they stood, or not accepted at all. In their own domain they were lords, touching all beyond the horizon, oracles.

After dinner she stayed on in the kitchen to help Kate with the work while Thomas and Jim stalked off impressively.

"You just sew you up a tick 'long about threshing time and bring it down here so's we can stuff it with fresh straw," Kate told her. "Be a feather bed you'll want too. Don't want to freeze next winter. Lon didn't leave anything like that up there, did he?"

"We haven't needed any covers yet," Lucile said. She puzzled Kate because she seldom answered directly. Ask her one thing, and like as not she'd veer to another.

"Well, you'll want a feather bed sure. I been saving whenever we wring a couple chickens, but there ain't enough yet. Tell you what you ought to should do—you ought to have Jim borrow him a gun and go up to Buckeye Lake this fall. It's geese that make a bed real warm. And not near so heavy neither."

"I'll tell him about it," Lucile promised indifferently.

Kate resented that in the girl, her assumptions of not needing advice. Personally Kate liked to be forehanded. It was all very well to talk out of the good side of your mouth when there was plenty to eat and you could leave your windows open at night, but you'd twist to the other when the snow came down. That was one thing she had insisted on doing the first summer she lived with Thomas, making her a bed that would be warm. Of course, she knew then that she'd have to make ready for her baby. But if Lucile knew what was good for her, she'd be having one the first year too. That was the way to make a man proud of himself—give him children.

Kate worked on in silence after her rebuff, her hands stinging in the scalding water. Thomas never wanted her to use much soap, said it spoiled the dishwater for the pigs.

Then, after a time, she forgot that she had been provoked.

"Got you any stone jars and tin cans to put up stuff?"

"Not yet," Lucile said. "Jim says there's some down cellar. Unless they're all broke."

"Hain't you been down and looked yourownself?"

"It's only a hole in the ground!" Lucile defended herself. "All dark and scary. Jim asked me to go down, but I told him I didn't want."

Kate snorted. The very idea of being afraid to go down in your own cellar! "Well, there's any crocks down there, you better get them up and have them washed," she said. "Cucumbers and ground-cherries and peaches and all kinds of truck's just aching to be took."

"I'll have Jim look," Lucile said again.

This time Kate did not attempt to renew the conversation. She felt she could afford to be somewhat charitable, since she was ten years older if she was a day. And it would take time for Lucile to learn there wasn't much mooning to be done around a farmhouse.

"I'll do what I can to help you out," Kate promised as she dumped the dishwater into the slopbucket.

"I'm awful thankful. You done too much already."

"Fiddlesticks!" said Kate. But she did have the feeling that she and Thomas could feel proud. They had almost a proprietary right to put in a word now and then.

4 Kate strove for Thomas's approval by detailing her conversation with Lucile as soon as she brought the girl into the middle room.

That they were in the middle room at all had rich significance. The door to the parlor was not only closed but locked. Jim and Lucile could not fail to know what that meant. The parlor was for guests of quality, the gesture of unlocking and ushering in as complimentary as volumes of words. Ordinary friends and neighbors might be regaled with a sight of ingrain carpet and postcard rack, but they hardly expected to be asked to sit. Even at funerals there was distinction. At such a time much of the space was occupied by the corpse, but the corners of the room were still adequate for the family and those who merited honor. The preacher, belonging equally to the quick and the dead, always stood in the doorway.

Kate's middle room was exactly right for the transition from kitchen to parlor. Because she had a mania for collecting things and a passion of continued possession, much of the overflow of miscellaneous furniture had come to rest on the very threshold of elegance. Three straight chairs, a chest, two tables, the head and foot boards of the bed in which Lon had died, a music box that the Gregorys had thrown away because it would no longer play, a revolving bookcase without books, and a round-topped, leather-covered trunk accounted for most of the litter. The potbellied stove stood off-center on its sheet of tin, the stair opening directly behind it. There was no carpet on the wide boards of the floor, but as Kate said, the cracks were so wide they would cut a carpet in two.

What saved the place from looking like a disused lumber room was the clutter of homely articles strewn over every surface: aprons, coats, boots, Thomas's rifle, the fan mill, coffee-grinder, candle mold, corn peg, best knives and forks, washrags hung on a string behind the stove, and the churn. Kate moved the churn with the seasons because she was finicking about her butter-making—she was already famous for her print.

She had hoped to have Thomas confirm her opinions about the necessity of providing feather bed and stone jars, but he was in one of his stubborn moods.

"Don't know why you can't live happy without them," he denied her. "Don't remember my ma having feather beds when I was a boy. And she always dried all her stuff. Ain't nothing much better to chew on than peach leather—that is, if you know how to make it."

"We'll get along all right," Jim put in. "Lucile's just hankering for a chance to go after the house."

"'Spect it'll need plenty a' goin' after," said Kate without much attempt to conceal her acrimony.

"What I'd like more'n anything else is an iron kettle," Lucile said with passive face. "I don't care so much about sleeping soft if I just don't—"

"Never said nothing about sleeping soft!" Kate stopped her. "Sleeping warm I was talking about! Anybody'd know you wouldn't mind having a hard tick under you. Or shouldn't—if you've done a proper day's work."

That brought on a long, awkward silence, during which Jim went over to dawdle with a few flints Thomas had carried in from the fields.

"Guess real Injuns made them all right," he gave his opinion. "That blue one is real pretty."

"Lots of them hereabouts," said Thomas. "Turned up six or seven together down in the far field one day. Didn't stop to pick them up 'cause I wanted to get through before dark. Not much good for anything but the kids to play with, anyway."

"Knowed a fellow saved 'em once."

Kate was a little more conciliatory when she saw Jim's interest.

"My pa had a whole box full of them things," she said, and shooed a fly out with her apron before she went into the yard to look for the children.

She was still out there when Thomas walked up the road with Jim and Lucile, the girl between the two men so that she could catch either arm for support if her ankle turned in a rut. Kate thought it was awful silly of Thomas. Such a procedure was enough to make a girl take on a little, to put on airs. She wouldn't step so high and mighty when she was carrying her first, and milking to do, bread to set, butter to make, washing to put to soak, and a man to satisfy before she could close her eyes.

129

5 Puzzled by Thomas's seeming interest in Lucile, Kate attempted to prove to him her clear superiority. She took immaculate care of her person, kept the house and the children pin neat, made him a mess of "ponhass" out of season, dropped words to the children that would let him know how strong she thought him. "Don't you go near that red colt now, Hocking!" she would warn. "Ain't nobody but your pa can handle a horse like that!" Or if she found him a little sulky some morning, "You've got to eat more, Thomas. Man can't do all the work you do around this place on nothing more'n six fried eggs and a plateful of potatoes."

She failed to charm him. Once, indeed, while he was letting his dinner settle, he looked at her a long time without speaking, as if he meant to say something nice. The mood passed quickly when Charlotte came in with a long splinter caught under her thumb nail. Thomas was almost brutal as he got the sliver out with his jackknife. "Don't see why they always have to run into all the trouble they can find!" he growled, his attitude clear indication that he thought Kate was to blame.

As the days passed and her craftiest plans failed to impress him, the suspicion crept into Kate's mind that he might be comparing her unfavorably with Lucile Brewster. Certainly Thomas was going over to the Brewsters too often. That was his prerogative, one that she had no right to question. But it would be hard for him to argue that every trip was made from sheer necessity. Hocking was old enough to run with bits of news and little articles. And it was not once in two weeks that Thomas gave Jim a day.

Kate began to watch him more narrowly, although she tried so hard to be casual that everything she said or did was suspicious. Long afternoons when she could not see Thomas in the fields she glanced repeatedly down the road, careful to hide herself behind the half-drawn blind. It was maddening that the gentle roll of the hill and the thick hedge shut off her view. In the winter one could see some parts of the Brewster yard and a portion of the house, but in summer nothing but the saddle-back of the roof. She was obsessed by the thought that Thomas no longer desired her, an obsession that daily fastened tighter on her mind.

6   And then one Saturday afternoon the merest chance proved in a moment that her fears were not without foundation. Thomas had lent Jim the bay horse to ride into town. Kate listened to the drizzle of talk in the yard before Jim left, distinctly heard Thomas promise to meet for a glass of beer somewhere on Columbus Street. He came in a half-hour later to ask in a matter-of-fact way if there was anything she needed. He seemed preoccupied, unresponsive, so that she had to repeat her order three times. "Don't guess I'll be back till late," he said as he went out. Kate watched him drive away, the little dappled mare sliding her slovenly feet through the dust.

Kate went about her preparations for Sunday, rolled out the pie dough and shaped the crusts before she went upstairs for a clean hairpin to aid in making a fancy crimp. The slant sunlight on the floor of the bedroom reminded her that she had meant to put the covers to air. She put the pin in her mouth while she carried sheets and comforters to the south window. Once there, she could not fail to look up at the great mound of Church Hill, all Linthorne now, from the lane clear down to Jordans. The children would have to go to the woods more often, she thought; they could learn more there than in school.

She was spreading the covers in the sun when her eye caught a slow-moving blur on the round hump of land behind the school. Kate strained to bring the object into sharper focus, the sun making her sneeze. When it disappeared in the trees, she was sure of one thing only—it had been a tall man and a tall woman.

She bit her lips to keep from crying and went at once to the east window in the back room to see if Thomas had stopped in at Brewsters. The added ten feet of height was enough to make the whole barnyard visible, and in it the hitching rack behind the house. There could be no question of what she saw, no question of the meaning. As she had feared, there was a little dappled horse tied to the rack.

Thomas was in Church Woods with Lucile Brewster.

X

1   That Faith began to cough as if she had lung trouble could hardly be construed as an added curse. It gave Kate something to think about, something physical, immediate, challenging. The child had never been well. Now, at five, she was a thin, angular, sad-eyed little girl who cried at every slight irritation, was cold even in summer, made no friends, shared no toys, suffered no reproof. Kate could not get her to eat. She tried coddling, indifference, threats, and failed with every method. A few mouthfuls were enough for Faith at any time. Nor did she like those foods that Kate especially wanted her to eat. If there was molasses cake or cream pie, Faith might always be persuaded; but soups, gravies, and all meats and vegetables she despised. She would as soon die as let her mother spoon an egg into her mouth.

Kate remembered what Celia Sapooney had once told her of the way children grew hale and hearty after they were measured. She was so much worried that she dared Thomas's anger and spoke to Celia in church.

Instead of a bonnet Celia had a regular flower garden on her head that Sunday, a paradise kept in place only by the ribbons under her chin. Kate thought the woman scandalous and hated to be seen with her, but the need of employing cunning in getting advice without Thomas's knowledge made her swallow her pride.

Celia was tickled to be so important. She started whispering behind her palm-leaf fan while the preacher was still hammering home, her voice a buzz plainly heard in the pauses of the sermon.

"She don't do it only in the afternoon, Mis' Linthorne. Funny that way she is. Time I took Adolph and Lotus she made us come

132

on a Friday. Good Friday's best, maybe. Don't know, but she just said for Bill and me to bring the kids down on a Friday right after dinner."

Kate was distressed, especially since Maude and Lena Spumm, twin maiden ladies who always came down from Lithopolis when the Reverend Mr. Schwartz was going to preach, turned halfway around to protest the discourtesy by pained faces and tiny shrugs.

"You tell me after church, Celia," she whispered. "I'll be out back of the coal shed."

Celia nodded, but every three minutes after that she thought of something that couldn't wait:

"Have her washed real nice and clean—old Tess is awful particular. I give Lotus a whole bath. You know she has to go to sleep afore Tess'll measure her! Got to pray every night afterwards and think real hard of the cure. Do it so hard it's just like holding onto something to bring down a baby. That's what she told me. You might not be able to understand her. She don't talk half of what she says so's you can hear. Don't Mr. Linthorne know you're a-fixin' to do it atall? Course, some folks say it's a-trustin' in the devil instead of God, but it's like I told Bill, I says, 'I'd be willing to trust anything would make them pretty angels grow up proper, and it don't hurt me none if you do call it the devil!' Well, I'll be a-waitin' for you right out where you said."

Kate was so mortified that she could hardly wait for the Doxology. She sent Hocking and Grover to their father, grabbed Charlotte in one hand and Faith in the other, and hurried out without exchanging a good-morning with anyone.

Celia had nothing to add when they met in the cinders and burdock out of sight of prying eyes, but she did promise to make the necessary arrangements.

"Won't cost you nothin', you remember that!" she kept repeating. "Take money for one of them gifts and you don't have it no more. Won't cost you a penny, not a single penny!"

"I'll give you something for your trouble," Kate promised, knowing full well that Celia was not above a bribe.

"Why, Mis' Linthorne! The very idee, to think of giving me anything! Ain't I always told you from the first that whenever I can do for you and yours, all you got to do is just put in a whisper? Why,

I wouldn't think of taking nothing! That's what's so pretty about it—they ain't no money passed. All you got to do for me is maybe just send over a ham or piece of tenderloin when you butcher next winter."

Kate felt stifled by the woman's nerve, her incessant blabber, offensive smell.

"I'll do what's right!" she said crisply, and hurried off so that Thomas would not start looking for her.

2   Kate would have preferred to wait a day, when Thomas would be in town. But when Celia came around on Monday afternoon to say that she had just come back from Sellerses and that old Tess would want Faith the coming Friday, she knew that she would have to chance going and coming without Thomas's knowledge. With adroit management and a little luck she would be able to fool him, since he was almost always away from the house the entire afternoon.

That Friday she was up at early dawn. She wanted to get as much work done in the morning as she could, so that even the potatoes would be pared in preparation for supper. Then if she got back late, she might still be able to have the meal waiting when Thomas came in. He was sure to fume if it was not—these long days he liked to get in several hours of work after supper.

Celia met her at the bridge over Hocking Creek, took the two older children on either side of her while Kate followed with Faith and Grover. Ordinarily she didn't mind walking them a mile or two, but today it was miserably hot, the heat haze undulant over the corn. To add to her discomfort, the children's hands were so sweaty that they kept slipping through her fingers. She had to snatch whenever that happened or the child would fall behind, the roadside flowers more attractive than the prospect of plodding on through the heavy dust.

"You mustn't be nervous now, Mis' Linthorne!" Celia called back when they were turning into the Cedar Hill pike. "Ain't no call to think the good Lord ain't watching down on people like Tess Sellers!"

"Best hush!" Kate warned. "Little pitchers!"

Celia took the rebuke gracefully, proud of her comprehension of such a riddling phrase. They marched on in cavalcade, the eight little legs striding sturdily and much more rapidly than the four big ones. Kate had thought once that she should carry Faith, but fear of the smudge the dusty shoes would make on her blue dress was an effective deterrent. After all, if Tess Sellers could do what she claimed, Faith would no longer need to be carried.

Naomi came out to meet them, her massive fat so wearisome that she could hardly drag one leg around the other. Kate knew her good nature from talking with her at church. What pleased her more was that Naomi evidently expected them.

"You come right on in out of this heat, you two!" she called as soon as they were near enough to hear. "My, but ain't it hot!"

"Fry a feller in his own grease!" Celia chattered amiably.

Naomi was appreciative in a blubbery way.

"Guess I got plenty to start the skillet," she said. "Now don't stop on the porch—door's open. You go right on in and sit."

Kate made Charlotte and the boys play in the yard. That would suit them better than the stuffiness of the house, even if it was cooler indoors, and she doubted if the measuring would take long. What Tess did she had never been able to get out of Celia. After many fruitless queries she had come to the conclusion that Celia didn't know.

It was dark in the parlor because of the drawn blinds, so dark that Kate hesitated just beyond the threshold, her eyes unable to adjust themselves after their struggle with the intense light.

"Just pick out a nice chair and sit, Mrs. Linthorne!"

She saw a chair dimly and sank into it, pulling Faith onto her lap. The child was frightened, crept close and buried her face, whimpering that she wanted to go home.

"Come now! Come now Faith!" Kate commanded, deeming authority better than persuasion. She was whipping herself in the same way; she too would like to run.

"Ma's out in the other room," she heard Naomi say sleepily. "She'll want you to bring her out there. I'll just go say you're here."

Kate waited apprehensively. Her eyes were able now to take in the garish richness of the furnishings, so much grander than her own. The Sellerses had real pictures on their walls, and not one motto but three. Those and the dried grass, the crystal ball, the gold-fringed scarf on the table, the massive chrome of Tess and her husband, old Zeke, and the real lace doilies put Kate in her place. It was a shame such an elegant room had to be partially spoiled by the enormous throat of the old open fireplace, but everybody knew that the house had once been a tavern and made proper allowances.

They waited a long time, Celia fidgety and reminiscing of her visit with Lotus and Adolph, Kate very grave. She conjured up all kinds of distressing pictures: of Thomas returning to find them all gone, of Tess bewitching Faith out of some kind of black book, of Naomi's blabbing. She knew now that she had been a fool to think that any miracle could make Faith like Charlotte. Some children simply were born pining and never quite forgot that they wanted to go back to heaven.

"You bring her on in now, Mrs. Linthorne."

She had neither seen the door move nor heard it creak. She felt suddenly very weak in the legs, very short of breath. She would be unable to go through with it, would have to run away. The old woman might claw her, hex her, might for very spite make her head swell or stop her veins.

But she was walking, walking, her feet wooden, her legs water, her heart a stone. The middle room was almost as black as night, both blinds and shutters walled across the sun. All she could see was a sort of couch in the center of the bare floor. Then out of the darkness, fantastic, inhuman, a spider shape crawled, every second creeping closer to her and the terrified baby. Kate wanted to scream, but her throat was too dry to form a sound. "You'll have to let her do it now! You'll have to let her do it now!" something within her kept repeating. She could not find the strength to resist. The long, bony fingers were upon her arms, upon her hands, were snaking over the withered body of her girl. She thought that Tess had already begun measuring when she heard her mumble, the tones like the rasp of dead leaves half heard on an autumn night as one swooned to sleep.

"Pretty, pretty, pretty. Mamma's chickee. Don't cry. Tessie don't hurt nobody. Don't want to cry. Tessie don't hurt nobody!"

That was all Kate could understand. She felt a little better, now that she knew the old witch was simply trying to make friends. But if she really wanted people to like her, she should roll the blinds and throw the shutters wide. She didn't have to be sensitive because she was toothless, her skin a sag of yellow wrinkles. All old people were that way.

She resisted when she felt Tess lifting Faith from her arms, but the hag was stronger than her age would indicate. In the dark there was a smell about the woman as of old apples in a closed room. "Let me have her now!" the husky voice vibrated in her ear, and she resigned herself to fate.

Then again Naomi was pulling at her arm and she was being led out into the room with Celia Sapooney.

"She's got to go to sleep before Ma can do anything, you know," Naomi told her to allay her fears. "Just you wait a minute or two and you'll hear her stop bawling like that." She appealed to Celia. "Ain't that so, Mrs. Sapooney? You know how 'twas with your kids."

Celia eagerly seconded her.

But it was no minute or two with Faith. A quarter hour passed, another quarter, and still Kate could hear the child's pitiful sobs. She became frantic.

"I'll have to get her and take her home!" she pleaded.

She was to find no help from Naomi. The big woman who looked like a rolled up bedtick creaked back and forth, back and forth, her eyes the eyes of a sick cow. If she heard, she showed no sign.

"Won't take much longer now, Mis' Linthorne," Celia assured.

Kate sank back with despondent eyes. She had heard her father tell of the time he had gone to a man to have the fire taken out of a burn. As she understood the narrative, the cure was instantaneous. One possessed of the power had simply to pass his fingers over the afflicted member and the hurt was gone. But that had been told when she was a little girl, so that she might have misunderstood. If only Celia had warned her, had given her some idea what the ordeal would be like, she would have steeled herself.

She heard the slow clock strike the hour. It would be getting late now. There was no longer any chance that she could beat

Thomas back to the house. She might have to tell him where she had been. What he would do was unpredictable.

But the sobbing had stopped. Then, from beyond the closed doors, there was the faintest rustling sound, as of a mouse running behind the wainscot. Kate sat frozen, her ears straining to hear. She saw that Celia was doing the same. There was a dark blob in the greenish patch of her face that told plainer than words that Celia's mouth hung open. After a long moment of black silence she heard Celia's whisper, "She's a-measurin' now, Mis' Linthorne! She's a-doin' it right now!"

Kate went hot, her heart pounding. She wanted to pray, but the words that came to her lips were mere jumbles of gibberish. Then, somewhat contemptuous of her weakness, she gave her brain direction, forced her lips to repeat, "Our Father," the Creed, "By Jordan's Stormy Banks I Stand," "Jesus, Lover of My Soul," the Doxology, and the Twenty-third Psalm. She was still lipping words, her hands hard clenched on the arms of her chair, when she heard the thin knocking on the other side of the door.

"You can go on in now, Mrs. Linthorne," Naomi drawled without budging. "Guess Ma's finished all she means to do."

Kate went, letting the door stand wide behind her. It was immediately closed, as if by some supernatural agency. She turned in the darkness to face the witch, all her horror returned, her hands instinctively raised to ward off physical harm.

"Take her!" she heard Tess's dry whisper, the sibilance like black frost upon her face. "You pray for her every night. She can get well if you think she can."

Kate needed no prompting to snatch up her baby. At that moment she had faith in nothing but sunlight. If ever she could but manage to get beyond the loathsome walls, she would begin to think that God was good.

She fumbled open the door, fairly ran through the room where Celia waited with Naomi. Out in the yard the three children came trooping to meet her, their eyes wide with wonder. "You get along home fast as you can scamper!" she commanded, and dragged Hocking by the arm when it seemed he did not mean to mind. She wanted to get them away, to get away herself. Never, never, never would she return to this evil place!

Celia came waddling after, her big hat bobbing on her head like a cork on water.

"Naomi won't think hard of you!" she chattered as soon as she could get her breath. "I just up and told her you was sometimes flighty like that!"

"I don't care what you told her!"

Celia was too dull to comprehend.

"I can just bet you don't, Mis' Linthorne!" she said as she perked up her flat face. "Know just how you feel 'cause I been through it all myownself. So happy that the good Lord is going to begin to love that pretty angel of yourn that you don't care about nothing else atall!"

Kate despised the woman so much that she would not say another word all the long way up Gregory Lane. Wanting to be rid of Celia made her change her mind about walking the road the whole way home. Instead she decided to enter the woods at the place the loggers had removed the fence. It would be longer that way, but cooler. There was this added advantage: she would be able to tell Thomas that she had only taken the children to walk in the woods.

"Thanks for all your trouble!" she said curtly when she took the children from Celia. "Guess it'd be some better if I didn't go all the way up lane."

Celia was a little hurt.

"Won't make no diff'rence to me, Mis' Linthorne," she said. "Bill, he ain't one to grumble if he's kept waiting a little while."

"I don't want you should go along!" Kate had to speak plainly. To soften the blow she hastened to add, "You see, if Thomas met you coming from the woods in that hat, he'd know something."

Celia was flattered.

"It is too precious pretty for anything but church, ain't it now!" she said. "Like Bill said when he caught me a puttin' it on, 'Land sakes, Cely,' he said, 'that ain't no git-up for Friday!' But I wouldn't let him talk me down 'cause I knowed you wanted me to look real fitten and fancy!"

"Well, you'll have something for your trouble one of these days," Kate promised, and pushed the children down the corduroy way across the ditch so that she would not have to stand all day.

139

Three more words from Celia, she felt, would be enough to drive her into maniacal frenzy.

3 Thomas had no dishonorable intentions toward Lucile. He had no intentions at all. If he had been inclined to rationalize, he would have known that a man who follows a maid does not hope eventually to be invited into the kitchen for a cup of coffee. Thomas rarely looked in on himself. He was capable of feeling sorrow, anger, lust, fear; he could weep at a funeral or laugh at ironic mischance; he could not calculate moral probability.

When he had first seen Jim's wife, his pulse had tripped a little more lively, but he took no pains to exchange words with her. Jim was fortunate in his choice, or wiser than Thomas would have thought. Thomas was glad the girl was so pretty. Such a delicious animal must have some flaw that kept other and richer men from wanting to possess her. He had once heard it said of women that, like horses, they were to be judged not so much by their eyes as by their teeth. That was why he tried repeatedly to make Lucile smile. When she did not, he was fairly certain that his surmise was correct.

He had no thought why he walked up the hill with the two when they left the house that first afternoon. Perhaps it was only that he was restless on Sundays. He didn't like to be with Kate too much. He was uneasy in her presence, afraid that she might discover some lack in him or busy her mind with suggestions he did not mean to accept. He had noticed that in women—their restlessness. They were never willing to let good-enough alone. If the house was an old-timer and so part log, they believed it should be boarded; if board, converted to brick; if brick, replastered to keep out the damp. Old and familiar chairs and tables that a man found serviceable no longer satisfied their artistic pretensions. Clocks should be oiled, even if they kept perfect time; the coat board moved from one side of the door to the other; the rug turned around so that it would wear evenly.

Thomas thought that Lucile was somehow different. It was nothing she said—she never bothered one with an opinion. It was not that she tried to flatter him, for she hardly noticed him at all. He was perplexed, but intoxicated. The first night when he came back home, he kept looking at Kate when her back was turned, trying to discover the something in her that irritated him. He didn't learn a letter to add to what he already knew.

But he could not keep away from Lucile. In the fields he would glance over at the Brewster place whenever he turned the team, his mind busily contriving reasons why he should walk across the line. He was scrupulous in the discrimination of good and bad. Fraudulent and flimsy excuses he cast aside—he didn't want to be taken for a fool. That was why he sometimes allowed half a week to pass between his calls, why he always had something of more than passing moment to talk about with Jim. He needed help in tending to a horse, had forgotten to mention that he had some poison good for the curculio, was hauling to the mill and would bring back whatever flour was needed.

He never went to the house. But with a single exception he was always successful in seeing Lucile. That was enough, just to see her, to watch her stately figure as she went down to the well, or trace the sweep of her bare arm as she threw corn to the hens. There was joy in being near her, even if she was unconscious of his presence. He gave no sign that he was disturbed, never dropped a syllable or permitted the least modulation of his voice. For all Jim knew, he was oblivious of his wife.

Then, after some weeks of such furtive visits, Thomas began to suspect that the attraction might not all be on his side. The coincidence of his calls and Lucile's stepping out of doors was almost too remarkable. Thomas was greatly pleased. He knew that he was considered handsome—too many people had commented on his figure for him not to know. There was no reason why she too should not think him one of the best-looking men she had ever seen, why she should not want to be near him.

To test his theory he began to alternate coming in by the front gate and stealing down the back lane. Never once that he passed the house did she fail to come out into the dooryard. And never once did she come out when she could not know that he was near.

Thomas took heart. The next time he came, he waited until Jim had gone back to the fields and then knocked boldly on the kitchen door.

It was a palpable lie—his wanting to see how the stove was

connected because Kate had been complaining about her flue. Kate had, indeed, said that there was too much smoke, but it had been only idle comment. Thomas made a ceremony of inspection, knowing all the time that Lucile wondered how he could take her for such a simpleton. At last he left off all pretense.

"Like it up here by now?" he asked in an attempt to be pleasant.

"I've always liked it," she said simply.

When their eyes met, she lowered hers guiltily, but she could not hide the color in her cheeks.

"It's real nice!" he said. "I been out this way a good many years now. I ain't never had no cause to complain."

At his casualness she seemed to take more courage.

"Course, it'll be a lot better when we have more things we need."

"Ain't nothing you're in want of I got, is there? I mean anything I ain't told you already you could have the use of."

She shook her head timidly, but her eyes were no longer afraid.

"I wasn't hinting," she said. "You been awful good. But it'll be a lot nicer when we got everything our own."

Thomas had to pretend to be going, but he had time for one pretty speech:

"Well, don't you be afraid to call in for things. Course, I wouldn't say that to most people, but you look like you got gumption right on top your good looks."

It could not stop there. Again and again he made excuses, glad finally to know that he needed little to recommend his presence. She talked beautifully, once the first chill was thawed out of her. He let her tell him of her schooling, of the years in Lancaster, the time two men had fought for her over in Millersport; of her father's death from an infection that followed a beesting; of her brothers, sisters, her Aunt Carrie, who must nibble at maple-sugar even in church. Nothing that she said was to him superfluous or silly. He loved the slight hesitancy of her talk, the deliberate way she strung her syllables together like bright beads on a chain.

"Tell you what," he proposed one day when she told him that she had never seen a hornet's nest, "one of these days I'll take you down over the hill where I know there's a big one hanging in a hack-

142

berry. Saw it last winter. Awful high, too. That's a sure sign there'll be deep snow, hornets up high like that."

"I've heard my father say that," she said.

It was no idle proposal in Thomas's mind. He waited and waited for a likely day, tried to anticipate a time when both Jim and Kate would be without suspicion. He had no thought of evil; all that he wanted to avoid was the latent evil in people's minds that resulted in loose talk. The difficulty was that Jim was seldom away from home. He drove into town some Saturdays, but Thomas generally went with him. If he did not, Kate kept good watch. Her eyes seemed to be sharper on Saturday afternoon than at any other time.

Then, without being planned for, opportunity came. When he left home driving the dappled horse that day, Thomas really meant to get into town as fast as he could push along. Not until he was going up the hill did the thought strike him to stop in for a moment to see Lucile. Kate would be unable to notice, would think him miles away—and Jim had already driven in.

He found her baking, her hands and arms floury to the elbows. She was in a hurry with her work, but that only made her more exciting. He had never seen her so active before, so full of zest for him.

"Mustn't work too hard!" he said, just for the sake of saying something.

"Do I look like I am?"

"You look all right."

"Like this?" She held up her hands and then broke into one of her rare laughs.

Thomas lost track of his intention.

"Tell you what I was thinking," he said slowly. "Was thinking there wouldn't come a nicer afternoon than this to go down see that hornet's nest I was telling you about."

"Hornet's nest?"

"Don't you remember?"

She seemed to disdain him. "I got lots of work to do," she said, and put the loaves in the baking pans.

Thomas was hurt. After all, he thought, he was going out of his way to be nice to her. If she didn't appreciate courtesy, then let her

143

get along without it. He had started for the door when she suddenly stopped him with her question, "How long would it take?"

Instantly he was alert.

"Oh, maybe an hour. Maybe just a little while longer."

Without another word she wiped off her hands, hung her apron over the back of a chair, and caressed her hair into place.

"Won't dare be any longer than that!" she warned him, and preceded him into the yard.

Thomas could not know that Kate saw them as they disappeared into the woods at the crest of Church Hill.

He was leading Lucile heaven knew where. There was no hornet's nest in any tree of his knowledge. But there were the deep patches of wood and briers, the ravines heavy with ferns, the oval glades where one would not have been surprised to start a deer. He was satisfied just to be with her. Never in his life before had he felt so masterful, so possessive. If there were time, he would like to take her clear down to Rock Ladder, to tell her—no, only Kate could know that!

"Shouldn't we be coming to it pretty soon?" Lucile asked when they were far down in the woods. She stopped, looked at him as if she knew he was lying.

"I'll get you back in time!" he urged her on.

What he intended to do, to tell her eventually, he did not know. There was always the possibility of saying they had missed the tree or that the wind had torn the nest loose. She would not be sure he had betrayed her.

"I don't believe there is any hornet's nest."

"Just you wait," he said. "You'll see."

"I wouldn't care very much if there wasn't."

He jumped at that. If she didn't care, she must share his feeling. He might as well out with the truth.

His heart was in his throat, but the mad words kept flooding his lips as he pulled her around to face him. There was no use trying to stop them. It might as well be told now as any time: he loved her, had loved her from the first! They would have to be careful! He had tried to fight down his feeling, had been unable to control himself.

When he had done, her cheeks were ashen.

"We'd better go home!" she said, and that was all.

"I can't help it—if I feel that way, can I?"

She shook her head. "I can't either—help it," she said. "But we'd better go home!"

For him the color had gone out of the day. All that dreary way back they walked in silence, hardly daring to touch each other.

4 It was a week later they returned.

After that they but lived for the times they could be together. They began to be stealthy, to appoint places to meet. For all their caution, Jim's eyes took on a strange look. One night he came home drunk, in his anger knocked Lucile down. He was humble the next day, of course, but he was no longer so open when Thomas talked with him. His answers to simple questions were entirely too subtle.

As for Kate, Thomas knew that she was suspicious. He got no decent words out of her anymore, nor did he give many. It maddened him to think that he had married a waspish woman.

Thomas stubborned himself against conscience deliberately. It was life, he told himself, life that could not, would not be denied. He had not invented the institution of marriage, did not especially believe in it. It was unnatural to expect two people to love each other alone forever and forever, to swear to God they would love no one else. Where was it written that the church or the law had the right to tie so hard that the knot could not be loosened! Even in the Bible it was written that Solomon had a thousand wives. And King David had even murdered a man so that he could get his woman away.

He was crafty, nevertheless. Either Lucile and he would have to be more circumspect, or they would have to run away. Thomas did not want to run. He would hate to give up the children. What would satisfy him better than anything else would be to have both the children and Lucile. The prospect of getting other boys and girls by her wasn't at all enticing.

On that Friday afternoon he meant to tell her of their need to be discreet. After dinner he went back to the upper forty, dawdled under a Kentucky coffee tree on the rise so that he could see Lucile when she left home. When at last he caught the glimpse of her blue dress, he took to the run and followed down the dry bed, going under the bridge, and so on down along Gregory Lane. Just above the first ravine, he struck off into the woods, making for the spot he had told her to meet him.

He was there before she came, as he meant to be, although her way was shorter. He trembled a little, could hardly wait until she was at his side. She was so beautifully trusting, so proud of his strength and knowledge. It would be impossible to tell her that they must give each other up, not to have her always.

He heard her coming then and made a place for her on the cool moss at the foot of the big bur oak. It was a spot they favored because the branches of the surrounding box elders swept so low that they were almost hidden.

"He knows, Thomas!" she said the moment she was in his arms.

He nodded, dumb with guilt. Now that she had come, he had not the moral courage to tell her that it must all be over. She was so eager for him, so ready to give herself whenever he wanted her. Kate had never been like that. It were better to drift than to go cross-current in hope of finding some dim shore, better to let happen what would happen. After a time, perhaps, both Jim and Kate would accept the inevitable.

All that afternoon as he lay tranced with her loveliness, Thomas pushed the ugly problem from him. When at last the sun lingered down the west, he knew they would have to be going back, even if the hours had seemed but minutes.

"Tomorrow too?" he whispered as he rose and held out his hand.

Her face was still full of unspoken ecstasy—she could only nod. He understood. If Jim went into town, nothing could keep her from the appointed rendezvous.

"I'll watch for you!" he said.

It was then that he heard a twig snap, afterward the *shush* of feet sliding through old leaves.

Thomas froze into immobility, held Lucile behind him as if to shield her from danger. He was of two minds: to lie quiet under the branches; to run in the hope of gaining the thick covert farther up the ravine. What deterred him was the knowledge that if they fled they would have to cross through the open for a good twenty paces. Sharp eyes would certainly see them. And if they were recognized, neither of them would ever be able to live the story down.

But if they stayed, what then? It might even be Jim, Jim come with a gun! If he was drunk—

"Come on, Lucile!" Thomas urged, suddenly panic-stricken. He made a careful tunnel through the branches so that they could not whip into her face. He knew now that there was more than one person coming up the ravine, was angry to think he should be caught in his own woodland. They were nearer than he had at first supposed, were walking softly, their feet only whispering the ground. When he heard the steps strike stone, Thomas realized that the time to escape was past. That meant that the strangers were already on the rock ledge no farther than fifty feet away.

"Get back! Get back!" he ordered huskily, and on the instant pushed his rigid body against Lucile to enforce his words.

His action was unfortunate. Lucile was off balance, her foot poised to clear an old limb, so that the slight shove sent her body crashing backward. In his endeavor to save her, Thomas too fell. The thin branches of the box elders crushed to earth—there was nothing to hide them.

Thomas made no attempt to rise, not even when his hostile eyes saw that it was the worst of all possible persons: Kate. She stood silent in the little bowl of sunshine, Faith in her arms, the other three children huddled behind her as if they expected a lion to rush from the thicket. Kate's face was hard, her full lips contracted to a thin line. Thomas wanted her to scream, to curse, to break into a torrent of abuse, to do anything but stand there in scornful silence.

When he could no longer endure her condemnation, he pushed over on his hands and got to his feet, his mouth sucking at a bloody scratch on his thumb. He felt dizzy and very weak, as if he had no skeleton at all. The dazzle of light around her made his eyes dance.

"Don't know what you think you're doing down here!" he said at last. The words broke from his lips and fell like dry twigs in front of her.

Her expression never changed a whit.

"You wouldn't!" she said. "Not you! I just wanted the babies to catch their father with his whore!"

Thomas never knew how or when she finally went on. All that he remembered was that he stumbled down the ravine over the way she had come, forgetful of everything but his own misery.

5 Kate was still up when he came in at eight o'clock that night. His face was green in the lamplight, haggard as the face of an old man. He would not look at her. For a long time he stood silent, a pace inside the door, as if he could not force himself farther. His throat had to be twice cleared before he could speak.

"I ain't asking you to forgive me!" he muttered. "And I ain't asking you to keep on living with me. But I just wanted you to know—to know that I been up and told Jim. And I give him his place back, lock, stock, and barrel. Don't know whether it'll make any difference between you and me, but I won't ever set foot on it again!"

When Kate glanced up, he could not meet her eyes. She was glad that he fuddled back out into the darkness, that he saw fit to sleep down in the barn.

She did not want to punish him. But she doubted if she could ever love him again. Certainly he would have to prove himself by more than a few words of empty promise.

BOOK TWO

I

1 Thomas was not reluctant to quit at noon—he was eager for the Last Day celebration. All morning long he had marked the blue and pink bonnets bobbing up the pike to the Mill school. From their dogged tread he knew that the mothers were burdened with heavy willow baskets, assurance of swollen stupor that would put a man in proper mood for the program. Thomas smiled when he thought of the treat he would add—bananas. He had smuggled six whole dozen home from town, had managed to hide them in sawdust in the cellar. Even Kate did not know. Her eyes would pop as hard as Celia Sapooney's.

There was good reason for his pride, he remembered, as he turned Dolly and Pete toward the barn. This was Charlotte's last term; she would be teacher next year. She could spell down Jake Frick any day, had, in fact, at the doings at the Fairview school last February. She wrote a nice hand, too, and had won half a dozen ciphering matches.

Hocking was someone else again. Great lubberly fellow, at twenty as big and strong as an ox, and as simple. He had never been able to get beyond third reader. Thomas thought he would never forget the first time he had sent the boy to town alone. Hocking hadn't said anything much when he got home, just pretended he had been husked all his life. Then at supper that night he let the cat out of the bag. "You know, Pop, some of them fellers in town thought they knowed me." "That so, Hock!" Thomas had remarked. "What makes you think so?" "Well, you know that fountain by City Hall. I was just standing there looking at it when some

151

fellers come along and yelled, 'Hi, Rube!' Must've took me for somebody else."

Thomas had kept charitable silence. Such humiliation could never have been Grover's. Smart as a blacksnake, that boy! Never a Last Day that he didn't get more headmarks than anyone else. And certificates, too. Seven of them in the house in the Bible, four of them signed by Frick and three by old Ebenezer Sprott. "The bearer has by diligence and attention excelled those of his class in Reading and merits my esteem" was the way they read. All green and gold like twenty dollar bills they were.

Thomas did not think of Faith. From year's end to year's end she was tallow white. Faith was her mother's charge, not his. Let Kate dose and bolus her, rub her with goose grease, give her worm seed, and sit up with her when she got spells at night. He himself had avoided her until her reality was that of the statue of the Virgin he saw above the door of the Catholic church whenever he drove to town.

Thomas's pleasure began the moment he entered the school-yard. For waiting there under the big cedar beside the patch of lemon lilies was the tall, bowed figure of the former master, Ebenezer Sprott. The old Quaker was a very benediction of a man. His cornflower-blue eyes lighted when he saw Thomas swing the gate, and his greeting was so eager that he hopped right through the lilies.

"Thee oughtest be ashamed of thyself to come so late, Thomas!" he reproached with mock severity.

Thomas shook his hand gravely.

"Thought sure I was seeing a ghost," he said. "You ain't teaching somewheres near by, are you? Thought you aimed to quit and settle down."

Sprott nodded so rapidly he looked like a woodpecker.

"Did so, did so, did so!" he explained. "Got a sweet little piece over near Bremen, all good bottom with running water. No better land this side of heaven, Thomas. Only I need thee to tell me how to get shut of the filthy pest that chokes it to death."

Thomas stood on one foot and wished he might for a moment be free to carry in his bananas. Once the cry was up, his triumph would be empty.

"Daisies!" Sprott almost shouted at him. "White daisies! Mow, grub, plough, burn, do whatever I will, they skulk right back on me."

Thomas took the old man by the arm and led him toward the door. While they ate they could talk at will, about more than daisies. Thomas knew no cure for them but patience and a strong back.

Despite the confusion and hilarity there was always something pathetic about the Last Day. As usual the children had been to Church Woods for flowers. On the platform there were coal scuttles of wilted wild Indian tulips, mournful anemones and hepaticas in all the inkwells. The great iron stove amid the huddle of desks was cold, the windows wide, and on the shelf at the back where there should have been a row of round, shiny tin lunch buckets there was nothing at all. Desks had been cleaned out, books strapped. Within three hours the spiders would be in sole possession.

Thomas expanded in the warmth of approving eyes as he brought his contribution to the table at the front of the room. Hands reached for him from all sides, and it was "Thomas" here, "Thomas" there, with "Mr. Linthorne" from the children. He knew his importance as a member of the Board, and as possibly the most successful farmer in the township. In return he was sage enough to know how much he depended upon the lives that were knit with his. Cory, Marty, Promise, Chenoweth, sad Joe Jordan, pear-bellied Wendell—they all loved and trusted him. Over in the corner of the room, sound as a nut at seventy, fine old Lute Tanterscham. His was an October face, wizened and winter-wistful, with apple cheeks and hoarfrost mustache. With his girls, grown women now, was a stranger, her frowsy blonde hair tied with a pink ribbon . . . Zeke Sellers, unchanged with the years. And behind Sellers, Harrison Schrader, who had named two of his boys Custer and Gorman. Thomas winced a little whenever he remembered. Adolph and Lotus Sapooney with Celia—still poor as Job's turkey, and with more gabble. The McGrubers, standing beside their Nellie and Logan.

And Judith Brewster! Neither Jim nor Lucile, only Judith. Thomas glanced around guiltily, covertly to be sure. Virginal, but like dark water, rather like slow fire was Judith. Thomas could never satisfy himself not to look at her, but he never dared look at her enough to satisfy himself either. He couldn't be sure. But Judith had been born early in '77, and that was right. Lucile had had no other child. Although she was but eleven now, each year made her seem more and more like another Charlotte.

Surely the Brewsters had suspicions! Perhaps Kate! And surely in time would notice the strange resemblance—the dark brows and eyes, the clean line of the jaw. God help Thomas Linthorne if ever Celia Sapooney got her imagination going like a windmill!

The impression of that Last Day was forever after etched on Thomas's mind. Slant April sunlight in shafts through the open windows, in pools on ribboned hair and pink gingham frocks; heavy men with brick-red faces, some of them in store-bought serge, some in no better than blue chambray shirts; smells stagnant in the room: of bread and butter, sweated bodies, cheap perfume, and the exotic smell of bananas; strained expectation on the faces of mothers as their darlings walked up to lisp a recitation, to be succeeded by smug approval, disappointment, indignation; the wheezy organ, raucous voices, clapping hands, shuffling feet. Patient endurance of the endless program, and young jubilation when it was finally ended. Then hand-clasps, promises to trade days, to write down recipes, send roots and slips of flowers.

Sharp in each detail as a new-minted dollar—and yet somehow hopelessly blurred. Blurred—in a face, an idea, a fear! Judith, Judith Brewster. Judith Linthorne!

Thomas was so abstracted that he walked home without a good-bye to anyone. After him ancient Ebenezer Sprott trotted to the gate, peered unbelievingly, his gnarled hands twisting tangles in his shiny black coattails.

2 When Kate burned newspapers to rid the house of smells after supper that night, Thomas was surprised.

"Company coming?" he asked.

"Nobody to bother you, Thomas. Just Ralph and Tom Tanterscham said in school this afternoon they might walk that girl cousin of theirs down to sit a spell. She's up here visiting from Sugar Grove 'cause her pa died."

Thomas bit his lip. He had seen the girl at school, had disapproved of her lackadaisically. Flossy, bleached yellow caterpillar, she giggled like a leaky churn! At that, she couldn't be worse than the Tanterscham boys. There was something wrong with those youngsters—only they weren't youngsters any more. Ralph was twenty-one, just one year Hocking's senior, Tom nineteen. They were big fellows, but sneaky.

Of course, Thomas thought, that didn't cut any ice off his pond—not unless Ralph really thought he was going to walk with Charlotte. First intimation Thomas had had of that was the winter day Lute Tanterscham stopped him on the road when he was hauling coal home from Hooker's. Lute asked him for his bushel of potatoes because Ralph had carried Charlotte home from literary society at Cunningham school. The old German was dogged too. Thomas had just laughed at him and his fool custom, but the encounter had set him to hard thinking.

Charlotte's haste to redd the table and the way Hocking bolted for the barn with a gorge of food still in his mouth brought Thomas sharply to his senses.

"You go get your catechism right away!" he ordered Grover. "If that's what's in the wind, we'll have to get a move on."

Grover would be confirmed in Lancaster this coming Easter. Thomas remembered with chagrin the impression Hocking and Faith had made when they were examined in front of the congregation. Preacher had to help them so much it sounded like he was guiding a pair of cripples down icy steps. Charlotte had been better, but the honor of the Linthorne name would never be clean until Grover rattled through the responses. And the beauty of it all was that Thomas had not coached him one-tenth as much as he had coached the older boy.

"We'll take the Commandments!" he announced when Grover put the catechism in his hand. "Set that lamp over here so's I can see better!"

Grover relaxed in the rocker on the other side of the room—it

155

was a game he enjoyed. He would wait stealthily while with heavy rumble his father fairly spelled out the questions, then leap like a bass at the lure. Ten minutes of such play, and he was sure of compliment.

"What is the first commandment?"

"I am the Lord thy God. Thou shalt have no other Gods before Me."

"What does this mean?"

"We should fear, love, and trust in God above all things."

"What is the second commandment?"

"Thou shalt not take the name of the Lord thy God in vain."

"What does this mean?"

"We should fear and love God that we may not curse, swear, use witchcraft, lie or deceive by His name, but call upon Him in every trouble, pray, praise, and give thanks."

Thomas nodded, but he could not follow. Such proficiency in piety was too much for his eyes and brain.

"What is the third commandment?" he faltered while he tried to race ahead to cover the answer.

"Remember the Sabbath day to keep it holy."

"What does this mean?"

"We should fear and love God that we may not despise preaching and His word, but hold it sacred, and gladly hear and learn it."

Thomas skipped to see if he could catch his pupil.

"Sixth commandment!" he ordered.

"Thou shalt not commit adultery."

Thomas started involuntarily. He had no choice but to ask the meaning. He hoped Kate was not listening.

"What does this mean?"

"We should fear and love God that we may lead a chaste and decent life in thought, word, and deed, and each love and honor his spouse."

There was commotion in the kitchen as Hocking brought in the foamy milk.

"Think they're coming," he drawled to his mother. "Saw somebody carrying a lantern down the road when I come in just now."

"Eighth commandment."

"Thou shalt not bear false witness against thy neighbor."

"What does this mean?"

"We should fear and love God that we may not deceitfully belie, betray, slander, or defame our neighbor, but excuse him, speak well of him, and put the best construction on everything."

The words fairly leaped at Thomas as he pulled the curtain aside and peered for the lantern. Sure enough, it was dancing down through the trees. Even as he looked, it made several wild gyrations in the air to indicate that the Tanterscham boys had seen someone at the window.

Thomas shut the book. "Guess that'll be all for tonight!" he muttered as he handed the catechism to Grover.

He didn't want to be caught. None of the Tanterscham children had been confirmed. It was too much trouble to drive into town, Lute had once said.

Thomas thought on the contrary that his insistence was clear evidence of Linthorne superiority.

Thomas watched the girl intently, although he pretended to be greatly interested in the *Dispatch*. He didn't have to be seventh son of a seventh son born with a caul over his head to see that Hocking was watching her too. Propped back at the kitchen table, Thomas could look right into the middle room, where for Elva's benefit Charlotte was fingering over the arrowheads and trilobites on the sideboard. Faith had disappeared upstairs as usual, but Grover was the biggest duck in the puddle. It seemed that Ralph had taken almost as much shine to him as to Charlotte.

"You going to stay until Easter?" Charlotte asked.

Elva giggled, her yellow bun dancing in the lamplight. "Land sakes, how do I know!" she answered. "Guess that's all up to Aunt Lottie. Says to me today, she did, 'You just tote up your plunder and hole down with us. No earthly use hard-scrabblin' down there in them hills. You ain't got no kith nor kin down there gives a bone button what becomes of you.'"

"Ain't nobody to walk with down there either," Ralph commented sarcastically.

Elva slapped him with mock indignation.

"That's all you know about it, you big smarty!"

"Is that so? Guess I saw that old widower that used to come around to ask you to ride to church. Didn't only have one eye."

"Ralph Tanterscham, that's a lie and you know it!"

Thomas cleared his throat to remind them that he was watching. He didn't want any scuffling in front of his children.

Ralph must have been reminded of civility, for he stopped his bawling and whispered something to Charlotte. Thomas saw her cast a hesitant glance toward the kitchen. A minute later she appeared in the doorway.

"You don't care if I unlock the front room and take in a lamp so that we can play the organ, do you, Papa?"

"I don't if your ma don't," Thomas consented. "What about it, Kate. Figure Faith's in bed yet?"

Kate was wary.

"I don't care if you go in there with them, Charlotte," she whispered, "but you take real good care of my lace doilies. And don't take the lamp with the flowers on it; take the other one."

Charlotte nodded dutifully and led in her guests.

Not until the organ was going loud enough to drown his voice did Thomas dare comment.

"Don't reckon she'll pull much double, if I know what I'm talking about," he said laconically. "You think she will, Kate?"

"She ain't all dry behind the ears yet, that's what I think," said Kate. "None of them Tanterschams is."

"Reckon I ought to say something to Hocking?"

Kate was firmly opposed.

"What's the sense of putting fleas in his hair?" she asked. "Best leave good enough alone. Chances are she won't think he's anything more'n a green persimmon anyhow if she just hangs around a little bit."

3   That next Sunday, Thomas was not so sure of Elva's eventual dismissal of Hocking. It had rained so sharply that the Linthornes could not go in to the Lancaster Lutheran church. When, about a half-hour before time for services, the sun came out, Thomas hustled the family over to Union Meeting House.

While the women went indoors, the men loitered in the church-yard for a last chew and chance to talk. That Sunday there was a new diversion. The bell bought secondhand after fire gutted the U.B. church on the county line had been hauled over by Balt Wendell, who had somehow managed to get it up the hill and to jack it up on four-by-fours. Balt stood over his treasure with all the pride of a father.

"Yessir, she's just a jim-dandy!" he was saying when Thomas came up with Hocking and Grover. "Reg'lar jim-dandy! Don't you say she is, Thomas?"

Thomas had to be critical before he could pronounce judgment.

"Sure it ain't cracked, Balt?"

Balt made a rapid denial. "Tighter'n a drum!" he said. "Didn't fall, just eased down gradual. Cracky, but me'n them fellers had a time digging her out, gol-dang if we didn't!"

They were an admiring group. Cory was there, and long-necked Amadias Pride, together with Sellers, Marty, Shreet, Peters, Schrader, and the miscellaneous boys belonging to all of them.

"Trouble was getting her up on the wagon," said Balt. "Just about all me'n them two skinny runts helping me could do."

"B-bet she don't weigh no more'n two hundred p-pounds, Balt!" Bill Sapooney challenged. "Ain't nothing' but b-b-brass!"

Balt was outraged.

"Two hundred pounds your grandmother's billygoat!" he retorted indignantly. "You just get up on them blocks and try budging her off!"

That started them. The story had often been told that Balt's father could throw barrels of salt weighing upward of three hundred pounds into a farm wagon simply by catching hold of the chines. Like stories were told of Balt, but today for some reason he refused to put his strength to the test. Rather, it seemed he wanted them all to fail in budging the bell.

Bill Sapooney made the biggest fool of himself.

"C-come up—c-c-couple inches—d-didn't it?" he panted, after he had succeeded only in heaving blood into his head.

"Nary a smidgen!"

"Did so. I got d-dirt under my finger nails."

"Hell, Bill," said Joe Jordan dolefully, "you didn't have dirt under your finger nails you'd be dead!"

Bill retired while McGruber and Schrader tried their luck. By bracing himself against one of the four-by-fours Matt Schrader finally managed to tilt the rim about an inch.

That egged them on. Shreet strained until the veins stood out in his head. A young chap named Henderson failed. Then for a moment none would make the venture.

"Why don't you up and try, Hocking?" Thomas heard a woman's throaty voice inquire. He knew without looking that it could be no one but Elva Uny. A decent woman would have gone straight into church, but she had had to follow Ralph through the wet grass to stand with the men.

Hocking flushed at her prompting, gangled awkwardly to the other side of the group. "You make Ralph try first," he said. Elva promptly pushed Ralph into the ring, but for all his sweating the bell was secure.

"Come on, Hocking!" she coaxed again. "You can do it if anybody can. You know what you told me about the way you lifted that stone your pa couldn't budge."

Thomas could have slapped her, even if she were not weaving a net for his son. He was vain of his strength, but not too vain. At forty-four a man might be excused if he gave over some of the heaviest work to his twenty-year-old son. Not that he could not have moved the hitching block if he had been so minded. Now, however, because of Elva's unfortunate remark, he would have to duplicate whatever Hocking succeeded in doing.

Hocking spraddled wide, braced his legs, for a second tautened. Then, slowly, he seemed to expand, to grow bigger, taller. The great cords on his neck stood out like braids. But the bell for an instant swung six inches from the supports, and with a dismal clank the clapper touched the rim.

It was past time for services—the women inside had come to the window to see what was delaying their menfolks, but church would have to wait now. Thomas had stripped off his coat and was rolling his sleeves before Hocking was well back in the admiring ring. All the men and most of the boys knew what was in his mind—that he must do as well as Hocking, or else give over his domination. On some of their faces he saw commiseration and anxiety written large. Their concern made him almost angry. They might as well have spoken aloud: they had for a long time looked up to Tom Linthorne, but there was now a new champion.

Thomas was meticulous in his preparations. He dug in his toes, stomped out a mullein that might make him slip, carefully surveyed the smooth metal ring to see how best he might get a purchase on it. He was breathing slowly, but as deep as he could.

"You b-better not try it, T-Thomas!" Bill Sapooney warned. "Take old fellows like me'n you an' we might bust our guts out!"

Thomas froze him with a look. He didn't like to have even his age compared with anything Sapooney.

His legs bowed, straightened slowly. He felt arrows of pain shoot along his arms and curve over his shoulders to lodge in the back of his neck. It seemed he must tear his arms out with the strain as the metal ate into the horn of his hands. Even greater was the mental agony of thinking that for all his effort he might fail.

"Wouldn't do it if I was you, Thomas!" he heard Joe Jordan admonish him.

Thomas reared back. The sweat stood in beads on his forehead, his eyes popped from their sockets, but from the cries of admiration and the sullen sound of the clapper he knew that he had done as well as Hocking.

He was half-dizzy as he staggered back to Grover's side, so blur-eyed that for a few moments he was oblivious of the whole group. When he did see and hear, he was amazed. A swart young scoundrel whose hair lay over his ears in black ringlets was nonchalantly straddled with feet on the four-by-fours, and in his hands as if sucked up by magic was the bronze bell. Once, twice, and a third time he swung it, and each time the clapper touched metal. Such an exhibition Thomas had never seen in his life. The man must be made of steel.

After that performance the clamor was all for Balt. He could hardly refuse now. A stranger had come in to carry away the community honor; he was the only hope of saving it.

"Come on, Balt!" they urged. "Ain't a-going' to hurt you none. Come on, ring it four times!"

Balt grinned, looked around foolishly. It was plain that he wanted to try, plain too that for some reason he held back.

"Come on, Balt!"

Balt capitulated. Hunched there in their midst, his little blue eyes crafty and his droopy mustaches curled about his mouth, he looked like a fat cherub that had just fallen from a brewery dray. He took off his coat and handed it to Marty, rolled his sleeves, fumbled open his celluloid collar, even slipped down one suspender strap.

"Ain't nothing' much to a job o' this kind!" he baited them while he made final preparations. "All a fellow's got to remember is to take it slow, get a good—"

How he intended to go on they never knew. There came suddenly over his face a look of blankest vacancy as he stared across the heads of those nearest the church. The next moment Flora Wendell was screaming from the open window:

"Balt Wendell, you old sheep! You come right on in here! What you up and fixing' to do, ruin yourself? You know your heart's bad! You come right on in here and bring them other loafers with you!"

Thomas got little out of the service that morning. He resented Hocking's continual gawking in the direction of Elva Uny, who was sitting with Ruth and Eliza, the older Tanterscham girls. He'd speak with him at the first chance! Might as well know soon as late that such a person could never become a Linthorne. No sense in Hocking's aiming so low he'd have to hoe with his nose the rest of his life!

Sadly enough, he couldn't aim very high. Who was there for him to marry? Lotus Sapooney was sixteen, but who'd want Sapooney? Kate had said something about the Marty girls, Etta and Luna. Nice enough, Thomas supposed, but they didn't strike his fancy. Turn out to be the picture-without-the-frame kind of women Spence Vitt was always laughing at. Darlene Schrader would have more life, but she wasn't exactly right in the head.

Finding someone suitable was Charlotte's trouble, too. High-stepper like Charlotte wouldn't want a bump on a log any more than Thomas would want one for her. She was pretty enough to draw flies, but the way she had about her didn't let them buzz very long. Ralph Tanterscham was the only one who had kept hanging on. And Thomas certainly didn't want Ralph for a son-in-law.

It was partly his reflection on Charlotte that kept his eyes turning in the direction of the curly-head who had swung the bell. The young fellow was sitting alone. Ory Shreet was in the same pew, but so far away that they couldn't even sing from the same book. Thomas was puzzled to account for the stranger.

When the benediction was spoken, he didn't wait until they were in the churchyard.

"Linthorne's my name," he said as he backed his man up against a pew. "Don't reckon you'd have much objection to letting me know yours."

"Sarple's mine. Jed Sarple."

"Knowed a family by that name once," Thomas said to make talk. "Lived down on Rush Creek when I was a boy. Your grand-pappy wouldn't have been old Jonadab Sarple, would he?"

"That's who he was all right."

Thomas held out his hand again.

"Wouldn't be hiring on for the season?"

"How much you paying?"

That made Thomas reflect. He had never hired, except by the day.

"Reckon fifteen a month and found would be about right, wouldn't it?" he bargained.

"How much if I find myself?"

Thomas was really nonplussed. "Well, son, to tell you the truth, you can't hardly find yourself. You hire on with me, you'll live right with the family. Tell you what I'll do, though: I'll make that twenty instead of only fifteen."

Sarple shook his head. "Been getting that," he said. "What I want's a dollar a day."

"Ain't never paid that much except during threshing and never seen it paid!" Thomas said with some pique. "Course, I ain't a mule-driver, either. All I want's a good day's work."

He walked off with little ceremony. He felt clumsy, not so much because he had not driven a bargain as because he could not express his real purpose. He needed no work done; he could manage

163

very well with Hocking and Grover to help him. What he really wanted was to test the man as a possible husband for Charlotte.

He was taken aback when Jed came that same afternoon. Thomas went out into the yard to talk to him, hired him on at twenty-five a month without a word to Kate. Jed promised to move up the following Sunday.

Thomas was happy when he came back to the house, but his elation was short-lived. Kate and Charlotte had been watching from the windows.

"That's that same fellow was in church this morning, ain't it?" Kate asked.

"Reckon it was."

"What's he want with you?"

"Ain't him wanting with me. I just hired him on to help out this summer, that's all."

"Hired him!" Kate gasped. "What in heaven's name you want with a hand? You beginning to feel puny?"

Thomas grinned. "Time he can't help me, maybe he can help you," he bantered. "Says he likes to do preserving and pickling."

He couldn't jolly Kate.

"Where's he going to sleep?" she demanded acidly.

"Where's anybody sleep? You can make up some kind of bed for him, can't you?"

"I can not! And what's more, Thomas Linthorne, I don't mean to! I ain't going to have any old tramps around!"

"Now see here, Kate, you don't have to act like that!" Thomas came right back at her. "That boy's just as good as you are!"

It was like a play, their making fools of themselves by shouting loud enough to tell the Sapooneys their business.

Kate had the last word, but Thomas allowed her to gabble. He was not so much interested in her reaction as in Charlotte's, and from Charlotte's face it was quite plain that her sympathies were all with her mother.

II

1   As Thomas anticipated, there was no great trouble about Jed Sarple's coming. It was always that way. Worries that gloomed like thundercloud warnings of storm vanished into thin air. "Linthorne luck!" people called it. Joe Jordan had the best comment: "Fellow like Tom Linthorne could put all his eggs in one basket, throw the basket downhill, and time he climbed down after it he'd find all the eggs hatched out into laying hens."

Thomas knew their envy and the hard lot some of them had. It did seem everything went right with him. He never had an animal down with cholera or blackleg, never had much smut in his corn, never lost his fruit. In dry seasons he always had enough water; in wet his land drained well. Linthorne luck! Linthorne luck!

Of course, there was Faith. Never up and kicking a good day in her life, you might say. Plenty people would be worried sick by her. Thomas wasn't, not much. Let the girl continue to straggle over and sing hymns with Celia Sapooney if she wanted to—it might do them both good.

To vex him there was this new girl running after Hocking. Thomas vowed he'd break that up. He didn't mean to tie his children down like some folks did, but neither would he let them run-hog wild. Lute Tanterscham hadn't let his oldest girls marry because he wanted to get his share of work out of them, and now he had a couple old maids. No, sir, Thomas wouldn't do anything like that! Just let Hocking bring a good sensible girl around, one who knew her place, and he could have her.

His real hope, however, was in the other boy. Thomas had never seen his like; he was never tired of watching him. Grover was always three steps ahead of everyone else. Take that little matter of the rabbits gnawing his apple trees. All the rest of the children knew he wanted to find some way to keep the vermin off, but it was Grover who ran home from school breathless to say that beet blood or the navel of a hog rubbed around the boles would stop the pest. Jake Frick had read it out of a book.

Thomas didn't want Grover to stay on the land. He wasn't heavy enough, never would have much meat on his bones. But that wasn't the main reason—Grover should be a teacher or a lawyer. In a year or two Thomas would be sending him over to Crawfis Institute to see what they could make of him over there. And if Grover did well at Crawfis, then he could go anywhere else he wanted.

2 His hopes for Grover began to mature on that long awaited Easter morning when the boy was confirmed.

It was a solemn and beautiful day for Thomas. He himself was up before dawn to walk the rounds through the dewy grass. Then at half past four he routed the girls and their mother because he knew that on this Sunday they'd have to fuss particularly with their clothes. Grover was excused from the milking; in his stead Jed drove the cows back to pasture. For breakfast they dipped into their coffee the baked twists of bread that Kate called "pretzels"—from her tradition they symbolized something that had to do with the Cross. Afterward Thomas helped Hocking curry the horses and brush them to a shiny gloss. The surrey had been washed on Friday, but the darning-needles must be picked from the fringe and the few hen-droppings scoured off.

The ride to town was sedate. The sun was splendid on the green hills, the roads clean and hard from Saturday's rain. Kate and the girls rode behind in starched white, Thomas and his boys in front, all of them in the dignity of solemn black. On Grover's knees the catechism lay open, and as they moved in slow processional through the green wheat and the spurs of woodland shot with the flight of tanagers, Thomas plied last-minute questions. There was no flaw in Grover's preparation. The Ten Commandments, the Christian Creed, the Lord's Prayer, Holy Baptism, the Lord's Supper—Grover was perfect in each and knew Scripture to prove his belief.

In the church, the windows a dim green-gold maze of stained glass saints and symbols, the altar half-hidden behind its potted palms and lilies, Thomas led his family right up behind the benches reserved for the confirmation class. He could not relax; it seemed he dared hardly breathe. The air was heavy with sachet, with the redolence of the lilies. When in the hush the organ began, his heart beat faster. It was time for the class to file in. Out of the sacristy they came, awkward, white-faced, the boys first, then the girls in their long white dresses, to take their solemn places in the pews directly beneath the pulpit.

The liturgical service and the sermon must be preliminary to the examination; it seemed they were interminable. By the time the preacher was finished, Thomas had wilted his good starched collar. It was almost a relief when the offering was lifted and the Reverend Wilme came out again, this time with his catechism in hand. Thomas hardly heard his remarks, was frozen with fear that things would not go right. Grover would get the first question because he sat nearest the aisle in the row of boys. And the first question was "What is the first commandment?" If only they were all that easy.

The minister was through now, waited patiently for a mother to take her crying baby out into the vestibule. His finger held the book open; his eyes were directed toward Grover.

"Grover Linthorne, what is religion?"

Thomas's heart dropped like a plummet. "What is religion?" The question wasn't in the book! He heard Grover falter, clear his throat, stagger through some inaudible words.

"Next," said Pastor Wilme. "What is religion, Roger?"

"Religion is going to church on Sunday," a towhead answered. "Next."

Well, what was it? Down the row of boys the question skipped, halfway across the row of shuddering girls.

"Religion is being a good Christian."

"Next."

Thomas endured nightmare. Once before, when Faith was confirmed, every one in the class had missed a question and the Reverend Wilme had gone right back to the adults sitting in the next row. Today the first adult who would be interrogated was Thomas himself.

"What is religion, Elaine?"

The little girl with coal-black braids was scared, but she was resolute.

"It's what you believe about God," she said as she struggled to her feet, and Thomas could see the way her fingers tore at her lace handkerchief.

"Why, of course," the minister seconded. "Religion is the way a man worships his god. You all know that! I've told you a dozen times!"

After that Grover scampered through the first commandment like a scared jackrabbit, explained the ninth, was the only one who satisfied the minister as to the person and office of Christ. Before Thomas completely recovered from his fright, it was all over and Pastor Wilme was announcing to his congregation that he was satisfied unless someone wished the class further examined. No one did, of course.

Thomas took careful note of the girl with the black braids. Elaine. Elaine what? He'd have to ask Grover. And if he ever got a chance, he'd do something real nice for her, maybe buy her a bonnet or a new umbrella.

"I ask you in the presence of Almighty God and the congregation here assembled: Is it your sincere desire to renew the vows of baptism, and to renounce the world, the flesh, and the devil? If so, then answer, 'Yes, it is my sincere desire.'"

From the long row of children standing before the altar came the almost inaudible response.

"Do you believe in the Trinity, Father, Son, and Holy Ghost; and are you resolved to continue in the fellowship and communion of those who are true disciples of our Lord Jesus Christ? If this be your sincere conviction, then answer, 'Yes, I believe and am so resolved.'"

"Yes, I believe and am so resolved."

"Will you be true to the teachings of our Lord according to the confession of our evangelical Lutheran church; and will you be obedient to the same until the hour of your death? If so, then answer, 'Yes, by the help of God.'"

"Yes, by the help of God."

Their confession made, they knelt while the minister laid his hand on the head of each, and repeated the passage that should never be forgotten. Thomas strained forward in his eagerness to hear the reading for Grover. There were many in his congregation who asserted that white-haired old Pastor Wilme seldom made a mistake. Those who in later life became untrue, were prodigal far from home, who resorted to drink, envied their neighbors, curled avaricious fingers around the wealth of others were often able to remember the prophetic warning of their confirmation verse.

The minister was close to Grover now—his hand in benediction on each head:

"Carl Troman: 'The fool hath said in his heart there is no God.' Mark Rhueling: 'He that by usury and unjust gain increaseth his substance, he shall gather it for him that will pity the poor.' Harry Zimmerman: 'Trust in the Lord with all thine heart, and lean not unto thine own understanding.' Grover Linthorne: 'For God shall bring every work into judgment, with every secret thing, whether it be good, or whether it be evil.' Lydia Langstadt: 'Fight the good fight of—'"

Thomas was satisfied. The verse would be written on the confirmation certificate. He would have Grover learn it that very day, would learn it himself. If Pastor Wilme thought that was all his boy should take with him, at least he had not detected any particular flaw in character.

At dinner that day Thomas put by Grover's place the gold watch and chain. It was a little more than he had done for the other children, but they had not been forgotten on their confirmation days. Hocking had had a silver watch, and each of the girls brooches set with brilliants that cost almost ten dollars apiece.

3 April and May were prodigal that year. Thomas took advantage of the weather, had Jed and the boys burn brush, harrow the fat fallows, mend the line fences. Potatoes had gone in on Good Friday; the fields would be ready for corn by the time the dogwoods bloomed.

In the house there was similar activity. Kate had good luck with her baby chicks, and with Charlotte's help set out a fine garden. Together they cleaned house, pasted new paper in the bedrooms, whitewashed the cellar, moved the stove out to the summer kitchen. Thomas was justly proud of their industry. Never a time did Kate send him in to market with fowls that were half plucked or butter that was streaked and striped. There was never such a butter-maker as Kate—all the town women insisted on her clover print.

With the exception of the Sapooneys all the neighbors were similarly busy. Spence Vitt got into his store of dried puffballs and burned them to drive his bees. He had a saying Thomas liked:

A swarm of bees in May is worth a ton of hay;
A swarm of bees in June is worth a silver spoon;
A swarm of bees in July is not worth a fly.

Spence's orchard was making him a rich man. He had planted more kinds of apples than Thomas could remember: Baldwins, Russets, Pearmains, Greenings, Ramboes, Bellflowers, Pippins, Limber Twigs, Swaars, Jonathans, and perhaps twenty others. He had cherries and peaches too, had even become a little fantastic in his cultivation of fine pears grafted on quince stocks.

Thomas loved the spring of the year for its promise of plenty, but loved it also for its bright vagaries. Sometimes when Charlotte came to the fields or when he walked the roads with her, she would tell him the names of the flowers he pointed out: cinquefoil, wild ginger, Solomon's seal, rockbells, partridge berry. Thomas gloried in the early roses, the rust-red patches of sorrel in the pastures, the twists of the nightshade on the worm fences.

Charlotte for the fields, Kate in the dooryard. This year her shrubs had bloomed riotously. In the three arbors the fairy-like beads that would plump into grapes were bountiful. The wrens had returned to the gatepost, the humming birds to the honeysuckle, the turtle doves to the willow trees. Under the lilac bushes the valley lilies were green mats.

Thomas was well content. Life had been good to him, God had been kind. His place was well secure.

4 In Lancaster one Saturday in early June he had evidence that a man's good fortune need not inevitably continue.

He had taken Grover with him as was his wont because he could expedite deliveries by letting the boy drive to the east side of town while Thomas himself trudged with two great baskets through the north end. As usual they met in the fountain square about ten o'clock.

This morning Grover had news: August Gregory had been robbed.

Thomas gulped when he heard. Gregory had once been the richest man in Bloom township, but was no more. Sciatica had robbed him of his vigor, and worry had brought his wife abed. The two had finally managed to escape the doctors, but Aug would go no more afield. Nor would he allow anyone else to till his soil. Two years since, Thomas had gone with an offer for the upper fields that lay directly across Gregory Lane from his great woods. He remembered his rebuff. But he had never ceased to hope because he knew that Marty, too, had an eye on the farm.

"How much did he lose?" he asked Grover anxiously.

"Three hundred dollars is what everybody says."

"What was he doing with three hundred dollars?"

"Don't know. That's just what everybody says."

Thomas kept his ears open. When he was waited on in the grocery, he brought the conversation around by direct inquiry.

"Hear anything about Aug Gregory's being robbed this morning?"

Fargot peered eagerly over his lenses. "Was a feller in here said something," he drawled.

"How much did he lose?"

"Well, it's all accordin' to what you want to believe. Some says one thing and some another. Story I heard was that he sold off his tools for cash. Got a mess of brand new tens and fives down at the bank. Either had his pocket picked or dropped his wallet before he got a square away. Just stood downtown in front of the barber shop and bawled. Feller finally had to drive him home."

Thomas was a poor companion for Grover when they drove north—he was thinking too hard. If Gregory was hard fixed, he might feel different about not wanting to sell. Marty would be smart enough to know that, would very likely make a good offer. Dirty shame for as fine a man as Aug Gregory to be in want. And Thomas wouldn't let him want—if it came right down to his getting along without. But on the other hand, Gregory didn't have much right to keep the land lying idle.

At home when he got a minute alone with Kate he put the matter up to her.

"You just don't understand!" he argued after she had scored him for being covetous. "Ain't that I want to get anything away from him without giving him full value. But you know—"

"I know that's only an excuse, Thomas Linthorne!" she said sharply. "You was the man I thought you were, you'd go right down there and offer to lend him what he needs."

"He won't never be able to pay back."

"What if he won't! You got enough to share up, haven't you?"

"Well, you don't have to get your back up!" he bridled. "I was only asking."

He was still irked an hour after. He wanted counsel, but neither Jed nor Hocking was about. Grover appeared after a time—he had been down cellar. Thomas hesitated, but finally asked his advice.

"Guess I'll have to lend Aug Gregory a little to tide him over," he announced as if the matter was settled.

He had Grover's reaction instantly.

"What for?"

"Well, he's Job poor, I reckon."

"Not your fault, is it?"

"No, it ain't none of my doin's."

"He wouldn't sell when you wanted him to."

"I know he wouldn't," Thomas admitted. "But—"

He went off without finishing, came back from the strawstack ten minutes later to find Grover sitting in the identical place on the stall. His eyes were bright.

"Look here, Pop," Grover said, "I been figuring a little about you lending that money to Gregory. You better do it."

It was so strange a reversal that Thomas stared. For a moment he thought Grover's opinion prompted by Christian charity.

"Why?"

"Well, it's like buying, ain't it? Way I figure is that if you don't lend, Marty will. First fellow to go down there'll likely come into the place when the old man kicks off. Heaven knows he can't last much longer."

Thomas felt a little ashamed for the boy, but he offered no rebuke. What Grover said was certainly true. Gregory would likely be stubborn about selling a few acres, but he had no children of his own to will to.

That same evening Thomas took a hundred dollars from under the mattress and walked down the pike.

5 Thomas was not patient to a fault. When it appeared that his children and the Tanterschams must be together every night, he sought an opportunity to talk with Hocking. He got it one day when they were making ready for the threshing crew.

"Be cleaning out your own wheat bin one of these days, I reckon," he began in an offhand manner.

"Reckon I will."

"All you got to do is find you a good woman."

Hocking labored in silence.

"You get the girl and I'll see to it you won't have to want for a little farm," Thomas promised.

He tried to be airy, jocular—and succeeded badly. Hocking seemed to sense something in the wind. When he spoke, it was with defiance.

"Guess if I did make a good pick, you wouldn't think so!"

"Well, I don't know. Take a woman like your mother, now—I'd say any man could see she had the right stuff in her. Charlotte, too, for that matter. She's a whole lot like your ma."

Hocking made a mighty dust with the broom and almost drove Thomas away.

"Guess Ma's all right," he admitted tactfully. "But if it was me, I'd never take Charlotte. I don't want my eyes scratched out!"

Thomas forced a smile. "Guess you're right there," he said. "Want good temper in a woman same as in a horse. What else you looking for?"

"Huh?"

"What more do you want? Fancy dresser, good looker, anything like that?"

"Guess it don't matter so much what the outside's like."

"Say as much myself," Thomas agreed. "Does sort of help to have a woman that's easy to look at—I'll admit that turned my mind in favor of your ma. But there's lots of other things just as important. Course, I was lucky and got more'n I bargained for. But if I had it to do all over again, you know what I'd look for? Just three things."

He paused provocatively to make Hocking question him. When the boy worked on sullenly Thomas had to repeat, "Just three things!"

"What?"

"Well, they're easy to remember because they all begin with 'C'. First of all, I'd take a girl that's clean. Kind that keeps herself and her house and kids in apple pie order all the time. Second, I'd want her clever. Ever notice your ma? Doing something all the time, and everything done right. Time we come to this house it wasn't nothing but four bare walls—and look at it now. Everything in it you can lay to your mother. It was her put the paper on the walls, stitched up rags for carpets, got the furniture together, hooked up all them pretties for the chairs—and did it while you might say she had a full-time job cooking, baking, scrubbing, darning, washing dishes, and taking care of babies. Third place, I'd pick a girl that was close and knew how to pinch pennies. Clean, clever, close—you just turn that over in your head!"

Hocking did more than that; he came directly to the point. It must have been a half-hour later when they were laying up a rough board shelter to be covered by the new strawstack that he said unexpectedly, "You don't like Elva, do you!"

"Well, I don't know her well enough to say either I do or I don't. She ain't exactly my type."

"It ain't you she'd have to marry!"

"That's right," Thomas forced himself to joke. "It ain't me she'd have to marry. Reckon maybe I'd pinch her like a pretty tight shoe!"

And with that parting thrust he calmly walked away and let Hocking make the best of it.

That night, however, he did something unusual: he made an excuse about his eyeglasses during family worship and shoved the book to Hocking. The device was none too successful, for by now even Jed knew that he could read as well without his spectacles as with them.

Hocking was a notoriously poor reader; he stumbled pitifully, had to be prompted on most of the words of more than two syllables. The family dared not remonstrate because they all knew why the text had been chosen.

"Who can find a virtuous woman, for her price is far above rubies.

"The heart of her husband doth safely trust in her, so that he shall have no need of spoil.

"She will do him good and not evil all the days of her life.

"She seeketh wool and flax, and worketh willingly with her hands."

Thomas sat by the table with his hand to his face, but instead of reflecting he was looking at Hocking through his fingers. The colored shade threw greenish-yellow ribbons of light upon the book and upon Hocking's face, intensified the blankness of his features.

"She layeth her hands to the spindle, and her hands hold the distaff.

"She stretcheth out her hands to the poor; yea, she reacheth forth her hands to the needy."

Grover and Charlotte were bored. They made little pretense of being attentive, smiled at each other from time to time, looked out the window when a rig rolled down the road. Pious Faith was disturbed at their conduct. Kate seemed nervous as a cricket. Her hands were rolled in her apron, but they kept twitching.

"She looketh well to the ways of her household, and eateth not the bread of idleness.

"Her children arise up and call her blessed; her husband also, and he praiseth her.

"Many daughters have done virtuously, but thou excelest them all.

"Favor is deceitful, and beauty is vain; but a woman that feareth the Lord, she shall be praised.

"Give her of the fruit of her hands; and let her own works praise her in the gates."

Thomas was so much irritated by the wretched reading that he was on his knees almost before Hocking had finished the chapter. After him the others crumpled down, and then when all was quiet he led them as they repeated the Lord's Prayer.

6 Thomas bided his time, hoping against hope that Hocking would come to his senses, but Elva seemingly had bewitched him. At nine or ten at night their laughter would echo up from the matted grape arbors. Or they would coax a horse from the Tanterschams and go driving—where, no one knew.

Thomas loaded Hocking with the heaviest work, called him an hour early, asked him to labor an hour after sundown in an attempt to make him listless as a suitor, but Hock's endurance was unlimited. On the hottest summer day he could stow hay in the broiling mows as fast as Jed and Thomas could pitch it up to him, only to clamor for them to get a move on whenever they took the corncob out of the water jug. Work seemed to make him happy, to supple his muscles for greater effort. He was a glorious animal, true Linthorne in bodily strength, and for his virility Thomas loved him.

In truth Thomas could not protest Hocking's attachment openly—it would have been mortal offense to the Tanterschams. For the same reason he could not often forbid Grover to go with

Ralph. Ralph would vote in the fall—for Cleveland, he said—while Grover was but fifteen. Mentally Grover was Ralph's superior, but that was hardly the reason the older boy sought out the younger. Thomas mulled over the matter, and at last found probable solution for the riddle in a theory of compensation: if Ralph could not have Charlotte, then he would at least woo someone from the same family.

He would have been horrified by the truth. Those dark nights on lonely roads, lurching along after Tanterscham's Callie or Dick, Ralph had a ready pupil. By the hour he would lecture Grover, his favorite theme the lure and anatomy of women, and his own incomparable personal charm. "All easy, once you git to know 'em, kid!" he would brag, and punctuate by an immense squirt of tobacco juice against Callie's rump. "All you got to do is act like you ain't a greenhorn! My God, kid, if I just had a dollar for every woman I've spread, I'd be a goddam millionaire!"

Grover learned fast. One night on a chance word from Ralph about a main of cocks to be fought in a big barn near Royalton, Grover mentioned the fact that he had a five dollar bill with him. Ralph drove like mad for the place, got there just in time to put the money on a red bird in the last bout. Grover was breathless with excitement—the barn was as near heaven as he had ever journeyed. All about him in the lamp-frosted fog of tobacco smoke were milling men with sharp, birdlike faces. Ralph pointed out as many as he knew: Brierley, the horse trader; Red Bratschalk and Lefty Loring, who enjoyed a local celebrity as prize-fighters; Lancaster swells like Foster, Penhock, Parke.

Their money placed, they scrambled to the vantage of a big packing case, from which position they could look straight down on the pit. Through the drifting haze Grover's eyes were sharp on each detail. He saw how the birds were spurred with steel, how they were set down, lifted, wiped clean of blood by their almost maniacal handlers. The red rooster was slain and he lost his five dollars, but he felt well repaid.

Coming home that night, Ralph prodded him to tell where he had gotten his hands on so much money.

"Hell, you don't have to be afraid to talk in front of good old Ralphie, kid!" he kept urging. "My tongue's fast on both ends."

"Well, I just found it, just like I told you."

Ralph went sulky and slapped Callie to a dead run. Grover was frightened then, thought his emancipation at an end. He tried to talk, but could not until Callie had to slow down on the long lift up Mill Hill.

"Guess you don't believe me, do you, Ralph?"

"Believe what?"

"That I found that money?"

As usual, Ralph spit an apostrophe. "Sure I believe you!" he sneered. "Just like I believe in Santy Claus. Giddep, Callie!"

Grover began to be panicky.

"Ralph! I didn't find it, not exactly. But I know where there's more, anyway."

If Grover knew where more money was hidden, Ralph knew what to do with it. Two nights later they drove again, this time to a poisonous house in a grove of catalpas. Ralph hitched to a tree in the front yard, led around the dark walls through a veritable jungle of bushes. At last the kitchen shades showed a faint green to prove that there was a lighted lamp inside.

Ralph knocked: twice, once, then twice again. At that he had to repeat his signal before the corner of the blind was drawn back. He knew what to do. As soon as he pushed his face against the glass, the woman inside began to fumble with the bolt.

Grover wanted to run, but dared not. He knew what Ralph would say because Ralph had said it a thousand times already: "Don't want to be a runt all your life, do you! Ain't nothing to be scared of!" For all Ralph's confidence Grover felt that his legs must surely buckle.

Inside he stood with his back square against the door and shivered. There were two women in the dirty kitchen, both about as old as his mother, both sloppily fat. It was not a hot night, but in the tightly closed house beads of perspiration stood on their foreheads and on their flabby dewlaps. Ralph had gone straight to the one who sat in a caned rocker and whom he addressed as Clymie. The other, between Grover and the table, kept rolling her head like a sow in the corner of a wallow. When she smiled to show a row of broken yellow fangs, Grover gasped.

"Come on, babe!" she fawned. "I won't hurt you none. You just ask Ralph over there. I won't hurt him, will I, Ralphie?"

Ralph added his voice, then Clymie hers. When all three of them failed to take the sick green from Grover's cheeks, Lydy got mad.

"Thought you said you was bringin' another man along!" she challenged Ralph.

Ralph rose to the occasion.

"God damn it, what's the matter with you, Grover!" he demanded as he got up and came across the room with his fists swinging menacingly. "You don't do what I tell you, I'll knock your block off!"

At home Thomas stopped by the boys' room with his lamp as he went down the hall. He scowled at their empty bed—he liked to know his family was safe asleep by the time he closed his eyes. Grover had asked if he might go with Ralph to an ice-cream social in Hooker, and in a moment of weakness Thomas had consented. Now there was a storm brewing in the southwest.

In response to a flash of lightning and the distant jar of thunder, he carried the lamp into the room, set it on the table while he went to the window to study the sky. When he came back, a moment later, his eye fell on the framed confirmation certificate. The paper had the effect of restoring his faith. Almost involuntarily he repeated the words, prefacing them with his son's name as he had heard them that first time from the lips of Pastor Wilme:

"Grover Linthorne: 'For God shall bring every work into judgment, with every secret thing, whether it be good, or whether it be evil.'"

III

1   That summer it seemed to Thomas as if life had become nothing but vexation. Charlotte could not get along with Jed, and Kate would not. The rascal was pleasant enough, tried hard to oblige. The fault was not with him; it was simply that he had to bear the blame for whatever went wrong. The minute Kate spied mud on her kitchen floor or saw a plate go out to the dishpan that had not been properly wiped with bread, she knew whom to blame. Before Jed the women were silent, superior. It was Thomas who heard their complaints.

If that was not enough to drive him mad, he might worry night and day about Hocking.

So that when the brawl with the Sapooneys came along, he was fit to be tied. Of all the people in the township he liked the Sapooneys least. Bill was a loafer and Celia a plain fool, and their brats, Lotus, Adolph, and the half-dozen younger children, were as like them as one row of corn was like another. It was degradation even to quarrel with such vermin.

On the same night that Grover came home soaked to the skin, the storm felled the rotten old oak behind the orchard, and for spite threw it squarely across the Linthorne-Sapooney line fence. Thomas had a good stand of corn in the big field, and although the howler had pushed it over a bit, he knew the sun would soon pull it straight. Consequently when he looked across to the mat of blackberries and mullein that Bill called pasture, he was a good deal disturbed. He could have called Jed and the boys to repair the damage in little better than an hour, but that section of the wire it was Bill

Sapooney's obligation to keep up. And for once in his life, Thomas vowed, Bill would have to get in an honest day's work.

He went over to the Sapooneys before breakfast, pounded until Celia finally came to the door. While he waited, he had time to see that the spotted cows were still in the muddy barnyard. They'd have to stay there until Bill got busy.

Celia was as usual like week-old gravy.

"Sakes alive, Thomas, come right on in!" she invited. "Bill, he's still snoozin'—he don't never seem to get enough sleep. Time he's awake enough to see daylight, it's night again."

Thomas sniffed whenever he set foot in the Sapooney kitchen. Celia never washed clothes or dishes. The plates were crusted with food from one week's end to another, in summer smothered with flies, in winter yellow with tallow. It was often told how years ago Celia had put in her place an officious neighbor woman who suggested washing up after every meal. "Two ways of doing things, old way and the right way!" Celia had snapped. "All gets mixed up in your stomach anyhow!"

Bill finally paddled downstairs in his bare feet, his eyes so bleary that he looked a little more stupid than usual.

"You s-say that tree's down!" he repeated for about the third time while Thomas tried to be patient. "Bet it got st-st-struck by lightning."

"Wind," Thomas insisted. "It's torn out by the roots."

Bill shook his head unbelievingly.

"T-tell you what, Thomas," he sputtered after he had been to the door to see for himself. "I bet I heard the crack when it got h-hit. S-smack! that's the way it went! Thought for a minute it was right inside my head!"

Thomas conceded the point.

"Well, it's a-layin' right spang over the fence, no matter what did it!" he said irritably. "I'll get a cross-cut and saw it up if you'll fix the wire."

Bill took up his plate from the table, rubbed it on his elbow a few times, and then ladled himself some mush.

"How about it? You ain't busy today, are you?"

"Well, t-tell you the truth, Thomas, I done promised Cely I'd

181

put her up a c-couple fly roosts over the table . . . Gettin' so dang bad we can't hardly eat."

Thomas snorted.

"T-tell you what I'll do: you just get that fence back and I'll p-p-pay you for it sometime. Won't we, Cely?"

"Pay nothing!" Thomas cut in. "I'll do just what I said I'd do—I'll saw up the wood. You want it, you can have it. And I want that fence back up by tonight. I can't have your cows running all over my corn."

He was as good as his word; he put Jed and Hocking on the saw as soon as he went back home. By the time he came in at noon, they had finished. The round cuts of the heavy oak bole were rolled up against the gap in the line, a bed of brush and branches tangled over them.

That afternoon when from the swell of his own pasture he saw that the Sapooney cows were grazing near the boundary, his anger grew. It was plain that Bill meant to do nothing. Fly-roosts! Thriftless, do-less, good-for-nothing loafer, that's all he was, he and his whole tribe!

Two days later Grover came running to the field to say that the Sapooney cows had gotten across to the corn.

Thomas saw red. For an instant he had the impulse to go into the house for his rifle, but he was sane enough to realize that his anger was not directed against the brutes. For all that, he picked up a stout length of hickory as he ran past the woodpile. Grover imitated him, outstripped him as they trotted down through the orchard where there was a stile. Sure enough, the cows were in the corn, smashing about with true Sapooney impudence. Sight of Thomas and Grover sent them lurching drunkenly down through the field, their half-filled udders slapping.

Thomas had to run a long arc to get around them before he finally managed to head them back. He kept yelling like mad as he beat back. Directly opposite the hole in the fence Grover waited, his club waving.

Just when it seemed the beasts would have sense enough to escape their persecutors by returning to their own lean pasture, one of them frisked about. That was too much for Thomas. He was after the animal like a fury. Whack! he brought his club down against the lean sides; *whack! whack! whack!* The frightened cow leaped forward out of the trampled corn, plunged for the barrier. The brush kept it from clearing the tree, and as it came down on its forelegs it struck the trunk, to crumple down with broken legs.

Thomas sent Grover to the house for the rifle as soon as he knew the beast could not be saved. It was an ugly business, but he meant to be resolute. Bill could butcher right where the cow lay, if he liked, and Thomas would say nothing to having the buzzards swooping around for a few days. Or else he'd send one of the boys down to get the fertilizer wagon. But beyond that, he wouldn't do a thing or pay a cent.

Celia came to the house crying while they were eating supper, and there was a scene in front of all the children.

"'Tain't like as if the good Lord'd blessed the two of us alike, you know that!" she kept sniffling. "Me and my man's always had a hard row to hoe."

"You never put your back in it, far as I could see," Thomas commented drily.

Kate checked him with an instant "Thomas!"

"Well, it's the truth, ain't it? I told Bill to get that fence fixed."

That made Celia burst out in another storm of sobs.

"He didn't have no extra wire," she quavered. "He hunted around all morning. Maybe you don't know what it's like to have to do without all the time!"

Thomas calmly ate a wedge of pie from Saturday's baking.

"Well, what do you and Bill expect me to do about it?" he asked when he had satisfied his stomach. "I'm not going to pay you for the cow, and that's that! . . . Not unless you pay me for my corn, and if you do it'll be the first thing you ever did pay for."

"Thomas!"

"We don't want no pay."

"Well, what *do* you want?"

"Thomas!" Kate checked him for the third time.

Celia was not daunted by his manner. "You know what it says

in the Good Book," she reminded. "You shut up your bowels of compassion, and Lazarus won't even dip the tip of his little finger in water for you."

"I don't want Lazarus to dip the tip of his finger in water for me! What do *you* want?"

Kate got up and left the room—if her protests were unavailing, she at least did not have to see Celia tortured.

"Why don't you give us a cow to make up for the one you shot. You got plenty."

Thomas swallowed her brass without gulping. After all, there was a little truth in what she said—she and Bill were as poor as blind church mice.

"I won't do that," he said. "But I tell you what I will do: you send Bill over here to work and I'll pay him a dollar a day until he's got enough money laid by to get him another cow. That's fair, ain't it?"

Celia puckered her mouth and walked right out into the kitchen. Thomas heard her slam the door without saying good-bye to Kate, rose to watch her bang through the gate. From the way she clumped along, he knew the answer to his proposal. Bill wouldn't be breaking his back for a mere dollar a day.

2 Not a fortnight later Muley, Spot, and Brindle began to tremble one morning when Grover drove them in to be milked. They managed to go back to pasture, but got down there, and were dead before night.

Thomas wouldn't believe that injury to his cattle might in any way be attributed to Celia. But by that time word of the Sapooney affair had walked the roads for miles in all directions, and others were more suspicious. It was Joe Jordan who insisted on the possibility of curse.

"Course, I know you don't set much store by evil eye and them things, Thomas," he said fearfully as they hung on either side of Thomas's wagon gate. "But you got to remember how Cely used to run after Tess Sellers. Maybe you ain't never heard, but she was down there for a week on end before the old lady passed on."

"What's that got to do with it?"

"Well, if what folks say is true, they know when their time's come," said Joe. "Can't pass it on to nobody while they're alive— what they know. And can't die without passing it . . . So maybe Cely—"

"You don't believe that truck, do you?"

Joe was injured, turned to go at once.

"Time you see what I've seen and hear what I've heard, maybe you'll believe a little too!" he warned. "You take it from me—them cows of yours was hexed. And I'll just bet she ain't all through with you, neither!"

His words gnawed at Thomas the rest of the day, with the consequence that he repeated them for Kate as they lay in bed that night.

"Don't think there's anything in it, do you, Kate?" he asked.

Kate was heartbroken about the cows.

"Don't know whether I do or I don't, Thomas," she admitted. "But you mark what I tell you: if I thought Celia Sapooney'd do a trick like that to me, I'd get my hands in her hair till she was bald as an egg! Muley was the best Jersey we ever had."

Thomas worried, described the ailment to whoever would listen to him. Most of them had had their judgment warped by Joe Jordan. Milk-sick, they'd say at first halfheartedly, and then veer off to mention Celia and show what they really thought.

"Tell you what we'd ought to do, Thomas," he heard a dozen times. "Ought to get us a gang together some night and run her clean out of the county."

Thomas put his foot down on that talk.

"It's like this," he explained patiently. "I'm not saying there ain't no devil. And I'm not saying that he don't give some folks that ask for it power to do things. But I am saying that if he picked on Cely, he's a lot dumber than he ought to be by now!"

Celia basked in her fame—it was the first time that anyone had shown a wholesome regard for her. At church she paraded a new turkey wing upon her discolored straw and stopped to talk to nobody.

A week went by, and then one morning Whitey lay dead in the pasture. Thomas shuddered when he went up to look at the animal. She had shown no sign of being sick the evening before. He had examined the pasture for poison without finding anything, but on the chance that he might learn what was causing the death of his cows, he went to the house for a butcher knife and returned to cut into Whitey's stomach.

What he found made his flesh creep—a solid hair ball more than two inches across. He had seen one once before down at McGruber's. "Witch ball!" McGruber had said when he showed it. The thing was incredible, but a lot of things were incredible that were true. *Hexed, hexed, hexed*—the word kept turning over and over, beating like a drum in his mind.

In his extremity Thomas saddled Dolly and rode up Locust Lane to see Como Cory. He hated to be a zany, but he was worried. If anyone could talk sense without scattering like a shotgun, it was Como. He was just coming in for dinner when Thomas arrived; gargantuan, lumpish, he sat on the cellar door and heard the whole pitiful tale.

"Got any stagnant water in that pasture?" he asked as soon as Thomas broke off.

"Brook's all the water there is."

"Any toadstools?"

"Puffballs. Never saw nothing else."

"Ever see any mold around the roots of the grass?"

"No."

Como sat and nodded his big head knowledgeably.

"Thought so," he said. "But you can just bet your life you got white snakeroot! Know what it is?"

Thomas had to think hard. "Can't tell offhand," he said. "But my girl'll know."

"Well, you take her out there with you. Better change your pasture until you're sure you got it all rooted out. Can't have trembles without white snakeroot, and that's the long and the short of it."

Thomas wanted to ask another question, but before Como's ponderous learning he felt like a simpleton. Not until he was in the saddle could he muster enough courage.

"You don't think there's anything in maybe being hexed, do you, Como? Guess you know what's going around."

Como laughed in his face. For the first time in his life, Thomas was happy at being affronted.

Whether Como was right or not, he lost no more stock after he had cleared out the snakeroot. He might be pardoned if he bragged a little, but his boldness made Celia an implacable enemy. Her tongue ran like a clapper. Thomas could have throttled her a dozen times because of what was reported back to him. To the Jordans Celia had related that Thomas visited every saloon in town whenever he went to Lancaster. Flora Wendell heard that the reason Kate had had no more children after Grover was that Thomas had caused several miscarriages. Marty laughed with Thomas at the story that Bill's indolence was owing to Thomas's having swindled him out of honest pay. The poor fellow had lost his heart for work.

Thomas didn't laugh at what Spence Vitt reported. Celia had been a long time with her tale to Cora, but the gist of it was that Grover was running wild with Ralph Tanterscham. Somebody had told somebody that somebody else had seen Grover and Ralph come out of a certain bawdyhouse on the Campground road. Celia made the most of the story, crunched it between her gat teeth, bounced it around as she bounced her beeswax or slippery elm.

"Course, I don't figure a word of it's so, Thomas," Spence said apologetically. "Only, I thought as how you'd like to know."

Thomas thanked him.

"Set any store by that Ralph Tanterscham?" he asked Spence directly.

"About as much as you could stuff up an ant's nose."

Thomas agreed. That same night he gave Grover his orders: he was to be home by eight o'clock, and in bed by nine. And there was to be no more driving with Ralph Tanterscham at any time.

Thomas had to wonder when he looked at the boy's innocent face. Grover seemed more puzzled than hurt. He had the soft brown eyes of a collie whipped for sheep-killing when he had only been chasing chipmunks.

3 Part of the fame Thomas enjoyed was that he subscribed to a Columbus paper. It was largely because of the articles about the coming Ohio Centennial and the coincident G.A.R. encampment in Columbus that he had resolved to go up to the capital in September. He had not told Kate how well he had perfected his

plans. Now with the loss of time and money he had been put to, it began to look as if he would be beaten out of his holiday. Work kept piling before him like mounting thunderheads.

But work or no work, when the first of August came around he must make his borage beer. It was a part of his pride; Linthorne wouldn't be Linthorne without the borage. Neighbors who helped with the haying or dropped in on Sunday afternoons during the dog days had come to expect the treat and had often tried to ferret out the recipe. Thomas wouldn't give it up any more than Kate would tell how she made her hypocrite cakes. He couldn't have. Into the brass kettle besides the borage went a conglomeration of spruce, spikenard, roasted corn, roots of yellow dock, sassafras, ginger— and whatever else struck his fancy. After he had boiled the brew long enough to satisfy himself, he added wheat bran and some of Kate's potato yeast to make it work. In a week's time it was ready. It rarely lasted more than ten days.

Thomas went down cellar for the cask one morning to surprise a large rat calmly eating its way through the apple bin. If there was anything Thomas hated, it was a rat. He had nothing in hand to attack the rodent, and by the time he could find a stick, it had scurried behind a pile of boxes. Thomas took down the rubbish to find a curving hole under the foundation. It was largely impulse that made him drive his stick into the burrow. To his amazement he rammed into what seemed to be a tin can. After a moment of trepidation lest he should have his fingers bitten, he tried to insert his hand, but the best he could do was touch the tin with his fingers.

Puzzled, he brought a spading fork from the barn and dug down to unearth the mystery. What he brought to light was an almost new baking powder tin. With rough fingers he pried off the lid, gasped when he saw the roll of crisp greenbacks hidden inside. As quietly as he could, he tiptoed up and let down the leaves of the cellar door before he came back to count the money by the light of the winter lantern. There was exactly two hundred and forty dollars in the hoard.

Thomas put the money in his pocket, carefully replaced the tin. Instinctively he knew—it was Gregory's money. If the tin and money had been old, he might have believed the treasure hidden a long time; but Gregory had lost new money, and the powder can was the identical kind Kate used. With a kind of cold rage he accepted the fact that someone in the family was a thief. Who, Hocking, Grover, Jed? Or one of the girls?

He was very casual as he went about work that day, but by appointing tasks he made sure that none of the boys went to the cellar. At supper that night he waited until Faith brought the Bible and then mentioned the rat in an offhand manner.

"Guess I'll have to put some poison down there," he suggested.

"You will not!" Kate protested at once, as he had foreseen. "I'm not going to be stunk clear out of the house. Them rats die in the walls, there won't be any living here. You can set traps, but you can't use poison."

"Well, I'll set traps then," Thomas agreed. "But I tell you one thing: I'm a-goin' down there tomorrow and plug up every hole I can find. No sense letting more move in on us."

As soon as worship was over, he got his hat and made excuse that he had to run down the road to see Spence. It was just dusk as he went out into the yard. Over on the crown of Church Hill the trees stood in black patches against a dun-gray sky lit by a single bright star. The fields were already stippled by fireflies, and the crickets were beginning to chirk.

Thomas looked only for assurance that the weed-grown road was dark enough to hide the fact that he would not walk as he had said. Satisfied, he circled the house, passed under the corner linden and the three plums on the west, and so came by stealth to the cellar. It smelled mouldy in the damp gloom as he sat on a box by the apple bin and waited. Overhead he heard the rain of feet as Kate and the girls began to wash up the dishes, then the heavier tread when the boys went out to see to the horses.

Thomas bit his lip and waited. He had no clear plan—everything depended upon the identity of the culprit. If it was Jed, he would have to make restitution and take the medicine of the law. Hocking would not be prosecuted, but he'd be cut off. Grover—

The outside cellar doors scratched as they were softly lifted. Mechanically Thomas arose, shivered as he strained to attention. He could not see his hand before his face, let alone see who crept down as quietly as a cat. He felt clammy as the body brushed past him. Whoever it was was used to such dark ventures, for he did not touch a single object on the floor. The intruder rustled down on the far side of the cellar. There followed a moment of silence, and the soft scrape of the tin as it was withdrawn. At that moment Thomas struck his match.

He hardly needed the light to know he had trapped Grover. Nor did he need it once he had proved his worst fear—his son's pitiful whimpering was enough to guide him. The boy seemed paralyzed, huddled on the floor, had to be half carried to the barn. Thomas dragged him along by thrusting under his armpits. On the way through the yard he passed Jed, who was carrying a bucket of water from the trough for Kate's dahlias. Hocking must have gone back to the house, for there was no light in the barn.

Thomas knew where he could find the blacksnake. Silent, implacable, he held Grover by the scruff of the neck and began to flay him. He hardly heard his son's cries of agony. Again, again, and a dozen times again, he brought the whip around with all the force he could command. The boy screamed each time the lash burned him, thrashed like a hooked fish, but Thomas had no thought of relenting.

He was still flogging Grover's limp body when through the open doors he saw someone running with a lantern who had been attracted by the cries. The house door, too, was open, and in the bright rectangle Kate stood silhouetted. She might peer now—she would know her disgrace soon enough. It were better that the boy had died than that he should have lived to this evil! Not even blood could wipe out the blackness of villainy!

It was Jed who had come running. His face was pallid as he appeared in the doorway, his eyes green in the lantern light. When he saw that Thomas meant to flog again, his mouth fell open.

"Don't do that, Mr. Linthorne!" he called out as the lash descended. "You'll kill him!"

Thomas had his teeth set; he ignored Jed completely.

"You'll kill him if you keep on!"

Thomas glared defiance. "None of your business if I do," he panted. "Go on back up to the house where you belong!"

Instead Jed set down the lantern and rushed in. Spent as he was by his exertion, Thomas could not stand up under the impact. Together they rolled in the inch-deep dust on the barn floor. Thomas tried to break loose, but the man was his master, held him pinioned fast. The iron muscles that bound him brought him back to his senses, made him able to think again. In a moment it seemed that he was as weak as water, the fury all drained from his heart.

"Let me up," he said quietly enough.

"You won't whip him no more?"

"I won't whip him no more."

Jed went immediately to Grover, picked him up in his arms and carried him to the house while Thomas trailed along behind. Under the Concord arbor they met Kate. She waited in silence for Thomas's word.

"I whipped him 'cause he needed it!" he said as he passed her.

That was all—it was explanation enough before someone not in the family.

Inside, with Jed gone and the girls sent to bed, Thomas told her the whole story while he put lard on Grover's welts and she held hartshorn. By the time Grover revived, Kate knew. She made no comment, but the tears no longer ran down her cheeks.

4   One consequence of that sad night's work was that Thomas told Hocking exactly how he felt about Elva Uny.

He and Kate had had a long talk about the whole business. The money could not openly be restored to the Gregorys without lasting disgrace; it would have to be given back a little at a time. Grover would have to be carefully managed: not disciplined too much, lest his spirit be broken; and yet held by a pretty strong rein. Jed would have his pay raised to a dollar a day. And Hocking would have to be prevented from making a fool of himself.

On a night when Elva scandalized everyone by playing leapfrog with the boys, Thomas waited up for Hocking.

"I tell you I won't have it!" he repeated for the tenth time as they argued in the kitchen. "That girl ain't decent!"

"You don't have no right to say that!"

"I'm your father—I guess that gives me a right! If she was, she wouldn't always be showing herself off to anyone that wants to look."

Hocking was both sheepish and angry.

"Trouble with you is you don't understand," he said. "She's just full of fun."

"She's just full of the devil! I tell you, Hocking, I won't stand for it!"

Hocking stood on one foot and then on the other, his mouth working. "Like to know what you're going to do about it," he challenged.

Thomas hated to resort to definite threat; he had vowed to avoid that.

"Listen, Hock," he tried to reason, "I been good to you, ain't I?"

His intended softness brought the bitterest words Hocking had ever spoken to him:

"Don't call it good to make me do all the dirty work while everybody else around here keeps his hands clean, do you! Don't call it good never to give me a penny without my going down on my knees for it! Don't call it good to try to run my whole life! Guess if I'm almost old enough to vote, I'm old enough to pick the girl I want to marry!"

His words stuck in Thomas's teeth. Afterward he would reason on them, and find them more than half right. But in his moment of anger there was no time for deliberation.

"You marry that girl and you'll get out!" he said bitterly. "I won't have her around here, wife or no wife!"

"Well, maybe I'll get out, then. Won't be any worse off working for myself than I am for you. Anyway, I won't have to hang around and wait for you and Mom to die before I get anything."

Thomas was too angry to go on talking. Better their words should sink in for both of them.

"I've said my say," he muttered as he went over to blow out the lamp. "I won't have it, and I want you to know it!"

Hocking didn't even take off his shoes downstairs. He clumped up ahead of Thomas loud enough to wake the dead.

IV

1 September came with skies smoky and often sullen, but the year was at prime. Everywhere there was color: of scarlet haws on the thorny trees, swollen purple grapes, orange bittersweet, blue chicory. In Kate's dooryard the white clematis burst to starry profusion. Cosmos, four o'clocks, golden-glow, marigolds flamed as if summer should never end.

But as proof of fall the roads were lined with goldenrod and wild sunflowers; boneset and blue lobelias bloomed in the moist places; of the Queen Anne's lace many blooms had curled to dried bird nests. The locusts were persistent in their sibilance; golden-tawny spiders spun across every fence corner. On fair days the frosted lips of the clouds were underlaid by deep blue shadows. Everywhere, in both the silence and the singing, was the stoic acceptance of coming doom.

Thomas raced the season, got in the second hay, picked the early fruit, made the bins and granary ready. Each year he loved more this time of year, loved the long knives whistling through the corn, the heavy loads that must be hauled to the elevator, the sorghum mill, the cider press. Now there was a different reason for his haste: he must justify to Kate his intended visit to the Ohio Centennial and the encampment.

The Columbus paper made him mad with excitement. There was to be a parade of Sherman's bummers up High Street with over a hundred loads of straw for the camp; on the way they would commandeer loads of chickens, apples, melons driven out from the side streets. Delegations of veterans were coming from Utah, Arizona, California. Governor Lounsbury of Connecticut and Lieutenant

Governor Brackett of Massachusetts were enroute to the capital with their staffs. Former President Hayes; W. D. Howells, the Ohio writer; General Lew Wallace; the Old Roman, Cleveland's running mate in the coming election; a thousand other celebrities would be there. "Cump" himself was coming, to sit on the reviewing stand where he could be seen by every one of the ninety thousand in line.

Thomas did his best to make Kate tell him to go.

"Listen here, Ma," he would remark excitedly, "the paper says they're going to have fifteen hundred school kids in red, white, and blue dresses make a big flag on the statehouse steps and sing."

"Are they?"

"Bet you it'll be real pretty."

"'Spect it will," Kate would remark, and very likely walk out to throw scraps to the hens.

By the fifth Thomas was desperate.

"General Sherman's going to be down here in Lancaster tomorrow, Ma," he said at table that night. "Look pretty good to him after all these years, I reckon. Born and raised right over on Main Street Hill."

"Guess maybe you'll have to knock off and drive over so's you can be there with the Ben Butterfields when the train pulls in," Kate said sarcastically.

Thomas didn't know what to make of her. She seemed mulish, as if she was disappointed about something. He tried to make her see his side of it by reading everything aloud he thought she'd be interested in; but the more he read, the worse she took on. What did she care that George Washington's coach would be in the parade or that it was valued at ten thousand dollars, that they were putting ten gas pipe arches across High Street with three hundred colored globes on each, that the stores and engine-houses were draped with bunting from cornice to pavement! Coates Kinney could recite his old ode, she doubted anybody'd listen!

Because of her opposition Thomas began to droop. After all, he didn't really have much business running off for two or three days—she was right about that. The encampment could get along without him—he had never gone to any other. There would be enough people to celebrate the landing at Marietta without his joining in.

By the eighth he had decided to abide by her judgment. Because he thought it would amuse her, perhaps partially restore him to her good graces, he called her in from the dishes that night to hear a little item about a prize quilt that was to be exhibited at the Centennial:

An offer of $1000 in cash has been refused for an elegant quilt, the property of Clay Hay Post, G.A.R., of New Carlisle, O. The quilt is composed of twelve squares, made and donated by the following ladies: Mrs. Governor Foraker, Mrs. General Hancock, Mrs. General Harrison, General McPherson's sister, Mrs. John C. Fremont, Mrs. General J. C. Black, Mrs. Frank C. Blair, Mrs. U. S. Grant, Mrs. Senator Sherman, Mrs. General McGinnis, Mrs. General Slocum, Mrs. General Gilson. Let the ladies who come here next week have an opportunity, by all means, to see the quilt.

"Fat lot you know about quilts!" she said the minute he was finished.

"I didn't say I did, did I?" he retorted. He was going to let it pass at that, while he went back to his paper, but something about the way she hung at his elbow pricked up the devil in him, so that he couldn't help adding, "Like to know what right you think you got to act like a sour apple all the time!"

To his surprise she burst into tears.

"It ain't like as if we didn't have the money, Thomas!" she blurted as she wiped her eyes on her checked apron. "And it ain't like as if the children wasn't growed up!"

"What ain't?"

That set her off afresh.

"What ain't!" she flung back at him. "You going off to Columbus without me, that's what! Never think of nobody but yourself all the time! You know I ain't hardly been out of this house in twenty years!"

She fairly put Thomas's head in a halter before she was through. He sat smoking without one word of rebuttal. When she finally came to a period, he had his question rounded and ready.

"Guess you'll be needing a new dress to go along up with me, won't you? And I'll have to get me a uniform ready-made. No time to have it cut out no more."

Kate could only stare at him—like a woman possessed.

"You mean that—"

"Why," he fibbed, "I meant to take you all the time. What'd you think, that I was fixing to lay out on the straw in one of them camp tents like—like them fellows coming from Kansas and way out west! Guess not. What I meant to do was rent us a room."

Kate kissed him, even though Faith and Charlotte had come to the doorway to listen.

"I'm awful sorry for what I said, Thomas," she repented. "I won't never say another word against you long as I live."

2 Never had conquerors moved on a city in more splendor than the Ben Butterfield Post in their brass and green plush coach with Sherman in their midst. At 11:30, when they pulled into the Columbus yards, Thomas and Kate were aquiver with excitement. Everywhere was the blare of bands, the jangling of bells. The station was a mill of men, an army with banners: "Tippecanoe and Pensions Too"; "Hail, Ohio"; "All The Way from Ioway"; "New York No 52"; "Greetings from Scranton." Everywhere in the turbulence was good-natured joshing, back-slapping. No introductions were necessary. "Hi there, soldier, will you work?" was the invariable query; and the answer just as silly, "Naw, I'd lose my shirt first!" Blacks scrambled in and out of the throng, crawled under legs for carpetbags and portmanteaus. Hawkers were out by the dozen, their merchandise mostly bamboo canes, armbands, boutonnieres. An enterprising Greek had piled a pyramid of long green melons just outside a hot-fish stand; an equally enterprising copper bawled out for him to move out of the way.

The Ben Butterfield boys and their wives packed tight around Sherman, lest he be recognized and mobbed. They were almost through the station when a tall fellow with an army roll of blankets on his back sang out, "By God, there goes Cump or I'm an Irishman!" Instantly heads craned from all sides, and the press of bodies began. Just outside the station doors an open carriage waited, in front of it a file of the Sons of Veterans. Sherman pressed toward it, ignoring the cries to shake hands.

Thomas used his shoulder to shield Kate from the howling

mob, kept his other arm around her to be sure she didn't go down. As Sherman passed through the file of young men presenting arms, a pretty woman in a pink bonnet fainted and was grabbed up instantly by a dozen hands. "Shake hands, Cump! Shake hands, shake hands, shake hands!" the mad cry persisted. One old granddaddy in some way managed to crawl through the guard, hung on the carriage steps even when the command was given to whip up. "Shake hands, Gineral!" Thomas heard him quaver. "Maybe it's the last time fer both of us!" Thomas reached for the graybeard just in time to drag him out from under the wheels.

They managed after a furious fight to get out of the press and to High Street. There were the arches, just as Thomas had read. Toddlers wore red, white, and blue dresses; wheelmen had their bicycles and tricycles laced with bunting. It had rained the day before so that the blue and red decorations had melted over the facades of the big three and four story buildings. No one in the crazy mob minded in the least. Curb to curb, the street groaned under the racing carriages and the great drays moving provisions and supplies out to the camps: bedding, tents, loads of potatoes, apples, even baked bread.

"Hi there, soldier, will you work?"

"Naw, I'd lose my shirt first!"

Thomas steered Kate around the pair, both of them drunk.

"Know where we're going?" he asked her.

She shook her head, but plodded straight ahead. They were both awestruck, afraid. Thomas kept one hand in his jacket pocket so that he could hold his money—he had read the warnings against pickpockets. With every step toward the center of town, walking became more difficult. Finally at Broad and High a burly brute with a three days' growth of beard openly made way for himself by shoving Thomas into the gutter. Kate bubbled like a teakettle as she helped him back to his feet, kneeled down to brush the dirt from his knees. He was aflame with indignation when a big hand smote hard between his shoulder blades and a bigger voice poured into his ear, "Hi there, soldier, will you work?"

Thomas glanced around sheepishly at the giant. The fellow was grinning. In an instant he forgot his anger.

"Naw," he said, "I'd lose my shirt first!"

"Didn't hurt you, did I?"

"Guess you didn't."

"All right. Who you for, Cleveland or Harrison?"

Thomas reddened—he didn't like to confess his politics before all the world.

"Harrison, I reckon," he admitted.

"You'd better be!" said the stranger. "That damn Cleveland vetoed too many pension bills to suit me!"

With that he went on, his big arms swinging bellicosely.

There was another such mob around the capitol as there had been at the station. They at last made their way through it into the rotunda and the wonder of the great seal set in the dome. Thomas had almost a proprietary air as he escorted Kate up to the chamber of representatives and afterward to the senate. They dared even peep into the governor's office, alive now with soldiers and uniformed dignitaries like all the other rooms and corridors.

"You know, Catherine, it all makes me feel pretty proud of myself!" he said nobly as they were coming down the east steps of the statehouse.

"You know, *what?*"

"Well, that's your name, ain't it?"

Kate laughed. "Now look here, Thomas, you just keep both feet on the ground!" she advised him. "No sense you making a plumb fool of yourself just because you're running around with a lot of other nannies that don't know where to go no more'n you do. Strikes me we better be finding us a room so's we can take off our shoes and rest our feet."

3 By night they were both so tired that they could hardly move. Thomas was out to splurge, and they had made a good beginning. In a hired rig they had driven to the camps—Neil, Hayden, and Dennison, then out Broad Street to the big tent of the Army of West Virginia, finally to the Centennial grounds. Kate was pretty sick of it all by the time they got back to the stables. Such a confusion of grandeur mixed with awful smells and noises was beyond her wildest imagination.

The camps were all the same: dozens of streets of tents latticed across open fields, each one as like the others as peas in a pod; stacks of straw from which weary men brought armfuls to litter down their beds; mounted aides prancing importantly through the mudholes; pine-plank mess halls, and accumulations of waste lumber for the campfires that would entertain notables each night; everywhere the idiotic "Hi there, soldier! Will you work?"

But tired or not, Thomas had set his heart on going to the Metropolitan Opera House. Kate admitted that the play there sounded pretty good: *Held by the Enemy,* with a man named William H. Gillette advertised as being the main character. She herself would much rather sit in the open to see the fireworks at the *Last Days of Pompeii,* but gave in because she knew the soldier piece would flatter Thomas.

At that, she was satisfied. This Mr. Gillette could certainly talk free and fancy. And the gaslights and velvet curtains and swells in their good Sunday clothes were enough to make a body's eyes water, without any play at all.

"I tell you, Thomas, they sure looked *some!*" she said enthusiastically when they were walking back to their room. "Real silk a lot of them had on!"

"Didn't look a bit better to me than you, Kate," Thomas said gallantly. "Sort of look *some* yourownself!"

It was his prettiest speech in years—it made them both happy. Hand in hand, they stood on a street corner while a raccoon and log cabin parade went by with streams of red fire. Thomas approved the partisans. If the magic that had put Tippecanoe into the White House had not lost its potency, Ben Harrison would be the next president.

4 Already at eight the day of the parade gave promise of being a stinker. Here and there along the curbs residents had set out pails and tubs of water, some with tincups, some without, but it was hardly fit to drink after an aide had allowed his horse to plunge into it. Nevertheless the men guzzled, much to the amusement of the stylish ladies with pigeon breasts who crowded the porches and flag-hung balconies.

"Hey, you got any idea where Twentieth Street is?" Thomas hailed a coachman who held in a fine span of bays before a greenstone mansion.

"Just kape right on the way yer headed," he had his answer, without even the courtesy of a glance.

Thomas kept on. Two ships of the naval battalion, the iron-clad "Mound City" and the monitor "Manhattan," pulled past him on their way to location, behind them a detachment wheeling a cannon made entirely from buckeyes. A little farther on he stopped by an iron picket to admire a covered wagon placarded with the fame of the Andrews' raiders. He had heard a hundred times of their luster, but they looked anything but famous now as they sprawled on the mangy grass under the limp trees and whiled away the time by playing Old Sledge.

Ants from a blue hill, jostling, grumbling, running aimlessly with lost eyes, thousands and tens of thousands of them. Soldiers, soldiers, soldiers, yelping, laughing, wiping the sweat from their eyes with red bandanas. They had driven the citizens hurrying downtown into the gutters, even a nurse with a parasol baby buggy. From all the side streets the blare of practicing bands and drum corps, a very fog of music. Twentieth Street might be. They had problems of their own, couldn't worry about the Sixth Division.

Thomas was humping madly over the tile pavements when sudden excitement brought him up short. There were Ohio men loitering on the walks here, all steamy hot and bored to distraction by their enforced idleness. As Thomas pushed through them, someone spied an old lady in black who had just limped out to her veranda. "That there's General Reese's widdy!" went the whisper. "She's Cump's sister."

All eyes were turned immediately.

"Who is?" a big fellow challenged. "Bet you a thousand dollars that's Mrs. Butler."

"Mrs. Butler your grandmother! Guess I know Mary Elizabeth Sherman when I see her. Didn't live in Lancaster half my life for nothing!"

That seemed to be authority enough. Someone started singing "Marching through Georgia," a hundred joined in, and before they got to the chorus there was a mad rush for the porch. Thomas was sucked into the mill, waited his turn to pump the old lady's hand. They should all have been shot when they hurrahed for the general right into her ears. Mary Elizabeth Sherman, the girl of old Lon Brewster's story, she who had leaped from the mountain to get away from her beau!

Thomas counted the day well spent already. Even if nothing more happened, he would have something to relate to his grandchildren.

5 Sixty, seventy, eighty, ninety thousand in line, blue bugs debouching from the side streets to crawl on a ribbon of gray brocade. Overhead the sharp tattoo of the sun, from the pavements the hyena laugh of silver bugles. Fall in! Fall in! The snarl of snares, boom of the big basses as another contingent added a longer tail to the snake.

One hundred and ten steps to the minute, tramping down Broad Street, tramping down old hatreds, tramping down the century, tramping down—

"Good-bye, Molly! See you down at the beer garden on High Street tonight!"

Dance of the flags, spume of light from the brass horns, impromptu chorus:

> *Gettysburg, Vicksburg, Sherman to the sea,*
> *Jumbled all together in a jolly jamboree,*
> *Goin' to keep Jeff hangin' from his sour apple tree*
> *Until we march through O-hi-a.*

Tramp, tramp, tramp, tramp, tramp, tramp, tramp—the whole earth hollow to the rhythmic boom of steel-shod leather. "Hello, John!" "Hi there, Mr. McIntosh! Be over tonight if I ain't too daggone tired!" "You come, anyway. Me an' Mary'll be a-lookin' for you!"

> *John Brown's body lies a-stickin' up its toes,*
> *John Brown's body makes you want to hold your nose,*
> *John Brown's body—*

"Hey, buddy, gimme a lip o' that cider, will ye? My feet hurt somethin' awful!"

Walks, lawns, balconies, and cupolas crusted with people, two hundred and fifty thousand of them in a city of only one hundred thousand. Mansions, carriage houses, all the pomp and dignity of wealth in brownstone and brick. Far down the street the boom of the mortars of the monitor, and the white pigeons wheeling in fright from the ledges of the cathedral. The gaping throngs at the curbs, once stiff-starched, now wilted as if they had just been squeezed from the rinse tub. As far as the eye could see the long, hot, wavering line of blue.

"Oh, de camptown racetrack's ten miles long—"

"Ain't half as long as my Aunt Clemmy's nightgown!"

"Your Aunt Clemmy's nightgown's any longer than this damn street, she ought to wind it around the—"

Oh, my darling Nelly Gray
Up in heaven she will say—

The big stone statehouse at last, its cheesebox rotunda red with the colors. Vendors, hawkers, mountebanks, trick riders—all luring pennies from the massed mobs hungry for added diversion. The counter-marching files returning past the reviewing stand and the saluting ranks of the Sons of Veterans.

Shake a leg now! Down Third Street, State Street, up High to circle the capitol square.

Twelve o'clock, one o'clock, two o'clock, three,
Sweat's a-rollin' down our backs like stinkin' yeller tea,
Feet a-feelin' flatter than the bottom of the sea,
While we go marching through O-hi-a.

"Come on, get a move on! Step it up a little! Step it up a little, can't you! Look like a herd of cows comin' home!"

Broad Street! One hundred and twenty beats to the minute for the quickstep past the reviewing stand. Heads up! Heads up! The massed north side of the pavement the color guard with the battle standards carried with loving care from the flag room in the rotunda. Antietam, Spotsylvania, the Wilderness—blood-stained, sabered to ribbons, riddled by canister.

Throats choked, hearts pounding. Up with the horns! Blow out your hearts, set the drums rattling as they never rattled before. *I have seen Him in the watch-fires of a hundred circling camps; I have builded him an altar*— The endless acclaim of the mob for each new wave of blue— Oh, that Lincoln could have lived to see this day— *Madam, I pray that our Heavenly Father may assuage the anguish of your bereavement*— Spines straight now, hands snapped at salute! On the right the reviewing stand, Sherman in the bay, behind him the fine white head of General Logan's widow— *It is rather for us to be dedicated to the great task remaining before us—that this nation under God, shall have a new birth of freedom*—

"God bless you, Cump! God bless you, Gineral! Sherman, Sherman, Sherman!"

With malice toward none; with charity for all; with firmness in the right, as God gives us to see the right! Thirty-eight stars in the flag, thirty-eight bright stars—and beyond the Mississippi perhaps a dozen others that would some day glow in the blue field. From Atlantic to Pacific, lakes to gulf, a perfect union, one and inseparable, now and forever!

6   Kate had promised to meet him on the steps of Dr. Washington Gladden's church, but Thomas had to fight his way to her. At five the blue stream kept flowing as it had flowed since eleven in the morning.

"Golly!" Thomas muttered wearily as he looked out over the desert of parched faces. "I didn't think there'd be this many people, Ma! Tell you what, we'll get home quick as we can, and cool off a little bit. Want to take you out to the fireworks tonight."

"You still got your money?"

"Course I got my money! What'd you think I done with it— throwed it away?"

"Well, it'd be a whole lot better off in my stocking!"

Thomas laughed at her. They had to go six squares east before they could finally get across the street, were both ready to fall by the time they came to Mrs. Marvin's boarding house.

Kate had her dress and top petticoats off and was watching Thomas snake down his suspenders when she saw his face fall. The next moment he was on the bed pawing his coat like a crazy man, his eyes wide, staring at the empty pockets. She needed no explanation—she knew the worst.

"Told you!" she said bitterly. "Always have to act like you know it all! Might've knowed there'd be somebody with light fingers who could tell you wasn't only a greenhorn!"

Thomas could have cried. All that he had promised himself— the fireworks, the Centennial, the ostrich plume to make Celia Sapooney's eyes pop when Kate went down the road was gone irretrievably! They would even have to borrow a few dollars to get back home.

V

1 Vanity and vexation, thought Thomas, and locked his mouth tight. It was early evening of the next day, a day that had seen him humiliated to beggary a dozen times. The affronts stuck in his craw. At the livery barn in Lancaster even Brierley had been condescending before he trotted out a sorry-looking hack. It was plain that he didn't believe Thomas's cock-and-bull story.

"Be there soon now, Thomas," Kate comforted when they passed Locust Lane on the way home. She patted Thomas's hand, made him rouse from his reverie.

"High time!" was his grumpy comment.

It was high time. Day had already lingered through yellow dusk, was going gray. Off to the north the wavy scallops of Black Man's Ridge looked like the back of a crawling monster. Barker's lights showed, then Brewster's and Jordan's. Around a bend in the road Church Hill humped up out of the night.

"Don't reckon you'd better say nothing to the kids about what happened in Columbus, Ma!" Thomas cautioned. "Wouldn't want them to get the notion we ain't dry behind the ears yet."

The old horse Brierley had hitched to their rented buggy made a long job of pulling to the top of Brewster's Hill, even had the nerve to try to muzzle a few heads of clover. Thomas was provoked enough to flick the whip.

"Just goes to show what a fellow can get into!" he said meditatively, without any thought that Kate's mind might be miles away from his own.

Before she had time to reply, their ears were assailed by the most infernal racket they had heard in months, even counting the brass bands in Columbus. All the fools in the county must be out with tinware and cowbells. Worse, the clamor had its origin just over the hill, almost certainly in their own dooryard.

This time Thomas really whipped up. The nag had enough left to scramble to the top of the rise, from where the home buildings loomed black against the sky. To their amazement the house was ablaze with lights from kitchen to parlor. It was too dark to mark anything with certainty, but Thomas could fancy the shuttle of bodies on the lawn.

"Now what in Jericho, Kate?" he asked with his mouth open.

"Reckon you know just as well as I do," she answered immediately. "It's bellers, that's what."

"You don't suppose Hocking—"

"I most certainly do. He's went and done it!"

Thomas saved his anger. He let the horse creep along at its own pace now—he wanted to get as much knowledge of the situation as he could. If what Kate thought was true—if Hocking had really married Elva Uny, he'd have to pay the penalty. He had been warned.

The lawn was alive with bellers; there must have been fifteen or twenty of them. Thomas pulled in under the poplar tree where his rig would be hidden by the screen of syringas in the corner of the yard. In the horrible tin-pan cacophony no one had heard him come. No one would have cared. The black figures kept running back and forth between the pine tree and the porch, one with a torch who seemed to be the leader keeping the din alive wherever it hushed for a second.

"Well, Thomas! You ain't figurin' to set here all night, are you!"

Thomas knew her mind as well as his own.

"Just been waiting to see if they'll haul Hock out," he said grimly.

He wasn't long in doubt—Hocking came out of his own free will. Instantly the clatter subsided. In the hush the lonesome crickets sounded eerie.

"What you want, you fellers?" they heard him bawl from the porch.

His idiocy was met by a scuffle of voices.

"You know what we want!" Ralph Tanterscham replied. "Either you're a-goin' to stand treat, or you won't sleep here tonight!"

To enforce the threat there was a rush for Hocking, but he was too quick. The front door slammed behind him, was bolted from the inside. The gang tried to break in, ran around to force the kitchen door. Thwarted in both attempts, they clustered together to debate strategy. Thomas knew their intention when he saw them boost someone up to the porch roof.

"Well, Thomas!"

He had no need for Kate to urge him—he was mad through. Not only must he be robbed, but he must have a fool for a son!

He carried the buggy whip into the yard with him, making no pains to employ stealth. At that his intrusion was a complete surprise. First intimation any of the rascals had of his presence was the sudden fury with which he reached up and began to flog the second figure shinnying up the porch post. "Get out!" he roared at the top of his lungs, and belabored those whose wits were sluggish. They ran like scared rabbits, leaving Tom Tanterscham trapped on the roof. In his panic he began to bleat, finally jumped over Thomas's head and limped off into the darkness. Thomas got the full benefit of a volley of curses.

In the shadows the gang reassembled while Thomas thrust Kate behind him and deliberated if he should go after them.

"Come on, stingy-gut, give us a dollar!"

"Get out!" Thomas shouted back, and ran forward to drive them. "Get clear off the place!"

Instead they began to throw at him. A tin can sailed past his head, a lump of cow-dirt caught him on the chin. To go after them in the dark was like fighting poisonous gnats. To make matters worse Kate kept pulling at his coattails. Out in the road a couple of the boys found his horse and buggy. There was wild hilarity as they scrambled to the seat of the rig and slapped down the reins. The frightened mare disappeared down the road, half a dozen of them screaming along behind her.

"Give us a dollar, stingy! Give us a dollar! Go on in and send Hocking out!"

The suggestion was enough to remind Thomas with whom he

had the greater quarrel. Kate was at his heels as he faced suddenly about and made for the door. "Now don't you go a-flyin' off the handle, Thomas!" she kept repeating as she tried to hold him back. "Don't you go a-flyin' off the handle!"

Thomas paid no heed. He leaped up the steps to the porch, used the whipstock to pound thunderously on the solid door. He didn't mean to wait, either. He knew where an ax stood in the corner of the smokehouse, and if Hocking didn't obey him, he'd use it.

2 Elva Uny sat in the best chair with her greasy yellow hair smack against Kate's best tidy. Hocking, more defensive, stood in the far corner like a prisoner at the bar.

"Well, what you aiming to do?" Thomas had at him for the third time. He had shut the door into the middle room—it wasn't decent that the other children should have to suffer.

"I don't know," Hocking drawled. "Farm, I reckon."

"Farm where?"

"Well—"

"Hocking means we ain't really got no plans yet," Elva put in. "He said as how if you just turned out your hand, you'd have room enough for us right here."

Thomas wouldn't listen to her. He hadn't looked once in her direction, could not have taken oath as to the color of her dress. Kate could have told that—dirty pink, and would certainly have added that as usual Elva had on no corset.

"You know what I told you, Hocking," Thomas said. "I meant every single word of it."

Hocking smiled slowly like some great dolt.

"I ain't saying you didn't."

"Well, you might just as well go now as later."

Hocking began then to play with the dish of pepper, cream, and sugar that Kate always kept on the stand to kill flies.

"Don't know what you got agin her," he tried feebly to argue.

"You ain't a-bein' fair, Papa Linthorne," Elva put in her oar. "I ain't maybe such a much, but I know when to come in out of the rain. And I'll take real good care of Hock, you see if I don't."

Kate had begun to soften despite her first indignation. Sight of

Hocking's confusion made her sympathize with the great over-grown boy who had only yesterday been her baby. When he saw the way her face kept twitching, Thomas knew he'd have to fight this battle alone.

"I don't care if you do or don't!" he answered the girl. "I won't make no secret of it: I didn't want you to have him, and I told him so. He knows what I said I was a-goin' to do if he took up with you. Told him fair and open. That didn't mean nothing to him, it don't mean nothing to me to have him around no more!"

"Thomas!"

"And what's more, he'll have to go right now!"

Kate cried, but Hocking only set his jaw.

"Told you he'd be like that!" he said to Elva as he pulled her up from the chair. "Can't be the boss of everything, he gets mad."

Thomas went white at the words. "Get out!" he commanded, and flung the door open so that they might see he meant what he said.

Hocking laughed nervously as a cabbage stalk came sailing into the light, held Elva behind him as they went slowly toward the steps.

Thomas slammed and bolted the door before they were off the porch, returned to hover over Kate who had slumped in the willow rocker. When she said nothing, either in recrimination or approval, he stalked past her and picked up the family Bible. Next to the title page was the page of records: births, marriages, deaths. Hocking's name was, of course, the first on the list.

Thomas studied a long time before he was sure of his will. It seemed petty to be headstrong, but with other children who must obey him it was foolhardy to be too lenient. Slowly, reluctantly, he got out his knife and cut out Hocking's name, then carried the tiny slip to the lamp and watched it wither in the flame. Kate sat im-mobile all the while, her mouth working, her tongue unable to form words.

In the silent kitchen, the girls and their mother white-faced and shaken, Thomas read Scripture:

To every thing there is a season, and a time to every purpose under heaven:

209

*A time to be born, and a time to die; a time to plant, and a time to
pluck up that which is planted;*
*A time to kill, and a time to heal; a time to break down, and a time
to build up;*
*A time to weep, and a time to laugh; a time to mourn, and a time to
dance;*
*A time to cast away stones, and a time to gather stones together; a
time to embrace, and a time to refrain from embracing;*
*A time to get, and a time to lose; a time to keep, and a time to cast
away;*
*A time to rend, and a time to sew; a time to keep silence, and a time
to speak;*
*A time to love, and a time to hate; a time of war, and a time of
peace.*

When he had read so far, he shut the Bible and looked at each of
them in turn.

"What I want you all to know is I told Hocking to go and never
come back," he said slowly. "And I don't want his name ever mentioned in this house again."

With that he rose and went up to bed while they all sat in frozen
silence. Kate and Charlotte were crying, but Faith stared straight in
front of her with a face like stone.

On the wall the clock proved traitor. "Hock-ing, Hock-ing,
Hock-ing, Hock-ing!" it ran on interminably. Kate endured the
torture until she could stand it no longer, then rose and stopped
the hands at exactly twenty-three minutes past eight. She had no
thought of the interpretation of her act. To the girls and Grover it
meant but one thing—that to her also Hocking was dead.

3   That autumn nothing went well with the Linthornes. They
heard of Hocking: how he had caught on as a tenant farmer
at the Orley place down on the Cedar Hill pike. They knew what
that meant. Orley's tenants were a byword in the township. They
looked starved, and they were starved. How Hocking could get
through the winter without anything laid by in barn or cellar was a
mystery.

That in itself was enough to worry Kate into bed, but it was not the end of her concern. As if to vex her, Thomas insisted on keeping Jed through the winter. If Kate had barely endured the man before, she hated him now. He ate Hocking's food; when cold weather came on, slept in Hocking's bed. And now there was no one sympathetic to her complaint, not even Charlotte. "Oh, he isn't so bad, mother!" she'd say whenever Kate brought her reproach. "He means well!"

Kate always met that with a "Humph!" Mean well! Hocking had meant well when he married Elva, and it had brought him only disinheritance. Thomas had meant well in turning the boy off, and he had brought down on his head not only the hatred of the Tanterschams but of the whole community. When people began to be silent to one's face, it was sure sign they talked behind one's back. At church there was never now the gossip and good fellowship there had been before. The Sapooneys, Brewsters, Tanterschams wouldn't speak—but they had reason for their disdain. What irked Kate was the way people like the Jordans, Sellerses, and Wendells acted.

And then, to top all the rest of the trouble, she had gotten a chicken feather in the apple butter. That was near the first of October, but the mishap preyed on her mind every blessed day. She always made nearly forty gallons of the spread, had orders in town for over half of it. Her reputation was based on the ritualistic way she did things; the aristocrats on Main Street Hill felt they could depend on her. What they would think if they found the chicken feather Kate could surmise. She couldn't go to each of them in turn and explain that Grover was stirring when a sudden puff of wind swirled the feather from the ground and dropped it right under his ladle.

The month of October wore on Thomas, too. Like Kate he knew the mesh woven about his name by evil tongues. He tried not to mind, tried to be as bluff and hearty as ever. He might have succeeded if it had not been for his own nature. Out in the barn he would find himself talking aloud, his justification uttered to Hocking, Lute Tanterscham, whoever he fancied the latest passerby might be. Somehow his arguments, though reasonable, always sounded hollow. "Pride!" he would often interrupt himself in self-condemnation. "Nothing but plain pig-headed pride!"

211

Nevertheless he held to his word. Hocking's name was not spoken—at least in his hearing. Neither did he apologize to the Tanterschams for the slur he had put upon Elva. As November neared and the contest between Harrison and Cleveland became more heated, Luther sometimes said a bantering word as he passed, knowing how Thomas meant to vote Republican. That was all that the families had to do with each other any more.

On election morning Thomas had a load of corn ready to haul to the elevator when Ralph Tanterscham walked into the yard.

"Voted yet?" he asked when he saw Thomas.

Thomas resented the strange question. "Reckon the election house ain't more'n open by now," he said.

"Republican, ain't you?"

"Always have been."

"How about that man of yours. He Republican too?"

Thomas would answer no more questions.

"What you beating around the bush for, Ralph?" he wanted to know. "Guess it ain't nobody's business but our own how we vote."

"Guess it ain't!" Ralph agreed, a little too saucily to please Thomas. "Only my old man sent me down to say that if you two are both for Harrison, and him and me for Cleveland, it ain't no sense going over atall. Can't do no more than kill each other's vote."

Thomas hesitated deliberately.

"Your father really say that?" he asked.

"Sent me over. Only he wants to know for sure, 'cause if you won't stay away, we ain't a-goin' to neither."

Thomas agreed to cancel out their votes without any more haggling. While they ate dinner that day he told Jed of the bargain he had struck.

That afternoon, however, while he and Jed were husking out from the shock, they saw Tanterscham's gray Molly frisk down the road. Thomas called Jed's attention—they both smelled a rat, although at that distance it was impossible to see who was in the rig.

"Best drive on in, I reckon," Jed suggested.

Thomas agreed. He didn't like the face of the thing; it began to squint.

Sure enough, the Tanterschams were still hanging around the election house when they drove up. Ralph looked crestfallen, but old Lute grinned from ear to ear. To Thomas's amazement he seemed to regard the whole matter as a good joke. "You shust vait!" he shook his finger at them. "You ain'd so schmardt!"

Thomas didn't know what to make of the business. It seemed that there was no ill will, that the words were spoken only in jest. A German gander like Lute Tanterscham wouldn't realize the seriousness of keeping a couple votes away from the polls in a close election, wouldn't comprehend that it might mean the difference between a Republican and Democratic administration.

For all that Thomas wondered, and was still wondering when the snow flew. On the night before Thanksgiving his straw rick burned and he barely managed to keep the flames from the barn. There was a light sift of snow on the ground, and for that reason Thomas walked the rounds the next morning to confirm his suspicion of incendiarism. Sure enough, someone had come up the run, crossed through the field behind the orchard. Jed denied that the big track was his, which left only four surmises: that it belonged to Bill Sapooney, Ralph Tanterscham, Hocking, or a tramp. One theory was as tenable as another; none satisfied.

When Thomas told Kate, she was very strange with him.

"I was you, I'd go right down and ask Hocking to come home," she said. "You got him on your mind."

Thomas froze. "You know I said I never wanted to hear his name mentioned again!" he reminded sharply. "I'll ask you to remember."

He didn't bluff Kate.

"I'll remember what I want to remember, and I'll forget what I want to forget," she said. "Only I won't do anything to keep you from acting the way you want. It's your sin, not mine."

Thomas bridled at that, but he couldn't get another rise out of her. He felt very desolate that day. He had counted on her support; if she turned against him like all the others, his cup of bitterness would be full to the brim.

4 On New Year's Day they had a real quarrel, the cause, Thomas's continued coldness to Ralph Tanterscham. Ralph had invited Charlotte to a watch party in Carroll the evening before, and Thomas had refused to let her go.

Kate was in one of her rare moods.

"It don't seem to make no difference to you she's getting so old that pretty soon there won't nobody take a second look at her!" she said tartly as she slapped pie dough.

"Don't matter to me if Ralph Tanterscham ever looks at her!"

"No, I reckon not! Or anybody else, for that matter. First thing you know you'll have an old maid schoolteacher on your hands!"

Thomas was amused. "She ain't only nineteen this year," he pointed out. "Born in '70."

"A girl ain't no spring chicken at nineteen, and don't you forget it! Trouble is you think Ralph ain't good enough for her. And if he ain't, then I'd like to know who is. Leastways he don't go off across country and sponge, like some other folks I could name."

Thomas tried to be reasonable.

"Guess you mean Jed," he said patiently. "You know he ain't got no home. And he don't sponge, anyway; he's as good a man as I'd want to come across."

"Always excepting your own son."

"See here, Kate," said Thomas sullenly, "I don't want to have a blow-up on New Year. Strikes me as how we could begin right, anyway!"

"Well, why don't you, then?"

"Why don't I what?"

"Go down and tell Hocking to come home. And stand out of Ralph's way."

Thomas got to his feet—this was serious business.

"I'm not taking my orders from you!" he said.

Kate thwarted him with sarcasm. "You know best about everything, don't you, Mr. Linthorne?" Her words stuck to Thomas like cockleburs.

"I didn't say I knowed best," he defended himself. "But I know what I think's right, and I do what I think's right."

"So does a mule!"

Thomas lost his head then. "I don't care what you think!" he shouted at her. "I've said my say about Hocking, and that's what goes! And I've said my say about Ralph Tanterscham and Charlotte, and that goes too! And when I need your advice, I'll ask for it!"

214

Kate was as mild as he was vehement.

"I wish you would," she said sweetly. "I'll have a lot of it thought up."

She left Thomas flat. He kept sputtering like a half-lit fire while she went about the business of baking. He knew he was making a fool of himself, but he certainly didn't mean to give up his principle. Somebody had to be the head of the house, and there would be no petticoat government in his. Kate would see it herself after a time—that Ralph wasn't a fit person to keep Charlotte company.

5 Through the processional of days they moved like strangers to each other. Except for the set of their minds, all things were the same as they had always been. On long winter nights Charlotte made leaf pictures from her accumulation of autumn rubbish: Niagara falls, a head of President Harrison, imaginary Swiss chalets. Sunday afternoons saw Kate set out her dish of tomato figs as she had always done. There were the same steaming footbaths for frostbite, the same sweet cream for chapped hands. When a skunk got under the porch, Thomas killed the scent by burning tar on live coals as he had done a dozen other times. Kate was even dependent enough to make her usual request for him to blow tobacco smoke into an inverted cardboard box to kill the lice on her house plants.

But all those things belonged only to the physical manifestation of life.

When spring came, Thomas escaped gladly to the fields. Out on the long slopes, sun in his face and the warm loam crumbling under foot, he felt free, as if he had escaped from unbearable bondage. Not given to worry, he nevertheless tried to be fair-minded. Attack his problem as he might, he reached but one solution—that he must not back down. It was unpleasant, of course, that there should be such great antipathy between Kate and himself, unpleasant that the neighbors must be alienated. But Hocking had made his bed and would have to lie in it. Ralph Tanterscham must be kept away from Grover and Charlotte. The Sapooneys must be made to realize the necessity of honest toil.

Only the Brewsters had the right of it with him. They had made him suffer for his folly more than they knew by their unrelenting attitude of distrust. He had been more than generous with them, had smoothed their way whenever he could. For all that, Jim's conduct had become ugly. This past winter there had been word three separate times that he was drinking again. Thomas feared that lapse more than any other. If Jim should lose hold on himself, become again the bum and rounder he had been before his marriage, then God pity Lucile and Judith.

6 One day when the wheat was yellow, Charlotte came to Thomas at noon as he was putting up the team. She wanted a party on her nineteenth birthday.

Ordinarily such a request would have been a little thing, but the fact that she came out to the barn showed her misgivings. They would have to invite the Tanterschams, Schraders, Sapooneys, Brewsters. Any one or all of the families might refuse to permit their children to come.

"What's your mother say?" Thomas asked as he unhitched.

"I don't think she minds," Charlotte said. "She wanted me to ask you."

"She tell you to come out here, did she?"

"No, she didn't," Charlotte answered firmly.

Thomas would have liked to say no, would have said no if the request had come from anyone but Charlotte. He was more than a little in love with his girl. In time Judith Brewster would have the same strong chin, the same dark cheeks flushed with geranium red, but her eyes would be more like Lucile's. Watching Charlotte as she stood in the open doorway waiting for him, strong in the wind as the wind was strong, Thomas knew his reluctant answer.

"What sort of doings you fixing to have?" he asked as he led the team to the trough.

"Well, there'll be a lot of people. Mother thought a lawn party would be nice. We could string lanterns."

Thomas nodded. "Would be real pretty," he tried to be enthusiastic. "Won't feel all cooped up like you would in the house."

A week passed during which nothing further was said, although Thomas knew instinctively that when he was away from the house

216

the talk was of little else. At the end of that time Charlotte came to
him again.

"I don't know what to do," she said. "Mother doesn't want me
to ask Jed. And I don't want not to because—well, it would look
too awful mean."

Thomas walked all around the hornet's nest.

"You ask Ralph and Tom Tanterscham?"

"Well, I sort of had to."

"How about Adolph and Lotus Sapooney?"

"I asked them too."

"Schraders?"

Charlotte thought she was being accused. "I have to invite the
people we know," she tried to defend herself.

"How about Judith Brewster?"

When Charlotte looked grave, Thomas knew that Kate had for-
bidden the girl.

"She's only twelve years old."

"Don't make much matter, does it? Wouldn't look right to have
everybody up and down the road and leave Judith out." He was
very circumstantial, matter-of-fact, but he knew he was not deceiv-
ing Charlotte one whit. That she should share his secret made his
face burn. "No, sir," he said with finality, "you have Judith same as
anybody else, even if she is just twelve."

Charlotte looked puzzled, was puzzled.

"You think I ought to have Jed, then?" she brought the conversation back to her question.

"Why, of course you ought. He won't be such great shucks at a
party, maybe, but there ain't no sense feeding your dogs so fat they
won't bark at tramps."

When Charlotte giggled, Thomas knew that he had made a
mistake in his metaphor. It was exactly what Kate always said about
Jed—that he was a tramp. Thomas knew better. One of the things
that puzzled him most in life was that women should throw their
combings at solid men and roll their hair on rats for every barfly
with handsome sideburns.

On the night of the party Kate was like a January thaw, but
Thomas did not mistake her. She was not content, only polite. It

was politic to pretend when honesty could result only in added ill-feeling. Lotus Sapooney could clack as well as her mother, and was equally willing. And what was true of Lotus was true in less degree of most of the others. As like as not they would be questioned as soon as they went home.

For all that, Thomas enjoyed the respite as he sat with Kate on the porch and watched the young folks out under the trees. Charlotte had used some of her own teaching money to buy the accordion-pleated lanterns, and she had not been stingy. There must be at least two dozen, all red and yellow, the tissue so thin that they tossed with every whim of the breeze. Under them the white muslin dresses were stained with softest color as the girls ran in and out of the rings playing "Drop the Handkerchief" and "Blind Man's Bluff."

They had all come, and Kate had met them graciously. Thomas had been watchful when Judith Brewster came down the road; he was afraid of what might happen. Nothing had, largely because Charlotte must have had the same fear. She had met Judith at the gate, had led her by a roundabout way to the lighted bedroom where the older girls were patting their hair for the last time. Coming down, the whole troop had gone out the back way to the well while Kate was in the parlor. It was all done so adroitly that it looked natural, even if it wasn't.

Now the game had changed again; it was "Hill-Dill," the one base an imaginary line drawn between the linden and the willow to the west of the yard, the other from the first pine to the fence on the east. "Hill-Dill," the "its" would cry, to send scuttling across the grass all those not yet caught. Thomas saw that the boys were pleased because the girls were so easily trapped behind the two peony bushes. Some of them seemed not to mind being roughly handled. Lotus Sapooney was the worst offender. Celia had fitted her out in a not-too-disreputable yellow voile, but it was so long that Lotus could trip whenever she pleased. That was whenever someone was near enough to catch her.

"Hill-Dill!"

"Reckon it's getting along about time for you to serve up, Ma," Thomas said drily when Mart McGruber got his hands on Darlene

Schrader and hugged her a little before he released her. Hang it, he hated to be a kill-joy, but such sport wasn't quite decent. It was hard to tell what young folks were coming to. In his day they had at least hired a buggy and gone off under a lonesome moon. Now they didn't seem to care a hoot where they spooned.

"Hill-Dill!"

"Guess you'll have to help me carry out," Kate said as she got up from her rocker.

Thomas was glad to have her need him. It was real nice, the way the womenfolks had things fixed, with board tables under the spokes of the three grape arbors. Kate had done things up brown: she had prepared not only marble cake and wine, but molasses pie and dried apple float as well. Thomas had to guess without success at the reason for such extravagance. Kate never liked to put on much show.

When the young people came trooping in answer to their call, he watched to see with whom Charlotte would walk. He was both pleased and disappointed—she was with Grant Schrader. Ralph Tanterscham hung back as if he didn't mean to eat with anybody in particular, and came at last with a cluster of the bashful ones that included both Judith and Jed.

While they ate, Thomas sat on the doorstoop with Kate. She was frostily familiar with him, had some pat answer for everything.

"Been a real nice party, Ma."

"Good enough, I reckon."

"Certainly think you ought to be proud of the way you put out."

Kate humped her shoulders. "Wouldn't be surprised if that cake's a little sad," she depreciated herself. "Get too much butter in it every single time I try to make it particular."

"Well, it looks like a real nice cake anyway."

They were startled by screams from the girls in the nearest arbor. One of the lanterns was burning. Thomas was closer than any of the rest, but they all came running after as he raced to slap out the fire. He was too late. The flames reached up for the cotton string on which four of the lanterns were hung, ate through it. In falling they all began to burn.

There was a mad rush to beat them out. Thomas saw Judith dart faster than any of the others, rushed to prevent her. The fire seemed to leap out at her flimsy skirt, to drown her scream. Like a living torch she began to run toward the gate, completely obsessed by fear.

Thomas hurled her to the grass, flung himself upon her, rolling her over and over. Nothing but his daring kept her from being horribly burned. The fire was out miraculously, her seared flounces and braids the only evidence that she had been endangered. She began to cry as he lifted her to her feet.

Then, from the back of the circle, he heard words that made his ears tingle. "Guess he ought to do for her," he heard Ralph Tanterscham say slyly. "He looks enough like her to be her old man any day in the year."

Thomas chose to ignore the remark, but he laid it up in memory. The words seared him as the fire had not. Through the sudden hush of the crowd he walked as a man doomed, his head hunched between his shoulders. Halfway to the house, he heard Lotus Sapooney's giggle break the spell that heard them all silent. He almost ran to escape into the darkness.

VI

1   That winter the cutters raced over the glazed snow as they had never raced before. Every night in December the lantern burned in the cellar to keep the fruit from freezing. Thomas melted tallow and beeswax together and stirred in lampblack so that the family would always go dry-shod, and Kate got into her muslin bags of tansy and horehound. Even Bill Sapooney worked to get in wood that he should have cut months before—he swore that he had seen the wild geese spelling ICE as they flew south over Church Hill.

In the slab shanty that Orley provided for his tenant, Hocking and Elva again froze and starved while they waited the baby that would come in March, but Thomas could not know. They were too proud to ask help. Some days they feasted greasily when Hocking had the good luck to find meat in his traps, but those days were far too few. Charlotte was their good angel. By sending through the teacher at Cunningham school, she could provide them with a few necessities without letting them know who befriended them.

Whenever the wind howled icily along the eaves as she sat in the snug warmth of the Linthorne kitchen, Charlotte thought of them and hated herself for being comfortable. She felt she could not confide in her father, for some reason would say nothing to her mother. But one night when the moon rode brittle through the sky and the thermometer dropped to ten below, she did something by stealth that neither of them would have approved. Onto the slab ice below her window, she dropped two of Kate's best comforters. Jed retrieved them for her, waited with the sleigh until she could sneak out. Charlotte pinned a five dollar bill to the comforters when she left them on the sandstone before Hocking's door.

So few were the miles between privation and plenty. At home the bins were full, the mows bursting. "Michaelmas day, half of your hay," Thomas always said, but the half would not be gone by Michaelmas this year. The end of the year saw him as well content as he had been for months. Kate was less hostile, the Tanterschams seemingly forgetful, the Brewsters and Sapooneys quiet. Balt Wendell had accosted him at the mill and had spoken about running a sugar camp together when the thaws came in February. Spence Vitt brought gifts of honey and wine. The debt to the Gregorys had been paid, and there was large expectation of being remembered when the old man should will. And partially because Charlotte was the teacher, but also because of the new esteem in which they held him, the neighbors asked if Thomas would use his box-sled to carry a load over to the spelling bee at Cunningham school. Joe Jordan had offered as the other driver.

Thomas shared the hilarity that bitter night. The moon was bright, the wagon bed deep with straw, the twenty-odd people behind him heavily bundled. Kate had stayed home, but Jed and Charlotte shared the seat. They sang as if their hearts would burst, most of the melodies maudlin. When he wanted, Thomas could boom like a bass violin; and tonight, to the great amusement of the children, he let his soul out. By the time they came to Cunningham, they were in little mood to spell.

But spell they did, and again Grover stayed up with the last Cunningham pupil. Como Cory was pronouncing the words, and having a hard time of it to keep up with the two racing thoroughbreds. *Phthisic, rheumatism, hyssop, ipecac, euchre, zephyr, victual, anachronism,* and *equanimity* they rattled off without batting an eye. Como couldn't floor either of them, finally gave up in chagrin and called the match a draw. While the women got into their big baskets of crullers and served up coffee in tincups, Thomas circled from group to group to bask in Grover's glory.

"That kid of yourn is sure cut out fer a preacher, Thomas!" old Bart Whitney commented as he stroked his white beard. "And that other one too, that Slivey kid. Goin' to let us all hear from 'em, that's what!"

"Won't be no preacher," Thomas smiled. "Lawyer, maybe."

"Well, he'll make a dang good somethin'. Got a head on his shoulders, you can see that."

Thomas was so intoxicated that he could not refuse Grover when he came around to ask if he might ride home in Ralph Tanterscham's cutter.

"What for?" he temporized. "Had a good time coming over, didn't you?"

"Yes, but he's got a new one. He just wants me to see how slick it is."

"All right, go ahead if you have to," Thomas gave in. "But tell him to be careful."

Fat chance of Ralph Tanterscham's being careful! As if to spite Thomas, Ralph waited until the two box sleds had pulled away, and then came racing down the road like mad. The gray rat of a horse he drove cut into the drifts to get around while the sled came perilously near going over.

Thomas bit his lip, but made the best of it. He could remember when Ralph Tanterscham used to gather fishworms in a bottle to melt into oil to make his joints limber. What he really needed was some fishworms oil for his brains.

2 On Christmas afternoon he had vicarious satisfaction for his grievance, and as usual he had to pay for it.

Because it was Christmas they were all in the house when Ralph arrived. Charlotte and Faith were cutting out Faith's new dress from the green wool Kate had bought for her present. Grover was propped up at the stove, playing hymns on a comb while he watched the progress of the checker game between Jed and Thomas. Kate was her usual self—she was never happy unless she was either cleaning up after one meal or getting ready for the next. She had decided on hominy and sausage for supper, to supplement what was left of the roast chickens.

Ralph came in after only a preliminary rap at the door. Oddly enough, he wore his store suit and coonskin cap, although it had been sleeting. Nobody stirred but Kate. To hear the to-do she made about the melting ice on Ralph's clothes, a person would think he had fallen into the river.

Ralph was both embarrassed and hostile, seemingly wanted to come over to the table where the girls were working, but could not because Jed and Thomas sat in his way.

"Oh, come on, take off your coat and stay a while!" Kate kept urging him. "Having hominy and hog for supper, if you've got a mind to the mess."

Ralph ignored her, kept looking at Charlotte. After a time the situation became so embarrassing that Thomas conceded the game and laid up the board.

"Have a chair!" he said roughly, and went past Ralph into the middle room. When Jed followed, Ralph grasped his opportunity immediately.

"Got something for you, Charlotte," he whispered as he came across to the table. From inside his coat he drew out a long, thin package that looked as if it might contain gloves or a fascinator.

To Kate's chagrin, Charlotte had to be stupid.

"Got something for *me!*" she repeated. "I don't know why."

"Christmas, ain't it!"

"Always have to act like the snake that got mixed up and swallered its own tail!" Kate scolded for Ralph's benefit.

Ralph held out the package, but Charlotte wouldn't take it. She flushed crimson, held her hands behind her as if to ward off temptation. Grover had to be officious by jumping from his chair and trying to push her.

"Coax her, Ralph!" he advised. "That's all she wants. Just wants to be coaxed like all the rest of them."

Charlotte boxed his ears. "You go sit down or I'll call Papa!" she warned. "And if it's any of your business, which it isn't, I don't want to be coaxed. I guess I know my own mind."

"Don't know much, then!" Kate sulked, and went out into the pantry to get away from her daughter's disgrace.

Ralph wouldn't retreat. "'Tain't much!" he urged. "Nothing but a little present. Come on, take it and forget about it!"

Charlotte felt pinned to the wall, but she still held back.

"I can't, Ralph," she explained quietly. "I don't like you well enough to take presents. I don't—I just don't think that way about you."

"It ain't a diamond necklace."

"I don't care what it is. I don't—don't you see, Ralph? If I took anything at all, people would talk. They'd say that—well, they'd just talk."

"Let them if they want to."

When she deliberately walked past him, he as deliberately caught and held her.

"Guess I ain't good enough!" he accused. "Guess that's what you mean—that I ain't good enough!"

"I didn't say that."

"I know what you said. Only it strikes me as pretty funny. You let a hired man lay right up against you all the way to Cunningham and back!"

"Ralph! Be quiet!"

"I don't have to be quiet. Guess I saw you when I went past. He was squeezing over against you as hard as he could squeeze!"

Unluckily he had his back to the middle door, couldn't see Jed come in. First intimation he had that Faith and Grover were not the only others in the room was that Jed spun him around.

"You don't say that to her," he told Ralph. "You say things like that to me."

Ralph dropped his package on the floor. He was scared, but he squared off. His fist caught Jed in the mouth, drew blood. Thomas was in the doorway by now, but would not interfere. When Kate came plunging from the pantry, he moved quickly to stand in her way. He was puzzled that Jed didn't seem to mean to fight back, only kept wiping the blood from his mouth as if he had been beaten.

That must have been what Ralph thought too—that Jed was licked. He watched his chance, when he got it moved in to strike again. This time he was not so successful. Jed simply grabbed the fist, twisted so as to throw Ralph up on his back, and the next moment had the door open. In full view of all of them Ralph sailed head over heels. Jed deliberately walked up to him, seized him by the scruff of the neck the moment he got his legs under him, and, like a terrier shaking a rat to pieces, ran him off the place.

In the house they all stood white-faced and spellbound, like mummies in a waxworks.

3 There weren't two ways about it—Kate would have her will this time. Merely exasperated, she showed spunk by jawing; determined, she turned to stone.

"It's either him or me, Thomas," she said with cold finality. "He don't go, I will! And I won't turn my hand to a lick of work until he does, neither!"

Thomas tried in vain to temporize.

"Pshaw, Ralph only got what he deserved!" he said. "Had it a-comin' to him for what he said to Charlotte."

"I don't care what he said. I ain't a-goin' to stand for any more interfering in my business! Uppity way that fellow takes on a body'd wonder who pays taxes on this place!"

Thomas got up and went out to the kitchen for a dipper of water in order to get time to think.

"Wouldn't look right, turning him out in the middle of winter," he said when he came back to the middle room. "He ain't got no place to go."

"Let him go where he come from."

Thomas slept on his trouble, but it was not his luck to dream any worthwhile solution. When at four in the morning he went out into the frost, Jed was before him with the lantern, as unconcerned as always. He seemed to have no idea what was up.

There was no breakfast waiting when they came steaming in from the chores. Kate wasn't about. Thomas finally routed out Charlotte and had her fry up a mess of potatoes and eggs, but he didn't feel like eating when the food came to the table. Jed was hearty—he never got up from table with his backbone scratching.

Thomas had a word in secret with Charlotte before they went

back out. "Your ma ain't sick, is she?" he asked hopefully while Charlotte pretended to be very busy.

"She's still in bed," Charlotte said. "I guess you know what's the matter with her."

"Ain't she countin' on getting up at all?"

Charlotte's face puckered as if she wanted to cry.

"You'd better do it—what she says," she managed to get out as she brought the dishpan from the hook. "Won't be any living with her unless she gets things the way she wants."

All that morning Thomas was a coward—he couldn't bring himself to turn off his man. He had come to depend on Jed's shoulders as much as his own, hated the thought of being forced into doing what he thought wasn't right. Twenty years ago he would have let Kate pack. Now it was impossible—their lives were like twin trunks from the same root.

Because of the holidays Charlotte was able to set out their dinner, but Kate's absence from table put a damper on all of them. As soon as they were done, Charlotte made some excuse to get Thomas into the icy parlor, faced him with stricken face.

"You've got to send him away, papa!" she said resolutely. "If you can't bring yourself to tell him, I think that—that maybe I can."

"What's your ma doing up there?" he asked as he hovered over her.

"She isn't doing anything. She won't even eat—she just sits and stares."

That decided it—without any more ado Thomas took the bull by the horns.

"Pretty short road that don't have a hill in it somewheres," he told Jed as they loitered in an empty box stall. "Far as I'm concerned, I'd just about as soon lose a jaw tooth as have you go. Guess Charlotte's pretty much the same way. Trouble is the missus gets notions once in a while. You live long enough, you'll know how it is."

Jed made things easy—he didn't seem to be at all concerned. Thomas waited in the kitchen while he went upstairs and threw his things together—he didn't have more than he could tie in a shirt.

By the time he came back down, Charlotte seemed to have flown the coop like all the others.

"Sorry I had to make a mess for you!" he said when Thomas was driving him into town. "Knowed Mrs. Linthorne never took much shine to me, but didn't know she felt that stubborn."

"What you aimin' to do?" Thomas avoided the miserable subject.

Jed laughed in a happy-go-lucky manner.

"Guess I'll catch on somewheres," he said. "Most generally do."

"How you fixed for money?"

"Got enough, I reckon."

Thomas wanted to ask a different question, but they were in the center of town and Jed was clambering down into the snow before he could blurt out the words.

"See here, Jed," he said as he pulled off his woolen mitten to clasp hands for the last time, "maybe I ain't got no call to say anything, but if not I won't do no harm. What I was a-thinkin' was— well, it's like this: you don't need to think you'll be plumb run off if you mosey out sometimes to see how things are a-gettin' along . . . Guess you know what I mean."

Jed only grinned, his big white teeth flashing.

"I won't get lost," he said. "You want to, you can carry that back to Charlotte."

He was gone then, and Thomas could only turn the horse. It was a desolate drive, the more lonely when he thought how things would be back home. Of one thing he was determined—no matter how things went, Grover would go away to school next term. The neighbors would likely think the Linthornes were trying to put on airs, and Kate might huff a bit because they were shorthanded about the place. But they'd all sit up and take notice in the end.

4   Charlotte ran away in May, the day after school was out. It was a clean job. She had confided in no one, had been as prim and prissy on the platform during the Last Day exercises as anybody could expect a lady teacher to be. One would think she meant

to hang on the rest of her life, that she hadn't a thought in her head not inspired by Quackenbush, Ray, and McGuffey. At supper that night she was her usual quiet self, except when she made them all laugh with a story about Lotus Sapooney's hard-boiled eggs that had been taken out from under a setting hen.

In the morning she was gone. Faith hadn't heard her get out of bed, although it was plain that Charlotte must have escaped before midnight. From her window it was an easy climb down the middle plum tree on the east side of the house. The trampled grass showed that Jed had waited for her there.

Kate accused Thomas of inspiring the plot, whereas the truth of the matter was that he was irritated because Charlotte had not confided in him.

"All your fault!" she started on him again when he came in for dinner. "Hope you'll like what you'll have to reap!"

"Don't know what you got sticking in your craw!" he grumbled back at her. "She didn't do no different than you done yourself."

"Yes, and you don't know how many's the time I wished I hadn't. Hain't seen nothing but trouble from the day I first set eyes on you!"

"Didn't see nothing much before, did you?"

Kate didn't really want to fight—her mind was too sore.

"You just don't know what she's a-gettin' into, Thomas!" she whimpered. "She won't have none of the pretty fixings she's been used to—and God knows what that man'll expect of her. Like as not he'll make her have a parcel of squawking brats that'll wear her thin before she's thirty!"

Thomas didn't mind her crying; he could always be philosophic when he saw her tears.

"She got a good man," he said doggedly. "Don't know what more you can expect. Certain sure he ain't the kind of fellow that'll plant acorns and count on sawing oak inside a year."

"He ain't nothing but a big overgrown animal! All he was and all he ever will be!"

"Well, that's either so or it ain't so," Thomas said judicially. "If he is, it's her bad luck, not yours. If he ain't, you got no call to fret."

They had a letter from Charlotte two days later. She apologized, but it was plain she wasn't sorry. She and Jed were on a little Rush Creek hill farm. They had a cow that Charlotte had named Muley after her mother's favorite—Jed was expecting her to calve any day. Charlotte wanted her dresses and things she had left behind when she ran off, would count it a big favor if Kate would pack them all in a big box so that she could send after them.

Instead Thomas loaded the spring wagon with all he could carry and drove down. Kate wouldn't budge, but she was anxious enough for news when he got back the next day.

Thomas purposely exaggerated. What he knew, and what Kate could understand from his indirection, was that unless they got better land, Charlotte and Jed would have a hard row. For all that, Thomas envied them. They both had acted like two kittens that didn't know their business in life was to grow up and catch rats.

5   It was a lonesome year—without Charlotte's voice the house was haunted by silence. Out in the fields, even, Thomas was puzzled by the strange sense of desolation that obsessed him. The meadows were vivid green because of the long spring rains, the pasture roses and trumpet creeper bright under the June sun. By the first of July the wheat was yellow and the blackberries had begun to plump. They were all unreal. Thomas saw as in a dream, shouted to the horses to prove himself awake.

Part of the trouble was, of course, that there was now no one to help him. Two years ago both Hocking and Jed had been blundering about, last year Jed alone had kept him company. With two or three in the field there would often be chance meetings in the fence corner where the water jug was hidden away beneath the elderberries. Stopping to talk a few minutes while they breathed the teams, they would hear sheep bells on the distant rises, halloos from far farms, the long whistle of the train as it crept north through the valley. Coveys of quail paraded along the margins of the field, crows croaked defiance from the woods, bright-striped chipmunks scurried away from frightening feet. Now, it seemed, all these things had been but imagined. While he rested the team, Thomas strained his ears to listen, as often as not was walled by silence.

He tried Grover at the plow, more to keep himself company than from hope of getting work done, but after a week or two let him go again to help Kate about the house and garden. Grover was no good in the field. Either he would burn himself up in the first hour or dilly-dally all the day. Try as he would, he couldn't run a furrow straight. Thomas released him without regret. There was little satisfaction in being a martinet.

What puzzled him more than his own stagnation, however, was the condition of the Brewster farm. Jim hadn't plowed, hadn't dropped a hill of corn. The wheat was yellow around the islands where the old shocks had stood, but last year's timothy field had been allowed to go to weeds. In the garden Thomas saw the bright sunbonnets where Lucile and Judith worked, but never sign of Jim.

July brought waves of heat to pull the corn out of the ground and fully ripen the grain. Although he complained of the drought, Thomas went gladly to join the threshers. Once again he was happy. For the tenth time he heard Tom Barker swear that one of his kids had rolled a hoop-snake home, listened to Cory's confusing harangue on the subject of free silver, laughed at the way Pride strangled because he wasn't provided with a mustache cup. When they were at Wendells's finishing up, there was a new topic of discussion: a fellow named Garshwin wanted to start revival meetings during August. Thomas didn't care much one way or the other because of his membership in Lancaster, but he couldn't sit back like a bump on a log.

"Trouble with a lot of them fellows is they want to make everybody think God's just a cranky old man out setting traps so's he'll have plenty skins to stretch on the barn door!" he said when the discussion grew heated. "Truth of the matter is—"

"Truth of the matter is they may be partly right," Amadias Pride broke in. "Take this idee of orig'nal sin, frinstance. Ain't a man here would ask a kid to pay up bills his old man owed. But the way the Bible reads you come down into this world so dirty you can't never do enough to get yourself clean."

"Like to know why you can't! Man tries his best, he certainly don't have to be much afraid!"

Arm to arm, elbows wide, their forks poised on end while with quick thrusts of their heads they gulped at the laden tines, they sat and shouted themselves hoarse. Bill Sapooney was the funniest—it took him so long to sputter that by the time he passed his "b-b-b-but" someone else had the floor. Thomas tried to keep his head, but it was hard with all the rest of them jumping on him. Just when it looked as if bitter words might be spoken, someone remembered how pleased Flory Wendell had been when Balt went down in '83, and how she had lit into him two hours later when she learned he was only snoozing under the pew.

In the general laughter Thomas escaped further persecution.

"You can all make danged fools of yourselves that want to!" he said as he got up from the table. "I'll stay home and sleep."

He heard the flurry of talk as he went out into the yard. He had a notion what would be said—he knew he was not as popular as he had once been. That was the pity of it: the world was full of people who tried to make a man color his life according to their own stripe, and who yelped he was bound for the hot place if he wouldn't!

VII

1 As ever Kate had taken advantage of the harvest to stuff the ticks and lay the front room carpet on fresh straw. Thomas wooed her by working the carpet stretcher, even fashioned a tin-can footstool that she covered with a strip of green ingrain. She was proud of the spot of color it made by her favorite cradle rocker, as proud as she was of her postcard rack with its gritty white icescapes that scintillated in the lamplight.

After the revival started they often sat together on the front porch at night so that they could join in the hymns. Zeke Sellers led, his cavernous bass somewhat sweeter than the chorus of frogs in the cattails down along the creek. There were always a half dozen of the old-time favorites before the harangue, songs like "There Is a Land of Pure Delight," "Rock of Ages," and "Nearer, My God, to Thee." Half asleep in his porch rocker, his body blissfully tired after his long day in the burning sun, Thomas would hear Kate join in the choruses. When he knew the tune, he sometimes sang with her in an apologetic way.

They wouldn't go across the road, although Faith and Grover were over every night. Thomas laughed up his sleeve at the stories the children brought home about the evangelist. Garshwin's black string tie and white bush beard made him look as sensible as a judge, but he turned out to be a ventriloquist and a rope artist. Both proficiencies attracted crowds. Each night before dusk the nearby families that wanted good seats would come stringing down the road, the barefoot children kicking up dust as they ran ahead, the menfolks loitering behind. Later the rigs began to arrive, some of them with sparks who brought girls from as far away as Carroll and Ringgold. Later still the hellions drove into the lot, to hang outside the doors and windows and hoot all through the service. From hear-tell they had their money's worth. Garshwin would have everyone laughing at his innocuous antics as he danced through the rope. Then, suddenly, the play would stop. *Whoosh!* the lariat would leap across the pews to entangle somebody's head and shoulders. "Another sinner caught for the Lamb!" he would yell as he pulled the noose taut. "Come right on up to the mercy seat, brother! God's a-helpin' me hold you fast!"

Such a travesty was hardly to Thomas's stomach. "Don't you play the fool and get down!" he warned Faith every night as she started out. "God ain't running no medicine show."

Faith was always as demure as a pansy, but Thomas wasn't sure how far he could trust her. He didn't have to be afraid about Grover. As like as not he'd be found outside the windows with the rock-throwers and shouters.

On the last night of the revival his curiosity finally got the better of him. It had been a boiling hot day, but with dusk a little breeze began to nuzzle the flaccid leaves. Kate kept moving her palmleaf fan as her rocker creaked back and forth across the loose boards, although she didn't join in any of the songs. When finally the sound stopped, Thomas thought she was asleep. He was surprised to hear her call him when he got up to tiptoe inside.

"Couldn't we go over, Thomas, maybe just for a little while? It's the last night."

Thomas hesitated—she had spoken his own mind. "Won't be no place to sit down," he pointed out.

"Well, we can stand up in back or along the sides."

Thomas grumbled, but he put on his shoes and buttoned his shirt. "Whyn't you say you had a notion?" he complained as they crossed the road. "Just about time for church to leave out now."

It wasn't at all; in fact it appeared the final service would last all night. Under the sick green light Garshwin was dancing like a Comanche, his long rope trailing behind him. His face was beefsteak red, his eyes bloodshot as he shouted sin into the far corners of the room. "Won't you come up and be saved, brother!" he roared at a cornstalk fellow who was a total stranger to Thomas. When the lout didn't respond, Garshwin did. "I'll be damned if I do, and I'll be damned if I don't!" his falsetto quavered back from the pew. He drowned the general laugh in another torrent of invective. Like a whirlwind he raced up and down the aisle, accusing, cajoling, threatening. Women wept. Up beside the pulpit Naomi Sellers and Flora Wendell ministered to the fallen who were laid in front of the altar.

Thomas was disgusted, but he stuck it out for Kate's sake. In the churning crowd behind the pews were fifty people he didn't know, most of them come only for the show. Thomas resented them, at the first chance led Kate down the aisle to a seat that had just been vacated. "What you think of him?" he whispered while they snuggled down together. "Reckon he's got the gift of gab all right!" Kate answered without committing herself.

The meeting dragged on interminably. Wagram gave testimony. They prayed for Serene and Margaret Promise, who were down and couldn't come through. Balt Wendell got up with sleepy eyes and began to tell what a wastrel he had been before he met Flora. Played cards every night at Hoster's livery barn. Drank, too, and smoked his stomach raw. It was only after he met the clean, sweet girl who became his wife that he began to see things straight. "Yessir," he grunted lethargically, "they ain't nothin' like religion. It'll do for every one of you folks here just what it done for me."

"Joy in your bones!" Garshwin roared to the chorus of amens. "Praise His holy name, brother! Praise His holy name!"

Thomas wanted to snicker. "She put him up to that, Flory did," he nudged Kate. "Tell by the way he acts."

The shouting slackened, but few went home. At ten o'clock the room was still sticky with packed, sweating bodies. Children lay on their mothers' laps, eyes tight. Outside there was periodic bedlam. The night was so close that it was impossible to shut the windows, but Garshwin paid no attention. He could howl down any hoodlum.

"Got enough, Kate?"

"Guess so," Kate yawned. "Best go up there in front and tell Faith to come on home, hadn't you?"

235

Thomas was shy. "Where's she sitting?" he asked warily. "I don't want to start down in front."

"She ain't far—only right up there with the Sapooneys."

Thomas waited until Garshwin had gone back to the altar. His right leg was numb as he shuffled forward; it made him limp. Awkwardly he stood in the aisle and motioned Faith. She was startled to see him, couldn't get free because she held the Sapooney baby in her lap. "What you want?" she kept whispering, so inaudibly he couldn't understand. "I want you to come on home!" Thomas said aloud.

"Come clear on up here, brother! There's more room at the mercy seat!"

Thomas fled before the maniac. His long strides had taken him halfway to the door before he saw that his way was blocked by Jim Brewster. Thomas froze, his spine like ice. Face to face, they stood like figures in a play, the contretemps the cause of their paralysis.

Jim was drunk, but he was the first to recover. "Listen, everybody!" he shouted. "Guess you all know me, most of you, anyway. I'm Jim Brewster. I just come over here to say—to say—"

Some of the men standing near tried to shut him up, but Jim lurched away from them, squeezed past Thomas, and ended up by bumping into Garshwin.

"Praise the Lord!" the evangelist panted while he held to a pew. "Go right on down front, brother—God's awaitin' for you!"

"I just come over here to tell all of you that—"

Jim paused dramatically, leered at Thomas who was still stiff. Kate had come back from the door, was poking her head through the fringe of men. In the dead hush they heard only the catcalls from the bums outside: "Put him out! He's soused! Put him out!"

Jim paid no attention, balanced his tongue and legs by supreme effort.

"—to tell you that Tom Linthorne there stold my wife! You ask him—he stold my wife. And what's more, he's the pappy of my kid. Only she ain't mine—she's his'n and he's her pappy. You just ask him!"

Thomas almost fell through the door. He forgot that he had come with Kate, that he was waiting for Faith, forgot everything but his own guilt. In the grove outside the trees whipped in the wind that swirled dust from the road. His throat felt dry—he kept gulping as he ran. Without conscious thought, he knew that Jim's open accusation would ruin him, would pull down the house and lives he had been so many years in building.

2
That was on Wednesday night.

Thomas had not foreseen Kate's reaction. "No sense you acting like a whipped dog!" she said drily when she caught him tiptoeing through the house. "What's done's done!"

He felt better when he knew she didn't mean to make anything of the mess. He couldn't understand her at all—she was as unpredictable as February weather. He had expected her to cry, to storm; instead she was so solicitous in the next few days that he felt queer.

He had not had to face any of the neighbors, and none had called in at the house. That in itself was not ominous—it was a busy time of year. Thomas wasn't afraid of the men. It was the women who made laws and set standards. Men might bluster, but they learned what they were supposed to think after the coal-oil lights went out at night.

Just at dusk Saturday he was coming up from the barn with the milk when he heard a strange crying sound from the direction of the Brewster house. He set down the milk pails, listened with all his ears. Save for the jarring of the frogs and the vibrant pulsing of the crickets, the night was very still, heavy with coming storm. There was no mistake—his foreboding was true. Either Lucile or Judith was crying. There was long silence between the plaintive moans; then, on an eerie high note, the clamor would begin again, to subside in a strangled sob.

Thomas shivered as if he had seen a ghost. The wailing of a woman had always made his flesh creep, even when he knew the cause of her distress. Distance and dark did nothing to add comfort. With vague certainty he accepted his own implication in the tragedy.

As quickly as he could, he brought the pails to the springhouse and hurried back through the dark to the line fence. Hidden there under the Osage orange, he waited for words that would give him direction. There were no words, for a long time nothing but silence. Then from the kitchen, where the only light in the whole house burned, the wailing began again, to mount higher and higher with the passing minutes. This time Thomas knew—it was Judith.

He wanted to break through the wagon-gap and go to her across the weed-grown pasture, but dared not. It maddened him, this perversity of man-made convention. She was his child, by Jim's own admission, by every line of body and every mood of expression she was his, and all he could do in answer to her need was stand in the prison of night, dumb to her pleading.

His forehead was beaded with cold sweat when he stumbled back to the house. He wanted to tell Kate, to ask her advice. He had to have some counsel or he'd go mad. Kate wasn't belowstairs, didn't even answer at first when he called up the well.

"Kate! Kate, you up there!"

He heard a door open, a step in the hall, then Kate's business-like voice, "What you bawling about, Thomas? Ought to know by this time that I have to help Faith take her bath on Saturday night!"

Thomas gulped for words without finding them.

"Well, I ain't got all night!" she scolded again. "What you want?"

Thomas didn't dare tell her.

"Just wanted to tell you it looks like maybe it's a-goin' to storm," he said lamely.

"Don't expect me to stop it, do you?"

"Think I ought to go out and drive the cows in before one of them gets struck?"

He heard the upstairs door slam—that was his answer. It was enough to satisfy him—at least it put an end to the matter.

3 The storm would break within a half hour. Thomas paced the yard in the sticky night, listening, listening. There was nothing now, nothing but the low growl of thunder over behind Black Man.

Overhead clouds scuttled across the faint stars, began to pile down toward the hills. In the southwest the sky cracked apart like an egg-shell; around the horizon and off to the north ran the phantom flutter of heat lightning. Thomas saw the white leghorns roosting in the peach tree, hurried to put them inside the henhouse. From the pasture the horses raced home, their hooves rumbling over the hollow earth. A sudden stab of fire etched them against the dark with streaming manes and tails. Thomas went on to the barn, shut them into their stalls.

When he came out again, the wind slapped him in the face. He heard the house door slam shut, the crash of a rocker as it went over on the porch. The next bright flash showed the willow tree like flowing water, its long branches stretched away from the storm.

He had to run for the house, was half drenched before he managed to plunge through the door. Kate bolted it behind him, ran to drop the windows.

"Grover home?"

"Thought you sent him to town with Jordans."

"Well, ain't he home yet!"

"Don't see him, do you?"

Kate pulled the shades and brought out the Bible, settled down by the kitchen lamp. It was so close in the room that Thomas could hardly breathe. After a time he could stand it no longer, must walk into the middle room to hold the door wide. The night was white; the wind enveloped him in fine mist. Already he could hear the slur of water down the cistern spouting, the puddled dripping from the eaves.

Above the storm Kate howled at him, "Thomas, you shut that door! You know lightning follows a draught!"

He indulged her fancy, went back to melancholy silence in the kitchen where the rain rattled furiously on the tin roof. Kate kept her lips moving as she spelled over the words of her talismanic charm—it was a part of her inheritance to believe that sudden death might be averted by drawing the shades and getting out the Bible. "Bet you the cellar's flooded," Thomas said when she caught him looking at her. She ignored his prosaic bravery.

He was worried, couldn't forget Judith's crying, wanted Grover to be home. Joe Jordan would likely keep him down there until the rain was over, if it would ever be over.

The wind kept rattling the windows demoniacally. At times the whole house seemed to sway.

Then, above the whinnying of the wind, he heard the sound of stumbling feet. He thought it was Grover, leaped to throw the door wide. Kate's lamp was blown out at once, but she didn't complain. Thomas pulled down a coat from the rack, held it across the door to shield her as she crept behind him. For once they both prayed for a flash of lightning. Out in the dark they heard Joe Jordan's voice. "Thomas! Thomas!" he kept shouting as he crept along the grape arbor, his eyes as blind as a bat's. They didn't have to be told he was scared. Never before had his voice possessed that high-pitched intensity, strident above the gale.

Thomas caught him at the edge of the porch, led him into the kitchen. Kate had a match ready, lit the lamp as soon as the door was closed. It showed Joe's eyes as big as saucers, his face milky. The water ran from him like melted tallow while he tried to get out something articulate.

"Grover down at your house, Joe?"

Joe nodded, and kept on nodding and nodding with slack jaw. He seemed to be afraid of Kate, couldn't make up his mind to speak in front of her.

"Ain't nothing the matter, is there?"

"It's Jim Brewster, Thomas!" Joe finally blubbered. "That girl of hisn's down there cryin' her eyes out. Her mammy's done run away and left her. She's all by herself."

Thomas almost shook the rest of it out of Joe.

"Where's Jim? What about Jim? . . . Ain't nothing the mat—"

Joe wouldn't let him go on, instead held his hand over Thomas's mouth.

"You'd best get your coat and come right on over," he babbled solemnly. "Can't never tell what might happen if he has to stay where he is all night."

As they went out the door, Kate's startled sob told Thomas that she had understood.

Thomas kept Joe's hand, pulled him along through the mud as if he were a baby. While they ran Joe kept blabbering incoherently. Thomas could make out only that Jim was down in his barn—it seemed Joe wasn't certain what had happened to him. Like as not he'd fallen somewhere while he was drunk.

In their haste they had forgotten a lantern, had to stop at Jordan's to get one. Mrs. Jordan was across the road with Judith, Grover said. He himself seemed unconcerned, his chief worry whether he could get home with a dry skin. Thomas ordered him out into the weather willy-nilly. "Shame on you!" he snapped when Grover hesitated. "Your mamma's down there without nobody to keep her company, and you know it!"

They crept by the Brewster house silently, waded ankle-deep through the mud to get down to the barn. Joe had left the door swing in his fright. It slammed in the wind that kept rattling the clapboards on the hen-house. Thomas was ahead with the lantern, thrust it before him as he stared through the open barn door. The place was empty. Jim had shoved his hay-rake and cultivator clear against the back bins as if he never meant to use them any more.

"Ain't nobody here atall, Joe!" Thomas shouted to be brave. His voice flung back at him, calling him coward.

For answer Joe only pointed, his long, skinny arm slanted toward a corner of the mows.

Thomas shifted his lantern, held it high over head. He saw Jim's feet first, then his sagging arms, his neck stretched to a full six inches by the rope that had cut into his flesh. He flinched when the light reflected from the staring eyeballs, fell back against Joe, who was shivering like a leaf in an autumn wind. "Figure he's dead, Thomas, don't you?" Jordan quavered. "Looks dead from down here!"

Thomas pushed him back out into the rain, then closed and barred the door.

"We'll leave him till morning and cut him down then," he said curtly. He felt sick inside, wanted to vomit, to get away from Joe, from the whole neighborhood. Instead he knew he could not, that the finality of this single act meant he must stay.

4   Dwarfed by the mass of hills momently discovered by light-ning, their strength puny to match the howling accost of the wind, Thomas and Judith crept along the slippery road, hand locked in hand. Thomas thrust a little ahead in the vain attempt to shield the girl. He had insisted she wrap herself in one of Lucy Jordan's shawls, but it was soaked before they left the yard.

If only Kate would receive her! She would need more than a dry nightgown and the pillow beside Faith. So much might be done by a word, the touch of a hand. Kate could hardly be blamed if she were not gracious. How much she had suffered already, how much more she must suffer with Judith actually in the house, Thomas had no way of knowing.

Here on the road it was useless to try to say a heartening word to Judith. Storm was master of the senses, buffeted consciousness into a blind, deaf, wordless thing. His face ran with rain. The wind sucked his lungs flat, pummeled him so that he lurched like a drunken man. By intuition he kept landmarks: the line fence, the sassafras thicket by the stile, the long curve home. He looked in vain for the house light—it would be hidden behind the grape arbor.

Lightning showed the wagon gate and the weed-matted ditch almost full of yellow water. Thomas counted a hundred steps be-yond, guided Judith across the plank that led to the pickets. He did not hesitate—he knew his duty. His concern was all for her, hardly more than child, so soon to be woman. No matter how Kate re-ceived them, no matter how silent or sharp she would be in the days to come, she could not bruise his spirit as she might crush Judith's.

In the lee of the porch Thomas drew her close, almost carried her across the flags. He wanted her to acknowledge him, love him; he needed her dependence as she needed his strength.

The arbor, the moss-slippery stoop, the door, the lamp—Kate. She stood in the very center of the room, calm, unsmiling, her hands folded in her apron. The light shone so obliquely that it did not reveal her eyes and mouth. Thomas could not guess her atti-tude. He was embarrassed, held Judith behind him.

"Brought Judith along home with me, Ma," he heard his lips stumble. "Guess she'll stay a few days."

He knit his brows, shook his head ever so slightly to show Kate she must not question. Judith had to step around him so that he might close the door. He made a great ceremony of the task, deliberately waiting until he heard Kate move forward. When he turned again, she was taking the dripping cashmere from Judith's shoulders.

"Well, I declare, child, you're wet as a drowned biddy!" she said with flat solicitude. And then to Thomas, "You better mix you up some whiskey and water. No sense taking your death of cold!"

That was their strange homecoming. Thomas reflected as he reached down the balsam bottle from the pantry shelf that some far day would be last, as this was first. Never stability, never the summit attained, to be held against time and fate. What must be endured by all of them before Judith said her last good-bye!

O wise Solomon! Thousands of years before he had perceived the heart of the mystery. "What profit hath a man of all his labor which he taketh under the sun? One generation passeth away, and another generation cometh, but the earth abideth forever."

5 He was to learn the price he must pay Kate the very next morning. She had fried pumpkin flowers waiting for him when he came in from the chores, but the set of her jaw and the cool deliberation with which she set out the cakes betrayed her mind.

"I don't want you should work today, Thomas," she said the minute he was finished returning thanks. "I want you should go down and fetch Hocking back home."

Thomas gorged great mouthfuls in silence.

"Reckon you know I promised Joe Jordan I'd sort of help him with—with what's got to be done down there," he jerked his head toward Brewster's. "Wouldn't look right if I was to back out."

"There's time in the day for everything that has to be done," Kate said quietly.

Thomas didn't bargain. If it weren't for pride, and the distressing presence of Elva the rest of his life, he wouldn't mind having Hocking come back. But to have to crawl to such a woman was as much as he could stomach.

Nevertheless he hitched up as soon as dinner was over. He

drove reluctantly, let the horse walk fully half the way. As he came out of Gregory Lane, he saw with surprise that there were gypsies camped in a wedge of woodland across the road from Sellers's. He pulled in, stared his fill without anyone's taking notice of him. He didn't like having the varmints around. Pack of common thieves— that's what all of them were! He had his say, he'd run them off. Ought to be on a reservation like Indians.

He was still grumbling when he passed Orley's and could see across the corn the mournful tenant shanty under its lonesome pine. He tried to prepare a set speech, failed in every attempt. That in itself made him furious—that he should be so inarticulate. He certainly didn't want it to appear that he was asking a favor.

Hocking was bronzed by the sun, a great brass giant in a sleazy denim shirt and straw hat that was almost blown to wisps. In his hands he held the bucket with which he had been going out to slop the pigs, as he had held it the past quarter hour when it might so easily have been set down.

Thomas was disconcerted by the faraway look in his eyes, his utter lack of words.

"Well, it's like that, Hock," he said for the tenth time. "Guess maybe I'm pretty hot-headed—only you oughtn't to hold that against me the rest of your life."

Hocking's expression did not change in the slightest.

"Guess we're a-doin' all right," he said coldly.

"Ain't nothing ever so good it couldn't be better."

"We're a-doin' all right."

It was a lie—nothing would ever go right with Orley's tenants. How could it? The man was a miserly, grasping skinflint, sharp as the edge of an adze. Thomas had heard of his agreements. Half the corn, half the grain, half the fruit, with the penalty of disproportionate shares in case a man was off sick or had sickness in his family. To hear Orley tell it, it was he and not God who sent rain.

"You won't come home, then?"

"Guess not."

Thomas shifted uneasily from foot to foot. For the first time he realized what Hocking had been through. It hurt him to know that his son was so set against him.

"Don't be so hard with me, Hock!" he pleaded. "I said I done

wrong. You want me to, I'll go on in and tell Elva the same thing. I
can't say nothing more than that, can I?"

"No sense pullin' up now. We're a-doin' all right."

Thomas had to be content with that as his answer.

He was more tardy on the road home than he had been in coming—he was afraid to face Kate. Worse, she might take out her spite
on Judith.

When he reached the turn in the road, he looked in vain for the
gypsies, was amazed that they could have picked up like butterflies
without leaving a trace of their recent occupancy. He thought for
a while that they might have gone to his woods, but there were no
wagons among the trees, no smoke that betrayed an encampment.

At home, however, he knew that they had not flown far. A swart
crone with a couple of yapping dogs at her heels was coming out of
the yard when he got there. She gave him the courtesy of a hard
look. Thomas returned her stare with interest, pulled in with a proprietary air. The grandmother ignored him, lackadaisically loitered
down the road toward Sapooney's.

Thomas went in without unhitching.

"What'd she want?" he demanded the minute he saw Kate.
"What'd that gypsy want?"

"Who said she wanted anything?"

"She tell your fortune?"

Kate ignored his question, and at the same time gave answer to
it. "You don't have to tell me—Hocking ain't coming," she said as
she walked into the middle room like a person dreaming. "And the
worst of it is that that ain't all!"

Thomas wanted no nonsense. He sat stolidly by the kitchen
table and waited until Kate should reappear. When she came out,
her face was so drawn he knew she had been crying.

"What'd that woman tell you?" he demanded again.

He had to fight to worm out her secret. It was not that the gypsy
had said things, but that she had refused to say anything. Kate had
given her a silver dollar, but instead of having her fortune read had
been frightened half out of her senses. The prophetess had taken
but one look at her hand before she quickly shoved back from the
table.

"Didn't say a single solitary word," Kate confided tearfully.

"Just kept a-shakin' her head like that and backed right out through the door!"

His bad humor was intensified when he went out to stable the horse. Down at Brewster's he saw a rig roll up behind the black tandem that the undertaker drove. Joe Jordan had promised to go in after the man, but had evidently taken his good-natured time about it. Sight of the equipage was chilling to Thomas. It meant not only the nausea of burial but the accusation of staring eyes. He would have to take Judith, and Judith would likely carry on as if Jim were her real father.

VIII

1 Two days after the funeral Kate was at him again—she
wanted to pick up and move to town. It was plain she was
afraid. In the house she hated to be alone, was always with Grover
or one of the girls. And in the dead of night when the house was
frozen fast in black silence, Thomas would hear the sharp intake of
her breath as she turned in bed. He bridled at his helplessness,
would not let her know that he had heard her sobbing.

But the more he thought of her proposal, the more certain he
was that he would never agree to it. This was his life—the land.
Here not only his few acres belonged to him, but the seasons and
the eternal hills as well.

All things familiar were dear. Under the eaves of the musty old
barn, mud-daubers and swallows had built for unnumbered gen-
erations. On the roof of the shed there were always racks of apples
drying in the sun; in the rose-bowered springhouse the icy runnel
of water forever sluiced around the crooks of milk set to cool in the
trough carved from the sandstone.

The year breathed like an animate thing—each dawn the world
was newmade. Spring stitched the meadows with fresh green,
bound fascinators of dogwood and redbud around the heads of the
hills. In the woods maidenhair and bladder ferns curled from the
rock ledges. By early June there were fireflies over the clover, white
pyramids of bloom on the horse chestnuts and catalpas.

Deep summer was more glorious. Over the tawny wheat red-
winged blackbirds flew from hedge to hedge; in the sky buzzards
hovered on the rim of the sun. The cattle grazed meadows streaked

with butter and eggs, bound with stake and rider fences heavy with bindweed and trumpet creeper. Monarch butterflies hung over the pleurisy weed, finches made fast to the sunflowers, hummingbirds darted over the pink heads of phlox.

How leave the patch of thyme that had escaped from some old garden, or the pennyroyal and wintergreen that were gathered so carefully each year? How give up the pull of the plow as it curled black loam, the tumult of threshing, of haying, the lonesome joy of wading into the sharp-bladed corn with heavy knife? Or the hoards of the year: berries and haws, hazelnuts from the thickets along the roads, greasy black walnuts, butternuts, shellbarks, wild grapes, persimmons, pawpaws that tasted like over-ripe bananas?

Autumn brought even more than these. After frost the woodlands were a spume of flying leaves. Thomas loved best the ancestral beeches, disfigured by welts of old emblems and initials carved by lost lovers. Autumn belonged too to the owls, to moons sliced from longhorn cheese, to hedge apples hung against sunset skies streaked like Ramboes, to great winged moths that fanned slowly out of the dark.

In November the weeds along the roads were often like white coral. Long days of husking out in the field or barn, or hauling fodder and grists, of fabricating metal and working leather, of standing guard over the cellar treasury of fruits and vegetables—these would follow, until it came time again to build a sugar camp on Church Hill.

How leave it all? Even the fantastic life of unknown creatures buried under old stones, the cloistered flock of pullets in their whitewashed nunnery, the dish towels spread to dry on the gooseberry bushes were part of his being. Never again to see sun-dogs with trepidation or to hear a neighbor's reluctant approval of a fine day as a "weather-breeder" would be to lose himself entirely. He could not go now. Here he had struck root, and here he must stay— until storm came to topple him.

2   Within a week they heard that a fine horse had been stolen over near Lithopolis. Thomas was almost glad; it gave proof to his opinion of gypsies. "Ain't nothing but thieves!" he said time

and again for Kate's conviction. "Couldn't steal, they wouldn't live!"

His blustering was never enough to satisfy her fully. Words could not hide the hostility of the neighbors. Sundays were proof. For years some of the poorer families up Locust Lane had carried their good shoes to church, had changed on the Linthorne front porch and left there the muddy clodhoppers they would want to put on again for the road home. Now they never ventured into the yard. Worse yet, the nearer neighbors, people like the Jordans, Barkers, and Promises, stopped calling in. When Thomas had work to do, he got help reluctantly. No matter how good the meal, the men were never loud at table as they should have been.

The unspoken antagonism only set his jaw the tighter, but it wore on Kate. To compensate for lost kindness, she became a fury of industry, drove Grover and Judith from morning until night. Thomas was concerned, but he tried to put on a good face. He resented most having Judith set to disagreeable tasks like cleaning the henhouse and carrying the watered sludge made from the droppings to sprinkle the melon vines in the garden. When he could, he relieved her. Once indeed he remonstrated, only to have the rebuke go clear over Kate's head. "Whistling girl and crowing hen always come to some bad end," she reminded him. He was wise enough not to press the matter. Judith had to pound up brick dust to scour the silver, sweep at least once a day with shreds of soaked newspaper, carry the slops to the pigs, and help with the milking and butter-making. Like as not Grover or Faith would loiter beside her while she lugged the heavy pails, seemingly oblivious that she was overtaxing her strength.

Thomas drove Grover whenever he found him loafing. The boy seemed willing enough, ran more often than walked, never lipped back. He was becoming more gawky and gangling each day, but was handsome for all his lankiness. Thomas could not be hard on him. When late summer gave way to September and it came near the time he must send Grover off to school, he almost gave up his intention. Grover's lack of flesh made Thomas think of him as a child, unfledged, innocent of the devices of the world.

"Guess we'll have to be thinking about getting Grover ready for Crawfis, Ma," he said to Kate one night, just to test her reaction.

He got what he did not expect.

"Don't know what you want to send him over there for!" she said. "Ain't nothing but a normal school. Thought you said you didn't want him to be a teacher."

"Well, he don't have to be, does he?"

"Whyn't you send him to Columbus? Reverner Wilme's always harping about that school up there."

Thomas sat in a brown study while he debated her proposal. Funny that he had never thought of doing that very thing! Doctor or lawyer, that's what he wanted Grover to be. He'd have to have Latin and Greek and a lot of other things he might never get at Crawfis. Kate's reason was, of course, something else again. Grover and Judith were too nearly the same age; she wanted to have him far enough away he couldn't come home every weekend.

"Guess maybe that's what I'll do—just send him up there," he said when he had satisfied himself. "Oughtn't to cost a whole mint of money."

"Cost enough!" Kate checked him. "Before you get your mind all set, you'd best write and ask. Or go in an' see Reverner—he could tell you."

Thomas stopped off with Grover that same Saturday. When he came home he was in as good spirits as he had been for days—to see him one would think he sat behind a four-in-hand.

"Three hundred dollars!"

"Well, we can afford it."

"Afford to move up there a whole lot better."

Thomas jumped over her protest.

"And he wants Judith to start in catechism this fall. Says if she—what's the matter with you?" He walked after Kate, forced her to listen to him. "Don't figure she ought to grow up a plain heathen, do you?"

"I ain't thinkin' about Judith at all," Kate said finally. "Only—"

"Only what?"

"Seems like you could do a little something for your own flesh and blood. I mean," Kate caught herself, "I mean Faith shouldn't have to take the little end of it all the time."

"Well, she ain't, is she?" Thomas hunched his shoulders. "Don't know what you expect."

Kate couldn't tell him. There was nothing to expect from Faith, nothing to do for her. She was like a shadow in the house, silent, undemanding, unassuming. Only the Sapooneys knew her. The families might be at feud, but Celia and Faith were too close to stay away from each other. Once a day, at least, Faith went down the road or across the fields. Working in the kitchen, Kate would hear her reedy voice added to Celia's rasp as they sang hymns together, two souls in limbo, waiting for the gates of heaven to swing wide.

3 Thomas rode to Columbus with Grover, proud of his knowledge of the capital. The college was out in the cornfields east of town, a mile beyond the car line. Grover carried his brown paper suitcase while Thomas lugged the heavier box of apples they had brought along. The day was sticky hot; by the time they came to the campus both of them were panting.

Three bare brick buildings, one of them a boarding hall, one a dormitory; fine arching elms; long tangles of grass around the yucca clumps on the lawn; shaggy-headed young men in turtle-necked sweaters carrying furniture, beating rugs, or simply sucking at big pipes; the hollow thud of a football as it rose lazily above the branches — that was their first impression, one that Thomas would always retain.

He was uneasy, wanted to get back home, but stayed to meet the *Hausvater* and help Grover register. After that formality they walked back in silence to the bare room that Grover must call home for the year. The furniture of the previous occupant had not been moved; it looked uninviting. Bare table, double bed with high headboard, washstand holding cracked pitcher and bowl, slop bucket, lamp painted with a garish skating scene — that was all, save for the big stove and coal scuttle.

Grover threw himself onto the bed at once, but Thomas took out his wallet and methodically counted out an even hundred dollars.

"Guess you can write for more if you get this all used up," he said as he handed over the money. "Ought to do until Thanksgiving."

251

When Grover shoved the money into his pocket without even muttered thanks, Thomas was embarrassed, stood in awkward leave-taking. He knew how Grover felt—as if he was being deserted. All about him were dozens of other boys, some younger, some older, but all unfriendly to a newcomer. Their voices as they passed up and down the halls were mocking.

"Want you to be a good boy now!" Thomas said as he edged toward the door. "You say your prayers and read your Bible at night, same as we do at home."

Grover smiled sardonically. "I ain't such a greenhorn!" he said as he untangled his legs.

"Well, you be a good boy!"

How could he say the rest, all that he meant to say? That he wanted Grover to find himself, to be a credit to him; that he expected him to study hard, and yet not study too much; that he must learn to conquer himself so that he might conquer others; that—

The door was shut behind him, and he was once more in the long dark hallway. Two little boys were bumping along with a heavy brassbound trunk, their skinny arms too weak to do more than scuff it over the pine planks. Thomas instinctively went to their rescue, dragging the burden the remaining way while they ran ahead to hold open their room door. He accepted their thanks, but could not say what was in his heart—that he wanted their real gratitude to be shown in kindness to his own lonesome boy.

He could hardly force himself to leave the campus, made once again the long circuit around the red brick buildings before he walked down the dirt walk that led to the car line. He felt empty as he walked, as if he had left something behind him, something that he must return for. Grover! Grover! He had his own battle to fight now, would no longer be able to rest on Thomas's stouter arm and sterner judgment. There was no longer any way to put force in his blow. If he proved to be true Linthorne, he would learn to plod ahead sullenly, to hew hard, set his jaw tight!

That was all Thomas's hope—that Grover would be true to his name.

4   When Kate insisted that Faith go into town that autumn so that she might attend high school, Thomas knew that the real motive was to get her away from Judith. He made no objection, simply wondered at Kate's whim. Lifelong she had not permitted Faith to get beyond reach of her apron strings; now it seemed that there was compulsion so great that she had decided to surrender her completely.

His advertisement in the Lancaster *Eagle* discovered what he thought was a good home for the girl with an antiquated spinster who lived on North Broad Street. Ladie Garland was the sole occupant of a big house set back under elms and maples on a green expanse of lawn punctuated with beds of elephant ears and scarlet cannas. A cast-iron dog had watched over the menage so many years that his back was covered with moss.

Thomas brought Faith home every Saturday when he went in to market, carrying Judith with him for catechetical school. On Sunday afternoon he had to drive her back again, but if anything he welcomed the extra trip to town. He loved the ancient stateliness of old Lancaster, the wrought-iron balusters and balconies, lawn lions, round towers, herring-bone pavements.

He had a strong sense of historical continuity. Under the massive Standing Stone north of the town, Indian babies had been born and old men had died in the Shawanese village, to it traders had penetrated from old Fort Duquesne, past it Zane had driven his trace from Wheeling to Limestone. Later stagecoach senators had stopped at the town's long white inns to stretch their legs while the horses were being baited. Grandees of the bar, the legislature, the army had been sired in the dreamy old mansions, had in turn married peach-bloom brides and fathered other proud sons.

What Thomas really loved was the sense of endless afternoon in the town, endless golden afternoon. Ghosts walked the pavements. On some broad veranda a Negro maid might be scrubbing the already white facade; under the tunneled trees straining teams might arch their backs against obdurate wheels; down in the public square merchants and country men might haggle—but these were pictures. Reality was in the sere leaves that the wind whispered down to yellow the flat-arched roadways, in the bent, deferential pensioners who came with slow rakes to pile and burn, in the acrid smoke drifting languidly across beds of lavender chrysanthemums. Endless golden afternoon!

Mount Pleasant was the symbol of all that the town meant to him. He had never climbed the Standing Stone, was satisfied simply to look at the scarred face of the rock. After rain the tawny cliff would be streaked with olive and violet, in bright sunlight it was orange and ochre, at twilight green shading to purple. Shaggy with forest trees at its base, it rose naked two hundred feet above their crowns, latticed with ledges and pocketed with nests of laurel, until, high above, it broke back sharply to form an island in the sky.

Thomas knew that Faith cared nothing for his companionship or opinion, and so never loitered with her. She was not even obliged to him for driving her in; in fact, seemed a little ashamed of him. "You be good now!" he would always say when he set her down on Ladie Garland's carriage block, but he knew he addressed a stranger. Faith rarely answered him. She would simply pick up whatever she had brought back with her, a basket of Limber Twigs or her tin box of clean clothes, and go in without once turning around. While she was swinging the door Thomas would *chk-chk* the horse and pull slowly away, his mind already busy with the intention to make a long circuit through the streets before he swung back home.

And so the autumn passed and winter came more lonesome than ever before. On rare days there was a meticulous bit of foolscap from Charlotte or a scrawl from Grover, but it was Judith who kept his heart alive. She seemed not to notice the hateful way she was avoided by other youngsters who had been told what they must think of her. At home she was always busy, always happy despite Kate's outspoken rebukes whenever the least thing went wrong.

Thomas loved her spirit, began to hope that Lucile would never come back to claim her. Call him "Mr. Linthorne" she must; but it was his right to rear her, and he meant to beg no man to think well of him for doing so.

IX

1 When Canaway's gelding was stolen in November, there were no gypsies about. Spence Vitt, who was now almost the only man who would talk with Thomas, saw something in the fact that the horse was spirited away on Saturday night while the family was in town. "Guess you won't let it go no further if I tell you what I think," he remarked while they sorted apples before his huge winter cellar. "Only I'll just bet you a dollar to a beer check the fellow that took that horse don't live farther away than you can spit."

Thomas was not very much surprised.

"Ralph Tanterscham?" he asked cautiously, and was answered by Spence's nod.

"Ever notice him? Always got more money than he knows what to do with. Never does nothing to come by it honest. Thing I'm wondering about is whether he's in with a gang. Was, all he'd have to do would be run a horse up to Columbus now and then. Easier than working, and a whole lot more money in it."

Thomas puzzled over the charge. It did look possible, now that old Lute was down flat on his back. None of the womenfolks would know what Ralph was about, and Tom Tanterscham would make the best kind of confidant to help Ralph lie out of any entanglement.

"One reason I sent Grover to school—to get him away from Ralph," he told Spence. "Didn't like the way things was going a little bit."

"Well, you'd best keep him there."

"Mean to," said Thomas. "Course, Christmas and times like

that he'll be home for a few days. Only it won't be like having him where Ralph can get at him every time my back's turned."

2 Grover had been home for the Thanksgiving feast only long enough to gorge himself and wear off the effects of his appetite, but on the twentieth of December he sent a letter saying that he would be down that same night. Thomas drove to Hooker Station after him, waiting impatiently in the cold until the train slid down under the valley fog. Grover was the only passenger to get off, but was so encumbered with luggage that it took him an eternity. The conductor pitched the last of his packages out on the platform.

"What you got in all them things?" Thomas indicated the parcels, as they stood shivering to watch the last lights burn out in the wispy night.

"Well, it's Christmas."

Thomas whistled. "Looks like you spent a mint of money," he half complained, and started to carry the stuff to the buggy. "Thought you said you was pretty well strapped."

"Oh, 'tain't much. Just a couple things for Mom and Judith."

Thomas made cautious observation as they rode home together. The boy was somehow changed, not so much in appearance as in actions and words. He seemed surer of himself, perhaps a little too sure. By the time they came to Locust Lane, Grover had blurted out that he belonged to a literary society and stood at the head of his Latin class. He recited a German declamation, further evidenced his erudition by a sing-song of declensions and conjugations. Thomas was uneasy before his paragon of a son, but also secretly very proud. The way Grover laughed whenever he finished one of his displays betrayed that he too was pretty well satisfied with himself.

"Guess you like it up there," Thomas observed happily. "Lot better than being stuck down here in the country."

Grover was watching for the house lights, didn't answer directly.

"Judith all right?" he asked unexpectedly.

"Was last time I saw her."

"Just wait till you see what I got her for Christmas."

Thomas set him down at the house, waited until Kate and Judith ran out to help in with the luggage. He didn't expect Grover to go along down to the stable, wouldn't mar his homecoming by the prosaic necessity of unharnessing and bedding down the horse. But while Thomas did the work, he thought hard of his son's words. It was something he hadn't exactly foreseen—that there should be any attachment between Grover and Judith. They both knew, of course, but for all that they might make fools of themselves. Only thing to save them would be to watch like a hawk continually, so that they'd be afraid of straying too far afield.

It was a good Christmas. Charlotte came home with Jed and their baby, so that Hocking was the only one of the family who didn't sit down before the roast goose. It was to Kate's credit that she treated Jed almost as well as she would have treated her own son. Thomas saw her wince once or twice when Jed called her "Ma," but she never let on.

After the meal they opened the presents stacked under the cedar tree in the front room. Thomas felt positively shabby when he discovered he was the only one who hadn't given. He was not used to doing for grown children, thought that Christmas was only for babies. But he would not be outdone, at the last minute went up to the bedroom and got into his tiny store of gold pieces hidden in the toe of an old boot. Each of the children had five dollars, Judith as well as the rest of them. Their eyes shone when he put the coins into their palms.

As Grover had predicted, it was his gifts that drew the most admiration. For Charlotte and Faith he had bought wood-burning sets, complete even to the tiny bottles of alcohol. Thomas got a jackknife, Judith a great fluted conch shell that might adorn her dresser or be placed on the mantle. Kate's present surprised all of them. The *Haussegen* was not new—Grover said he had bought it secondhand, and it was hideously framed with some sort of rococo beading from which most of the silver paint had peeled, but it was so immense and glaring that the German words fairly leaped out of the frame. Kate had to correct Grover when he pretended to read the inscription, intoned it herself while they all listened, a bit awe-struck:

Wo Glaube da Liebe,
Wo Liebe da Friede,
Wo Friede da Segen,
Wo Segen da Gott,
Wo Gott keine Not.

"Means if you love each other like you should there won't be any jawing and you'll always have peace around the place," she trans-lated. "Where on earth you get it, Grover? My pa had one with them same words. Hung right over the bench where he made shoes all day."

Thomas thought Grover was a bit too mysterious in his answer.

"Oh, I just picked it up," he said airily. "Like I said. Saw it in a window downtown in Columbus and thought maybe you'd like to have it."

"Well, I should say I do!"

Thomas had a chance at Grover later when they were out in the barn together.

"How much you pay for that picture you got Ma?" he asked point-blank. "Cost a pretty, didn't it?"

Grover looked sheepish. "Didn't pay anything at all," he ad-mitted. "It was just on a wall up there—fellow gave it to me. Only I couldn't tell her that—not at Christmas."

"How much you pay for all them other things?"

"Why?"

Thomas didn't want to be rude. "I just don't see where you got all the money," he said quietly. "Always said in your letters you was hard up."

Grover shook off the query with a shrug of his shoulders.

"Worked for it," he said.

Thomas could not challenge him. But he was not convinced, not perfectly satisfied. Grover's industry had never been remark-able at home; it would be wonderful elsewhere.

3 As usual there was a great deal of visiting in the week between Christmas and New Year's Day, jaunts over the ice to bees and parties, a watch meeting to face the first moment of '91. No one came to the Linthornes. After Charlotte and Jed went home, quiet was so continual that the house might have been untenanted. Faith was always with her mother, Judith generally busy with some appointed task. Thomas tried to keep Grover company, invited him along whenever he went to the barn or drove to town, generally to be refused. Grover was jumpy, restless; it was plain he fretted for companions nearer his own age. Thomas permitted him to walk Judith across the road to singing school, but he wouldn't hear to it when Grover suggested driving her into town to the watch meeting.

"Don't know as I want you to go yourownself," he said. "You ain't no fit age to be up all hours of the night."

"My gosh, Pop!"

"Well, you ain't! Have to be in bed by nine at college, don't you?"

Grover laughed at him, seemed to enjoy his joke the rest of the day. In the end he won Thomas over, got permission to use the gray horse and the cutter. Thomas thought for a time of asking to go along, but would not when he saw how happy Grover was to go alone.

He did sit up. When twelve struck, someone in the recesses of Black Man came out with a shotgun and blew up the sky for a full quarter-hour. Thomas went out into the yard to locate the sound. Spence had said something of a couple of new families back in the hills, briar-hoppers who lived worse than the Sapooneys. Thomas didn't like to have them near—in some vague way they were menacing.

By one he had read six full chapters of Job and was dozing in his chair. He made coffee to keep himself awake, remembering that other vigil long years before when Barker, Jordan, Tanterscham, and Sapooney had kept him company. It would be Lute's turn next—none expected him to last through the winter. Thomas wondered if he'd be invited down to Tanterschams to sit up. He'd like to perform that last office for the old fellow, but would likely be snubbed. All the Tanterscham women had their backs up.

Two o'clock. Where could Grover be? Even with long leave-taking a watch meeting could hardly last beyond one. The drive home would take no longer than another hour. But the hands were crawling, crawling! Thomas was alert now, wide awake. Time after time he went to the door to listen down the road, only to have his expectation disappointed. He became chagrined, then angry, at last fearful. The gray was a good trotter, but she might have shied at something in the road. At several places there were steep slopes down which a cutter could turn over a dozen times.

At ten minutes after three he heard the jangle of bells, then the blur of voices out in the road. Thomas went in through the cold rooms, pulled the curtain aside to stare out. There was not one sleigh but two, drawn up side by side. It seemed that there were two people in each of them, certainly Ralph and Tom Tanterscham, to judge by the voices. Thomas was amazed at their effrontery, then horrified when he saw them carrying a limp figure into the yard. In a flash he knew the worst—the scoundrels had gotten Grover drunk.

He would not go out to meet them. Waiting in the dark middle room, he heard them fumble the kitchen door open. They made no secret of their shame, were loud as they staggered in with the body. Tom backed in first, himself unsteady, his neck purple in the lamp-light. "Where you goin' to put him, Ralph?" he hiccoughed. "Just want to drop him on the floor?"

They seesawed across the room, Ralph's hands under Grover's armpits. Behind walked a tall, thin man Thomas had never seen before, his only burden Grover's hat. He seemed ill at ease, kept glancing around as if afraid of surprise, once even nudged Ralph and pointed to a place beside the stove.

Thomas waited until they had put Grover down, and so got between them and the door. He said nothing, only stared while their mouths gaped. Ralph was the first to recover.

"Guess maybe he got a little bit more than he could carry home all by himself," he said flippantly. "Be all right in the morning. We just run across him and brought him along."

"That's a lie and you know it!"

Ralph's flushed face lost a little color when he smelled danger.

"Ask Tom there!" he brazened. "Ask Crab . . . Ain't that so, Tom? Didn't we pick him up in Deckle's saloon?"

Thomas ignored him, only walked over to the stove and came back with the poker. He was white mad, but he meant to keep control of himself. Once and for all he meant to have it out with the Tanterschams, to let them know they had to let Grover alone.

"You see this!" he said as he held the iron under Ralph's nose. "I'm a-tellin' you, and you'd best mark my words: if I ever catch you with Grover again, I'll mash your head in! Now get out! All three of you, *get out!*"

They skulked past him, left the door wide when they went out into the night. Thomas followed hard after them. They were already in their cutter when he got to the road, had disappeared before he turned the gray into the yard.

He made a short job of stabling, hurried back to the house to see if he could rouse Grover from his stupor. The rest of the night he sat by him, kept cold cloths on his head, forced black coffee between his lips whenever he appeared to be stirring. When at half past five Kate came down, he was still at the sorry task. He was vindictive as he told her what had happened. "That's your Ralph Tanterscham!" he fairly shouted at her. "Good-for-nothing loafer—that's all he is! Like to break every bone in his body!"

Kate kept her temper and her tongue.

"You'll wake Faith up," she warned coolly. "No sense carrying on like a crazy man."

Somehow her quiet only irritated Thomas the more. He was still muttering at eight when Grover finally opened his eyes, looked at them in bewilderment for an instant, and then shuddered back to sleep, as if he could not face the horror of his own guilt.

4 Nothing more came of the incident until spring. Grover was pitiable when he went back to college, so shamefaced that he and Thomas exchanged no more than a half-dozen words on the way to the train. Letters that came from him in subsequent weeks were apologetic, not full of the nonsensical braggadocio he usually wrote.

The whole township knew of the episode before it was two weeks old. The Tanterschams, who had lied about their part in the affair, were heard with relish by those who had already begun to flout Thomas. The story they told was that they had found Grover lurching about the Lancaster streets. They were good enough to carry him home, only to be threatened by a madman in the Linthorne kitchen. All that saved them was that they had been able to wrestle the poker away.

Thomas did nothing to correct the impression they made. He told Spence the truth, but Spence had not been misled. It was Spence who reported that Celia Sapooney was running the roads with a dangerous mouthful of gabble. At Lucy Jordan's quilting she had suggested that if they all knew what was fit and proper they'd see to it that Judith was taken away and put in the county home.

Thomas bit his lips when he heard that. "Don't think there's any danger, do you?" he asked Spence anxiously.

Spence wouldn't say one thing or another.

"Wouldn't worry too much if I was you," was his slim consolation. "Guess everybody knows Cely pretty well by now."

Everybody did know Celia, but hate and fear were powerful agents to distort judgment.

Miraculously Lute Tanterscham hung on through the winter. When the March winds blew the sky clean, Thomas heard one day that the neighbors were going in to plow. That in itself was curious, with both Ralph and Tom at home to carry on the work. But it was more peculiar that none had stopped in at Linthornes to ask a team. Next to Spence Vitt, Thomas had lived closest to Lute Tanterscham through more than twenty long years.

He smarted because of the slight. On Wednesday morning he was of two minds: to ignore the bee entirely, or to stomach his pride and go down. Sight of Joe Jordan dragging along the road brought decision—he had not been asked, and he would not go where he was not wanted.

As the sun crept up the sky, however, he thought better of sulking. Like as not the affront was not intentional; certainly old Lute had not inspired it. Bill Sapooney, who never did a lick of work himself and for that reason contrived that others should do two, might have called the men together. Or Spence Vitt, knowing how shorthanded Thomas was, might have excused him from the added chore.

Thought that he might be called a shirker sent Thomas down when the sun had almost touched ten. He felt strangely uneasy; the nearer he came to the old red brick under its dark layers of pine, the more he was prompted to turn back. He might have done so if he had not been seen. Two fields over Barker came along the rise with his black geldings, spotted Thomas on the pike, and for some reason pulled in until Marty came abreast. Thomas lifted his arm in greeting, was tardily answered. That told him the truth, but forbade him to go back for fear they would boast they had driven him away.

There was no one about the house—the solemnity of approaching death kept all the shutters fast. Even the white hens scratching in the lane seemed to be silent, deferential. Rags came out sulkily from the back porch, gave one premonitory bark, then recognized Thomas and stretched lazily in a patch of sun.

Thomas went on down to the barn. He looked in as a matter of course, began to congratulate himself that he could drive on without the necessity of talk when he saw Ralph and Tom running down the lane from the field where the men were working. Thomas waited nervously—of all people in the world he wanted least to see them. As they came nearer and shuffled to a walk he saw that Ralph's dark face was expressionless, Tom's beet red. Ralph waited to speak until they were no more than ten feet away.

"Anybody ask you to come down here?"

"Asked myself, I reckon," Thomas said casually.

"Well, get your damn plugs off this place!"

The words stung like wasps. Thomas thought bitterly that if he had not been fool enough to inveigle himself in the nasty predicament, there would be no need to defend his pride.

"I didn't come down to have words, Ralph," he tried to be calm. "Thought maybe you could use another team."

"We can't!" Ralph snapped immediately. "Get off!"

The two brothers stood menacingly on either side, Tom's mouth working, Ralph's tight-lipped. Thomas could understand their hostility, but they were not masters of the farm.

"Well, you going or ain't you!"

Thomas smiled wryly in an attempt to mask his anger. "Didn't know you'd fallen into the property already, Ralph," he said sarcastically. "When did your pa die?"

If his words were unwarranted, Ralph's action was more so. Without warning he began to pick up stones and cobs and hurl them at the horses that had been lazily switching their tails in the sun. The team took fright, lurched down the lane dragging the heavy plow, Ralph at their heels.

Thomas finally caught up with him, nearly pulled him off his feet. He was so choking mad he felt like slapping the ruffian to the ground, did not only out of respect for Lute. He couldn't see Tom come up from behind him with the yard length of fence rail. The blow caught him in the neck, drove him to his knees. Before he could recover Ralph's fist banged against his forehead.

Staggered by the assault, Thomas groveled on hands and knees. He felt dizzy, sick, as if his insides wanted to lurch out. When he did finally push to his feet they rushed him again, kneed him as they dragged over his body. He fought back as gamely as he could, but he was hurt so badly he was no match for them. Not until he was beaten to a jelly did they stand back and let him limp down the lane to his team.

They were still standing with clubs in their hands when he finally got the horses turned around. Thomas held to Bill's harness, staggered by his assailants drunkenly. He but half-heard Tom's nervous self-congratulatory laugh, Ralph's parting thrust, "And see that you stay off, too!"

There was no need for the words. Thomas would not take even a last glance at the dark house. When Lute's life faded, all that had ever been bright in his relations with the Tanterschams would be smirched by bitter black hatred.

5 On the night before Grover came home for the summer vacation, the gray mare dropped a long-legged piebald foal with a face so freakishly marked that he seemed always to be winking. Thomas had been up all night with the horse, had to drive after

Grover at ten with no more than a mouthful for breakfast. On the road home he could talk of nothing but the foal, must take Grover down to the barn before he even went in to kiss his mother.

Grover was at once taken by the colt. "Darned dude!" he said admiringly as he hung over the stall. "Ain't that just what he looks like, Pop?"

"'Spect he does, a little, maybe."

"Let's call him that."

"What?"

"Dude!" Grover almost shouted.

Thomas could hardly force him to carry his suitcase to the house. "Always wanted a horse marked with a patch over one eye," he kept repeating. "You'll let me have him, won't you, Pop?"

Thomas had no such intention. "We'll see," he put Grover off. "Now you run on in and say hello."

Grover seemed to think that was patent enough. From that day he never referred to Dude except as "my horse." Thomas allowed the appropriation, in time came to use the words himself. "That's Grover's horse!" he would always point out whenever anyone referred to the piebald. "Two of them fell in love the minute they laid eyes on each other."

In truth Grover had made a wise choice. As the summer advanced, Dude straightened out, plumped into the sleek contours of a thoroughbred. Thomas had put the mare to a roan stallion named Merry Boy, as fine a horse as Black Belle had been. Something of the sire showed in the son. Dude's shoulders were heavy, his legs long and slim, his chest a drum. Grover could hardly wait for the day he might go astride. He discovered that Joe Jordan had an old saddle, traded him a shoat for the leather, and spent the greater part of a week rubbing it to some semblance of its first gloss.

"Just go easy!" Thomas always warned whenever he saw him cast longing eyes at the colt. "He ain't a-goin' to run away."

There was more danger that he might be stolen. Thomas said nothing of his fears, but he nailed the barn tight, and on a trip to town came home with a big iron padlock that would withstand a sledgehammer. "No sense locking the door afterward!" he commented when Grover helped him rivet in the staples.

Grover was proud in his possession of one of the keys. He wore it in place of his watch fob, made a ceremony of going down with Thomas to see that everything was right before they went to bed. On the hottest nights he grumbled at leaving Dude in the pasture. At that he was not more apprehensive than his father. Thomas put the horses far back from the road so that thieves would think twice before they indulged their fancy.

6 When he was not worrying about the horse, he might worry about Judith. Like Charlotte, she had matured early; now, nearly fifteen, she appeared to be a grown woman. Thomas said a crafty word to Grover now and then so that he would not get notions about the girl, but he could not keep the two of them apart. They went to the hills for blackberries and came home full of chiggers; in the garden batted potato bugs into round tin pails; even helped a little in the fields. When Thomas threshed, he had to send Judith away from the separator—it seemed she was happier there than she would be in the house. It was noticeable that Grover didn't work long after she had gone.

That night Thomas thought best to drop Grover another hint.

"Guess you'll sort of hate to go back when school opens up this fall," he said as they sat together on the porch.

"Oh, I don't know," Grover said immediately. "Why?"

"Well, you won't have Dude around. And I guess you'll miss Judith some, too."

Grover made a peculiar noise in his throat as if he had thought better of something he meant to say. "She's awful pretty," he finally stammered. "Guess maybe I will miss seeing her."

"Well, you remember she's your sister!"

Thomas knocked out his pipe and went in without further parley. He wanted Grover to think rather than talk, to come to a full realization of the relationship. It would be confusing to him, of course. For long years Judith had walked with pigtail braids, nothing more than the wistful daughter of a pinched family on the neighboring acres; now, suddenly feminine, she must be denied because her veins ran with the same blood as Grover's own.

7 It was a day almost at the end of summer that Kate came downstairs one morning with tears in her eyes. Thomas stared at her as she fished in her apron pocket and finally brought out a string of black beads with a silver crucifix on the end of the strand. "Know what that is, I reckon!" she said in a hard voice as she threw the rosary to the table. "Found that on the floor beside Faith's bed. Slipped out of her hand when she dropped off last night."

Thomas picked up the beautiful beads, let them run through his fingers.

"What you make of it?" he asked.

"Why, it's plain as the nose on your face! That woman she's been staying with in Lancaster's a Catholic!"

Thomas gulped, but he kept silent while Kate explored every mournful possibility.

"No need you getting all riled up about it!" he said to quiet her. "Ain't no harm in her having a rosary to say her prayers with if she wants one."

"Ain't no harm? You mark my words, Thomas Linthorne, you let Faith go back there this year and she'll turn on you, just as sure as you're knee-high to a grasshopper!"

Thomas didn't relish that surmise, but neither would he consent to break Faith to his will.

"You just let her alone, Ma," he counseled hurriedly when he heard the girls coming downstairs. "That's the only way she can get peace of mind—well, I won't stand in her way."

Kate's mouth hung open as he went out the door, but he had time to think over his decision before he went back for dinner. It satisfied him—he wouldn't consent to keep Faith at home or change her boarding place. It was a person's own business how he made his peace with God; he should do it the best way he knew.

X

1 It was just twenty-five years since they had been wed. When April came back with fitful sun, Thomas remembered one day because of the blaze of dandelions in all the fence corners. There had been dandelions then, robins moving north, the purl of water through every woodland. Twenty-five years! He had missed voting for Lincoln by but one year; now he was nearly fifty. And Kate, who had been as willowy as a sapling, was inclined to be lumpish.

Twenty-five years! It was good he had not forgotten—she certainly would not forget. He would have to do something handsome for the anniversary, although he had neglected all the others. She should have a new black dress, and shoes, and a hat. Perhaps gloves—she would like those. And—the idea struck him with the sudden force of inspiration—and they would have their picture taken. The best photographer in Lancaster should do the work. Perhaps he could even tint the faces. There would be a gold frame, not too heavy, and yet impressive enough. After all these years there would finally be a portrait over the mantle.

He fairly ran to the house with the idea, tingling with the same excitement he used to feel when as a boy he pulled a flopping small-mouth out of some ferny pool along Rush Creek.

The photographer was a small man with wiry gray hair who walked around them critically as they posed before the garish back-drop of swans afloat before a Grecian temple. Thomas sat poker-stiff, afraid even to move his eyeballs lest he be rebuked. His collar pinched him, but he dared not move his chin to shove it down.

Three times already the photographer had had to adjust his black bow. His right hand clawed uneasily at the ornate chair arm, his left held his gray felt just below the looped links of his gold watch chain.

"Don't spraddle your legs out that way, Mr. Linthorne! Pull them together!"

Thomas obeyed immediately. Behind him, her hand on his right shoulder, Kate stood as timid as a mouse, her olive face sadly beautiful above the stiff black ruching and white cameo. In the dressing room she had even dared dab her cheeks with powder, the first she had used in her life.

"Ready, I guess," the photographer said in a disgusted kind of tone. "Want you to smile a little. Not too much, you understand! No sense looking like a sick horse."

His head tunneled under the black cloth and Thomas froze to absolute immobility. Nothing happened. The muscles around his mouth ached from the unnatural way he was holding his lips. When he saw the man's head pop back into sight, he thought the ordeal was over, tried to get up. He was shouted down—the photographer was almost out of temper.

Thomas rued the day. It was all over within three or four minutes after that, but he could not breathe easily until he was out in the waiting room.

"What I want is a great big jim-dandy!" he explained while Kate stood by admiringly. "Something we can hang on the wall in the front room."

"About two by three?"

Thomas figured, nodded consent.

"And I want a right good frame, too. Something like that one over there."

The picture he indicated was old ivory, the frame a concave that looked to be solid gold.

"Cost you twenty-five dollars, that one would," said the proprietor. "You want something a little cheaper, I can—"

"I want one just like that one there!" Thomas said emphatically.

"Want to pay it all down?"

Thomas left two tens and a five. He was acrimonious as he led Kate down the long flight to Main Street.

"Hear that fellow talk, you'd think I wasn't nothing but a stinking cheap-skate!" he kept muttering angrily. "Acted like he thought he was going to be beat!"

Kate had to flatter him back to good humor. They had the long day ahead of them in town, and she meant somehow to get to a dry-goods store, something she would never accomplish if Thomas was nursing a grouch.

Thomas saw the proofs when he came into town on Saturday. He was surprised at his likeness, tremendously impressed. The plate showed a strong-jawed man whose hair and mustache had just begun to go iron-gray; beside him a prim-looking woman in many black flounces. It was Kate to the life, and if Kate, then it must be he also.

"Tell you what," he grinned as he handed the proofs back, "I sort of changed my mind a little bit. What I want's three of them pictures instead of just one."

This time it was the photographer's turn to be impressed.

"Don't mean all framed alike, do you, Mr. Linthorne?" he asked hopefully.

"Every single last one of them. Don't you make no mistake now—I want frames just like that one over yonder."

He was well pleased with himself. One of the pictures should be Charlotte's, one Grover's. It would look nice in his room at college, be something the other boys would envy. Faith would be slighted, but you might say she was still at home, at least a good part of the time. And as for Hocking—well, if ever Thomas sent one down there, Elva would very likely use it to prop the privy door open.

2 It was well that he be pleased about something—heaven knew his moments of elation were becoming more and more rare. Time hadn't healed the resentment of the neighbors, had, if anything, made them more critical. Met on the roads, they spoke in such a perfunctory manner a person would think they begrudged their breath; passing by the house, they never looked in. Even Judith had begun to feel the sting of their tongues. She tried to keep a brave face, but it was plain to Thomas that she thought of herself as alien, unwanted. She had no one to confide in, must have been

gravely offended that Kate often talked to Thomas in low tones and gave up the conversation the moment she entered the room. She could not know that it was not she but Faith who was the subject of concern.

For Easter, Thomas induced Kate to buy Judith a fine white lawn—he wanted her to be proud when she was confirmed. He had looked forward to the holidays, but Grover brought no gladness with him when he came. He seemed moody, worried, stalked about the house in dismal silence. Only his horse seemed able to interest him. On Saturday, Thomas let him saddle and ride to town, secretly glad to be able until bedtime to escape his haunted eyes.

Grover stammered his secret on Sunday afternoon just three hours before he was to start back to school—he needed money, was in debt for more than sixty dollars. He chewed out his dismal information with averted eyes, tried to brighten the picture by suggesting that he be allowed to sell the colt. After all, he would never need the horse. It would take him another year to get through the academy, four more until he was graduated from college. By that time Dude would be too old to be of much value.

Thomas's heart sank, but he tried to keep his words level.

"You got me fair beat, Grover," he said slowly. "Been thinking I give you more'n enough to get along on already."

"You don't understand, Pop. It ain't that—you see, I just owe some fellow and he says he's got to have it soon as I get back."

"What did you do with the money?"

"I didn't do anything with it—I just owe it." Grover kept twisting his toe in the ground while he hung onto a fence post. "You don't understand—it wasn't anything I just had to have. I—well, I guess I sort of got in dutch."

Thomas lifted his son's chin so that Grover had to look in his eyes.

"You'd be a whole lot better off telling me the truth," he said. "I ain't made of money, and you know it. But if there's anybody you really have to pay, I want to do the right thing. You just tell me the truth."

The tears streaked down Grover's face when he saw he was caught. He hadn't meant to do anything wrong, he said. But one night in January, Ralph and Tom Tanterscham had stopped in at the college. They had played cards, and Grover had lost. Ralph had acted like it was all right for a while, but in the last few weeks he had been sending letters saying he needed every cent he could get hold of because he wanted to go out west.

"I could make it up to you," Grover kept repeating while Thomas stood rigid with anger. "Honest, Pop, I didn't know I was doing anything wrong. You just give me the money to pay him back and sell Dude to make it up that way."

Thomas shook sense back into him.

"Now, see here," he commanded roughly, "there's just one thing I want you to do, and I want you to do it right away! You go down to Tanterschams and tell that skunk that if he ever asks you for a penny again, I'll run him clean out of the county! He knows I mean what I say! Go on, I want you to repeat them very words!"

He had to march Grover to the gate.

"Don't you take no back-talk, either!" he ordered. "You don't owe him a cent, not one red cent! You tell him what I said!"

He stood by the yellow rosebush until Grover was out of sight, boiling to think the boy could be so stupid. And to think that the Tanterschams had followed him to Columbus, played him for an easy mark! The two of them deserved hanging, would very likely get it in the end. Just let them once be caught red-handed in their thievery, and the jig would be up!

Grover came back home looking queer, and he still appeared jaundiced when it was time for him to leave. He had the big picture to carry as well as his suitcase, but for the first time didn't want Thomas to drive him to Hooker Station. "Maybe there's some place you and Mom want to go tonight," he suggested once in half-hearted protest. "I can walk just as well as not."

Thomas insisted on driving him over. Grover was nervous, talked a little too fast and laughed in a falsetto born of semi-hysteria. Thomas pretended not to notice. He wouldn't ask what had happened at Tanterschams', regarded the incident as closed. The least said about some things, the better.

"I want you to be a good boy now, Grover," he said earnestly when they saw the train coming far down the track. "Promise me that you will."

"I'll be all right, Pop."

"You won't never gamble no more?"

"I'll be good."

It was as much as Thomas could expect. He saw Grover swing up the steps like an acrobat, caught one last glimpse of his face as the cars pulled away. Grover's eyes blinked a little when he saw his father—and then he was gone, the lonesome whistle of the train Thomas's only assurance that Grover had not been an apparition.

Six miles down the track at Carroll, and beyond that again at Canal Winchester perhaps, other sons would leave their fathers to clamber aboard, like Grover taking with them more than they left behind.

3 They were in bed early that night—Kate had the toothache. She kept turning and twisting so that Thomas could not sleep, complained that the whole side of her head was neuralgic. Alum and salt brought no relief, nor did the toothache gum Thomas had bought her in town. Ten o'clock struck, eleven, and still she writhed in agony. Thomas lay awake, looking through the window at the moon riding a saddleback of cloud. It hurt him for Kate to suffer, more than if he suffered himself. Finally when he thought of heating an iron in hope that it would quiet her, he crawled out of bed and went out through the hall in his nightshirt. For an instant he had the thought of taking the wall-lamp downstairs with him, but did not because it was too hard to get back into the bracket.

At the bottom of the flight he stopped short for an instant— there had been a noise that sounded like the creak of his wagon gate. He went to the kitchen window, could see nothing. His imagination was getting the better of him—he would have to get another dog.

There it was again—only this time not the wagon gate but the tread of muffled feet. None of the stock was wandering about; he had shut them all tight for the night. His mind raced to the uglier possibility—that the Tanterschams had come after Dude. It would be like them to think they could get their money that way!

Thomas brought the rifle from the middle room, threw a shell into the chamber while he inched open the door. In the cool draught he stood like a ghost, his eyes straining through the darkness. There was certainly someone fumbling with the barn door. The persistent metallic scratching sounded as if the hasps were being pried loose.

Thomas went down through the grape arbor as quiet as a cat. From the covert of the woodshed he had a clear glimpse of sky against which anyone who passed would be silhouetted. To help him the moon, which had been hidden for a time, came out from behind a dirty wool cloudbank, flooding the barnyard with blue-silver. Thomas meant to give no warning—his intention was not to scare the prowlers away. The Tanterschams could not beg immunity forever.

It took them an unconscionably long time. While he waited Thomas leveled the rifle over the cordwood, sighted along the barrel toward the aperture in the trees. The sky was going dark again, would hardly be clear bright for another half-hour.

At the instant he thought of going on down at the risk of being attacked, he heard the barn door grate softly shut.

His heart pounded louder than the muffled feet of the horses. It might not be the Tanterschams after all—there was noise enough for an entire gang. Like black mist he saw the first horse poke his head from the square silhouette of the barn, then another, and another. Riding them were three men, evidently the three who had been in his kitchen on the night they brought Grover home drunk. Ralph, Tom, and the skinny man.

The rifle went to his shoulder automatically, pointed its ugly nose toward the horse that showed patches of white. Ralph would certainly ride Dude—the colt was his particular prize. Thomas took careful aim, squeezed the trigger back carefully. A scream answered the spurt of flame, then the thunderous roar of hoofs as in the black dark the hoofbeats blurred like rain on the kitchen roof.

Thomas ran for the lantern, heard Kate stumbling downstairs.

He didn't wait for her. Dude was still clattering around the barnyard, had somehow missed the wagon gate in the stampede. Thomas went warily. There was a chance the fallen man might only be winged; he would certainly be armed. Kate caught up with him at the yard gate, her breath short.

"What on earth's the matter, Thomas?"

"Shot a thief, that's what!" he answered gruffly. He wouldn't tell her it was Ralph Tanterscham—she would know soon enough.

In the dancing light they at last saw the black bulk of the figure, his legs outstretched, arms thrown up over his head. Thomas went swift then, lifting the lantern shoulder high.

The concentric rings of yellow light were like a golden frame. His eyes wide staring, Grover lay flat on his back, his head drilled from temple to temple.

4 Long Joe Jordan came into the yard like a walking dead man, Lucy in her best black at his heels. Their faces lowered, they knocked solemnly at the door, stepped inside fearfully when Judith opened for them. Their eyes traveled the worn cracks in the floor, crept up the chairs on the far side of the table, came at last to the blanched faces of the big man and plump woman who sat there. The ten feet between were a mile to travel, but Joe and Lucy were resolute. "Have my sympathy, Thomas! Have my sympathy, Mis' Linthorne," they said with dark voices as they reached out workworn hands.

Have my sympathy, have my sympathy, have my sympathy! That same night the Sapooneys, Vitts, Wendells, Martys, Promises, Canaways, Barkers, McGrubers. *My sympathy, you have my sympathy, my sympathy!* People from as far away as Hooker and Lithopolis, the hill families on Goose Ridge and Black Man. Endless, real, heartfelt words from mouths that hung open in mute agony. *Have my sympathy, Thomas! My sympathy, Mis' Linthorne. Mr. Linthorne, you have my sympathy!*

Como Cory was the last one—he came early on the morning of the funeral. "Thomas!" he said simply as his arm went out like a great bear's around Thomas's shoulders. "Don't grieve, man! You've got to remember—His ways are past finding out!"

Thomas broke down then, cried like a child. Como stayed with him, wouldn't go home until after the burial in the afternoon. He talked quietly, hopefully, saw the gold in the gray. "You mustn't give up, Thomas!" he said many times. "You don't know what it's all about, and I don't know what it's all about, but there's reason behind it—that's one thing you can be sure of. God didn't want things to be this way, He wouldn't let them."

Thomas rested on him as on a rock. The darkest hour of his trial was still to come, but Como had heartened him for it more than any other man could.

Although the casket would not be opened, Thomas would not scant the other solemnities. There would be a service both at the house and at the grave. He sat on a chair by the door that opened to the porch so that he might escape easily if he could not bear the ordeal. None but the family were in the room with the coffin, only Kate, Faith, Charlotte, Jed, and Judith. Hocking had not come home.

Promptly at two-thirty the Reverend Wilme began, his voice low-pitched but penetrating enough to carry to those in the kitchen and on the front porch. Through the hymn and the prayer Thomas's face was marble. The short, jarring sobs of the women left him utterly unmoved—he had already suffered too much. Out in the middle room Celia Sapooney from time to time brought out a long wail, only to be stifled by Bill's ready hand. Thomas could see them from where he sat, beyond them Balt Wendell and Flora, their eyes hollow.

When it came time for the sermon, Thomas gripped hard the arms of his chair. The pastor took a long time finding the text, cleared his throat before he read solemnly:

"For God shall bring every work into judgment, with every secret thing, whether it be good, or whether it be evil!"

Thomas choked—he could stand no more. Out in the blossoming peach tree beside the lot where the rigs were hitched, a robin was chirping the passion of spring, forever new, forever fugitive. Thomas went toward it with hungry eyes, his brain prowling for any possible refuge. After him Como Cory stalked down the path. He had not been inside, had waited on the porch, sure that this moment must come.

5 And on the kitchen wall in the desolation of twilight after his return from the cemetery, the *Haussegen:*

Wo Glaube da Liebe,
Wo Liebe da Friede,
Wo Friede da Segen,
Wo Segen da Gott,
Wo Gott keine Not.

Was it true, could it be true: that love came from belief, was followed by peace, peace by blessing sent from God, so that one knew no want? He had believed, and in his rough way he had loved.

But there had been no lasting peace. Always when it seemed that life could oppose no further thorns, there had come a day to tear his heart again. Not that he thought he was more deserving than all others. They too had their trials, their moments of weakness, of enveloping blackness. There was hurt in all hearts. Purpose in life, it seemed, was vain, desire void. Let a man aim high or low, there was no surety of success. Chance and fate pulled forever against him; in the end there was only death.

In such a scheme there was no reason for belief, no place for God!

Unless—unless defeat answered the riddle of the seeming formlessness. Man might be meant to struggle, even to go down in the unequal battle. Drought, blight, storm, hunger, lust, slander, hypocrisy, hate—these were antagonists too formidable, to say nothing of bitter chance. If there was a good God, He knew that. What if struggle was His intention? What if He wanted men to be tried, to be baffled, beaten, to despair of physical accomplishment? The field had to be broken, the iron molten, the orchard lopped, the wheat winnowed, the stream prisoned above the mill. Perhaps it was the same with man's life. From defeat greater endeavor must be born, from tears increased purpose, from despair hope. Why should a man fall but to rise again, die but to live?

That was what God must admire—strength that would pull his creature up from the ground when he was knocked down, courage that would not let him give up. God would not punish defeat. He would punish only the coward, the quitter, the man who would not try.

Perhaps that was the eventual evidence of faith, the only peace—to go on. It might yet be demonstrated that Kate had been gifted with intuition when she made them all learn the words of the motto, wisdom fixed in memory by the difficulty of the alien tongue:

Wo Glaube da Liebe,
Wo Liebe da Friede,
Wo Friede da Segen,
Wo Segen da Gott,
Wo Gott keine Not.

BOOK THREE

I

1   One day in the summer of 1903 Bill Sapooney came hobbling
with his tongue hanging out—there was a car stuck in the
mudhole right in front of his house. "B-borrow me your team, T-
Thomas!" he begged. "Won't t-ta-take nothin' much out of them.
Fellow said he'd hand me over five d-dollars if I got him out."

Thomas wasn't inclined to trust Bill with the big blacks—he
had owned them only a year. "Just you keep your pants on," he
said when Bill kept dancing on the doorstep. "We'll get him out all
right."

The Searchmont was mired to the hubs, looked as if it had skid-
ded into the slough with all the impetus gained from the descent of
the long hill. In the weeds stood a big man in a duster who swore
volubly all the while Thomas was hooking up the log chain. Thomas took as much of his profanity as he could stomach.

"Guess maybe it'd be a right good idea if you'd just hand over
that ten dollars now, mister," he said drily. "Sometimes these
horses get a fool notion they don't want to pull a lick."

"Who in hell said anything about ten dollars!"

"I did. Course, if you don't want to pay that much, reckon nobody'd care a whole lot if you just set here all night."

The owner grew apoplectic, but he paid. Thomas pocketed
the money before he snagged the car to dry ground, stood grinning while his victim cranked the motor furiously. Only when the
Searchmont coughed out of sight did he notice Bill's wry face.

"Here, Bill," he said casually as he handed over the money.

"You get you a couple wheelbarrows of gravel down in the creek bottom and dump in that sink hole of yours."

Bill's eyes glistened avariciously. "D-do that, Thomas!" he babbled. "Do anything you say!"

Thomas went on home with the thought that the incident was closed, but again he had mistaken Bill Sapooney. Instead of breaking his back hauling gravel, Bill used the ten for a down payment on a team of jacks. One of them was wall-eyed and the other foundered, but Bill treated them like a pair of brothers. All that he asked them to do besides rescue work was pull out the sled each night with a couple barrels of rainwater on it.

"Man's got sense enough, he d-don't have to work!" he boasted. "Hell, T-Thomas, I ain't never had me a c-c-crop like these here autemobeels!"

2 With early fall the devil-hunters up on Black Man were at their sport again. The din of their fear made the night hideous, wore down the patience of everybody with a grain of sense. Men, women, children, and toothless old grannies, the flotsam that had washed up from the counties farther south, prowled the dark with dishpans, iron kettles, homemade drums, and cowbells. They crawled under the schoolhouses, broke down the corn, tore through the fences. Farmers who had at first been inclined to laugh began to talk of shotguns.

What worried Thomas most was that Kate needed her sleep— she had been ailing for several years. Judith did all the work now. "They just fair pesticate me to death, Pa," Kate said without much complaint whenever the racket woke her in the middle of the night. "Don't see why if they want him so much, old Nick don't come right down and oblige them."

Thomas was furious when the rascals trampled his patch of ginseng. He hadn't really believed the advertisements in the paper about twenty-five thousand dollars as payment for no more than a half-acre, but he had been interested enough to plant the weed. He was piqued to find the crop a total loss, the patch no more than a swirl of footprints.

3   The dinner bell rang so insistently that Thomas left the team in the field. He had been a little anxious about leaving Kate alone in the house, but she had insisted because she was afraid Judith would give up her intended trip to town if Thomas stayed at home. Hurrying in along the north lane, he did not stop to reason that if there were anything seriously wrong with Kate, she would not be able to summon him so forcibly. But he was a bit chagrined to find her on her feet at the stove when he reached the house, laboring for breath.

Somebody out on the front porch wants to see you," she said without looking at him. "Guess maybe you better spruce yourself up a little bit. There's a bucket of fresh rainwater out on the bench."

When she locked her lips after that, Thomas scented something distasteful. He was full of unpleasant conjectures when finally he came back into the kitchen, slicking down his hair with the heels of his hands. The visitor couldn't be an agent or salesman—he had trained Kate to take care of such pests herself.

From the middle room he saw the rig in the road, evidently a livery outfit. Then through the honeysuckle vine he spied the long green dress and wide hat of a modish woman who calmly waited for him on the front porch. Thomas's heart sank. With a presentiment of trouble beyond expectation he quietly let himself out the side door and dragged around to the front of the house.

Lucile rose slowly as he stood at the foot of the wooden steps, held out her lace glove as she smiled in her old sleepy way. Thomas could hardly take her hand. He stumbled a little as he went up to stand beside her, his words of greeting choked back into his throat. She hadn't changed much, not nearly as much as Kate and he. She looked thirty-five instead of fifty, her skin still peach satin and the corners of her eyes unwrinkled.

"Wouldn't have had any trouble knowin' you anywheres," he finally managed to stammer. "Guess I—well, you sure ain't changed a whole lot!"

Lucile smiled, sat down again while he stood uncomfortably on the far side of the porch.

"We all change," she said softly. "Everything changes, even our names. You'll have to call me Mrs. Townley."

Thomas couldn't find a word to say. He felt ashamed, wanted to escape. Instinctively he pulled out his dirty bandana; now he twisted it in his hands as he stared down at his clodhoppers. What Lucile must think of those and of his patched jeans would be a pity!

Lucile rescued him from his stupor.

"It shouldn't be hard for you to guess why I'm here," she said. "I want to know about Judith. Is she at home?"

Judith! Her words stabbed Thomas to the heart—he knew their full import. After all these years Lucile had come back to take from him the only child he had left.

"She ain't right now," he said as he tried to think ahead to some evasion. "She went into town to sewing circle. It's every Wednesday afternoon."

If anything, Lucile seemed to be relieved by his information.

"It's just as well," she said. "It's really you I want to talk to. I want you to let me take Judith back to Philadelphia with me."

Philadelphia! Half a continent away! If ever Judith went that far, he would never see her again. She might as well be drowned in the depths of the ocean.

"Guess you're forgetting she's twenty-six," he said.

"I'm not forgetting—I've counted every year." Lucile dropped her eyes, arranged the folds of her dress. "You see, Thomas, I know I haven't any claim any more. It isn't that I want her for myself, or that I want to take her away from you. It's only that I think I can help her a little."

Thomas's mouth grew tight at that.

"Didn't know she needed any help!" he said gruffly. "We been good to her. She's happy."

"Is she?" Lucile raised her eyes. "Is she—really and truly happy? Isn't there a—you know what I mean. You know she hasn't been asked to marry. Don't you see—if she went away with me, there wouldn't be any doubt about her! She'd have a chance to get the things you can't give her, no matter how hard you try."

Thomas fought hard to down his hurt. Must he lose Judith, too? Charlotte escaped to a home of her own, Faith a nun, Hocking lost, Grover dead. The house would be desolate if it held only the two of them again. But this time it would be unlike their first year, when blood was young and hope securely anchored.

"It ain't for me to decide," he said, thoroughly miserable. "You'll have to ask Judith."

Lucile rose, held out her hand again.

"I want you to ask her, Thomas," she said. "I'm going to stay at the hotel until Saturday. I know you'll do what's right."

Thomas stood on the porch until the Negro had flicked her away, his eyes lost. She could count on him to do what was right! Right! All his life he had been wrong in doing what he thought was right!

The sky was a great tub of shelled corn when he walked Judith down the road that same night. They sat on the bridge together, his words strange echoes of those that had been so hard for him to hear.

"You got nothing here to look forward to," he argued listlessly. "Come a day when you don't feel so young no more, you'll want somebody near you to depend on, maybe bone of your own bone. I want you to have all that, Judy! Ain't nothing in this here world I don't want you to have! I can't give it to you—you know that. Maybe she can."

Judith wouldn't listen to him. When in the starlight he saw the tears streaking down her cheeks, his voice choked up.

"You think about it, anyway," he said as they were walking back home. "I ain't a-goin' to say another word, one way or the other."

Two days later Thomas filled the wash basin with hot water, propped the triangular piece of cracked mirror on the kitchen sill, and shaved right after breakfast. Kate and Judith both cried as they kissed each other. "You mind, now, I want you to write!" Kate called as Thomas started Dude toward the gate. She tried to smile bravely, but Thomas knew her well enough to whip up.

As they topped Brewster's rise, they saw she was still in the doorway, her hand fluttering a last good-bye.

4 Alone again, they huddled close against the winter of the narrow years. Thomas made many mistakes in his courtship, but not the mistake of permitting Kate to wear the kind of flat black bonnet trimmed with glass grapes Celia Sapooney recommended. "Pshaw, you're still a spring chicken, Ma!" he always said when she complained. "Look just as fresh as a daisy."

He bought her a kersey jacket trimmed with velvet and yards of braid, when winter came added a muff and a lynx boa that was meant for a far younger woman. He was proud of her appearance, always thrust her forward at church. "No sense hanging back," he urged her. "Reason people stare is they like to see you."

They went everywhere together, to balloon ascensions and harvest-home festivals, band concerts and weddings, at least once a month drove down to Charlotte's to spend the day, made the long trip into Lancaster expressly to ride the street cars. Thomas even became so enamoured that he helped in the house. "Corn'll keep, I reckon," he would say when he saw Kate's task was to dry the curtains on a sheet pinned to the carpet. He didn't like to have her stooping too much—it made her complain of her back.

Or they would sit by the stove long winter evenings while she covered with crocheting burnt-out light bulbs he had brought her from town, fashioning balloons with square baskets attached that he tacked on strings suspended from the ceiling in the parlor. "You sure got a gift, Ma!" he would admire her handiwork as he got up from his chair, yawning a little. "About ready to climb the wooden hill?" As like as not she would insist on fixing a few eggs and a pot of coffee.

In those days his favorite quotation became the proverbial wisdom of an old calendar:

A little farm well tilled,
A little barn well filled,
A little wife well willed.

He often repeated the words to remind her that she would never know want.

One summer he even bought season tickets to the Lancaster Chautauqua. They drove in every night for a week. Kate was as enthusiastic as he, while her strength lasted. They cackled together at a funny play about two pairs of twins that were always getting mixed up, applauded the Tyrolean bell-ringers, marveled at the electrical wizard with his queer towers of apparatus.

By the end of the week Kate was so worn-out that she could

hardly move, but Thomas wouldn't miss the last night speaker. "You don't understand, Kate," he said when she hung back. "This William Jennings Bryan can talk rings around anybody. You know he ran for president—that ought to tell you."

Kate went. The night was hot, white, breathless. Bryan dripped with sweat, poured himself innumerable glasses of water, rolled up his shirt sleeves. His jaws sagged, the loops of his black bow came undone, but his periods were rhythms of long mellifluous syllables like cascades of golden thunder.

That night Thomas was very silent on the road home. Not until they came to the dark screen of trees along Church Hill would he confide to Kate what was in his heart. "You know, that's the way I always had an idea Grover would be," he said emotionlessly. "Guess maybe he might've been able to talk that fellow down."

Kate only patted his arm. It was almost the only time he had ever spoken of Grover, and it was senseless to try to add to his words. The only evidence of remembrance was that once each year they went with scarlet peonies to the pine on the hill where at long last they too would be laid.

5   When Kate came down, Thomas was not overmuch worried. He was able to get Darlene Schrader in to do the work, thought that a few weeks would be enough to get Kate on her feet again. Instead the weeks turned to months.

Celia Sapooney angered him. He found her in the bedroom one rainy afternoon, her consolation hardly hopeful.

"Guess maybe you hadn't ought to make her talk too long at one time," he said tactfully when he saw Celia sitting at the bedside as bleak as a raven. "Wears her out too much."

Celia took the hint, creaked to her feet immediately.

"Just one thing you better know, Mis' Linthorne," she said as she paused a minute by the footboard. "You're called in the night, don't answer!"

Thomas saw Kate's tragic eyes. "Don't rightly know what you mean, Celia," he said for her.

"What I mean is you hear somebody calling you like this: 'Kate!

287

Kate!', and you answer, you'll die while they get well!" Celia whispered. "Was a woman I knowed over near Pine Hill once did that very thing. She didn't last no time atall!"

Thomas shut her out before she could elaborate, but the damage was done. When he came back to the bedside, Kate had turned so that she need not look at him.

"You don't have to worry about nothing Celia says," he blundered. "Guess you ought to know her by this time."

Kate wouldn't answer. She lay with her eyes sealed, her breath as slow as if she were asleep.

6 "Sick abed and worse up, that's how I feel!" Kate might answer inquiry on those days she felt good enough to sit in a chair, but Thomas began to have misgivings for all her spunk. Summer had fled and frost now nibbled at the golden beech leaves, the day's sun was short and powerless to burn, along the fences the goldenrod was gray. Folks meeting on the road when they saw how the year lingered reminded each other portentously, "Green Christmas and White Easter make a fat graveyard." It was well to be warned. The dogs and horses went with sleek coats, the pullets had not molted, there were thundershowers in late November.

"Looky here, son," Thomas said the next time Cranford drove out from Lancaster in his brassy Duryea, "seems to me you're aholdin' something back you ain't got no right to keep! I want to know, and I want to know without any hemmin' and hawin': just what's the matter with my woman?"

The doctor was a young man, fairly competent, but not yet old enough in experience to know how to talk to a man so blunt.

"You don't have to worry, Mr. Linthorne," he said equivocally. "I think maybe we'll be able to pull her through all right."

Thomas winced at the words.

"What do you mean—pull her through?" he asked, badly frightened.

"Well—" It was plain that Cranford would rather not commit himself. He teetered from one foot to the other, his black case banging against his tight pants.

"Might as well let me know the worst of it, son."

"Well, it's just like I said: you don't have to worry. Her kidneys are pretty bad—she's been having a lot of trouble on that account. Might take some time before she feels like herself again."

Thomas stalked away from him, suddenly abject. He could read a man's face as well as his words—he had read Cranford's. In sober truth the young fellow should have declared that Kate didn't have one chance in ten.

On the first of February 1907 he cranked up the telephone and got a call through to Sugar Grove so that Charlotte could come in time. He never liked to use the balky thing, always shouted into the transmitter to make sure he could be heard. With Charlotte on the road, he could go straight down to summon Hocking—it was Kate's dying plea.

Now that the long-feared moment was at hand, he was calm, fully master of himself. He drove rapidly—he had seldom lingered with a good horse in front of him. Greetings from the roadside he returned with a wave of his hand while he showed the neighbors a good face. Something told him that he must not let on, must act as if nothing was wrong. Nothing was, except the emptiness in his own heart. After winter the grass and dandelions would be as green and yellow as ever, the ironwood as frosty lavender, the clay as stubborn. Neighbor would loiter with neighbor, girls send lacy valentines to their beaux, children escape half-naked to the fields and woods. Only in his life would there be change.

Hard to anticipate, it would be harder to realize. Seen in prospect, the years were so long; in retrospect, so short they might not have been at all. Reality! Reality! Where and what was reality! In no place permanence, in no place rest. One was swept on as by the waters of a millrace, ground as the grist. All the lost years—of struggle and blessing, despair and reconsecration: could they be treasured as a record of success? It was written that there was strong confidence in the fear of the Lord, and that His children should have a place of refuge!

Kate had been the lodestar through all his years—she would be no more. What moments of weakness he could remember when he had depended on her, of doubt when she had capped his words

289

with intuitive certitudes. All his faith had been inspired by her; there was always red sky when her sun went down. "Oh, Kate!" he kept moaning aloud as his mind winged space to the shell of a woman dying in coma in their front bedroom. "Oh, Kate!"

Mercifully Hocking himself answered the knock. He shut the door behind him with awkward hands, waited for Thomas to speak.

"Your ma's dying, Hock. I just thought maybe—maybe you'd want to see her once more before she goes."

He was glad he had been able to manage the words without emotion—if Hocking came, it should not be because of pity.

"Heard tell she's been right puny," Hocking said slowly.

"Best get your coat on and drive right back with me."

Hocking hesitated, his sleeve raveled by the wind as he stood on the cold stoop. It seemed two forces fought in him for mastery: the old, of home and all that home held dear; the new, of mistrust and hatred rounded by the years. In the end only the stronger could win. Hocking bolted back into the house for his coat.

"How long's she been down?" he asked when Thomas whipped out of the lane.

Thomas made him certain of many things. Now that his boy was with him again, their bodies pressed close together under the heavy blanket, he wanted there to be complete forgetfulness of misunderstanding born of pride.

"Hock, I want you should come home!" he said finally. "You know how lonesome it'll be after Ma goes. You can't go on not forgiving me forever."

They were turning in by that time and Hocking was showing his nervousness, so that Thomas got no answer. But from that moment Hocking walked with lighter shoulders, knowing he need no longer truckle to Orley's will.

II

1 Thomas moved down to the Brewster place when he realized
how many children Hocking had fathered. There was Claudia,
born in 1890; Maude, three years younger; then Arietta and Ade-
laide, twins. Lucy was ten, Elva nine, Mary seven, Kate but four.
Worse yet, Elva was again pregnant. "'Tain't my fault," Hocking
returned stubbornly when Thomas reproached him. "What I want's
a boy. Going to have me one or know the reason why."

Thomas thought that the reason why would very likely be Elva's
death. Her teeth were gone, her hair stringy, her face fully as bad as
Celia Sapooney's. From morning until night she slatted around the
house barefoot, her shapeless dress torn in a dozen different places.

Thomas smiled wryly when he went up once to find the big
picture of Kate and him gone from the front room, in its place nothing better than an ugly calendar. He wouldn't remark about the
slight, but he did scout around to see what Elva had done with the
photograph. He had a long search—it was gathering cobwebs in
one of the cellar apple bins.

His only gain from Hocking's coming was a collie pup from the
litter born that spring. Dog and horse—it was about all he wanted
any more. Hocking worked the big black team, but Thomas hadn't
let him possess Grover's horse. Dude grew fat in the Brewster pasture. Fifteen years old, he could still outrun any crazy automobile.
Thomas hardly used him as much as was good for him. Sometimes
they went to town no oftener than once a month.

That winter Thomas made himself as comfortable as a worm in
a cocoon. His Turkish rocker stood beside the shiny revolving

291

bookcase that held Kate's Bible and his new Ridpath; on the corner table lay his stereoptican, a set of foreign capitals and another of national parks in the box beside it; and on another table at the head of his leather couch swung the big fluted horn of his phonograph. Sometimes Hocking's girls came down on Sunday afternoon to play with the puppy and see the slides, but Thomas insisted they keep their fingers off the cylindrical wax records. It was his prerogative to be concertmaster; he always teased them before he sent them home satisfied.

2 When spring came back again, he left the work entirely to Hocking. There was a strange lust in his blood—he wanted to be on the roads. The drive to Charlotte's was no longer enough; he would no sooner be home than the hills called him again.

One sunny afternoon in Lancaster he got a flea in his ear. "That's the thing you ought to do, Thomas," white-haired old Matson told him while he idled at the grocery. "Get you an agency for the *Stockman and Farmer*. Fellows like you is what they're looking for."

Thomas wrote that same night, had a reply within a week. He was important with his blanks and sample copies, bought a handsome leather case to keep them from the dust of the roads. As a sort of joke he sent in subscriptions for everybody within a mile, thinking how puzzled they'd be when the paper began to come to them regularly. The money-order was a whopper, but it made him happy. He'd have to hustle if he wanted ever again to equal that week's work.

3 His hair grew white as the years drifted by, but that was the only change. When Balt Wendell and Zeke Sellers dropped off in the same month, Thomas pinched the skin on the backs of his hands, looked to see if his throat was getting any thinner. He felt as if he might last a century. Despite his coddling himself, his arms were as strong as ever.

Within a radius of twenty miles he became as well known as the weather, had the children flocking from the houses whenever they spied Dude trotting down the road. Wherever he went he was welcome—often the extra place was laid at table before he set foot in the house. Thomas treated his hosts to wonder. By the hour he would spin his yarns: of the Plummer Hill mine fire that had been burning since '84; of the haunted house and stone barn on the Pleasantville pike that two of LaFitte's pirates had built, and of the shadowy gold that still clanked there on windy nights; of the old canal, the high-walled cemetery deeded to the President of the United States so that the family within would never be disturbed, of Old Man's Cave and Wildcat Hollow. Long before he was ready for the bed prepared for him, Bounce and the children would be asleep on the floor.

Actual sales of the *Stockman* were not many. Thomas grew anxious at times when he found poverty or sickness and dipped into his bank balance to remedy it. He didn't like to think that the day might come when he would have to ask Hocking for some tiny return from the fields. Heaven knew that with ten mouths to feed besides his own Hocking needed every cent he could lay hand on.

Thought of the uncertainty of the future sent Thomas one day to Charlotte's. He was always glad to pull into the hill farm, from which Jed had fairly wrung a good living, but this time he was all business.

"Tell you what's on my mind," he said when Charlotte sat with him under the thick wild grape vine that hid the porch from the sun. "Got a notion I'd better be getting in to see a lawyer."

He was glad that Charlotte didn't try to jolly him. In her green gingham she looked the picture of Kate as she rested with hands folded in her lap. She had kept her figure—she didn't look forty.

"You do whatever you think's right, Papa," she said quietly. "What I thought was that everything was already settled. I mean, there's no reason why things can't go on just the way they are now."

Thomas shook his head. "Wouldn't be fair," he said. "Course, I want Hock should keep the farm—guess you know that."

Charlotte was puzzled, couldn't see what he was driving at.

"It's about the big woods on Church Hill," Thomas explained for her. "You see, Charlotte, truth of the matter is I always wanted that to stay Linthorne. Only Hocking ain't had no boy, and your name's Sarple. Only—" He broke off; there was no way out of the dilemma.

"Perhaps Hocking'll have a boy yet," Charlotte reminded him.

Thomas shook his head again. "Won't if he knows what's good for him," he said. "Thing I was really wondering was if you'd mind just going on calling it Linthorne Woods after it's deeded over."

Charlotte did her best with the melancholy occasion. As soon as she could, she got him into the house for a feast of homemade bread and ground-cherry preserves.

"They're just like Mamma used to make, but don't you spoil your supper," she warned when she saw his eyes sparkle. "Won't be but another hour or so until Jed'll be in."

4 Elva had had no child after the one born following Kate's death, but when in answer to Hocking's invitation Thomas went down one night to help dispose of the watermelons that had lain all day in the icy springhouse, he saw she was big again. She was like a death's head at their party—the children could do nothing to please her.

"Don't you throw them rinds on the grass, you dirty pig!" she shrilled at eight-year-old Kate. "Think all I got to do is clean up after you, you got another think coming!"

"She ain't a-doin' no harm!" Hocking tried to mollify her as he brought the child over between his knees. Thomas saw he was embarrassed.

"That's right—you go sticking up for her! Fat lot of good it does me to try to learn them right with you around to stick me in the back all the time! Know what's good for you, you'll keep your mouth shut!"

Thomas didn't like the way Hocking laughed at her, slowly, deliberately, as if Elva were a freak in a tent show.

"Know what's good, maybe I'll keep *your* mouth shut!" he said, and ignored her further tirades.

Thomas made him walk down the road when he was ready to go home.

"Want to go sort of easy on her when she's like that!" he warned kindly. "She don't mean nothing—she's just got a little more than she can handle right now."

Hocking walked silent for a long time, the smoke from his corn-cob blue in the moonlight. When he did speak, his mouth was full of venom.

"She ain't nothing but a dirty slut—that's the whole trouble!" he said bitterly.

"Don't say that, Hock."

"Well, it's the god's truth! I've put up with just about all I'm a-goin' to stand!"

Thomas trod carefully, fondled the silky ears of the dog as they stood under the great silver poplar in his front yard.

"She don't mean no harm," he said again and again. "You just be real nice to her until after the baby comes along, maybe you'll take up with her again. No sense her doing any work anyway, not with all them girls around to do it for her."

He sat worrying for a long time after Hocking went home. Nothing had hurt him as much as this, not even the knowledge that Spence was selling because he had to take Cora to town.

After that he cut short his excursions, kept a wary eye on the way things moved on the home place. Whenever possible, he himself tried to make the road easier. When the well failed, he scoured the county to find someone who knew how to trail a hazel wand, in the end paid out of his own pocket to have a Lancaster firm drill for water. Whole days at a time he entertained the younger children, setting them astride Dude for plodding rides around the row of fruit trees. Whenever he had a word with Hocking, he pointed out some good in Elva, a task that made his brains ache.

"Get you a boy this time sure," he promised for her. "Better be fixing up a good name to call him."

"I don't care what she calls him," Hocking would answer sullenly. "Call him Woodrow Wilson if she wants to. About all the sense she's got!"

Thomas prayed for Elva's time to come. No difficulty he had had with Kate had ever been as bad as this slow, consuming fire of hate that was eating through Hocking's heart. The fields showed the boy's indifference. He failed to make a second crop of hay, let the corn stand until it appeared he didn't mean even to shock it, turned the pigs into the orchard to eat the overripe apples as they fell from the trees.

And then one night without warning he was gone. Thomas knew the worst when Mary and Kate came down with tear-stained faces to ask after their father. Hocking had once or twice said something about the war that sounded queer. The likelihood was that he had lost himself by running away to Canada.

5   Thomas was one and seventy when he went back to the plow. The world was new to him, a brawling, jumbled, discordant jangle of hatreds and fears through which men hurried breathlessly to their deaths. Only the hills were the same, the hills and the sweet smell of the loam as the share furrowed it. The buzzards still hovered over Black Man, the great clouds still creamed up like soap bubbles in the west, the snakes still lay sunning themselves on the warm rocks. By the time the pear trees showered down their milky petals, he was sure of himself again—he was not so old that he would fail the seasons.

He wanted not to fail—there was a Linthorne born at last. Elva had called the baby Conrad, out of pure spite, it seemed, since there was none she knew who bore the name. Thomas entered no word of protest. When Celia Sapooney tottered over one afternoon, he saw her in time to prevent her doing damage. "You just get you some rabbit brains to put on that little fellow's gooms when his teeth begins to come through," Celia was advising Elva when Thomas came in. He didn't pretend to be ceremonious with her. "Bat brains are a whole lot better," he said deliberately. "Come over to your house and fetch some one of these days."

That put an end to the gabble—Celia was gone in less time than it takes a frog to dive into a pond. Since Bill went home to the good Lord, as she always said, Adolph had been keeping her in style. She had roses on her hats the year around.

Thomas labored to keep pace with the seasons. He got in the full forty acres of corn, saw it knee high by the Fourth. The threshing revealed his true loneliness—almost all the old faces were gone. Wendell, Cory, Sapooney, Canaway, Barker, McGruber—the names remained the same, but the features were fraudulent. What irritated him most was that some of the young whippersnappers insisted on calling him "Grampa." They were almost deferential in their rough way, shoved him aside from the heavier work, ceremoniously passed him the meat first at table.

It became his joy to outdo them.

"Funny thing to me you can't get no more'n fifteen bushels off of that piece," he would remark when he heard their complaints. "Got nearer twenty-two myself."

"Yeah, but look at the kind of ground you got."

"Humph!" Thomas would taunt. "Can't take nothing out of the ground you don't first put into it."

For all that it was an unequal race. The second year was harder than the first, the next more difficult still. When he went home one night in '17 to find Dude dead in the pasture, the heart went out of him.

6   It was a Sunday afternoon in late June, a day so muggy that the moist heat swirled like water over the fields. Thomas had lain on the couch for a while to rid himself of a headache, but could not rest. He thought he might keep his temples from throbbing if he got out under the trees, but even there the air was stifling. The wasps that kept darting down over the fallen plums troubled him; in his attempt to escape molestation he went back to the house for his hat.

Bounce protested any excursion into the brassy sun, dragged along with hanging head, his long tongue curled out of his mouth. At the stile behind the barn he yapped fearfully, tried to make his master turn back from the clover. Thomas held up a strand in the barbed wire so that the dog could crawl through, went on along the margin of the field toward the worm fence beyond which was the big square of wheat. The grain stood thick and deep in the yellow sun, its color accentuated by the long hump of Black Man, green-black under mountains of creamy clouds.

The undulation of light made Thomas dizzy—he had to hold to the rail to steady himself. In his head the hammers kept pounding, ringing against his ears. He had been a fool to come so far—it would cost agony to get back to the house. Bounce crept close to him through the matted grass, whined as he lifted his head to lick the gnarled fingers on the rail. Thomas was grateful for the solicitude—it was plain Bounce knew he was in trouble. He made a fainthearted attempt to pat the long nose, had to grasp back quickly to keep from falling.

The noise in his head whirred louder—it sounded for all the world like the roar of the old separator Zeke Sellers had once owned. Instinctively Thomas looked up to confirm his fancy, at the same moment heard the blur of voices. Before him the hills of Black Man swam into violet. Then with great effort he was able to focus the long swell of the wheat. His heart leaped at what he saw. It was no fancy, no mere roaring in his head. They were threshing, threshing as they used to thresh forty years ago. Only the dancing of his eyes had kept him from seeing the separator set down in the corner of the field, no more than sixty rods beyond the honey locust.

Against the long sweeps the teams pulled steadily, relentlessly, on the platform above the whirring cogs a great barrel-chested fellow with red hair who kept them at their pace. It could be no one but Gorm Schrader! Zeke Sellers fed the sheaves—it was easy enough to recognize him. And the others, laughing and jesting as they hauled in from the far rises, who were they? Thomas blinked his eyes to make sure he was not mistaken. He knew every face—Spence, Como Cory, Tom Barker, Lute Tanterscham. Bill Sapooney leaned on a fork as he sputtered something to Sellers, who paid not the slightest attention.

His eyes were clear now, the pain in his head gone. He was across the fence effortlessly, his legs strong as they crushed through the fringe of standing grain. Suddenly he saw a trim woman in a pink sunbonnet come through a gap in the Osage orange, in her hands one end of a pole on which was slung a big stone jug. A lanky boy followed her. Thomas shouted—it was Kate and Grover, come out from the house with fresh water.

He began to run with long strides, his body light as the wind, and at the same moment they saw him. "K-keep on a-comin', Thomas!" he heard Bill Sapooney yell. "G-got room for another hand over here!" Gorm slacked the horses, jumped down from the platform to join the others who were clustered about the wagons watching him. Then as the cogs whined silent and the belt stopped, they were all trooping to meet him, their eyes shining, their voices loud with banter. Spence had snatched up Kate's end of the pole, but Grover dropped his and ran ahead—he would be the first to meet Thomas at the rendezvous under the honey locust.